# LOST KIN

# LOST KIN

## A NOVEL

## STEVE ANDERSON

YUCCA

F

Yucca Publishing books may be purchased in bulk at special discounts for sales promotion, corporate gifts, fund-raising, or educational purposes. Special editions can also be created to specifications. For details, contact the Special Sales Department, Yucca Publishing, 307 West 36th Street, 11th Floor, New York, NY 10018 or yucca@skyhorsepublishing.com.

Yucca Publishing® is an imprint of Skyhorse Publishing, Inc.®, a Delaware corporation.

Visit our website at www.yuccapub.com.

10 9 8 7 6 5 4 3 2 1

Library of Congress Cataloging-in-Publication Data is available on file.

Cover design by Zubothan Mahaathev of Dreamz23
Cover images courtesy of Shutterstock

Print ISBN: 978-1-63158-081-9
Ebook ISBN: 978-1-63158-088-8

Printed in the United States of America

# LOST KIN

# One

Harry kaspar knew he shouldn't be heading into a bombed-out neighborhood with a plainclothes Munich cop he didn't know, not alone, not with night falling so fast. It wasn't standard operating procedure. He took the risk because plainclothes had a hot tip he could not ignore.

"There has been an incident, sir," the cop had said. "Your brother may be involved."

A destroyed city street at dusk harbored an urgent sort of menace, like a dense old forest just ravaged by giant wild beasts that could return at any moment. The larger ruins loomed as jagged high glaciers about to break apart and plummet down. The cop, a detective, plodded on ahead evidently content to let Harry trail him. Now and then shadowy figures shuffled by, the homeless, the refugees, all the cursed who had somehow survived to see the fall of 1946. They had their rickety carts, their distended packs on their bony backs. They paid Harry no mind, not intimidated anymore by his American conqueror uniform of waist-length Ike jacket, officer's cap, and belted overcoat. His getup only made him feel more like the easy prey in this ravaged forest.

Or maybe it was because plainclothes had found him at home wearing a purple velvet smoking jacket. It came with Harry's billet, a requisitioned city mansion—small and modest as mansions went, but nevertheless . . . The Captain Harry Kaspar who first arrived in defeated Germany in the spring of 1945 would never wear such a getup. Harry didn't see combat, but he had seen death after the war was done. One killing was even his doing. In his previous post with US Military Government in the small, secluded Bavarian town of Heimgau, Harry had fought back against a murderous American deserter by liberating a train full of plunder the predatory fiend had stolen. The man exploited Harry by using the alias of Colonel Eugene Spanner. Harry had to kill the sham colonel using his bare hands and a dull army pocketknife. He gave all the loot—the valuable personal belongings of exterminated Jews—straight back to Jewish refugee survivors. His renegade operation was illicit by strict application of military law, but he would do it all over if he had to. No one would guess Harry capable of any of that now on this dim late afternoon in October. As he answered his front door for the cop, he was even holding a snifter of the mansion's Armagnac to go with that smoking jacket. His new brown horn-rimmed glasses (genuine, no Bakelite for Harry) were fashioned by a skilled *Optiker* in the Seidlstrasse—Harry justified this by knowing the work won a local artisan one afternoon free from rubble clearing. The hard truth was, though, Harry was becoming as infected as any victor turned occupier. Rank, passport, extreme wealth, full access to the PX, and so much more—sooner or later, every last one of them inherited the stale, complacent powers of old.

The cop had given his name as Dietz and held his Criminal Police badge up to the light streaming out from Harry's foyer. Harry peered through his specs at the unique *Kripo* shield with the Munich coat of arms—a hooded monk taking a vow. Knowing from fake, he felt at the brass plate and the pin attached to the back. Here was a bona fide city detective. But Detective Dietz didn't want to come inside.

"I've been out in the cold too long. I'll only get warm," Dietz said in German, speaking low as if making a telephone call from a stranger's house. "*Herr Kapitän*, I request your presence for a certain, well, sensitive matter."

"What does that mean?" Harry replied in German. "Please be clear, Detective."

This was when Dietz knocked him for a loop. His brother might be implicated in a crime. *His brother?* Harry did have an only brother, Maximilian. Max. But the fool had returned to their native Germany in 1939, and no one had heard from him in years. Back in America, Harry and his parents had disowned Max. Harry was stunned to hear his brother mentioned, but he kept it inside. He had learned never to wince. The slightest tell could turn a man from conqueror-occupier into someone's sure mark in an instant.

Harry took the offensive: "How do you know? Tell me. Do you know him? What's his name if you know him?"

"I don't know him. I know little about this, you understand. I only report."

"You're doing it for someone else. Someone you want me to meet. I see . . ." Harry nodded, easing up. "What it's about?"

"I can't discuss it. Not here. We must hurry, please. Oh, I must ask for your utmost, shall we say, *Besonnenheit*."

"And it's utmost discretion you want? So you want me to come alone. That's what you mean. You're acting solo on this—moonlighting as it were."

"*Ja, klar*. This is what I mean." Dietz flashed Harry a smile of reassurance, but it fizzled out. "Please. It's not far. I'll wait here for you to change."

Harry had requested the transfer out of rural Heimgau to help curb his mounting fear that some unforeseen operator would pin his deed on him, or blackmail him, or worse yet come seeking revenge. He had even paid off a formidable Military Government clerk to push the papers. In his Munich post, he was a Branch E (Munich) Liaison Officer with Regional Military Government of Bavaria. Military Government—MG for short—had him observing local authorities and writing boilerplate reports while often having to step in and play minder in a pinch. He was just another gilded middleman for proclamations or promises, the former delivered in quadruplicate and the latter avowed in smoky clubs. Find your lost faith in me, German. You can depend on us, refugees. The post did give him a certain freedom, though, and on this evening he was going to use it. Normally he'd grab a jeep or even a sedan from the motor pool but that meant signing for the vehicle and chaining the steering wheel with a padlock if left out on the street. So he had let Detective Dietz lead him on foot.

Dietz trudged farther into the neighborhood with his head down and shoulders set, as if he were a boy needing to show his father right where he'd lost his ball. Drops of an early wet snow grazed Harry's cheeks and spotted the layer of grit that had plastered the streets ever since wartime air raids began destroying ninety percent of old Munich. He had made one error—he hadn't changed out of his deerskin loafers hand-made from a master *Schuhmacher* in the Kaufingerstrasse, and the bones of his toes ached from the chill in them. An odor like rotting chicken parts persisted in the biting damp breeze. Harry kept his nose closed and an eye on all. The building facades turned more skeletal and the hills of debris grew higher. The passing locals seemed more on edge here. People glared and crossed each other's paths, kicking rocks and rags clear. "Goddamn winter coming," a little girl muttered.

Dietz halted at a corner, pivoting one direction and then the other as if he'd lost his way. His long shadow cloaked Harry, and Harry was glad for the darkness. In the daylight he would stand out bright and vivid here like a hand-painted porcelain figurine on a trash heap. He carried his large black leather attaché with platinum buckles clamped under his arm, the padded strap tight on his shoulder. He had learned to be ready for any eventuality. It was why he had eased up hearing Dietz "report" to him, because underpaid German police often moonlighted as intermediaries for all manner of transactions. The mention of Harry's German brother might only be a lure. Tonight's "incident" could simply prove the usual opportunity—*Kompensation*, some preferred to call it. A certain acquaintance has come into a particular Gutenberg Bible, or a reasonable facsimile thereof, and said acquaintance would like to make Harry a solid offer. That or a most charming and discreet frau with a past wished to become a man's obedient wife. Morphine. Child selling. Who knew? A sensitive favor might be asked in return. That or someone knew more about Harry's past than Harry liked. Which was why his breast pocket held the M2 auto pocketknife he'd bought off a paratrooper to replace the GI-issue model he'd lost disposing of Colonel Spanner. He also owned a stubby little Mauser HSc, which concealed better than his service Colt. He left the piece at home. Discretion was discretion.

Dietz, his face bent forward as if sniffing, turned to face Harry, and a stray working streetlight cleared the shadow off Dietz and his plain clothes. He wore a tattered overcoat dulled by that all-pervasive grit dust, a common accessory for Germans these days. With the wet snow spattering it, the fabric almost shined golden in the sallow light. Dietz had a broad face that could have a second chin in better times. Here it only bore sagging jowls, lined features, sunken cheeks. The loose skin seemed to hang in waiting, ready for some meat to cling to again.

"There is a tunnel, through the rubble," Dietz said.

Harry could have stopped Dietz right here, made him fess up. Maybe it was time. Maybe it should have been time. He felt the pocketknife against his heart. "After you," he said.

Dietz led Harry through a blast hole in a building, making sure Harry ducked his head. All went pitch black for a moment, and then they were creeping along a low passageway that zigzagged around heaps of debris and passed interior courtyards. Small fires crackled here and there and a radio hissed, its channel lost, a few mocking laughs clanged in the air, and Harry heard faraway clip-clops of people navigating over loose bricks, step by cautious step. The passageway darkened and Harry and Dietz descended beneath all of it.

The cellar room was about the size of a standard kitchen. The four lit candles hinted at blackened sandstone, bricks stacked into beds and benches, a pile of hoarded wood. A moldy stench hit Harry's nostrils. Dietz cleared his throat and stood aside for Harry to see.

In the far corner, a man lay on a board flat on his back. A long blade extended from the stomach.

Harry didn't know what made him feel more nausea—seeing that blade in the corpse's gut, or realizing the dead man could be Max.

Blood splattered the dead man's face. His mouth was stretched open as if about to take a big bite. With all that blood and contortion, it was tough to make out the man's looks at a glance. The first thing to do was confirm. Harry scanned the corpse, keeping his back to Dietz. He saw crow's feet and a little white in the longish matted hair. Short in height, wiry build . . .

Fading memories of Max crept back—memories Harry had let die. Max was older. If Harry was twenty-eight, that meant Max would be thirty-three now, or was it thirty-four? Max had darker features than Harry did yet they looked enough alike as boys that people mixed up their names. No one mistook their different demeanors. Maxie was always the affable one. His brother had bigger bones, a higher forehead, had grown taller. Max was not near as slight of build as this corpse. If this were his brother, he'd eat his handmade loafers. He sighed, with relief.

"This is not your brother," Dietz said.

"It's not, no. Well? What's this all about? Is he here somewhere?"

"No. There is a young woman, in the next room."

Unease swelled in Harry's chest. He looked toward the splintered doorframe off to the side, a rectangle of dimmer light. "She did it?" he said.

Dietz shrugged. He was only reporting. Harry wondered if the cop felt queasiness at all.

"Then tell me why the hell I am here. My feet are cramping in this cold."

"The young woman in question, she asked for you. She knows your name and title exactly. 'Captain Harry Kaspar of the US Military Government,' is what she said."

"And, don't tell me: She claims that I have a brother."

"It's more than that. She says that she *knows* him."

"Is that so?" Harry said in monotone.

"This is all that she will say. She might be Russian, but it's hard to tell. You wish to question her?"

"Not quite yet. Let's let her calm down a little."

He would have to get to the bottom of this. A stranger who might just be a suspect knew about Max. Not even his American colleagues in MG knew about his brother who chose Nazi Germany over the Land of the Free. Who else could be on to him, on to the both of them? Fraternizing with the conquered enemy was still an offense to many, even though Harry's only crime was one of kinship. It was a clear weak point in his polished-up armor. The realization brought back his nausea. He swallowed, hard.

The blood had run off the board, soaking into the earthen floor. The fingers had clenched into claws as if clutching items since removed. Harry unfolded his blue silk hanky and used it to tug at the one unbloodied finger. It didn't budge. Rigor mortis would put the death at about five hours, he reckoned.

"This death is too fresh for rigor," Dietz offered. "It must be cadaveric spasm—with the shock of a murder like this, I would not be surprised."

"You're the expert." Harry had an unlit Chesterfield on his lips. Smoke and nausea didn't seem the best allies here, so he reinserted the cigarette in the pack and produced his horn rims. He slid them on, thinking that Max would never wear glasses like these.

He concentrated on the long blade in the man. It was a type of sword and slightly curved and etched with swirling patterns. The handle was a dark wood with no guard but a hooked knob on the end. It certainly was not the Nazi fashion. It looked like something older and rougher, made for actual fighting and killing.

The dead man's US Army fatigues were GI issue, but the olive drab was faded, the hems frayed, the stitching worn fuzzy. Duds like these were for deserters at large, or prisoners, or VD cases getting the treatment.

"You check for dog tags?" Harry said.

"There were none," Dietz said.

The collar was pushed open and unbuttoned as if someone had checked that already or yanked off the tags. The man's eyelids were still open, the eyeballs spattered with blood. A man gored past death, worn-out fatigues, the blood—it all took Harry back. Something about him, inside him, wanted another crack at a grim but simple deed as he had done before. It was direct action and panacea all in one.

"Would you call that a saber?" he asked Dietz.

"Oh, but certainly. Looks like something Slavic, if not from the Orient. A cavalry piece perhaps? And it's sharp—look, the thing's gone right into the board there." Dietz shook his head at that. "Also, this man? He looks too old for a GI."

Harry nodded, pleased Dietz had noticed. He held up the rectangular Daimon flashlight Dietz lent him and inspected the room. In the opposite corner stood a small cast-iron oven, its door open for embers that needed stoking. In another corner, an opened suitcase held potatoes, turnips, and something wrapped in brown paper—often this was a hunk of meat or bread. There were two canteens, blankets, and two more of the sabers in their sheaves.

Harry shined the light back on Dietz, who didn't blink. "Heck of a thing we got here."

"It's another lovely day in Munich."

"You're moonlighting. But you could have run the girl in just the same."

Dietz sighed, a puff of air that smelled of meat (brown paper bundle confirmed). He spoke lower again: "How can I alert the *Polizei* first? This incident, it involves an *Ami*." An *Ami* was an American. The fledgling reformed German police could not act on American crimes or crimes against Amis before alerting US authorities. Dietz had a point—the uniform, at least, was Ami. Dietz also had a knapsack at his feet now and it was bulging. The young woman had likely given him one of those brown paper bundles to smooth things out for her.

Harry turned off the flashlight. "Listen, Herr Detective—what's your first name anyways?"

"Hartmut."

"Hartmut." Whenever Harry needed to test a German, he acted his most American. Thus using the first name. It always threw them off guard. He placed a hand on Dietz's shoulder. He smiled. "I'll say this once: You need to take this matter to the MPs, my friend. At least find a public safety officer in MG. I'm not the kind of Ami you need, see—"

"Because you're a born German."

"Yes. No! I'm a naturalized American. How do you know that?"

"Everyone knows," Dietz said. "And, I can tell from your German."

Dietz was testing Harry too. Harry couldn't blame the detective. Harry asked him, "Just how did you get included in this anyway—"

"Neighbors came to me. I live nearby." Dietz added a shrug.

"You really are not acting on police authority?"

"The authority here, it is not yet clear."

"Despite your brass badge."

"I needed you to trust me. For her sake."

"How did you get my address?"

"We police are not so very powerless. We do have lists."

"What makes you think this girl knows my brother?"

Dietz let his hands slap at his sides and he gave a grimace that Harry knew all too well. It meant, are you sure you're ready for this, American occupier?

"Lay it on me," Harry said.

"Well, the girl, she said she knows about you as well. Something vague about a train of plunder."

Harry started this time, openly, and his mouth might have dropped open. "A what?"

"That was the point when she stopped talking," Dietz added.

She knew about the train job. It was one step away from knowing about Harry doing a man in. Max the apostate was one thing, but Harry's own history was a stomach punch. *Just what game was this girl playing?*

"I see," he said, turning away from Dietz. Thinking it out. He wondered if it could be blackmail, and irritation smothered the unease in his chest. He placed the Chesterfield back on his lips and lit up. If the dead man had clearly been a GI, Dietz would have had to call the MPs or US Constabulary. But who really knew with that shabby uniform? There was a gray area here, probably just enough.

He faced Dietz, glaring. Dietz held up his hands as if to say, I'm just the messenger here.

"Do we have an ID on her?" Harry said.

"She has no papers, nothing. She could not have been here long."

"And she's Russian, you say?"

"From the sight and sound of her, yes—something like that."

"What about sad sack here? Anything on him at all?" Had he already asked that? Harry's mind was in that other room now, ransacking it, digging at how she could know of him.

"Nothing on him. I can check our lists if you wish. But as I say, I cannot—"

"Cannot act without first alerting US authorities. I know, I know. Listen, Dietz. Hartmut. Before I—we—go any further with this, could you just wait in here a little while? I'm going to speak to her." Harry handed Dietz the rest of his open pack of Chesterfields. "Please."

Dietz took the pack and made it disappear under his thick sleeve as if Harry had just traded him bogus meds on Old Town's shadiest corner. As much as the man would've liked to smoke one, it would gain him so much more out on the street. "But, of course."

Harry carried two candles into the next room. The young woman sat on a bench made of bricks, her back straight against the wall. Harry set the candles on a charred end table and the room doubled in light. She wore a grubby white headscarf, a blue shawl around her shoulders, gray wool blouse, surplus German army trousers, and boots. Smooth skin. The room was cooling with that oven ignored and yet sweat glistened on her cheeks, neck, collarbone. She was more woman than a girl, Harry saw—nineteen at the most, a little too gangly, but it was probably from malnutrition rather than puberty. She had dimples and a delicate nose and crooked teeth and her eyes were hard with thick, dark gray irises, two silver rings that reflected the candlelight. Harry was certain he did not know her. If nothing else, he would have remembered all the lugs and two-bit Romeos aiming for a shot at her.

He pulled a stool over but a leg fell away, firewood now. He squatted so they were eye level.

"I kill man," she said in broken German, the accent Slavic. Harry waited for more. She repeated it louder and made a stabbing motion with one hand.

"You killed him? Down here? Over there?" Harry said in slow German. "It was so easy for you, with only one hand?"

She shook her head and thrust the imaginary saber with both hands, heaving forward, getting her back into it. Sharp gal: She understood more than the words. "This man, I take him around the corner," she said using the German idiom for murder.

Harry pulled another pack of Chesterfields from his attaché case, shook out a cigarette and offered it to her, a real prize. She waved it off.

"Why do it?" he said. He reproduced her two-handed stabbing motion. "What for?"

Harry expected her to claim any manner of violation—rape, heirloom theft, the murder of her child. He would give her the benefit of

11

the doubt. She only glanced away, consulting the pockmarks on the wall. Her chin hardened up, the dimples vanishing.

"I know you understand me," he added. "Who is he? Let's start there. American, is he?"

She nodded, eyes to the ground.

"Yes? Look at me. That a yes? No?"

"He is evil swine. A Judas." She spat, a little too close to Harry's deer-skin loafers. He really should have worn his sturdy old brogues for this.

"All right, we'll hold onto that thought. So, who are you?"

She shook her head.

"Then where did you come from? And why am I here if you're not going to tell me anything? When you're the one who came asking for me?"

She ripped off her headscarf, her black hair tumbling down to her shoulders, and wiped her sweat with it. Harry had seen some cold feet in his time here, but this girl was getting frostbite and fast. She was practically panting now as if running away already.

"Easy, easy . . ." Harry stood and made himself big in case she tried to bolt.

Wet had filled her eyes, and a tear rolled down one cheek. She let the tear stay. She'd been out on her own a while, Harry could smell it on her, like freshly tilled earth with a little compost thrown in. It wasn't offensive, just opened his eyes a little.

From his attaché case he drew his chrome thermos, twisted off the red cap, and poured hot coffee in it—real coffee from the PX, its steam gleaming with candlelight. She cradled the cap-cup with all ten fingers as if it was made of fine porcelain and filled to the rim. As she sipped, she studied his Ike jacket with its thick hems concealing the buttons, his captain's bars and patches, taking it all in with wide eyes as if she had never seen an American uniform up close. It was the look the Germans used to have. It was still amazing to him that this no-nonsense US Army wool could appear exotic to anyone. He wondered if she was new here.

"Are you a refugee? A Displaced Person? Supposing you are. We can get you to the UN relief people, they can get you food, send you home—"

She jerked back, eyeing the way out, definitely not what Harry expected. Usually the mention of UN relief brought the same response as a stack of Hershey's bars.

"Home no good? Okay okay, not yet we won't. All right?" He added a smile.

She nodded and handed back the thermos cap. Now she stared at his face, at his features, but in a different way than she had at the uniform. He said in English, not caring if she understood, "Way I see it? Someone on this block fingered you. They heard screams maybe. Told the cop they knew in the neighborhood, Dietz. But why didn't you run? You could have. Paid people off with your goods. To me, that means you consider yourself accountable somehow."

As he spoke her head lowered, and she stared into her lap. Harry wondered what a girl like this must have been through. She could not help what she does now. What she does, it runs her. He understood that much.

Another tear. It splashed on her wrist.

"How do you know my brother?" he said. He didn't dare give away Max's name yet. If she didn't know it, this might end right here.

She sniffed and stared back at him. Stalling. He figured she too was contemplating just how much to give away.

Meanwhile, Dietz waited in the other room and likely couldn't hear them because someone was pounding away at the rubble above, the dust floating down from the bowed beams.

Irina moved closer. "Please, you remove eyeglasses," she said.

Harry shrugged. He could see without the horn rims just fine; they were little more than reading glasses. He pulled them off.

She studied his face, closer. She could see the freckles on his cheekbones better this way, and those sagging eyelids of his he'd

13

always hated because he suspected they made him look sleepy, lazy. Her eyes sparkled. A corner of her mouth turned up in a half smile.

"What?"

"May I see hands?" she said.

Harry slid his specs into a pocket and held his hands out with knuckles up, like a guy about to get a manicure. She flipped his hands over and her eyes searched his palms as if scanning a book for a passage. Then she slapped his hands away like a mom confirming a kid's washed hands. "You stand." She stood.

Harry stood and gave her a little joke salute. She was under his height of five nine, but with a proper dame's heel on she could face him nearly eye to eye. She studied his earlobes and his head. He'd neglected to comb his hair in his hurry to leave and his cowlick in back was probably sticking straight up.

She laughed.

Harry rolled his eyes. "That's quite enough, sister," he said, but smiling as he patted down his hair. Her laugh faded and they studied each other, their faces slack. She muttered something in her language and gave him that look again, nodding as if recognizing him.

"Irina. My name is Irina," she said.

"Yeah? That's a nice name. And you know my brother."

"Yes, I know him, Mister." She nodded to confirm it.

"Forget Mister. You asked for me by name. You know about me."

She shook her head. "Not here," she whispered. "Not with dead man. Not with police."

Dietz had surely heard the laughing and the German surely would not know what to make of it. These casual Americans joke around even with murder suspects? Harry went back into the adjoining room and made a straight face to reassure Dietz, who stood and replied, "So. I can watch over the body while you call your authorities. You will need at least a jeep for her and for the stiff there."

Dietz would gladly do that, Harry reckoned. Hot sips of fresh American joe or an officer's pack of finer smokes was well and good, but the detective had also stumbled on a swell little score—while he waited he could help himself to the goods in here. Harry couldn't blame him. This whole busted city, this whole country, hell, most of this continent was back to caveman rules.

"No? Then, I go and bring the MPs for you?" Dietz added.

Irina stood in the doorway, her eyes fixed on Dietz, ignoring the corpse in the dark. Harry shook his head at Dietz.

"Then what is it, *Herr Kapitän*?" Dietz said.

"I might have another job for you," Harry said.

"Oh?"

"Can you find a way to get the corpse to your morgue incognito, or somewhere safe, just to . . . keep him on ice for a while? Nice and quiet, like. And do not worry, I'm fully responsible. You're just following orders."

Just following orders—always an unfortunate word choice, but there it was.

All expression had emptied from Dietz's face. Harry had expected this. Just like their conquerors, every German, from a blind grandma to a jumpy little Hans, had learned never to show too much excitement. Harry pushed his attaché open wide, placed the thermos back inside, and produced two packs of Lucky Strike and two cans of Spam.

"What about preserves?" Dietz said.

"Berry jam? Marmalade? It's all in the PX. You just say the word. Consider this only a down payment on the lease."

Dietz grunted, and a smile slipped out. "What about her?"

"She's my problem. But I'm asking you to keep quiet about her too. It's part of the *Kompensation*. Deal?"

# Two

THE YOUNG WOMAN WHO CALLED herself Irina was not going to come clean easy. Harry had learned to be patient in such situations. After that meat grinder of a duel he'd survived in Heimgau, he could well understand her state. As for him, seeing that long curved blade in a man wearing US Army green certainly gave him a jolt. But it also evoked the nightmares he used to have about nearly being killed in the same grisly manner he had killed a man—run through just like that apparently bogus GI in the cellar, but again and again and again. In other nightmares, he could not protect anyone from being killed as hard as he tried. His parents. Max. Babies. He had woken screaming, sweating. The more he prevented death, the less he prevented it. Situation normal, all fouled up. But those nightmares had waned with time. He couldn't imagine what it was like for a refugee on the lam, always running, always worked up, feeling eyes on you all the time over your shoulder, the monkeys riding your back with razor claws.

If he pushed this girl Irina too hard, he would only bring it all back and she would hightail it. She needed her rest, and she needed comfort, and then he would find out all there was to know about Max. Harry brought her back to his billet by flagging a ride from one of the off-duty GIs who cruised around in requisitioned German cars serving as private taxis—a Joe gives an officer and his Gretchen a ride, Harry pays Joe double, and no one's the wiser. By this point Harry was holding Irina up, she was so tired. She had gazed at the dark mass of his modest mansion against the night sky as if it was a castle in a dream. It stood on a secluded avenue near the vast English Garden, whose woods and meadow lawns the Allied air raids had scorched so thoroughly that much of it looked like Central Park after a wildfire. Harry had a fine view though, looking onto a surviving thicket of birches and oaks. The mansion was two stories of decorative modern style with strong clean lines, a patinated copper roof, and chalky stucco-over-sandstone that looked more like something out of fin de siècle Paris than the pastoral yellows and rosés Munich's buildings had flaunted before the age of smoke damage. Art Deco, most called it, some Art Nouveau. It was definitely a bastard. As with most mansions here, as with Harry's previous billet in Heimgau, the home had a nasty provenance. It belonged to Jews the Nazis had forced abroad or shipped away, then to a Nazi party fat cat before he too vanished. But what could Harry do? Live in a barracks? They were inheriting what came before.

Once inside, he got Irina to a secluded upstairs servant room far from his master bedroom. The narrow feather bed swallowed her, and soon she was snoring. Then he had to assure his German housekeeper Gerlinde that his visitor in need was not after her job even though the girl was young enough to be Gerlinde's daughter but with twice the looks. It was a private matter and Gerlinde was to feed the girl and get her whatever she required, within reason.

"Fräulein Irina needs her rest above all. That comes first. No matter what she tells you," he instructed Gerlinde.

"All in order," Gerlinde replied with a curt nod. "I'll stay till she's well."

That evening as Irina slept, Harry retreated to the den with its dark wood paneling and shelves and brass sconces. He had a broad desk to match and a leather sofa laden with tassels. He sat there with a whiskey, cupping it in his hands like hot soup so he could think.

Before Dietz made off with the corpse, Harry had the detective retrieve the saber from the body and wipe it clean with a rag.

Dietz had protested that this was destroying evidence. For his worries Dietz got to keep much of the goods in the cellar, with Irina's blessing. Harry kept the saber. The other two swords went with him too, bound to his attaché case. He was taking a chance by keeping a murder weapon. But this way Dietz could know he wasn't going to leave the detective hanging with a corpse and an unsolved murder. They could share the shame. In any case, Dietz might simply have hawked the saber on the black market—just tell a GI it belonged to a Nazi and the deal was licked.

Near midnight, Irina started awake. Gerlinde put her in a quick bath (so Gerlinde could change the grimy bedding, no doubt), and Irina was sound asleep again. Harry poured another whiskey. The day was Friday the thirteenth. He just had to laugh at that. He was not superstitious and he wasn't even naïve, not anymore. Those first months in Heimgau had sure sabotaged his idealism. Yet he was on to something here. He had not thought about Max for so long. So many times he'd reminded himself that he shouldn't want to see his brother ever again, not after all he'd put the family through. Then, after he transferred to Munich, he found himself wondering and he used his status to do some discreet asking around. The Military Police told him they had nothing on a Max Kaspar. He tried the local Counter Intelligence Corps office—the CIC. CIC had nix. MG was no help to him either. He had limited access to records; that got him nowhere. New files showed up all the time, but he wasn't counting on it. He told himself he'd go try the British zone one day or even the French. He never did. Max was surely no Nazi, yet who knew where he'd ended up? His brother might have become desperate, or dependent, or simply fallen in love. And Harry had to stay wary of bigger players who could know more about Max. The US zone bigwigs, War Department mucky-mucks, and gung-ho CIC agents always held the best trump cards and those sorts of operators could seize a man's final chips at any time. All it took was one weakness.

Harry toasted himself. Here he was feeling alive again, all thanks to a girl with nothing to lose. He drank, and he felt a warmth that he was sure was not the whiskey.

Mail lay on the desk. He brought the small stack over to his lap—*Stars and Stripes*, the new Munich paper, and more of those humble letters from locals crafty enough to try his home address with shady opportunities and thinly disguised bribes. Those made good fire starter. One letter was from the US Army confirming that his deployment was ending mid-November, a little over a month away.

He still had time to reenlist, but something had held him back and what happened tonight did not make the decision any easier. He took another drink, for strength. If he was going out with a bang, he didn't have much time to find the firecrackers.

The next morning, a Saturday, it was all Harry could do not to wake Irina up first thing. He stared out his vast rear windows at the frost sparkling on his terrace and small classical garden. They were getting frost every morning now. He thought of the frost on all that Munich rubble, melting and trickling down in, then refreezing and clogging crevices as the snow came down to blanket all. The best you could do was not slip on it. The worst, not let the weight of it smother you for good. He closed his eyes to the thought. Sleep had not helped him. He'd started awake twice in the night thinking, *I could lose my post over this corpse, this girl.* Dishonorable discharge. End up in a stockade even. Some desperate snake could use it to brand him a born kraut lover or even worse a Communist. Un-American. Such were the times, again, already. War didn't end all fears; it only started new ones, and every Joe and Fritz was looking for a scapegoat. And that wasn't even the worst of it, he did not forget—someone could pin the train job on him and his killing Spanner or even frame him for the murders Spanner had done. It all made Harry wonder what came first: Irina murders a guy and then comes looking for him by way of a plainclothes cop, or she's already looking for Dietz and then has to murder a guy?

He heard his housekeeper out in the hallway. "Gerlinde? Come in here, please."

Gerlinde planted herself in the doorway, her gray hair pulled back severely. It was her attempt to tame the frizz, he guessed. She shook her head at him.

"What's the matter?"

"Fräulein Irina is roaming the upstairs looking out windows and rubbing her hands together. She will not rest anymore. I told her."

"She's up? Why didn't you . . ."

Gerlinde held out her hands in confusion—he'd never instructed her to inform him.

"It's okay. Tell you what, why don't you bring her down here to me?"

Gerlinde padded off, shaking her head again.

She ushered Irina into the main living room. Irina's skin had more color, her hair was up in a loose bun, and Gerlinde had lent her a simple blue smock that, owing to Irina's emaciation, was so baggy that Irina kept pulling it back onto a shoulder and so short she kept tugging down the hem. Harry had on civvies—brown trousers and gray wool sweater. They sat in broad tapestry armchairs grouped at the base of a column, and in another world might have been two travelers chatting in a hotel lobby. Harry tried small talk in German. Irina confirmed she had slept well, yes. Gerlinde was washing her clothes. Another tug and pull at the dress. Was she hungry? No, Gerlinde had fed her well.

Then Irina sat up straight. "Thank you, *Herr Kapitän* Kaspar. For the nice sleep. I want to say this to you."

"Call me Harry."

She stared at him.

"So who was he?" he said. "A Pole? A Yugo? German?"

Irina hugged herself, with apparent worry, and seemed to lose a third of her size. Her feet even came up off the floor.

"Go on, you're safe here. Not with dead man. Not with police. Remember?"

"*Max* know English," she blurted in English. "He know it well. To me, he sounds as you. American man."

So she did know Max's name. She had hit Harry so fast with it that he just glared at her to go on, to give him more. He needed details, confirmation. Was Max alive? Her eyes, avoiding him, found another window. As she gazed out, she reported instead on what she had heard about Harry. It was only the basics—Harry had hijacked a train of plunder and he gave it to good people. Waving her arms, her voice rising. Harry kept his blank face. Even hearing this, her simple and relatively harmless version of the tale, it shot through him as if he'd touched an electrified fence. His Heimgau posting was like the Wild West and seemed about as long ago sometimes. Yet the farther he got from it, the stronger he knew it would return to haunt him.

"You risked your life, yes? Yes?" she said, stabbing a finger at him. "For others you do this."

Some Americans had heard rumors of it, but none knew the names involved as far as Harry could tell. One thing he had learned about those under foreign control: They often had more information than the occupier did—the occupied, the refugees, and the down-and-out were the real experts in the know. It amazed him how they were able to spread news, as if they shared access to some secret wireless television apparatus. There were days when he wished some fellow Americans knew just what he was capable of. They might even appreciate it. His girlfriend Maddy Barton might know the rumor, but she certainly didn't know it was he. And why tell her? She wouldn't believe it, and that wasn't her fault. What clues had he given any of them? None. Handmade horn rims and a mansion do not a rebel make.

"I'm asking the questions here," he said.

Irina smiled. "You know what you are? You are *Kudeyar*," she said, what sounded to Harry like "cool-jar" and obviously from her

21

native language. Then her eyes widened and she waved hands. "I mean to say, you are like hero of legend your people call Robin Hood—"

"Says you," Harry said, his voice rising. "Robin Hood? Someone told you that word. Someone from the West. The same person who told you about me. Was it Max?"

"Please? I can't . . ."

They heard footsteps, from down the hall. Harry kept at it. He leaned forward. "Who told you to find me?" he barked. "Was it Max? Well, was it or was it not my brother?"

She said nothing. She bowed her head.

Harry stood over her. "We don't have a lot of time here, get me? Sure, the body's on ice. But ice melts, honey, and the water it runs fast."

"Please. I promised him."

"That right? He promised me some things. Promised my parents. Tell me, or you can tell it to the MPs. You understand? *Militärpolizei*. Oh, we're not done. There's the CIC—that's the Counter Intelligence Corps to you, and the US Constabulary too. You really don't want the likes of them. They wear yellow scarves, think they're God's own cavalry." He'd grabbed her wrist, squeezing it. He didn't want to play it this way but here it was.

"He's in danger," Irina muttered.

"What?"

"They are all. They can't escape . . ."

The footsteps neared—and came faster, more clipped than Gerlinde's.

"Who's they? Escape what?" Harry said.

Irina started to choke up.

"Oh, no, don't start with the tears, sister. I'm no soft touch. I took you in, but you want me to help? You got to come clean."

Irina glared at him, and for a moment Harry figured he was going to get a spitball between the eyes. He let go of her wrist, she shook her hands as if she had icy water on them.

The footsteps had stopped. Maddy Barton was standing in the doorway, hands on her hips. Her bright blood red, Chinese-style silk dress was such a contrast to the brown and gray room it was as if a spotlight had been turned on her. Her lipstick was even redder, which the fresh powder on her cheeks only emphasized. Irina sat up and gazed, more in awe than in fright. Irina probably hadn't seen a striking dame all dolled up like this for years, if ever. Harry had seen a lot of them ever since the occupation began to require more Girl Fridays than GI Joes, and he had managed to stay clear of them until Maddy Barton came along. You could call her his girlfriend, but he wasn't too sure anymore. Yesterday Maddy had wanted to go to another of those parties Harry couldn't stand, all visiting committee congressman pressing the flesh and hinting at buxom Fräuleins for hire, the sycophantic adjutants there to keep the correspondents drunk, most officers risen three ranks or more in the time Harry had remained a captain. Maddy went anyway. Harry stayed in, and for his trouble got a plain clothes named Hartmut Dietz knocking on his door.

A long thin Pall Mall hung from Maddy's red nails. She was only now coming home from the big shindig.

"Have a nice time?" Harry said.

"Wouldn't you like to know." Maddy's eyes narrowed and upped and downed Irina. She left a pause where in kinder times she might have introduced herself. "More house staff?" she said. Not a bad jab, if only Irina could understand it. "We could use a good laundry girl," she added.

"She's a refugee," Harry said, adding, "she's a DP," since a DP or Displaced Person by definition was someone who suffered from the Nazi regime and needed care according to policy and regulations and common goddamn decency. DPs were likely just one step above a local German in Maddy's eyes, but every bit helped. Harry had put up DPs before. "It's a liaison issue of mine. She's got nowhere else to go. Yet. Only be a couple days."

"That so? Shame. Might want to keep one around next time," Maddy said, her eyes fixed on Harry, "'cause you could use the house help," and with that she pivoted and continued on down the hallway, the clip of her heels then rising up the stairs.

Leaving Irina to stare at the doorway. She had slumped again. Harry thought about saying something about her long black hair, how it could be styled to look like Maddy's. He didn't know if that was what a woman wanted to hear in such a situation. Harry did know that Maddy's cold-shoulder barely hid the keen curiosity of a muckraker. She could have worked for Hearst.

He waited for Maddy's footsteps to fade upstairs and said, "The way I see it? You're not able—out of coercion, fear, what have you—to talk about this. So I'm going to have to report it."

Irina's chin dropped. "Report?"

"Uh-huh." It was another bluff, but all that Harry had.

Meanwhile, aromas of real coffee and bread wafted into the room. Out in the hallway, Gerlinde hurried past bearing clothes on one arm and a tray piled with food on the other. Maddy was putting his housekeeper through her paces again—standard operating procedure after lasting the whole night through.

Sweat beads had formed on Irina's forehead.

"Unless you can tell me more," Harry said. "See? We help each other."

Irina looked up, her face green. She tried to stand but whirled around wobbling, as if to vomit. Harry bolted for her, caught her going down.

"Gerlinde!" he shouted, "I need help here."

Nothing came out but a dry heave. Crouching, Harry held Irina in his arms, cradling her. "You better not be playing me for a fool," he muttered.

Irina groaned. Her heavy breathing hinted at what had had almost come up—Gerlinde had fed her precious liverwurst and radishes.

"Oh, that's a tough break. Not used to eating like that, are you?" he said.

Irina stared with glassy eyes, her eyelids heavy. A wan smile spread across her face. "You do look like him, as a man. And he said this about you too."

She moaned. She passed out.

Gerlinde and Harry carried her back to her room. Noon passed. They let her sleep. Harry returned to his den, pacing around the furniture. He would have had things under control if Maddy hadn't made her big entrance. Maybe he shouldn't have put the screws on Irina like he had.

Then he remembered what Irina had said: Max told her that his little brother looked more like him now.

Which, Harry realized, meant Max must have seen him at some point. With his own eyes.

He bolted over to a window. Was that why Irina was looking out? Max was watching them?

Peering out, his forehead to the cold glass, Harry only saw a lead gray sky and woods gone dim.

"Herr Kaspar!" Gerlinde rushed in, her shawl trailing off a shoulder and she didn't care, such was the pale shock on her face. Harry knew what was coming.

"The girl—she's gone," Gerlinde said. "Not one trace of her anywhere."

# Three

Harry considered the tight spot he was in and decided that the neighborhood where Detective Dietz of the Munich Police had led him to Irina and a corpse was not the ideal spot to search for her. Returning to the scene, as it were. He went anyway, on foot. He could have headed out to a bar or a show instead to get his mind off things, but then he'd only rub shoulders with the usual Americans complaining about conditions. And Harry would choke back his anger again. You want conditions? Step out of your clubby clubs and staff cars for one moment and look around you. Smell it, if you dare. And try to remember why you are here in the first place. Besides, he didn't feel much like running into Maddy.

This neighborhood, he knew from his backgrounders, was once a stronghold of Munich's working-class Socialists until the Nazis purged it. Then the Americans and Brits bombed it. Tough block, tough luck. At least last night's wet snow had ceased. He manned a street corner and stepped in place to keep warm and plied passersby with Lucky Strikes and Hershey's, nothing shady here, just a curious Ami with a few questions, but none of the locals knew a thing about a Russian girl lying low. He only got shrugs and more shrugs. And he kept seeing the same refugees shuffle past as if they, having nowhere else to go, simply traveled concentric circles around the center of Munich.

He was starting to feel like one of them, the way he was running around for nothing. It was pushing four p.m. on Saturday—a good three hours since Irina made a break for it. Harry and Gerlinde had searched the mansion. Irina had taken only her clothes, a sandwich Gerlinde had set out for her, and all three of the sabers—Harry had left them leaning against his bedroom dresser. And she somehow snuck out of that creaky old mansion quieter than the mice Harry could hear from two floors away.

Daylight would be dimming soon. Harry found the block with the blast hole in the building and crept through the rubble tunnel back to the cellar. He could hear it well before he entered—a young German woman had moved in with a mob of children who, instead of tugging at Harry's pant legs, huddled shrunken in the shadows with their big drooping eyes on him like old owls. Harry took a good look around. The place was picked clean, of course, right down to the board that served as the dead man's final resting place—busted up for firewood no doubt. The woman knew nothing except the one indisputable fact that her husband would return from the Eastern Front, where he was a POW, he'd return any day. Sure, sure, Harry told her.

"You know a Detective Dietz?" he asked her. "From the neighborhood here? Yes, you do?" He gave her a can of spam. "Don't save it for when your man comes back. Give it to the kids. Promise me." She promised.

Dietz's block was only two over, the woman told Harry, but to reach it, he had to backtrack around a giant rubble pile that led him in yet another circle until he discovered a detour through a courtyard. Dietz's building looked lucky. It had shrapnel scars and smoke-damaged sandstone but compared to the surroundings looked like a *Residenz* instead of the dull tenement it was before the bar lowered to such deep depths. As Harry neared Dietz's corner, he spotted the police detective waiting on the curb. Harry almost expected it. The cellar woman's eyes had lit up at Dietz's mention, which meant Dietz had a reputation. Word would pass fast to him while Harry circled.

Dietz was slapping his hands together as if he'd just come out for the fresh air that wasn't so much fresh as refrigerated grit. "Herr Kaspar?" he said. "Surprised to see you passing by."

"I'm sure you are."

"Just heading out."

"Of course you are. Trading? Or is it work?"

"Are they not the same thing?" Dietz said, adding a laugh. He was scanning the surrounding rubble and its various openings, trying to hold the smile.

"Don't worry, I'm alone."

"Are you sure?" Dietz's eyes fell back on Harry.

"Herr Dietz—Hartmut, I'm Military Government, remember? I'm here to look after you."

"And this is why you leave me with a corpse my colleagues are itching to ask me about." Dietz was speaking lower now.

"I told you it'll be worth your while."

"That is not what I mean," Dietz snapped. "I don't want to lose my job."

"You won't. No one will."

Dietz stole a glance back at his building. "I did not tell you my address."

"What was I supposed to do? Waltz right into police headquarters? So calm yourself."

"All right, all right," Dietz said. He touched Harry on the shoulder, which was very un-German and un-conquered of him, but then a year and a half into an occupation was a strange, neutralizing time. He flashed a smile. "So. Should we take a walk?"

Dietz and Harry strode around a corner and into a better-off neighborhood, passing shops with actual windows and signs (most reading Closed or Out of Stock, but who was counting?). They had ridden a short stretch on a packed streetcar, Dietz hanging on the outside with the rest of the sorry German men, Harry warm inside as befitting an

American although the local riders' shortage of soap didn't mix so well. Now Harry and Dietz kept big smiles on their faces as if just a happy Ami and German out on a stroll. It could have been a photo in *LIFE*.

"How's the Fräulein?" Dietz said through his teeth.

"She's okay," Harry said. "She needed rest. Been through the grinder, that girl."

"She tell you about it?"

"Not yet. She needs time. So I need time."

They crossed a small square before a bombed-out church, the only blemish on the neighborhood. Groups of men, huddled with their backs facing out, halted their black market food trading to watch Dietz and the American captain pass. Dietz raised a hand to reassure them but didn't look their way.

"The body?" Harry said.

"In a drawer. Safe for now. I had to remove the uniform, for discretion's sake. Please do not ask me to destroy it."

"Of course not, it's evidence. Are you crazy?"

Dietz snorted. "No, but everyone else is."

They reached the Isar River, just south of Old Town. Harry led them to a bench along the bank, lit up two Chesterfields, handed one to Dietz, and told him just to smoke the damn thing for once. They puffed and looked out. The Isar rushed by as brown and frigid as ever, but that didn't stop people from hauling water out of the river in buckets and cans and rusting helmets while others attempted to wash clothes. Women lunged for the scraps of wood that drifted by—such valuable firewood. Amazing they weren't all dead from hypothermia, Harry thought. Just looking at that water seemed to make the temperature drop ten degrees.

Dietz shook his head. "The blood is all over that corpse of ours. A mess."

"I know. Look, thanks for this. I know it's not easy."

"*Ach.* What is?" Dietz spat a loose shred of tobacco. "I couldn't wash him, mind you, because blood is evidence, and who would want to waste the cleanser in any case? I fingered around as best as I could with a bright light and a good lens." He sighed at the memory. "Well, in the end it was the uniform that gave us a clue."

"What sort of clue?"

"I thought, is it not odd this man has no dog tags, paybook, papers, nothing private on him? Not even a photo of loving mother or one of your 'Dear John' letters. Quite suspicious." Dietz picked another tobacco shred from his teeth. He stared at Harry doing it. "There was a name, on the trousers: Earvin Posey."

"Funny last name. So?"

"So, your Mister Posey is no flower. He's on our list of known Ami deserters in the region, a list that your Military Police gives us."

Harry wasn't surprised. A good number of GIs in Germany had deserted full time to commit rapes, attack the locals, extort, plunder, and smuggle, among other vices. It had started during the war, when some probably had their reasons. Spanner had reasons that almost got Harry killed. But nowadays it was just one more symptom of their complacent yet unsettled occupation of endless duration. Idle hands, working away. "What else you got on him?"

"He was listed as violent and dangerous." Dietz shrugged at that.

A craft was coming down the river—a log raft laden with women and children hugging their bags and a man standing, somehow, pushing the raft along with a wooden post. It was like something out of Mark Twain, if only . . . The sight hit Harry low in the gut, and he clasped his hands together and waved them to wish the raft refugees luck. As they passed they just stared back, exhausted, wet, freezing.

Dietz glared at the raft as if simply annoyed it distracted Harry. "It makes me want to know more about this girl of yours. Does she belong to the Poseys of our fine world or to a pathetic journey like that raft there?"

"I'm working on it, I told you. Getting to the bottom of it. It's my responsibility."

"I understand. I do believe you."

They stomped their feet and smoked, not so much for the relaxation but for the warmth that was in the smoke.

"*Shashka*," Dietz said.

"Come again?"

"It's what that type of sword is called. They're from Russia and White Russia, Ukraine, The Steppes. Take your pick."

"Thanks, I'll check it out."

"Good, because our corpse cannot stay frozen long."

Dusk fell as Dietz led Harry on a different route back through Old Town. A crew of men was clearing rubble in the dim purple-gray light. All were stooped, their shoulders sagging, the thick, oversized white letters PW on the backs of their dark coveralls seeming to weigh on them as much as the debris they heaved. Bored GI guards watched over them. These prisoners were hard cases and possibly SS, since most German POWs in the West had been released long ago. Harry made a mental note to look up whether Dietz had been in the Wehrmacht. Asking him about it now wasn't exactly going to cement the man's loyalty. As if reading Harry's mind, Dietz walked with his head down, his hands deep in his pockets.

And Harry thought of his brother again. He reminded himself to keep a clear head. Invoking Max's name could still be some kind of swindle—Irina hearing somehow that this flush Ami had a lost brother and she'd tried to exploit the info. Everyone had an angle, if only to survive. Around here lost relatives were used like gold bars or more valuable currency such as a rare fresh potato or the promise of one. Harry had considered everything. Deduced. He was no fantasist. But, lacking hard proof, he simply had to go on instinct. And then his gut kept reminding him that Irina had recognized him in the same way a distant relative recognizes family. He could tell from her eyes. Hell, he almost saw Max's twinkle in her eyes.

It hadn't escaped him that Dietz appeared to be admirably discreet himself about mentioning his brother. The detective had not even brought it up today.

Dietz had strode ahead. He entered a side street and faced Harry catching up. "Should we split up here?" he said.

"Sure. Probably best we don't stay together too long. But, I have a question: You ever hear of a German named Max Kaspar?"

Dietz's head cocked to one side. "Spelled like your name? With K?"

Harry nodded.

Dietz's head cocked the other way.

"Okay, you can cut the act now. He's my brother," Harry said.

"Ah. Of course."

"I appreciate your keeping things quiet—'on the QT,' we say. I just . . . I only have so much time over here, so I supposed maybe it was time I started looking."

"The girl did not know where to find him?"

"No."

"He look like you?"

"As kids, sure, but now?" Harry shrugged.

"Kaspar . . . Max Kaspar," Dietz muttered. He shook his head, deep in thought.

"He is—or was—an actor." It was hard to imagine his brother doing anything else. Max was Maxie. Maxie played. Harry remembered that Max worked hard but never let you see it. He wasn't political and hardly an opportunist, except when it came to champagne for breakfast, rich sauces, and dames that purred. Harry added, "Max had come back over here from New York. He had some success in Germany, I heard, before . . ."

"Before" meant before 1942, before Stalingrad, after which the promise of Hitler's Greater Germany descended down a black pit faster than people could claw and climb. Harry couldn't imagine Max in a soldier's uniform even on stage. But the times had turned the most unthinkable notions into Technicolor gems. By the spring of '45, Hitler was demanding that children and old men take up arms for the Final Victory.

Dietz was still shaking his head, probably less at his failure to recognize the name Max Kaspar as much as at the sad choices that people make. "No. I don't know the name. I wish I knew of him. For you. I am sorry."

# Four

HARRY WALKED SOUTH FROM HIS MANSION, edging along the English Garden. He wore his uniform and kept his head up, his shoulders squared. Cap under an arm. Let them see his face, anyone and all of them, whoever might be watching. Irina herself could even be tracking him from behind statues, pillars. Max could be. If Harry didn't spot them first.

It was now Monday morning, October 16, 1946. Harry had spent all day Sunday looking for Irina, in the train stations, on the big and small squares, and along the main avenues where hordes of refugees trudged in and out of Munich. He asked at checkpoints and in crowds. Nothing. *Nichts*. Irina still had to be in Munich. She was his responsibility. He had taken the risk. Others might have thrown up their hands, Harry told himself. He could have turned the corpse in, confessed to bungling it, and taken his lumps. Taken his chances. Since he only had a month or so left, a dishonorable discharge would hardly have been worth the carbon quadruplicates, he reckoned, and he overcame his late night fears this way. Or, he could have paid Detective Dietz to find Irina. Dietz knew people an Ami never could. But Harry didn't work that way. He wasn't the sort to sit and wait for answers. Maybe that was why they had never promoted him after Heimgau, he thought. He didn't delegate enough. Didn't make others do the dirty work. *They could stuff their powers of delegation*, he thought.

He hurried along, turning onto the broad Ludwigstrasse, daydreaming about what he would say to Irina once he found her. He would be understanding, yet firm. He would demand to be taken to Max but any way she wanted it. In the meantime, he had to be careful. He stopped before a plate-glass window to observe the street in its reflection. This was what spies did in pictures, but he wasn't exactly sure what to look for. Would someone trailing him be across the avenue, or on down the sidewalk? And what about shadows?

After Sunday's washout, Harry had come up with a new angle. Military Police headquarters had a prime location where Ludwig's grand avenue funneled into the Odeonsplatz, the opera house, and Old Town. His uniform was pressed for his visit and he would've pinned on more fruit salad if he had any—anything shiny helped with the MPs. The marble and iron lobby resembled a post office or bank. A sergeant sitting erect behind a polished oak desk the size of a jeep took Harry's name, asked his business, sir, and directed him up a staircase. Harry never cared for these MPs hard cases, but they were all right, he reassured himself, just a little rule-bound and tightly wound up. Then they made Harry wait longer than the Germans who passed in and out. Harry watched the sergeant talk on the phone about him. And Harry's skin started to heat up. Then they sent him on to another clerk behind another jeep-sized desk, this one a stone-faced sergeant major who sent Harry on through a back courtyard to an adjoining building.

They were sending Harry to a major who might help, stone-face had told him.

Outside, Harry lit a Chesterfield and exhaled some of his heat. He wondered why they were giving him the runaround. Maybe it was because he was German-born *and* from Military Government— all eggheads, Commies, and silver spoon do-gooder types making nice with the conquered krauts, to name just three of the wholly untrue assumptions. Maybe, like dogs, they had even smelled poor detective Dietz on him. What he wanted to do was tell them about his seizing a certain train and taking out one of worst perpetrators in the US Zone of Occupation on his own when it seemed no one else would lift a finger.

He pinched his smoke out and set the butt between cobblestones for some lucky German employee. The adjoining building was a squatter replica of the first, two stories instead of four, and had no guards or jeeps for desks. Harry wandered the lobby and found a staircase.

At the top, Major Warren Joyner stood waiting. Harry saluted and Major Joyner waved Harry along, practically shoving Harry into his office with a hand so thick it felt like a baseball mitt.

"Sit down," Joyner said. Harry pulled over a worn metal chair. The room looked like file storage more or less, all mismatched file cabinets and tables piled high with folders and ring binders. The desk was pushed up to the window, facing it. Joyner grabbed his wheeled desk chair and swung it around to face Harry, grunting as he sat down, and the chair back knocked at the desk, which in turn banged the window. Joyner was an actual cop back home, Harry had heard, a former town sheriff from Oregon. He looked the part with his paunch and large ruddy face. Harry could practically see the star badge and ten gallon hat. He could also figure out what was happening to him. The Military Police didn't want to hear from Captain Harry Kaspar of MG with another of his pressing inquiries so the desk sergeants had called the adjoining building to tell Major Joyner that Captain Kaspar was coming to see him. Because Joyner was too hardline even for the MPs. Harry knew the jokes about Joyner. He was Sheriff Joyner, gunning down black hat krauts at high noon. He didn't care whether a man was in the Party or not. Some of the worst Nazis in temperament weren't even party members, so denazification was never going to touch them. The Americans' denazification policy was being de-emphasized, but Joyner refused to get on board. He was obsessed with rooting out Nazis whether a big shot brownshirt or the corner grocer and would just assume take one down an alley and snap a neck than waste the paper for a report. Joyner's hate for the enemy remained strong and steady in a time when GI Joe and one-star general alike were warming up quite nicely to the fresh Bier, the curvy Fräuleins and especially the locals' eagerness to please and work their fingers to the bone. The fact was, they'd say, your average German's spic-and-span was closer to apple pie than any other dish in Old Europe. These were the hypocrites, Harry recalled, who two years ago wanted to pave over the whole country with Portland cement. Now they wanted to live in its fairy-tale castles, buy its factories, ship home the finest glass, china, and silver. But a man like Joyner wasn't fooled. He was still looking for that big score of SS malefactors who were all too often getting away and blending back in. Some even had the brazen balls to pass themselves off as DPs, concentration camp inmates, anti-Nazis even. The game was far from over, the pickings still ripe. All Joyner had to do was nab one of the bastards. But he wasn't getting much help these days. The Military Police had new challenges. The Black Market. Refugee smuggling. Communist agitators. Deserted GIs. GIs making more dough than the one-star generals. Harry, swallowing hard in Joyner's metal chair, reminded himself he was lucky they hadn't tossed him to the CIC or the US Constabulary. He had stayed clear of the major mostly because the man hated Germans, even ones in American uniform. He wasn't surprised to get Joyner now. Joyner wanted to make Germans pay. Harry, the born kraut, helped Germans find their way. Enjoy yourselves, boys.

Major Joyner held out his big hands. "Well?"

"Well, I'm not sure you can help me, sir."

"Why not? I'm the new contact for Military Government," Joyner said, spitting out the name as if he'd just swallowed a horse fly.

That nasty fly was telling one sick joke. Whether Joyner's new duty was true or not on quadruplicate somewhere, Harry could not know. Not in the little time he had. Not if he didn't want half of the bigger building to know what he was up to. He and Joyner were stuck together like two schoolboys on recess who hadn't been picked for the big ball game.

"In that case: I'm trying to track down a name." Harry volunteered details: The German police were hearing this name was behind some recent stickups and worse. Harry was trying to help the cops out. It wasn't lying as much as feeding what needed to be fed.

Joyner had listened with his lips pressed together. "I have my own lists," he said. "Some big Nazis, sure, but mostly two-bit SS who might be slithering around. Who you lookin' for?"

"That's just it, sir. I'm afraid it's not a German."

Joyner's face reddened and Harry expected a blast of hot air to follow, Joyner detesting that not even a sorry German-American liaison from MG wanted at his special lists.

"It's a deserter, a repeat offender," Harry added.

Joyner belted out a mighty laugh. The air hit Harry now, but it was warm and sweet from whiskey. The major punched at the air one way, then the other.

"Sir?"

Joyner leaned forward, hands pressed to his knees. "Those damn fools in that other building, they went and matched us up because they figured you're angling for some tin-pot Nazi—probably even figured you'd want to get one off easy, so they'd play a little joke on me."

"That's not my game."

"And they got no clue." Joyner slapped his knees. "So. It's a sad sack you're on to, and a deserter to boot? Well then, they're missing out. Hell, I'll help you." The major kicked away his chair and moved around the table. He heaved over a couple binders.

"Major, look. I can understand your position. But just because I'm German, it doesn't mean I'm swinging the other way like everyone else."

"Say no more . . ."

"You have to finish the job we came over here for. You're honest about it. And the SS? They still have it coming, way I see it."

Joyner faced Harry. "What do you know about it?" he said slowly, like a record player running down.

"I wish I had something better for you, is all. If it leads to that, you'll be the first to know."

"All right. Fair enough."

Joyner flung open a binder. As he flipped pages, he told Harry what he'd learned about most deserters. There were thousands—tens of thousands of them across Europe. The smart ones who had skipped the front line during the war settled down with a Gretchen and learned the local language, usually in France or Belgium or Italy where the situation was less heated. But a deserter looking for trouble? They ran many scams but the hustle offered no sure goal, no safe harbor, and to keep pulling it off they scored uniforms and identities they often discarded after a few jobs. Harry knew a thing or two about that, but he wasn't about to tell it to Joyner. He focused on how Posey fit. The man Harry saw had died in worn fatigues—even for a deserter, it would be the last thing he'd want to be found in. He must have been really down on his luck.

"Want to give me a name there, Captain?" Joyner said.

"Posey, Earvin." Harry began to spell out the name—

"Earvin Posey?"

"I believe that's it."

Joyner slammed the binder shut. He turned to Harry. He grinned, his teeth big and square. "Your Earvin Posey was a deserter, and he was at it a long time, too. Since before V-E. He made it on our lists all the time way back when. Real wild one."

"*Was*, sir?"

"The hoodlum was found dead months ago, down south in Austria. In the British zone they got there. Faithless scum like that, serves him right."

Maddy was hollering for Gerlinde. Harry heard her as he entered his foyer. He followed the droning whine upstairs to his master bathroom and opened the door. A wave of hot steamy air fogged his glasses.

"Just pour it right on in, Linda honey," Maddy said from the bathtub. Calling Gerlinde Linda was Maddy's way of being thankful. The city's shattered water lines rarely delivered enough hot water, so whenever Maddy felt like a bath she commandeered his and had Gerlinde boil and lug hot water up the stairs. Maddy was full of real American can-do—the only problem was, it was often someone else's can and not much of Maddy's do. "Linda dear?" Maddy repeated.

Harry yanked off his glasses but still couldn't see where the steam haze ended and the bathroom's white marble began. "It's me," he said from his fog.

"Oh. But she was bringing me more hot. It's getting cold." Maddy had switched to her pouty voice, the one she'd used the first night they met to tell him how much she missed home. Later she used the same voice to tell him how much she hated it back home.

"You're going to wear her out," Harry said, his hair itching from the sudden sweat.

"Aw, she can take it. Tough fraus like her, they're out rebuilding this whole city—this whole stinking brick pile of a city." Maddy splashed water to drive her point home.

"That's exactly what I mean." Harry moved closer. Maddy's contours appeared among the white marble blur, a bloom of rosy flesh like the flower frosting on a cake. He passed her and cracked open the window.

"Hey bub, what's the big idea?"

"Cold air. You ever take a real steam? Mixing it up, hot and cold, that's the real tonic. Too much of one thing is bad for you." Harry had made his voice softer. The last thing Maddy liked was a lecture.

Gerlinde came bursting through the door panting and grunting but somehow the steaming water didn't slosh out the pail. She squinted at Harry through stray strands of thick gray hair.

40

"That's enough," Harry told her. "Set that down here and I'll take care of it."

"What about your lunch?" Gerlinde said. "You must eat."

"No. Not now. Get some rest. You can go if there's nothing pressing to do. Clear?"

"*Alles klar, Herr Kaspar.*" Gerlinde glared toward the tub, sighed, and shuffled out.

Maddy had dunked herself. Harry stood at the edge, making sure not to catch a toe on the tub's clawed feet, and saw the pink of Maddy's shoulders and chest and knees and thighs showing through the remaining daubs of bubble bath foam. She emerged, spit out a long stream of water, and stared up at him. He smiled for her. She showed him a pink breast, the areola a brighter pink, and submerged it. No smile.

"I missed you Friday night," Harry said. It was the truth. He'd last seen her Saturday morning when she came home from being out all night to find him questioning Irina. She'd stayed in her bedroom and probably slept right through Sunday as far as Harry knew. She had demanded her own room from the start, and he'd left her to it long ago.

Maddy shrugged, sending water sloshing. She gave his uniform a nasty once over as if he should've worn a tuxedo to her bath. How dare he remind her of work? She had come over as a WAC, but Harry had only seen her wear the uniform in photos. Instead of rotating home she'd signed on as a secretary for the Munich PX, a position she referred to, if she had to, by its official designation of administrative clerk. She apparently reported to an office across from the Wittelsbacherplatz, just around the corner from just about everything in town and just about everyone in the know.

"Did you get your reenlistment?" she said. "That where you've been?"

"The papers can be pushed, if need be," Harry said.

"Can they?"

Harry knew what she meant. People who dared to push can push them.

"Where did you stay?" he said. "After the dance."

Maddy's official billet was a hotel suite she shared with four administrative clerks. She hadn't slept there for months. Her room there was storage for clothes, a dressing room. The four had a little racket going in the fine garments of top Nazi cronies' wives and mistresses and daughters. It was amazing what lavish furs, gowns, and lingerie the fat cats' women had been wearing while the rest of Germany starved, and burned, and died. But that was a failed Democracy for you.

"My place," she said. "And it wasn't a dance. It was a party."

Harry chuckled. "That's funny. I'm trying to imagine you clearing stacks of minks off your bed at three in the morning."

Maddy snorted. "Why don't you stop trying, and pour me some of that hot water?"

Harry lifted, poured. Maddy closed her eyes as the steamy water swirled around her, enveloping her, the foam bubbles whirling.

"Now, the window please?"

Harry shut it, and the muggy warmth hit him before he could get back to the tub. Maddy raised a gam and let it hang over the side. Harry thought about stroking it. He thought about stroking a lot of her. Maddy watched him, smiling.

"Where's your refugee girl?" she said.

"I don't know. She hit the road apparently." Harry stared at her. "You didn't scare her away, did you?" It was just possible, if Maddy had bothered to get out of bed to do it.

"Me?" Maddy touched her red nails to her neck. "I really don't see how I could. Or why I would. We could have become fast friends."

"You might have learned something. About this place. Been through a lot, that girl. Seen a lot."

Maddy drew the leg back under water. "I bet."

"Not like that. It was on the level, Madd."

Maddy let out a little cackle of a giggle from deep in her throat. Her lips shined red from heat, no lipstick required. "I know: You tell me where she went, and I'll tell you where I was."

"I wish I could tell you." Harry wiped sweat from his cheeks and neck.

Maddy was sweating, beads of it running down her cleavage.

"What are we doing here, Madd? Huh? What?"

Maddy's hand rose from the tub and reached for his. It was so warm it didn't feel wet.

She told him to go wait in her bedroom.

He did it. He folded his uniform over a chair. She came in and slipped under the silk covers with him, her heat surging through him as he caressed her, and she him, both of them sweating again and damping the sheets. She moaned and turned from him. He ripped away the silk, entered her from behind.

Afterward they lay still, on their backs, letting their bodies cool.

"There's that big shindig Wednesday," Maddy said.

Regional Military Government was hosting a reception for another delegation of visiting congressmen and VIPs from major business and industry. A medieval manor and its vast grounds south of Munich would serve as a proper bulwark against the rubble, the stench, all that displaced poor. The main entertainment was horse racing of all things, featuring thoroughbreds formally owned by Nazis, and bird shooting was promised. Maddy had been talking about it for weeks. The swell soirée would go into the night. She was bringing multiple outfits. It was to be the last outdoor function before the cold weather hit full force. It was also a last chance at landing an even better position.

"It starts in the afternoon," Maddy added.

"All right," Harry said.

But then Maddy's voice went beyond pouty to a new, and Harry had to admit, sympathetic tone that he wanted to kiss and scream at the same time. It said: "All I ask, Harry? Just go to one party with me. Just dance with me, dammit. A girl needs a good ole whirl out of her man occasionally."

It meant: *We—I—just can't go on like this, Harry honey. We're hitting a dead end here.*

Harry wondered if this was her real voice. It had to be in there somewhere, and it would eventually claw its way up to the surface just like the rest.

And then she said, "Sometimes, it's like you think the war's about to start instead of it being over. Is that what you're thinking? You know something that I don't. Something that keeps you on edge like this."

Harry considered telling Maddy the whole truth. Not just about Irina, but about that train job back when the world was simpler and still sick of war. She'd see he was not who she assumed he was. Not down deep. He was going to lose the fluff and fat he had gained in Munich, and if she didn't like it, she could hoof it. They could all hoof it. He ruled out telling her, or anyone, about Max though. He had too much to learn first.

He lay there staring at Maddy. She had fallen asleep with her mouth open, an unlit Pall Mall stuck to her lipstick. The truth was that he didn't know exactly who she was either. In her resentment at him, who knew whom she'd tell? The PX alone got the word out faster than Radio Munich, not to mention the nine plus shindigs she attended a week. He wouldn't be surprised if she tried to kick him out of his own mansion.

He was getting a chill lying there. He pulled on one of her swanky plundered robes, gathered up his uniform, and skulked back down the hallway to his room.

By the time he was eating the ham-and-cheese roll Gerlinde had left out despite his clear orders to the contrary, that bum named Earvin Posey had returned to oust Maddy from his brain. So the bum had died twice—once in Southern Austria and last Friday in

Munich. Talk about down on his luck. Posey was no Posey, Dietz had said. How right Dietz was and didn't even know it. Too bad the man found in Posey's GI fatigues wasn't talking. Harry needed talk. A revelation. Even if it was hearsay, it might just lead him to Irina. He thought about that as he popped the rest of the roll in his mouth and licked the mustard from his fingers.

These days, in this broken town, only one thing made people talk like a barker, a crier, a confessor. He thought about Maddy's swanky robe, and it gave him an idea. Down in a cellar storage closet he found the mansion's smartest duds, more of the surplus left by the previous owner. He chose a black wool overcoat with sable collar and a bowler hat, but he decided against spats—he wanted a hint of old money, but that was too much. Back upstairs, he slathered on eau de toilette and a hair tonic that made him sneeze. He wrapped his neck in a scarf of lavender cashmere.

And out he went. He hit the streets and felt passersby watching him, the rare silly rich man, some eyeing him for what he appeared to be and others for what they could take from him. He added American flavor by putting on his gleaming horn rims, chain-smoking Chesterfields with a cigarette holder, and tossing the butts as largesse.

On Sunday, he had done the quickstep—he had hit all the obvious spots in his uniform, wearing down his soles. Today was the masked ball. He would try the darker mirrored haunts and let his costume do the talking. The edges of Old Town had what he wanted. He tried the black markets on squares, corners, and down alleys. He had the cigarettes, chocolate, and enough dollars for flash but didn't need them. The getup alone made them come to him.

He hit up the Displaced Persons from the East, former forced laborers who'd refused to go home. "I like to buy sabers," he said in a simple German he accented with American Rs. "You know anyone who sells fine sabers from East?"

They directed him to squats, cellars, and more black markets, each with fewer Americans and Germans than the last. No one had sabers, but that didn't stop them from suggesting yet another spot. One pair even showed him the way like boy guides in old Casablanca, hoping for a cut, any cut.

"A girl named Irina sells sabers. You know her?" Harry said and described her. And they nodded, yes, oh yes.

Six hours later, it was all Harry could do not to rip off the soft silky greatcoat and toss it in the gutter. He had struck out, his sword hunt leading to nowhere but a lean-to behind a shell of a warehouse where another widow with at least six children gave herself to GIs for a syrette of morphine, or Pervitin pep pills, or even a rotgut poteen if they had that.

Darkness came and a chilling wind with it. Harry had fled his dead-end tour. He was now blocks from his billet, heading home. A boy in short pants ran by. Harry halted him, pressed the silly bowler on the boy's head, wrapped his neck in the cashmere scarf and sent the boy on his way. Harry coughed again, having smoked so many his pipes were raw. He spat into the cold wind and it sprayed. A girl named Irina? He might as well have said Dorothy Lamour. He had his dance, but they had theirs, and they were leading for a way, any way, to part the rich American dupe from his cabbage. Right now, someone was probably crafting a fake saber out of some old Nazi sword, hoping for the return of the soft touch. *Amerikanski* sucker.

"Pardon, sir. Good evening. You were looking for a saber, isn't that right?"

Harry stopped, turned. A man stood behind him. He'd spoken in German with a thick Slavic accent. He wore a threadbare army overcoat and scruffy felt Tyrolean hat with a shredded feather, had a longer beard like a farmer, thick wire glasses held together with Leukoplast tape, and more gaps in his teeth than teeth. His hair and beard were streaked with gray. Harry had seen him earlier, hanging on the fringes of the sucker seekers.

"You followed me," Harry said.

The man nodded.

"Well, I'm not looking anymore." Harry turned to press on. He would take the back way home and lose the man.

The man followed. Harry stopped, sighing. The man shuffled up to him but kept his distance. The moonlight shined on his glasses, revealing cracks in the lenses.

"You all had your chances," Harry added.

"But, I did not want anyone else to hear. You must understand, it would have spoiled the show."

"I understand. They were working me hard. Who wants to make enemies, that it?"

"Correct."

"Well, I'm all out of scratch," Harry said, "and I don't even have a butt left."

"This is no problem."

"So what is it, then? Out with it."

"You seek a girl, you said. Yes? I know of this girl you seek."

# Five

THE NEXT MORNING HARRY SAT in a jeep before a bare plank barricade, revving his engine, waiting for the guard to return. He had reached the Displaced Persons camp at the Standkaserne just north of Munich center. Most of the DP camp premises were former concentration camps, Hitler-Youth schools, army bases. The Standkaserne was a former barracks. Keeping Jews and forced laborers from the East in such encampments was tough to swallow, yet they provided the best sites for them to be fed, get medical attention, and be easily repatriated. The Standkaserne DP camp seemed less distressing than most. The new guardhouse looked more like a pine wardrobe set outside, and the flimsy barricade of bare stumps and one unpainted board just might stop an intruder in a wheelchair.

The man on the street with the Slavic accent had told Harry to try this DP camp. Their encounter had lasted less than a minute. The man was standing back, his face shrouded in hat, glasses, beard, darkness. His description of Irina included details Harry didn't mention yet the man didn't know Irina personally, he assured Harry—he was simply a humble admirer of young woman and had seen her trying to sell the sabers Harry spoke of. All had laughed at her. The Slavic man told Irina she needed to sell to Americans, but she was afraid of Americans. She said they would send her home. Harry asked the Slavic man where her home was, then where his home was, but the man was already backing up into the dark night. Harry said he could warm up in Harry's mansion. The Slavic man waved his hands and said, "No, please, but thank you, I can assure you there's nothing more I can tell." Then the Slavic man took off in a sprint and Harry lost him at the next corner. It was strange but all Harry had needed.

He had a new jeep from the motor pool and wore his uniform. He'd decided to go with what he was. He wasn't a civilian, not just yet.

He tried the horn. Still no guard came.

He got out, pushed up the bare plank, almost got a sliver for his effort, and drove on in, passing the scraggy trees that lined the main avenue and then along the mix of dark wood bungalows like giant garden huts and larger stucco structures. Homemade signs bore a mix of Hebrew, Cyrillic, and an English with strangely formed letters—probably dictated by an English speaker but painted by a non-English speaker, he reckoned. He only passed a few people going in and out of the nearest buildings, in twos and threes, shoulders relaxed as if they were shopping.

Three old sedans and a rusty truck were parked on a long rectangle of crushed gravel. Harry parked there and continued on foot, passing no one but a group of girls who were laughing and skipping along. A two-story building bore a sign that read UNRRA in familiar black letters, from stencils borrowed from the US Army no doubt. It stood for United Nations Relief and Rehabilitation Administration—the people now entrusted with caring for the Displaced Persons. Harry expected a line out the door, but there was no one here. The front entrance was open. He walked on through, poking his head in doorways. He saw empty desks. The sounds of stray typewriters sent him to more doorways, and upstairs, and finally to a sign that read Administration Office in English.

The room was crammed with tall wooden file cabinets taking up one wall, a metal desk, incompatible office chairs strewn in a rough circle, and shelves and stacks of shoe boxes with numbers and names—what looked to Harry like makeshift post office boxes. Crammed, yes, but organized well. He respected that. He also saw no dust. He sat in one of the chairs facing the imaginary rest of the group circled in the other chairs, feeling like a man too early for a meeting. One wall had a map of Europe with old and new countries, their various displaced and repatriated peoples marked out in colored arrows that crossed and re-crossed each other's, while the wall behind the desk had a large chalkboard on which different nationalities and nation groups were listed along with their approximate numbers and status, Repatriated, Still Displaced, Permanent Refugee, In Transit. It looked a hell of a mess to untangle.

Footsteps. Harry stood. A woman marched in. She had short blond hair. She stopped in the center of Harry's imaginary circle with her arms cocked back, staring around the room as if looking for anything that Harry had touched or moved. She wore a shirt of muted blue-gray plaid, trousers tucked into her socks, and ankle boots. Her eyes landed on him.

He smiled at her. "Good morning."

"You left dirt in the hall. Or is this mud?" she said in English with a slight British tinge.

Harry looked down at his brogues, checked the soles. "Little of both. Sorry."

"So what is it you want?"

"Actually, I was looking at your chalkboard there."

Her eyes found the chalkboard, but her head had not moved.

He kept smiling. "That for your camp, or for the region?"

"Region. Camp network. Same thing."

The woman walked over to the desk and sat, looking at papers in an inbox. The light from the window bathed her there. It was a shame that those blond locks weren't longer, Harry thought. It would go all too well with her fair skin. Good thing she wore the military look, he wanted to tell her—she would be too distracting otherwise. And those greenish-blue eyes, too.

"Know what always gets me?" he said. "We have to put these people up in former barracks and detention camps. A concentration camp? Why when Germany has all these palaces and castles. Supposing we put them all up on the grounds of some former lord or monarch or what have you?"

She lifted a memo to read. "You're making conversation," she said after a pause. "This is what you Americans do. I have no time for it."

He dropped the smile. "I'm not making conversation. I'm gathering information."

He told her his title and function and reported the closest thing to the truth—he was here checking up on suspect Displaced Persons.

"But, your authority does not cover DPs specifically," she said.

"No. It does not."

Her chin ticked up a notch. She set the memo back in the inbox.

"Is it hard to keep track?" Harry said. "All those people, coming and going?"

"Of course. Many go unaccounted."

"How do you mean?"

"Some choose to go their own way."

"But, you know about them."

She shrugged. "The ones who pass through here? Sometimes we do, sometimes we don't."

"Still, it's all reported."

"Of course. I report what I have to UNRRA, and to the central office, and they relay our informations to your Military Government. Captain Kaspar, please, now I am very busy—"

"Name's Harry."

She nodded but only to disguise her eyes rolling, he noticed.

"Those boxes behind me," he continued. "What are they for?"

"They are, how do you say? 'Dead letter' boxes."

"So the recipients are dead, or they only missing? What about repatriated? Or the ones gone their own way?"

"All of those."

"I didn't get your name," Harry said.

"Lieser."

"First name?"

She let in a pause where she might have sighed. "Sabine."

Footsteps, voices. A group marched in bearing clipboards and files, a mix of men and woman. They stood at the desk smiling and chatting in English of various accents, waiting their turn to ask questions of their Miss Sabine Lieser, all bearing the chatty warmth of an office gang fresh from eating a special lunch. They ignored Harry. One woman raised her eyebrows at him in that way that said, *Sorry to disturb, but you clearly had no appointment.* This was a tight crew, Harry saw. Sabine Lieser had probably asked them to show up in case she needed backup.

Within minutes, they had filed back out. Sabine could handle this alone, was surely the consensus. She lifted another memo from the inbox and read as if Harry had left too.

Harry sat back down. "So, you're the one in charge?"

A single nod. "The boss is at a conference."

Harry cleared his throat. "Listen, Miss Lieser, I'm looking for someone."

"Who isn't?"

"That's good. You practice that?"

"Practice?"

"Never mind. She's Russian, I think, possibly from Ukraine or something similar. Might have just come in. I was going to check the hospital but thought I should respect your authority."

Sabine stared. Not even a flinch.

"No? Probably about nineteen. Peasant clothes, definitely. A looker but malnourished."

"This could be anyone. Sorry."

"Anyone a year ago. Before the mass repatriations. But not in the last week. She reportedly was here yesterday. You would've definitely noticed her, seeing how this place is like a ghost town."

"Well, I don't know her."

"She might have been with a man."

"Ah, now we make such progress." Sabine's grimace made the sarcasm sting more. "And what does this man look like? You have his name?"

"A little taller than me. Darker hair but similar features." Harry sighed. "A name, I don't have."

Sabine waved at the air, dismissing his inquiry.

"Do you know what a *shashka* is?" Harry said.

"No."

"It's a type of saber. She'd been seen trying to hawk a few on the black market."

"That does not concern me. Who told you she was here?"

She would laugh if he told her it was a bearded man on a dark street. "The girl's name is Irina," he said instead.

She laughed anyway. "Captain, do you know how many young women from the East are named Irina?"

A tough thought hit Harry: This Sabine probably thinks he's just looking for a refugee wife. It was the latest fashion for GIs and brass alike. He sat up and said, "She might be in some trouble, this Irina."

It got another laugh from Sabine. "Then she would not come here. It only attracts attention. Here you get labeled, and when you get labeled . . . others take over. Policies. Directives. Out of my hands, you see. One hopes this young woman is smart enough to know that."

Harry sighed again. He studied the board again and the maps that had been re-colored. "You have other records, surely. Files and dossiers. Ledgers. Any of those identify individuals by name, sex, and so on? A photo even."

"Some do, some do not. Most are many months old now since the large repatriations are well over. It's as I told you. No one new has arrived. So, please, if you would be so kind . . ."

She stood—her desk before her like the armor on an antitank gun. *Go back to your Military Government*, the stance meant.

Harry crossed his legs. He produced a Chesterfield and set it on his lips. He offered her one.

"I do not smoke."

Of course you don't—you accept it, and you barter it. Even prim UNRRA officials did that. She really was an odd duck, this one.

"Ever heard of an American named Earvin Posey?" he said.

"No. I would remember such a name."

"Let's try another angle. Know of any specific DP groups that are in trouble? Any, say, gangs, or rackets that might be competing?"

"Sure, I know of many. But I don't know of any who are here."

Harry leaned forward, his forearms on his knees. "Listen. Miss Lieser. I came here because you're one of the last camps in Munich that's had a large number of non-Jewish DPs. Slavic DPs, specifically. But, apparently, I'm all on my own here."

Eyeing him, Sabine sighed. She sat down. "Captain Kaspar, you must understand, I do not mean to be uncooperative. We have a good camp here. I would not ruin it by letting in elements that disrupt. We, I, owe it to these people who survived. Who keep surviving."

She had held up her hands and kept them there. And, then, oddly, she was smiling at him. It was a nice and wide smile and it flushed her cheeks. It made Harry look at her neck, too, and she noticed that and turned away to face her board, to the arrows of peoples displaced.

"You understand?" she added.

"I think so. But, mind if I have a look around your camp? Since you have nothing to hide."

"Of course I do not. Shall I provide, how do you say, galoshes?"

"Funny. That's a joke, right? No, I'll just try and be more careful."

The day seemed brighter as Harry walked out, the cold draft more refreshing. He replaced his horn rims with aviator sunglasses and headed off into the depths of the camp. He passed what had to be a school building with children playing on the front steps. Another building was a performance hall of some sort—from inside he heard violins tuning and pianos jangling. On a wide-open area once used for military drills, men and boys played soccer while girls marched in formation singing. A hospital was half-empty, and Harry counted more nurses than patients. The smell of fresh cooked cabbage and aromas of spiced meat wafted from a kitchen house. He studied all the faces. He peeked in, walked through every building. He heard Slavic languages but saw no one like Irina. He talked to children, old ones, even the sick. All looked to be in decent shape, many recovering here since the end of the war. Almost all seemed to be Jews. More signs were in Hebrew here—or was it Yiddish, in Hebrew script? He really should know that.

He had been at it for at least an hour by the time he rounded the back road of the camp where the garbage dumps and a grimy workshop stood, stomping along now to make up time, the sweat itching under his hair and beading on his forehead even though it was barely fifty degrees out. He was wasting his time here. It was inefficient, ineffective. Irina could hide anywhere—could be hid anywhere. But then again, he recalled, the Slavic man had offered the info and refused payment. Why would he do that if this place had no meaning?

At the farthest corner of the camp, Harry found a secluded courtyard flanked by two identical old yet pristine warehouses. A large black Mercedes was parked there. A uniformed man and a woman stood at the rear fender. Sabine Lieser. The officer's uniform was so unfamiliar it took Harry a moment to realize it was Soviet Army—olive tunic with those stiff shoulder boards and standup collar, high peaked cap with red band and star, flared-at-the-thigh jodhpurs and riding boots. Two junior officers with plain caps and no riding pants stood before the car's hood smoking and drinking from a flask.

Harry kept back at the corner of one warehouse, the scene tinted green from his sunglasses. Then the two junior officers strode off to the shade of the opposite warehouse and began urinating on its wall with their backs to him. He marched across the cobblestones.

Sabine and the Soviet officer were gesturing, pointing at each other. Sabine pushed at the man's shoulder.

"Hey, hold up there," Harry said.

Sabine turned on her heels. She was smiling, laughing. Harry had expected arguing. He forced out a grin. The Soviet officer faced Harry smiling. Harry gave the Soviet a relaxed salute, which the Soviet returned with a larger smile and a broad and childlike sweep of his open palm, what he must have thought was an American-style wave. The junior officers had closed up their flies but kept their distance.

"I was just, uh, finishing up here, Miss Lieser," Harry said.

Sabine spoke in Russian to the Soviet, shook his hand, and marched over to Harry.

"Busy morning," Harry said.

"When is it not?"

"They just show up like this unannounced?"

"What, like you?" Sabine said. Her smile had dropped away. She kept on going past Harry.

He followed, fighting the urge to take another look at the Soviets behind him. Sabine turned at the first warehouse and found the main path back. He caught up to her. "Maybe I was hoping to meet them. You don't see too many Soviet Army visiting."

"You don't want to meet them," Sabine said, her voice hard.

Only now did Harry realize that she was speaking native German. He switched to German. "And here I took you for a Scandinavian," he said, adding a chuckle.

"Is that supposed to be a compliment?"

"I'm not sure. A lot of officials are Scandinavian, is all. And your English, well, it fooled me—"

"I'm Bavarian—a Municher in fact." Sabine spat out the words, glaring at the path ahead.

Harry could understand. Her English sounding too good to be a German's. His German sounding too good to be a real American's. In another age, these would've been compliments. But when a war just ended, and the two languages were enemies?

"Try being an Ami but born over here," he said. "Everyone thinks you're either a spy or a moron."

Sabine walked on, deep in thought and hugging herself from the wind blowing through the trees lining the path. Harry endured the silence wanting to comment on the weather, always trying to fill all calm with blather just like an American. He held out for a good minute.

"You must be damn good at what you do," he said. "UNRRA hasn't let many Germans work for them let alone run the show."

"I had the English. My background checked out."

"You must have been squeaky clean, or . . . So what were you, before?"

"A nurse."

"Oh, yeah, which hospital?"

"It doesn't matter. It's not there anymore."

He suspected air raids—American B-17s by day, British Lancasters by night. "Right. Tough break," he muttered.

Sabine led him onward down a side path to a table under a fat birch tree. She sat and blew air out her cheeks, running her fingers through her short hair.

Harry had a Chesterfield in his mouth, unlit.

"Got another?" she said.

"I thought you didn't smoke."

"I don't, well, not indoors anyway."

Harry shook one out and lit her with his Zippo. "How do you know Russian?"

Sabine sputtered a bitter laugh and a billow of smoke. "How could I not, this job? This war."

"*That* war, more like. It's been over a while."

"So it has. After a fashion."

She pulled a soft blue scarf around her neck. The sun had broken through, sending shafts of light on through the trees. It seemed to Harry that her blouse had opened a little more. The sun hit her skin there, just so.

"Tell me something," Harry said. "This Irina girl I mentioned. She's afraid of Americans, or at least of our authorities. And how. Like certain Germans were when we Americans first came. Any German with something to hide."

"It depends on who she was. Her past. Whom she knows even."

"Of course, but why?" As he said the words, he felt a chill run up his armpits. He wondered why Max would be scared. What would he have to hide?

"Well, I can think of one reason," Sabine said.

"What? For her, you mean?"

"Of course I mean her. Is something wrong?"

"No. Go on, please."

Sabine nodded behind her, toward the way they'd come. "Those men back there."

"The Sovs?"

"Yes. They're Soviet Repatriation Mission."

"I didn't think they were the Salvation Army."

"They are not that. Surely you've heard of this unit? They have one overriding aim—to take back all those from the Soviet Union who ended up in the West because of the war."

Harry nodded. A year ago, there had been millions of Displaced Persons, but the Americans and British had worked hard to ship them home under the policy of Repatriation. Only the Jews were allowed to stay owing to their special status as Holocaust survivors. Harry knew the official line—the Western Allies were helping out a valued ally who, through its great sacrifice and grim persistence, had made all the difference to hasten the defeat of Germany.

"You Americans and British, you cut a deal with Joe Stalin at the Yalta Conference," Sabine added. "Doesn't matter whose side they were on before, during, after. Stalin wants them all back except the surviving Jews and the so-called 'ethnic Germans,' whom he's now evicting to the West in droves." Her voice had hardened again. A soft vein bulged on a temple. "So many—too many—were sent back against their wishes."

Harry had seen numbers in reports. He had heard stories. But he wanted to talk about a missing girl. "In my previous posting, we had refugees but we didn't do much repatriation and it wasn't my watch in any case, so let's get back to—"

"Who knows what it was like for those who were forced back?" Sabine continued, stabbing at air with her cigarette. "Off they went on convoy trucks and freight trains, back to their home territories, to their new Russian and Soviet masters. You must understand. Stalin's henchmen collect people like children gather ants. We know what happens to the ants. The Soviet doesn't just want major so-called traitors to the state. They want everyone. From all over Russia and White Russia and the Balkans, Poland, what have you. And you gave them to the Soviet because you cut a deal, and Americans honor deals."

"That may be. Still, as far as I understand it, the worst really is over. Regular Soviet citizens don't have to return against their wishes now."

"Ah, but there are still, how do you say, policy exceptions? You must give up a few bones so you can keep the whole stew."

So that the Americans and British could consolidate their holds over their own zones of occupation, she meant. "Well, you know more than I do," he said.

"One must in my position. So, no, they are not your Salvation Army, Captain Kaspar."

"Still, for bird dogs on the sly those Russians kind of stuck out."

"You should've seen them a year ago. They had bullhorns, red flags, even a band. Pied pipers, yes? So that all would follow them into the trains. Back then, they were a big show. The circus." Sabine shook her head. "The people didn't want to go back. They sensed . . . something. But they got caught up in it. We did all we could—"

"You were there then? Here?"

Sabine nodded. No words followed.

Something about that made Harry want to hold her tight in his arms. "The summer and fall of '45 was no picnic anywhere," he offered.

"No. But we mustn't forget today. And now? They are sly vultures." Sabine added, in a discreet voice that sounded like it was coming over a wireless on low volume, "I think that they are SMERSH."

"SMERSH?"

"Soviet Intelligence. NKVD, GRU, whatever they call it now. In any case. I give them nothing. I only smile, make a joke. I'm just trying to keep them at bay."

"I noticed. And you didn't need your army of office colleagues this time," Harry said.

"Please?"

"Never mind." Harry was used to Germans not getting his Americanized humor, but with Sabine it was different. He felt self-conscious about it as if he was visiting a professor in his office. No, it was more than that. It was as if he was being assessed, as in a job interview.

Sabine held up her Chesterfield, inspecting the butt. "So, your camp search—are you satisfied?"

"Not really. I could be back."

"I'll be here."

"Good. You okay now?" Harry said.

"Better, yes. Thank you. Truly, Captain—Harry, is it?"

"Right."

They shared a pause. Sabine stretched her legs and leaned back and her bangs had just enough length to fall away, off her face, and again Harry imagined that blonde hair long, and longer, flowing down her shoulders.

"You know, you could always go over my head," she said. "Go straight to UNRRA HQ, or to your Military Government."

"And what would that gain? I mean, why come all the way out here just to muck things up?"

"Yes. It was my hope you might say something like that."

# Six

Two days later, harry worked through his office inbox and took the usual questions from his secretary but his mind was combing through his trip to the DP Camp at Standkaserne. He couldn't have admitted to Sabine Lieser that he was looking for a girl involved in a murder, especially when he himself was sitting on the evidence. On top of that, it was a girl who might know his own brother. It wasn't a chance he could take, not with a dame who showed fewer tells than the Army poker champion of the European Theater. Besides, Sabine Lieser was right about Irina. A woman like Irina would never show up at a DP camp and risk revealing full identification—and a woman like Sabine would probably never let her. Of course, Sabine Lieser had wanted him to understand that. She probably did know something about Irina, however, even if she didn't know her by name. He'd have to keep an eye on this Frau Lieser, and not only to watch that lovely neck of hers glow in the sun.

His office was just across the Isar River, a fifteen-minute stroll over the bomb-battered Luitpoldbrücke. His drab but undamaged three-story building stood one block off the proud Prinzregentenstrasse, on the corner of Geibel and Schumannstrasse. They shared it with struggling German accountants, lawyers, and architects as well as a bustling USO office annex on the ground floor. His second floor had offices for three other liaison officers who, like Harry, had responsibility for Education and Cultural Relations, Property, and Civil Administration divisions. They had a team of German secretaries who acted as translators, confessors, and occasionally intermediaries in black market deals. At the far end of his hallway, a once dormant office now housed someone called the US Trade Council Representative according to the door plaque that was just hung. Harry had only seen whom he assumed to be the new man once, from the back as he stood at his door. He wore a dark overcoat draped over his shoulders and a wide-brimmed hat. No one had seen any staff and no one knew the representative's name.

Harry tried to keep his office fairly spartan, to show his visitors he was on the level—what you saw with Captain Kaspar was what you got—but within weeks after arriving it was a lost cause. Soon Germans and refugees were bringing him gifts in thanks for his liaison work and, seeing the gifts already in his office, more of them brought him more presents and increasingly in anticipation of fine liaison work—in their favor, of course. Harry had hand-painted beer steins, embossed glasses, fine porcelain and silver, photos and homey paintings, and all manner of homemade schnapps. He had banners from untold number of small clubs for everything from horse riding to stamp collecting. Not to be outdone, those few Americans who required Harry's influence over local issues brought him glitzy Nazi regalia, stateside booze, and nifty gadgets. The Nazi kitsch they could keep. He did keep two radios—one a portable, a Zeiss camera, and a few bottles of Johnnie Walker. He welcomed a new Underwood typewriter only because his old Underwood was sounding like a piano. His was a warehouse of good faith and form, he assured himself, and much of his bounty he redeployed to smooth over unhappy parties in his liaison assignments. Sometimes he would even see an item return, which he took as a good sign—the good faith and form having come full circle, something that should happen more here but did not. Headquarters knew all this and didn't want to know. As long as he got the job done. It wasn't as if he was negotiating interzonal treaties, allowing the return of major complicit industries, or whitewashing war criminals.

The folder on Hartmut Dietz arrived with the morning mail. Harry had requested all the records MG had on the detective, but it was only one page. The dates and specifics were vague. Dietz was a beat cop before the war. Raised Catholic, the regular allegiances. He'd belonged to a club that played skat and poker. He had a wife. During the war he ended up in the German Navy (he, a landlocked Bavarian, such was the irony of wartime duty) and had never joined the Nazi party, which might have been a favorable sign a year ago. Since then, though, Harry had seen how the cruel aftermath of the war could change a man more than any party, persecution, or even combat. The hunger alone could twist one's soul like a pretzel.

Harry ate a cheese sandwich at his desk and read up on the current pleas he had to manage. A Munich parish hoped to print its own newspaper. A soccer club wanted their field back from the armor regiment using it as a parking lot. A theater group wanted to put on open performances in the English Garden. His job was to shuttle between parties, helping each to reach an agreement, and then report the outcome. It wasn't horrible work, but it sometimes made him feel less like a spokesman than just a spoke. Before his transfer the previous April, he was heading the whole of Military Government in a small town. Sometimes he wondered if his Munich transfer had amounted to a demotion, or simply velvet handcuffs. Sure, he had pushed for it, but he always suspected someone in MG or even CID or CIC knew about the train job and was happy to install him here until his service ran out, so that he could do no harm. Who was harming who? He had helped them to no end—he'd rid them all of a bad egg that they'd never dared touch. If that was harm, then the Nuremberg Trials were a beauty pageant.

Concerns about Hartmut Dietz filled his head, displacing daydreams of Sabine Lieser. He lit a Chesterfield and pulled over one of his five keepsake ashtrays. An uneasy heat was rising up from his stomach, and the itching smoke didn't help at all. It was already

Wednesday afternoon. Three o'clock. Almost five days had passed since he'd asked a plainclothes German cop to break major regulations and put a corpse on ice for him.

Detective Dietz needed to know the score. Harry owed him that. He slid Dietz's page into the folder, the folder into the outbox. Then he grabbed his coat and headed out, leaving his butt to burn itself out in the ashtray.

First Harry tried Dietz's flat. Down in the lobby, he rang and rang the bell but no one answered. An old woman told him that Herr Dietz was not at home. Police headquarters was his next stop, the *Polizeipräsidium* building pocked with bullet holes and shrapnel and blackened from fires gone mad. In its front courtyard stood the scorched statue of an old general, still riding his horse despite centuries of error and self-destruction. Harry strode inside and passed through an entry with walls still marred by pockmarks and burn smears and the wood trim beat-up, no doubt from the Nazis who had hauled out their goods and burned files and fled back in '45. He followed a hallway lined with crime scene photos and found an open floor of desks like in an American-style police department. The uniformed police looked the part, too—they were wearing a new American design of royal blue with open collar. Without their *Deutsch*, it could have been Chicago or the NYPD. Sometimes it seemed that "rebuilding for democracy" was nothing more than stylizing a movie set.

A young cop at a check-in desk eyed Harry as if trying to identify a plane in the sky by silhouette. Harry said in English, "I'm looking for a detective named Dietz." Young cop flipped open a directory. At the two nearest desks, two cops chatted. Their German was thick with Bavarian dialect, but Harry got the gist:

"Who's this Ami come around?" said one. "Coming to nab the mystery corpse?" said the other and they chuckled. "Well, have at it. Take a good while to defrost, that one."

Harry kept his eyes on the kid cop, pretending not to understand.

A hand pressed on Harry's shoulder. Hartmut Dietz stood next to him. Without adding a word, he turned Harry back the way he'd come and led him outside.

They stood out on the little square, on the opposite side of the scorched general. A cold light mist was coming down, forming a wet sheen on Dietz's thin hair. The detective looked pale in the gray light, his face stretched in a scowl like someone had just kicked him in the shins.

"Never!" Dietz barked. He had a hand out as if ready to karate chop. "You were never, ever, supposed to come see me at work."

Harry felt the same scowl coming on. "Is that right? And you were never supposed to talk about a certain corpse."

"Who said I was?"

"Don't give me that. I heard those bulls back in there."

"*Ach*, those drunks? They don't know the score. They shit out their mouths."

"Sure, and they were jawing on about that other corpse I lent you. I got a million of them."

They were shouting into the mist. Dietz's voice broke. He buckled over in a nasty, screeching cough. Harry let him, gave him a pat on the back. He walked Dietz down the street, and Dietz pointed to a sign down around the corner where they found a tiny pub with three tables. Harry ordered two schnapps and a bottle of water from the hunchbacked man who shuffled out to them.

Dietz choked back the booze. He slid a butt in his mouth. Harry yanked it out. "Those things will wreck you when you're howling like that."

"How you think I got wrecked?" Dietz said.

"Yeah, and the war had nothing to do with it," Harry said. "You, in the Kriegsmarine? The Navy's a tough posting for a Bavarian landlubber."

Dietz slammed down his glass with a pop. "What, now you're looking me up when I put so much trust in you?"

"Relax. Just wanted to make sure you're who I think you are."

"I'm not a Nazi. What are you going to do, sick Sheriff Joyner on me?"

Harry wondered if Dietz had been following him. Then again, Major Joyner was an easy guess since he was the locals' preferred example of the relentless Nazi hater. Whenever a Nazi who'd escaped justice was beaten in the night or found dead, people said it was Joyner. They both feared and admired Sheriff Joyner depending on their affiliations. So Harry let it go. He and Dietz had traded enough accusations.

He gave Dietz another pat, on the forearm. The schnapps had given Dietz's eyes a soft glaze. "You first," Harry said. "Okay? I'm listening now."

"Okay. I should tell you that I've done a little digging of my own. Don't look at me like that. It was discreet, so don't worry. Your girl Irina wasn't telling us everything, it seems."

"Go on."

"It turns out another shout was heard there. Shouting. A man. Which makes three voices total. That means there were two men and one woman."

"Says they."

"But I trust them. It was neighborhood people. They confide only in me."

Harry sat back, sighed, sipped. "Well, that's more than I was getting on my end. Thanks."

"I don't know if I can say you're welcome."

Harry tried a laugh. "Hey, you're the one who came to me."

Dietz shrugged at that. They swirled their schnapps. It really wasn't bad stuff once Harry got into it—straight corn like they drank up north, but smooth. A year ago, they were still drinking potato swill in joints like this.

"What did you find out about me?" Dietz said.

Harry related what he knew. Dietz nodded along. He told Harry that his Navy life consisted of land duty along the North Sea,

guarding ships in freezing weather and then diving for cover twice a
day from Allied bombers. They lost more men than the submariners
had lost, he reckoned.

"And before? You were a cop," Harry said.

Dietz nodded. "A very young cop."

"Most of the Munich police were Nazis. We allowed few back in.
You passed muster."

Dietz shrugged again. "I might just as well have joined the party
because that's what you did to advance. But I was too busy having a
good time." He added a laugh.

Harry lifted his drink and touched it to Dietz's. They met eyes;
Germans always met eyes when they drank. Dietz said, "You're not a
regular Ami, you know. You play by different rules."

It was Harry's turn to shrug. He rotated his schnapps glass with
fingertips, two full circles. "I thought about dumping the whole
thing. The fact is, my duty might end soon, and I don't know how
far I can get with this—"

"End when?"

"A month. Maybe two."

Dietz grabbed at Harry's elbow. "No, Harry. You must follow
this, see where it goes."

"I was hoping you'd say something like that," Harry said, though
he hadn't meant the part about giving up. He was only testing Dietz.

"Can I call you Harry?"

"Sure you can."

Dietz called for two more. They arrived in seconds.

"They know you here," Harry said.

"That they do."

Harry lifted his glass. He set it down. "Look, supposing I told
you—and I think I owe you this confession—that Irina got away?"

"No!"

"Yup. She fled. I can't find her anywhere."

Dietz's face went slack, but his eyes held their soft glaze. "Well, then, you'll just have to keep at it. We have some time—not a lot, but some."

"Will do. Thanks."

"I had to mention it to a couple of my colleagues—about the corpse, I mean. Pay them off. You know how it is. I couldn't just stash a corpse anywhere. Especially at the morgue."

"I understand. It's all right."

"A corpse is quite a burden."

"You said it."

"What the devil's wrong with us, huh, me and you?" Dietz said. "We should be working together. Helping people."

"Sounds fine to me," Harry said.

They raised their glasses again. This time, though, Dietz didn't look Harry in the eye.


On his way back, Harry passed the Old Town black markets hoping to spot the man with the beard and Slavic accent. Coming up empty, he returned to his office to find chaos. Three Bavarians from the soccer club had almost come to blows with the German employees in MG Property Control Section, and Harry had to sort it out. He reached home by seven that evening, bone tired. Gerlinde had gone for the day, leaving the mansion in darkness. Harry went to turn on a light. He sensed someone in the house. He stood in the foyer, listening.

It was Maddy. He could smell the sweet perfume one of her superiors got her on a Paris junket. She knew so many majors, colonels, and generals, all rearguard types who'd never seen combat but rode desks like gladiator chariots except their shields were their puffed-up chests done up with medals of every color, the swords their sharp tongues and stern memos, the feints and thrusts their back-room whispers and leaks applied with extreme prejudice. Opponents cowered, colleagues awed, and mistresses swooned. That was the way Harry saw it, but Maddy had them figured out in her own way.

She sat in the near dark of the main living room. Harry sighed, laid his overcoat on the foyer table, and walked in to her. The air in there was so stale with tobacco that even her sweet French water wasn't cutting it. The remains of a once raging fire smoldered in the fireplace and cast Maddy in silhouette, orange on one side and blue gray from the window on the other. The line down her center was as black as the deepest cave.

Then Harry remembered—the big party. At the castle. Regional Military Government was pulling out all the stops. It hit him low, like a bowel cramp. "Shit," he muttered. "I'm sorry. I completely forgot."

Maddy said nothing. Harry let his hands slap at his sides. He moved to the middle of the room, facing her. Her legs were crossed. Across them lay her coat and her gloves.

"There was a car here for us?" he said.

"Was."

"I just don't know what to say. I had a tough afternoon and it was evening before I knew it."

"Did you?" Maddy said, but it wasn't a question she wanted answered. Her voice was cast in iron. Harry expected no less. He felt for a side table and flipped on a desk lamp. He was now standing to her side, but she was still staring at the spot where he'd been standing. She wore a plunging, pale blue dress that elongated her cleavage and made her skin gleam as if powdered. Her eyes were bloodshot, the rims pink. She had wiped her mascara off. She wanted him to see she'd been crying over it. He went over to the buffet and poured himself a whiskey.

"Don't worry," Maddy said. "I'm not going to blow my top this time."

"I'd deserve it if you did."

Maddy snickered. Her teeth looked yellow in the light. "What's the big idea, Harry? Huh? Tell me that much."

"I'm not sure what you mean."

"What's your game?"

"I told you. Hard day. Actually, it was kind of funny—couple soccer players just about clocked our clerks in Prop Con—"

"Spare me," Maddy cut in. "I don't care about that."

Harry nodded, sipping his whiskey. "It's about time we get to the heart of it? Is that what you want?"

"You don't have any friends," Maddy began.

He knew what she meant. The other three Americans on his floor stuck together with their all-night poker, officer's club golf, and hunting trips in the Alps. Harry only saw their secretaries these days. He shrugged. "They stopped inviting me."

"But you wouldn't go anyway. Not even if they asked real nice."

Harry nodded. "I guess that's why they stopped asking." The fact was, Harry had led her on. He had arrived in Munich telling himself he was ready to relax and play the big city American officer. Blend right in. That was when he met Maddy. But he lost too much at poker, suffered through too many hangovers, and paid the Germans and refugees far too much scratch for their goods. What shook him more was that he feared he could become like the American types he had fought head-on in Heimgau, and even like someone he had always suspected his brother Max might have become in Germany—a decadent hanger-on. What other explanation was there for his lost brother, even if Harry couldn't find the records for it? Death or imprisonment were too tough to fathom. And if his brother had been a certifiable Nazi, then the world had no hope at all. Harry scaled back his high life before long. Some called him a sucker, a soft touch. Others, practically a heretic. He could say one thing about Maddy— she had judged him in her own way, with her own eyes, and had stuck with him while others left him to play in his one-man band.

"We're different, that's all," Harry added. "I was on the ground at the end of the war. Ground Zero. Most of these new officers were not."

"Tell it to yourself, Harry. What I don't get? You were a captain then. You're still two bars."

Harry's skin heated up as if that fire was still blazing in the fireplace. He lifted his glass to hide his scowl. "I told you, didn't I tell you? They stopped giving out the bars and stars like penny candy once the combat was over. Besides I don't do this for the silver and gold, some extra fruit salad on my chest."

Maddy laughed, a howl from her belly that threw head back, exposing her throat to him. "You put in all this goddamn duty. You command a town after the surrender. All that swag in your office, and you're still two bars?"

"I told you, Madd," Harry muttered, clenching his glass to his chest.

"And here's what I don't get—what you been up to lately when you're not in the office. You're out hitting the locals' black markets,' and then the DP camps? You're not food office or refugee desk, and yet you choose—choose—to visit a DP camp off duty? And all the while, all the while, you're running around with some shady Munich cop?" Maddy had said all this with her lips curled as if she'd just drank cod liver oil.

"Who says he's shady?" Harry said.

"He just looks it. You know what I mean."

He knew. Maddy was sharing a common outlook among Americans. Germans who didn't amuse them or serve them directly weren't even Nazis; they were just dirt. They were subjects who needed to be kept in their place or they'll start leering. Harry threw back two quick gulps. He imagined himself hurling the glass into the fireplace.

"And then," Maddy continued, "you're obsessed with this DP girl?"

Harry faced a window. He didn't want her to see how she was getting to him. He wasn't surprised she knew any of this. With all those friends of hers, she had more voices keeping her up to date than the radio, and this big city was a small town. "You do not know what you're talking about," he said. "But you're right about one thing: I mucked up the works real good by forgetting your party—"

"To hell with the party, Harry."

"All right. To hell with it."

"Fishy cop. That girl, probably a communist for all you know. And the rest of it? I just don't get you. You're running around like some private dick, but you're certainly not that. So what are you? You know what I used to think? Why you choose to go your own way?"

"What? Tell me what you thought."

"You're scared. Because you're scared of moving up."

Harry laughed.

Maddy matched it with a grimace. "You're headstrong, that's for sure. The ones who know a thing or two about Germans say it's the Prussian in you. But I don't buy that."

Harry's smile had fallen away. "You didn't give up on me. I'll give you that."

"Yeah, I didn't. Until tonight. And then I realized it, why you don't move up in rank and don't want to."

"Oh? Why don't you tell me?"

"Because it keeps you anonymous."

Harry didn't answer. His teeth were clenched und wouldn't unlock.

"You get your rank elsewhere. Another way. Because it's all—this whole solo dance of yours—is precisely the opposite of what it seems."

"Meaning?"

"You are involved in something." Maddy was clawing at the chair arm.

"*Meaning?*"

"You're not who you say you are." Maddy had raised her chin in defiance. "And you want to know what else? I'll bet you haven't reenlisted either."

Harry glared back, helpless.

"You told me you would, but you haven't. And you know why? Because you got something big that's going to keep you in clover after—after you get that uniform off maybe."

Harry fought the urge to laugh again, just to spite her. He set his glass down instead. He sighed. "Maybe you just never knew me."

They stared at each other, eyes fixed. It was more like a staring contest than some sad yet loving stalemate.

Maddy said, "You're running some kind of racket, aren't you?"

"A *what*?"

"You heard me."

"I heard words." Harry threw back the rest of the whiskey and let it burn.

"Okay, maybe it is an operation then." Maddy stood. She faced him.

"Look, you're sore at me," Harry said. "I understand. But, and I hate to disappoint you, there's nothing to it. It's like I told you—"

"What is it? Meds? Whores? What? Maybe one of those fine art rings. Or, maybe it's something more . . . important. More unusual. Maybe you're covering for someone. Maybe you really aren't who you say. No. Goddamn do-gooder like you, maybe you're more the cloak-and-dagger type."

"Me?" Harry said. "You're saying I'm some kind of secret agent?" He laughed again.

Maddy's cheeks had puffed up like stones, her eyes wide and glaring, reflecting all the fire that was left. "Go on, go on," she continued, "out with it." She stomped her foot and grinned at him, her teeth shiny as if slathered with aspic. Harry knew the grin. She writhed her hips into position, smoothing them out with her long fingers. She was preparing herself for him, for it. Talk about a racket—what could be more of a racket than she was running?

She moved in. Harry backed up to the buffet. The warmth left from the fire made his face feel stretched dry. He could tell her anything—he was into church artifacts or diamonds even, selling them back to the states APO for a killing, using the girl Irina as a messenger. Sure, why not? That or he really was a spy, sure he was—he was

74

sneaking around the Soviet zone incognito and running a network by way of the black market and reporting straight to CIC or even to Wild Bill Donovan of the Office of Strategic Services. Never mind that the OSS had been disbanded and Harry didn't even know who the new secret agents were.

He held up a hand, stopping her.

"What?" Maddy said, smiling now, one of those sultry, full, barely parted lip jobs that really made him want to open those lips with his tongue. If she took one more step, his hand would feel the warmth of that gleaming skin and would buckle, and he'd be kissing her before his brain knew what hit it. She said, "What is it you really do, honey? Just tell me."

Harry kept the hand up. "I'm going to tell you the truth. There was a murder. This Irina girl had seen a man get killed. It looked like she did it, but I don't think she did. I just feel bad for her. I don't want to see any innocent punished for something they didn't do—or, in her case, something she might have been forced to do. These poor bastards have been through enough. I have some good clues. I think she has been at that DP camp. I just have to . . . dig deeper. So you see? There you have it. That's my racket."

Maddy was shaking her head at him, her forehead pinched. She stepped back from his hand. "No, there's something else. Something behind it. Someone."

He couldn't tell her about Max. He couldn't tell anyone until he knew the score. Sweat itched under his wool uniform. The anger was rising up in him like a lava bubbling in his brain, burning behind his eyes. He let it. It was the only way to keep her backing up. He let his lava thoughts tumble out as words: "You think you're above all that. Helping people, it's like some virus you don't want to catch. Just like the rest of them."

"What? No, I only figured . . ."

"Figured what, Madd? Figured I was another Joe you could push around? I'm just another of those silky pillows you collect."

Maddy stepped back to the middle of the room, shocked. She seemed to have lost inches in height. Harry followed her. "That's it, isn't it?"

"No. No, it is not." She pulled on her coat slowly, dragging it on over her shoulders as if she was ready to trudge out into a bitter snowstorm. Her skin had gone pale, as if already out in the cold.

"I'm not what you wanted," Harry said. "See? We're getting to the bottom of it now, aren't we?"

"Maybe a fella shouldn't get so sore," Maddy muttered.

"At least I know I'm trying. But can you say that about yourself?" The sweat ran down his face but he let it, tasting it salty on his lips. "Huh? Can you? What are you good for here?"

Maddy buttoned up her coat, her jaw hard. "Go to hell, you."

"Me? I'm going to hell? Then I'll have a lot of company."

She clenched her fists, glaring around the room like the tough dame looking for something to throw. "You're going to regret this. You'll see. You'll come crawling back."

"You think you own this place. This country, this people. You think you own me."

Headlights shot around the room from outside. A car was pulling up.

Maddy flashed a wild grin at him.

"That's the car," Harry said. "You told the driver to come back."

She glanced out the window and her grin flashed at him again, like a neon sign on the fritz.

"You're going to that party anyway," he said.

Maddy threw her shoulders around and stomped out, for the foyer.

"But you aren't going to let me go, are you? That's your move. You're really showing me up, aren't you? Pull some more of that rank you cherish so well." Harry followed her to the door.

She flung the door open and her heels popped at the stairs as she rushed down and out.

Harry was grinning now too, almost chuckling, anything to hold back the anger. He bounded back inside and over to one of the windows and watched the car just as it was turning around, crunching gravel. He had expected to see a man in the back seat with her but all he saw was her, sitting rock-hard and upright, a cigarette in her mouth and her lips tight around the holder. Her face was still pale, and the night cast dim, damning shadows on her proud face.

"Think I'm an impostor? Take a good look at yourself," he blurted at the cold glass as the car sped off.

# Seven

"Ever been in a stockade, Kaspar? *Well? Have you?*" shouted MP Major Warren Joyner, his fists balled white. It was only Harry and Joyner in a cold, windowless basement room in Joyner's building, another swell hand-me-down from the era of Nazi police no doubt. There were concrete walls a brownish gray, a metal table and two chairs, a caged lamp above, and one dandy of an iron drain in the middle of the floor.

"No, sir," Harry said from his seat at the table. He kept his chin up. *Act like you've done nothing wrong*, he'd reminded himself.

"Well, you're damn fucking close." Joyner paced around Harry in his chair. Twice now one of his large fists had sprung open and slapped at the wall as if he wanted Harry to be that wall. It was Thursday the eighteenth now, already evening. The call to Harry's office had been harmless: A Major Joyner needed Captain Kaspar right away, a clerk told Harry. He had crossed back over the Isar River on foot and Joyner met him out on the street and pulled him along by an elbow and down to this basement, heaving the metal door open like it had been stuck for years. Harry, expecting the worst, had removed his glasses.

He could hear the air pumping out Joyner's broad nostrils as the major paced. Joyner stopped before the table, facing Harry. His sleeves were rolled up.

"I have the corpse," he said.

"Corpse," Harry replied. Not even like a question. He only flinched inside, but it was like a dull blade.

"Do not fuck with me," Joyner said, "do not." Harry expected a scream, but this was a low growl from deep within Joyner's gut. His face showed red blotches. "I got *your* corpse, Kaspar," the growl continued. "I got it back, I should say."

Harry kept his hands under the metal tabletop and pressed to his thighs so their shaking wouldn't give him away. He made his eyes meet Joyner's. "Sir, I'm sorry—but with all due respect, I'm a little confused."

Joyner's thick fingers wrapped around the opposite chair back, wanting to twist the metal like a rope of licorice. "I see. And is that because you want to fuck with the United States military even more than you already have?"

Harry dared a sigh. "Look, sir—will you just sit down? Please?"

Joyner, glaring, plonked into his chair and his belly met the table, driving the table frame into Harry's knees.

"I know what you're thinking. You think this born German has gone native," Harry began. He brought his hands to the table and spread them out. "But the truth is, I was helping a refugee. Young woman by the name of Irina. Slavic—might be Russian, Ukrainian, not sure yet. A poor DP all out of options. Her family doesn't know where she is," he added, improvising, and realized he could've been talking about Max. "So, there are no Germans involved for me to protect."

"As far as you know."

"Yes. True. But I'm betting on it. A girl like this doesn't know Nazis. Appears to me she did the deed but in self-defense, if at all. I screwed up. Supposed I could figure out what happened, maybe save her some grief. I haven't. I'm certainly not the best private dick."

"Are you as bad a betting man as you are a shamus?"

"Sir?"

"You truly have no idea who can be behind this, do you?"

"Do you? With all due respect?"

Joyner laughed. "You think I would tell you?"

"No. And why should you?" Harry sighed again, eyeing his pack of Chesterfields on the table. His fear waning, the dull blade withdrawn, he was realizing how lucky he was. Joyner could have jailed him and asked questions later. He could have let Legal Division or CID deal with him. Wash his hands of Harry. But not Sheriff Joyner. True to his legend, the man was doing it his own way. If he got others involved—the paper shufflers, the brass, the patronizers—they'd only muck up the works.

"Go ahead. You can smoke now," Joyner said. As Harry lit up the major added, "Damn sticks are bad for you, you know. No one wants to talk about that. No one wants to hear it. But I'm telling you, some day? People will get it." He shook his head. "People think I'm crazy. Sometimes I think I'm the lone wolf."

"I know how you feel, Major," Harry said.

Joyner looked away. They sat in silence. Harry stabbed out his cigarette after two puffs. Joyner watched him do it. Harry added, "Sir, if you don't mind me saying, I can understand how you would not trust me. How you can never accept people here. They're either greedy, backstabbers or brown noses. And that includes a good deal of true-blue Americans nowadays."

Joyner snorted.

"But the rest, these DPs like this Irina girl? They suffered more than anyone. Almost as much as the Jews, some of them. And they're barely surviving now. So I had to give her the benefit of the doubt. I think you know what I mean."

Joyner nodded, his eyes on the table.

Harry thought of Max, wondering what his brother the actor would think of his performance. Max had told him the best ones always came from the heart, from a truth. In this moment, Harry felt that.

"Can I ask a question?" he said.

"Shoot."

"How you found out about this?" Harry thought better of mentioning Dietz by name. The detective might still be in the clear.

Joyner set his hands on his belly, his fingers interlocked. He shook his head at Harry. "Acting on a tip-off."

"Anonymous?"

"Is there any other kind these days? For Christ's sake."

Harry told Joyner more details including the possibility of an accomplice, but he left out Dietz and of course Irina's mention of Max. Joyner, for his part, said the Munich police had no clue who brought in the corpse, but they promised an inquiry. Fat chance of that, Joyner remarked—the police were more worried about scrounging toilet paper than codes of procedure.

"Do you have an ID on it?" Harry said.

Joyner shook his head. "Only thing saving your ass? That corpse probably isn't American. Uniform's too old, for starters. Hell, the sorry bastard wasn't even circumcised."

Harry understood it now. Joyner was left with what few other American officials would want—a corpse that wasn't American but, owing to the uniform and a total lack of clues, was stuck between US and German jurisdictions. Joyner was probably just as angered by having the thing dumped on him. But he wasn't one simply to pass the buck and dump it on the CID or CIC either. He wouldn't trust them any more than any other agency. Harry could commiserate.

They were doing a hell of lot of commiserating, he and Joyner.

"Was the tip-off straight to you?" Harry asked.

Joyner only shrugged, his lower lip jutting out. The gesture confirmed it for Harry. Again, it all came back to Irina, and what she knew, where she'd been. Harry told Joyner a little more, reporting his attempts to find Irina and his visit to DP Camp Standkaserne.

"So. Do you know any more than that—than I do?" Harry said.

"I'm . . . still working on that," Joyner muttered. He heaved himself from the chair with a grunt and shuffled over to the door. He was wheezing as if he had climbed stairs.

"Sir? Everything okay?"

"Everything's jake."

Joyner opened the door for Harry. Harry followed the major down the dim hallway and past a desk that had a guard when they'd arrived but was now empty.

Outside, on the courtyard, the air stung their cheeks. Harry buttoned his overcoat up to his neck. "That's it, sir?"

"Yep. That is all."

"Better get a coat on, Major, if you're heading back to your billet."

"Not just now. Got some work to do yet."

"All right, well, I'll keep you posted. I am sorry for any trouble."

Steam pulsed from Joyner's nose. He seemed to consider Harry with a mixture of anger and fatigue, as others might a flat tire.

"I'm recommending a reprimand for you," Joyner said. "And I'm making it as severe as I can."

"I understand, sir." Harry's chest tightened a little, but what could he do? It could have been much worse. He had obstructed evidence. He had harbored a suspect.

"But, I'm keeping it in a drawer—my drawer that only I can open. In case you foul up again." Joyner's mouth had curled down on one side as if he needed to spit. "Now I don't want to hear about you running around like some private shamus anymore. Are we clear? You're a liaison. You make sure the USO and Munich caterers union are square, schoolchildren get the new textbooks, all parties are happy. That's what you do."

Unless you have something only Sheriff Joyner can use, the major was also saying.

"Understood," Harry said and turned to go.

Joyner grabbed his elbow. "And one other thing. If I find out any Germans are involved in this, don't even need to be Nazis, you are going to end up in a stockade. And for a good goddamn while."

"Yes, sir."

"Damn right. Now, go on home and smoke another cigarette if you have to. But don't say I didn't warn you."

# Eight

Harry headed off into october's coldest night yet spewing angry gusts of cigarette smoke. Some snake of a weasel had sold him out, warning Sheriff Joyner as if he himself was the murderer. He didn't like being dealt double, not since it almost cost him his life back in Heimgau. Joyner said it was anonymous but it was still a hot tip because it fingered him. All he was doing was trying to help a girl. And hoping to find his brother—he could admit that to himself.

He pressed on through the northern edge of Old Town, his hands deep in his pockets to stave off the wind and the chill it carried.

He considered marching right into the *Polizeipräsidium*, but his reasoning won out. It would help no one to make a scene.

Near the main train station the night was coming alive with people, carousing, nightclubs. He peeked in bars, beer gardens, and cabarets, scanning the crowds. He recognized faces. But not the face he needed to see.

He backtracked toward police headquarters. A couple side streets over was a club that didn't have a name. Different types slapped different nicknames on it. The building's outward-facing facade made it look like a charred hull. A neatly swept path through the rubble ran deep inside to an inner courtyard. Officers came and went, Fräuleins on their arms. Harry stuck to the darkness of the courtyard's arched entrance. Three young toughs stood watch at a nondescript red door, the usual United Nations of bouncers—a foreign DP, a German, and an ex-GI, all wearing suits worth more than their life savings before the war. Harry slapped his face and hair into place. He put his horn-rims on. Another group passed through heading for the door, shout-ing and laughing. Harry gave one of the young American officers a good slap on the back, and the poor sap was so full of booze and wild visions of naked blondes that he took Harry for someone he must've been drinking with all afternoon and evening already.

And Harry was in. The door led to a cellar, which cleaned up all right. They even had a chandelier. Harry sat at the bar, a slab of cool gray marble. He rested a hand flat on the calming surface while his other hand cradled his second whiskey. The place was trying to be more than it was, and the action was no different. On one end, a band of elderly Germans (classical musicians, Harry guessed) sweated to keep up with their bandleader, a black American. At this early hour the small dance floor in the middle held only Fräuleins with painted faces who shuffled together out of boredom, casing the scene. At the other end was a card game at an oval table—boyish American lieutenants, gaunt civs in rumpled suits, and a sole Soviet liaison officer at one end with only a frown for company. More painted Fräuleins worked the perimeter eyeing any winners, but they mostly got each other's eyes and they weren't too friendly. A mishmash of poker chips, European currencies, and occupation dollars lay before each player, and Harry guessed the biggest pile added up to less than a carton of stale Camels.

Hartmut Dietz, with his modest pile of mishmash, occupied the end opposite the Soviet. He hadn't seen Harry over in the dark at the bar.

Harry turned away from the room and stared at the bar mirror, his reverse image just another object among the bottles and glasses and revelers reflected. He reconsidered how to handle this. Major Joyner had warned him, sure, but the major never said he couldn't do a little cleaning up. A hard case like the major would understand—he'd make a kraut squirm a little, see what shook out. Joyner would certainly want to know the score if he was in Harry's brogues.

Harry downed the rest of his whiskey, pushed off the bar and onto his feet. He swayed a little—he hadn't eaten for hours and the juice had gone straight to his head. He shouldered through the crowd into the light of the room, parted the two Gretchens zeroing in on Dietz, and placed a hand on Dietz's shoulder. Dietz turned and see-ing Harry, rose up. His chair leg caught Harry in the shin and Harry stumbled back, pulling on Dietz's shoulder for support.

Dietz fell down with him. A Fräulein screamed. Men shouted. Dietz howled for air but nothing came out—the fall had knocked the wind out of him.

"It's okay, folks, I know the man," Harry said, holding up a hand and forcing out a chuckle, his face reddening.

Pretending to help Dietz up, he pulled the detective close by the lapels and growled, "What's the idea, selling me out like that?"

Hands clamped on Harry's shoulders and jerked him back-ward—two big goons were pulling him out of there. "He's a friend of mine, we stumbled is all," Harry told them but they said noth-ing. They had him by the arms, his heels off the ground. "Big idea? Givin' a kraut the benefit of the doubt over me?" he joked in desperation.

They pulled him up the cellar stairs, heaved him out into the courtyard, and then joined the bouncers to light up, ignoring Harry now as if he was a bag of garbage they'd set out.

The cold sobered Harry up. He shared a laugh to himself as he smoothed out his wrinkles. He guessed it could have been worse. He could be holding his jaw right now—in pieces.

He decided to wait ten minutes tops. After about five, Dietz emerged from the cellar and stood off to the side in silhouette. His overcoat collar was pulled up high, and his hat leaned forward shielding his eyes. Harry could almost see him as a Gestapo man he never was, or at least the young cop he used to be. He was watching Harry like Harry didn't know he was there—like he stood behind one-way glass.

Harry held up a hand. Finally, Dietz walked over. "What happened in there?" Dietz said softly in English as if reading a letter aloud to himself. "I did not understand what you meant."

"What I meant?" Harry said. "The corpse—it's gone. That's what."

"Gone?" Dietz's hands sprung from his pockets. He put an arm around Harry and led him out onto the street.

Harry halted Dietz and stood him against the building's scorched facade. "Military Police have it," he said, keeping it vague—he'd let Dietz show his stripes.

The detective switched to German. "You say that like the stiff just got up and walked away."

"I wish that were true," Harry said. "But here's the thing: Someone tipped them off."

"What? Well, it wasn't me, I can assure you." Dietz looked both ways down the street and over Harry's shoulder. He pushed back his hat, exposing his eyes glossy with anger. "Who the hell would do this? I want to know."

"That's just it, isn't it? I don't even know. Anonymous tip, they say."

Dietz snorted a laugh, shaking his head.

"You can laugh. Surprised I'm not in the hoosegow." Harry's face was in silhouette now, and Dietz searched its darkness. Harry gave him nothing.

"I tell you. I did not tip them off."

"Prove it," Harry said.

"Am I not proving it?"

"You tell me."

"I'll try, Harry," Dietz said. "But you'll have to come with me."

Dietz walked Harry in silence through the dark streets.

"Where we going?" Harry said.

"Home. I'm tired," Dietz said.

Harry waved down two GIs in a jeep who dropped them a block from Dietz's street. Harry had not expected to go home with Dietz.

Few Germans wanted their occupiers to see inside their hovels, for they offered windows onto their true lives. Harry had seen fur-wearing opera stars harboring whole families in helpless squalor and what looked like hobos out on the street living in princely comfort.

Dietz's floor was the third of six. The old egg crate of an elevator wasn't working so they trudged up the stairs in the dark, Harry having to feel his way with starts and stops but Dietz climbing with an even, deliberate rhythm. From the floors they passed, Harry heard cackling, music playing, arguing. He smelled cheap perfumes, sundry tobaccos, mold, and that unmistakable fetor of rotting vegetables. Dietz's floor was quieter. He knocked at his door in a pattern of two short knocks, then three shorts. They waited. From inside they heard the same knocks in reverse. Dietz opened the door.

The front room was dim, illuminated only by the low light from an adjoining room. A woman stood before them wearing a plain dark apron over a pale dress. Her features were too hard and bony for attractive, but her wide smile made up for some of it. She shook Harry's hand. "Frau Dietz. Welcome," she said.

"My wife, Lila," Dietz said.

"Nice to meet you," Harry said, turning away to see four small children peeking around the doorway of the adjoining room, their sexes indistinguishable because of their towheads and bowl haircuts. Harry waved at the kids and they vanished. Dietz didn't call them back out. There might even be more kids back there, even a complete other family or two.

Harry turned to catch the sharp look Dietz's wife shot at her husband. She excused herself and Dietz followed, excusing himself for a moment, and Harry, his eyes adjusting, inspected the goods lining one wall: a few worn burlap sacks and old suitcases full of who-knew-what, several pieces of tarnished silver and porcelain, what looked like cheap paintings, and some of that ubiquitous Nazi kitsch (daggers, medals, armbands, caps) the newer GIs liked to send home. These were standard black market goods and Dietz looked to be doing all right, but it was no El Dorado. And who knew how much it cost to feed those kids alone? Their ration cards certainly weren't cutting it. A dark mood fell over Harry. He felt a fool for barging in on Dietz at that card game. Who the hell did he think he was? He had a mansion all to himself. And he had gotten Dietz into this in the first place.

When Dietz came back in, Harry was eyeballing a small print of Hitler defaced with bullet holes. "You'll get a lot for that Adolf print," he said.

Dietz nodded. "The vandalized kitsch is the height of fashion now. You need a drink?"

"Last thing I need. I might attack you again."

Dietz led Harry through a narrow galley kitchen to a classic German eating nook of etched wood, the benches built into the wall on three sides like a booth out of an old pub. On the small table stood a small electric heater unit with no housing—it must have been ripped from a German jeep or car and rewired. Dietz switched it on and his wife brought them ersatz coffee. Harry only took half a cup so that they wouldn't run out as soon. There was always that fine line between charity and condescension; the only thing worse was to refuse the hospitality. He wouldn't drink it in any case. Lila could discreetly reuse it.

"I found you down at that card game," Harry said once Dietz's wife left the room. "That right there could confirm you sold me out. Says, you're an operator first, a cop second."

Dietz laughed. "Did you see my winnings? Dead currencies and cracked chips worth no more than cig stubs. I'm just getting by, Captain. Would I live here if I was not?"

Dietz showed Harry papers confirming this was Dietz's family domicile since before the war. He showed Harry photos of his wife looking twenty years younger though most were only taken six, seven years before.

"How did you know I was in that club?"

"A hunch. I knew they sometimes let in Germans but only ones with respectable jobs."

"I see."

"I didn't mean to bowl you over," Harry said. "Just clumsy of me."

"I know." Dietz sipped his coffee.

"I was worried I couldn't get in," Harry said. "But they let you in."

Dietz sighed. "I play cards, yes. To survive. Some of the winnings I spread around, to make my job—my life—easier. How do you think I kept that corpse on ice as long as I did?"

It wasn't every day a German admitted how they had to please and even kowtow to keep the wheels greased. Dietz was trying his best. But he needed coaxing.

"You have certain friends," Harry said. "That what you're telling me?"

"I wouldn't call them that." Dietz spoke lower. "How should I say this? I have a suspect background, Captain. The report on me you saw? It was—how do you say?—favorably corrected. There, I said it. I was never in the Party, that much is true. But before, in the first couple years of the war, I was in a military police battalion. In the East. I didn't like what they were doing so I managed somehow to get transferred to the Navy of all things. As far away as I could."

"How did you pull that off?"

Dietz shrugged. "Quit doing your job. Run card games on duty. Get in a fight or two, preferably with an NCO. All the sudden they don't want you. I was lucky. Some end up in a penal unit."

Harry nodded. No one was a saint. Saints were for suckers. "Since I got you on the level, let's talk about the corpse. Funny thing was, they never asked me my police contact—who I asked to keep the corpse. That means they already knew, or they don't care."

Dietz slumped. "Isn't it obvious? They must know or assume I was the contact."

"Then why not go after you? You don't seem too worried—"

Dietz banged on the table. "Worried? What do you know about it?" he growled. "It's well beyond your 'worried,' I can tell you, and it's like this every waking moment . . ." He let the words trail off. He rubbed his fingers through his hair, and Harry could see his head through the thinning strands—pale, clammy skin that didn't look comfortable to wear at all.

"All right, all right," Harry said. He set his hand on Dietz's forearm. Dietz let it stay. He mumbled something in Bavarian dialect that Harry didn't catch. It almost sounded like praying. Harry removed his hand and said, "The way it looks to me? They're keeping it low-key for now." By *they*, he only meant Joyner, but Dietz didn't need to know that. Joyner had given Harry a break, and Harry felt a loyalty to this major who was really another loner like him. "They didn't ask me too many questions, don't seem to be making a case of it," he added. "I expect they'll want to know whatever I find out—even though they told me to quit searching."

"Well? That's authority for you," Dietz said. He made a gesture with his index finger, revolving it around as if spinning a globe.

He scooted closer. He held up a cigarette, his hand shielding his lips, and spoke English in a whisper—not even his wife should know what he was about to say: "You want to know about my so-called 'friends'? I do help out your brass from time to time, and even your intelligence. But it's more like an informant—on Germans, yes, but often on Americans and everyone in between."

"Sure. Who doesn't?" Harry quipped.

"*Gottverdammt*, listen," Dietz snarled. "What you should know? I could have turned you in for your ridiculous stunt. Holding on to a corpse—how foolish? But I believe in what you see in that girl—in Irina."

It sounded less like a warning than a cry for help coming from Dietz. "I appreciate that," Harry said.

"Good. Because I would lose my status if anyone knew I was telling you this, Captain."

They were staring at each other, eyes level. "So I guess we're on even ground," Harry said.

"We will never be that," Dietz said. "But, it's the little things that matter in the long run," he continued. "That's what I found out during the war. It's not what such and such a bigwig says, or what two or three nations' big dogs boast about around a table. They're just taking care of themselves. It's what happens here on this uneven ground that makes a difference. It doesn't always conform to the big dogs' so-called pledges and treaties, their so-called decisions and principles. But you know what? They can go piss themselves."

"Fair enough." Harry picked up his cup, then set it back down. "Can you tell me any more about Irina?"

Dietz shook his head. "She paid me to help find you that night. That's it."

"And you don't know why she came looking for me?"

"All I know is that a fellow was killed. I'm like you. I don't think she did it—at least not alone. There's more to it. Someone behind it. You know it, and I know this. So you must keep searching for her."

"Who says I'm not?"

"Please. Captain. I only mean, you seem to hide it. It's nothing to be ashamed of."

"Who says I'm ashamed?"

"Very well. Let's call it agitated."

"Have it your way," Harry said.

Dietz was rubbing at his leg.

"I didn't hurt you back there, did I?" Harry said.

"No, no. You could have hurt yourself worse, what with those bulls they have for guards." Dietz shook a hand as if it got burned.

"Yeah, guess I'm a lucky Joe tonight." Harry stood and picked up his cup to help clear the table, but Dietz waved him off the chore—Harry was his guest here. "Thanks for inviting me into your home," Harry said. "And do thank your wife."

Dietz stood. "Very well. But it was nothing."

"And, promise me you'll tell me anything you know. Or find out."

"I will, Captain. And you tell me if you discover who sold you out."

"Deal."

Dietz held up a finger. "Wait, this reminds me—about those sabers? I asked around a bit. Word is they're probably something like, how do you say? Cossack."

# Nine

*SO MUCH FOR DIETZ SELLING ME OUT*, Harry thought. He had no other suspects. There was no reason to consider Maddy Barton. She would sell him out in anger; he didn't doubt that. But she couldn't have known about the corpse, since she didn't stoop to know any Germans who might have tipped her off let alone resort to a vulgar cowboy like MP Major Joyner.

Besides, Maddy's social schedule hadn't given her the time for it. As he expected, she never returned from the party that night they fought. He couldn't blame her. He had lost his head and loathed that he had. He understood that, down deep, his harsh reaction to her probing likely stemmed from wanting to conceal Max. He still had not told Maddy he had a brother. All it took was one reckless soul to point a finger at him or Max. Such were the times. The war didn't end fear and want. Some needed a scapegoat to stay alive while others stood to gain from it. It didn't matter if the pointing was so off-target it was like a B-17 dropping its load on a hospital.

Maddy's tenacity wasn't that different from his, just turned on its head. The more a person had to lose, the sharper the claws. So Harry employed thicker armor against her stabs. On Friday the twentieth—a week since he asked Dietz to hide the corpse, and two days since the party—he instructed Gerlinde to have the contents of Maddy's room packed away in the mansion's garage. He told Gerlinde to enlist trusted help and make sure none of Maddy's belongings were missing, not even a hairpin. The garage was safe and watertight.

Both Harry and Gerlinde had keys for Maddy in case she showed up demanding entry. Meanwhile, Harry had a letter sent to her office and her apartment. In case she missed those, he copied the letter a third time, put it in an envelope with her name on it, and taped it to his mansion's front door:

> *Well, it looks like we're through, Madd. I hesitate to be so hard about it but there it is. You know it's run its course and I know it, too. It seems we're on two different paths here, you and I. That's not a judgment on you. It's just the score.*
> *You know I'm doing you a favor. It was a good ride while it lasted, and I'll cherish having ridden it with you.*
> *Love always,*
> *Harry*

He included a postscript about her belongings in the garage. He was trying to make it easier on both of them. He was really doing her a favor. If her things were still in the house, only more drama would have ensued because neither could have helped themselves from having one last go, whether it was a shouting match or another roll in the sack.

If pressed, he might have told Maddy a bitter truth—he didn't have time for her now. His search for Irina and Max had sparked something in him. Life was too short. Lives had to be saved. And winter was coming. How many more would suffer then? He wanted to be the man catching the fish and not the one eating it. The last time he felt the spark, that fire, he had solved the torture-murder of three decent civilians—and then avenged the murders of two men he'd urged to help him in his fight. That the sick bastard behind it all ended up to be an American was a small shock to an immigrant like Harry. He had chosen America and expected more from it. These days, he knew better. A country didn't matter. The cold fact was that all over, in every damned country, too many suffered at the mercy of a few bullies who presumed they ran the rest.

Dietz was right. This was no time to hold back. With the corpse off his hands, Harry realized he had nothing to lose. Friday afternoon he had a full schedule of appointments. He canceled them all.

He hit the black markets, plazas, and known hangouts of DPs, always with the same message. "You know a young woman named Irina?" He described her in detail. "She's in real trouble but I—the US Military Government—have good news for her. We are granting her an amnesty." He flashed papers from his fancy attaché and added a big Ami smile. "It's official! Amnesty—*Straferlass*! But that's not all. There's a huge reward for finding her."

On Saturday he was at it again—brandishing that attaché with both hands as if it held gold bars. He was like one of those mothers of German soldiers still traipsing through train stations in droves, never giving up asking if someone, anyone had seen their sons who'd gone missing on the Eastern Front circa 1943. If he had a photo of Max, he would hold it up just as they did. Then he started asking about Max by name.

"Anyone know Maximilian Kaspar? He was an actor. He lived in America. Surely someone's heard of the man?"

If any Americans saw him or heard him attracting attention like this? Let them wonder. Let them report him. This was all or nothing.

He got nothing.

That afternoon, he ended up at the Standkaserne. He'd parked his jeep and was walking down the main avenue when Sabine Lieser stepped out from one of the linden trees lining the way, as if the two of them were playing hide and seek among the trunks. It made Harry smile. But Sabine had her hands on her hips, and she hurried him along. She sat him in a nicer office tucked away in a first-rate Quonset hut. The metal blinds were half closed, creating strips of light that made the chromed steel table between them glimmer and dressed Sabine with their gleaming. But she wasn't exactly glowing.

"What in the devil do you think you're doing?" she said. "Don't act like you don't know. You run around offering rewards? Calling out her name, Irina's name? You could bring real trouble."

"I wasn't calling out her name—"

"Don't give me that."

Harry leaned forward, letting the light flash in his eyes. "Well, I don't have too many options, do I? If you haven't noticed."

Sabine stared a moment, her body rigid as if those strips of light had strapped her in place. She broke free and stood. She went to the window, separated the blinds with two slim fingers, and peeked out. She turned the blinds closed a little more, almost shut. She sat back down in her chair, crossed her legs, and clasped her hands around her knee.

"I have decided," she said, "that I want you to know something. The Nazis imprisoned me."

A slight gasp escaped from Harry, and he hoped it didn't sound like laughter. "I'm sorry."

"Do not be. The Nazis didn't like Socialists and they were always striving, so incessantly, to show us just how tough they were. The Gestapo kept tabs on me. They never held me too long—a few weeks at a time, and about a year once."

"A whole year?"

"But then the war turned for the worse and they had bigger fish to fry—literally—and German 'undesirables' such as I were not a priority."

"That's where you were a nurse? In a prison hospital."

Sabine nodded. "I did what I could. I had been in nursing school. They made me drop out." She crossed her legs the other way. "In any case. I wanted you to know."

"I appreciate it," Harry said.

He wasn't sure what to say, where this was going. Their eyes darted around but kept finding each other.

Sabine planted her feet to the floor, slapped her thighs. "So. All that running around? You must be hungry. You can eat here, in the mess. The food's quite good."

"I'm fine. But thanks." Harry's appetite was boring a hole in his stomach, but he wanted to show her he wasn't just another pampered Ami needing platefuls of good chow around the clock.

"You've been among Slavic DPs," he said. "Do you know what *Kudeyar* means?"

Sabine's head raised up. "I do, actually."

"What?"

"*Kudeyar* was a folk hero. An ataman. I mean to say, *Kudeyar* was a Cossack—a Cossack type of Robin Hood. But one who can lop off heads while he's at it."

"With, say, a saber?"

Sabine squinted at him. "How do you know this?"

"About *Kudeyar*? Irina told me. Silly girl, she said I was like that." Harry added a chuckle. He hoped it wasn't too cocksure. He wasn't used to strutting like this, but Sabine seemed to be drawing it out of him.

"What are we talking about here?" Sabine said. "Sabers? A saber's an object. I'm not interested in objects, especially ones that kill."

"What are you interested in?"

"People," Sabine said.

"So am I," Harry said.

"You're not going to give up, are you? Tell me that."

"No. I'm not. I won't."

Their eyes had found each other's and refused to dart now. His followed the lines of her face, her mouth, and returned to meet her gaze.

"Irina was here," she said.

"She what?"

"I told her she could not stay."

"When?"

"When it was too dangerous for her."

"Why didn't you tell me?"

"Could I trust you? I was not so sure." Sabine threw up a hand.

"It's tough to trust. I understand. But is she still here, in Munich?"

"I believe so, yes," Sabine said. She looked away, consulting the blinds.

"Give me a clue. Anything," Harry said.

Sabine was biting at her lip. She glanced at him. Harry glared back. She lifted a cigarette pack from the tabletop between them. Harry placed his hand over hers, keeping the pack down. She stared at his hand a while as if reading his veins like a fortune-teller. His hand warmed with anticipation. She pulled her hand away.

"Go to the English Garden," she said. "Wait there. They will find you. Go now."

Harry's mouth was dry. His knees ached. He sat on a bench in the English Garden, the bench biting into his back. He should have taken up Sabine on her offer of food, he understood now, because he'd been planted here over an hour and no one had come to him. He had the bench to himself, looking out on a meadow. He paced around the bench to keep warm, for the tenth time. He sat again, but the bench bit again and he was all out of sitting positions.

The last of the day's sun broke through, warming his face. A dusting of new snow sparkled, in patches. It was bright, and it made him close his eyes.

He woke, sometime later. How long had he been asleep? The sun was sinking, the scattered clouds dimming to a dark purple like bruises on the sky.

A slip of paper lay on the bench next to his right hand, anchored by a rock. It was a note:

*Nationaltheater. 17:30 hours.*
*—Irina*

Harry checked his watch. He had fifteen minutes.

He jogged out the south end of the English Garden and navigated the remains of the Residenz, that demolished palace of former Bavarian monarchs, the classical garden's paths lined with scrubby grass, blackened statues, and fountains. He kicked clear loose cobblestones as he found his way through the shadowy piles of rubble and considered the piles his friends for once because the Residenz stood between Major Warren Joyner's MP building and the Nationaltheater, and rubble like this provided good cover. The Nationaltheater was a carcass, a blackened maze of columns and busted half-columns like some junkyard Stonehenge, the remnants of floors above left hanging like the last leaves on a November tree, the roof all but gone. A statue was lodged upside down in debris, the head submerged. Harry headed deeper inside, using the columns as cover. As darkness came, light flashed from all sides, from passing cars, surviving streetlights, a stray spotlight or bonfire, a collage of rays and shadows monstrous and looming, the beams so sharp they looked like they could slice a torso in two. Harry tiptoed along, one foot and then the other, having to feel each step so that it wouldn't give away.

He only stopped at what he took to be the center of the place. He waited. He sat on a block of marble—he'd get soot on his butt but that would be the worst of it if he were lucky. He heard a siren in the distance, the clip-clop of a horse cart out on the Maximilianstrasse, and then voices, but far outside. Feet were shuffling out on some sidewalk. A distant crunch of glass. He heard nothing inside here. The stone and marble made it colder, just like inside a real building, and he got a chill. He turned up his collar.

"Heinrich," he heard.

It sounded like it came from his right, but it was hard to tell with all the dark angles, hollows, echoes. He stood but kept to a crouch. "Who you calling Heinrich?" he said in English.

A little laugh, with a strained high note like a worn bell. "Why, you, of course."

"The girl—where's Irina?"

"She's safe. I do appreciate your concern."

It was decent American English, but Harry heard the rough edges. The voice seemed to have moved, though Harry heard no footsteps. Tricky fellow, this one.

"Says you," Harry said stalling, peering into the darkness, hoping for more stray light.

"But, that is your real name, isn't it, Heinrich?" the voice said in German.

A white shock shot through Harry's chest, sucking his stomach so tight he wanted to gag. He knew this voice, this laugh.

"The name's Harry," he snapped.

That laugh came again. A hacking cough came next, like marbles on metal, but the laugh would not give in.

"Max?" Harry blurted. The coughing continued. Harry moved toward the laugh-cough, tottering, his heels wobbling on rubble.

A convoy of trucks passed outside, sending in beams of headlamps.

And Harry saw the long shadow of his brother, stretching out from behind a column, the distorted shape flickering and quaking from the wild barrage of light.

# Ten

Harry stood dead center inside the ruins of the Nationaltheater and peered into the darkness, searching the columns for the source of the shadow. It had vanished after the convoy of trucks passed outside. The laugh and the coughing had stopped.

Then a head showed from behind a column, obscured by more shadow, an eclipsed half face. "It's all right. I'm alone. Let me see you," Harry said.

"Sure, sure."

Max stepped out into the dim evening. One shoulder looked higher than the other did. He had a stoop?

Max took two steps forward, Harry took three.

Harry clanked open his Zippo, held up the flame. Max's face had creases. Those once soft and happy cheeks and brows were heavier, which made his eyes look sunken. His brother now looked like their handsome grandfather when they were children. Yet it was all Max. He wore a scarf checked with purple and gold and tied like an ascot. It compensated for his jacket, which had a mix of old buttons and various color threads mending the buttonholes. Hanging off his shoulders, like a cloak, was an old German Army greatcoat dyed black to look civilian.

"That's quite enough," Max said.

Harry clanked shut the Zippo.

"Tell me I look good and I will box your ears," Max continued, adding a smile, and it was still Max's smile, the way it stretched wide open and curled up at the same time, bringing those wide eyes back out of their deep sockets. He came closer, dragging a wooden stick that tapped at the debris. A cane?

"Your leg hurt?" Harry said.

Max looked at the cane as if someone had just thrust it in his hand. "Oh, this? Why, it's just for effect. A prop." He threw the cane, it clattered away, and he held out his arms for a hug.

Harry held out a hand instead and Max didn't flinch, ever the smooth actor. He grasped at Harry's forearm with one hand and gave Harry a firm handshake with the other. Their eyes were almost level. Max's eyes used to be higher, Harry recalled.

"I had you a little spooked," Max said. "Admit it."

That was Max—always with the taunts and gags. Harry couldn't help thinking that it was good to see Maxie still had it. "Not a chance," he said and added a smile.

Max smiled and held out his hands as if to say, *I gotta be me.*

"You're alive," Harry said.

"You say it like it's such a bad thing."

"I don't know what it is. It's been, what—eight years at least? All the same: It's good to see you, Maximilian."

"Please, do not call me that or Maxie for that matter, and I will not call you Heinrich or even Heino like it used to be." Max stood back a step and gave Harry the full once-over. "You're a real Ami. Looking well."

"Thanks. Where's Irina?"

Max nodded, a half smile on his face. "Still the same Heinrich though, aren't you?"

"Harry. It's Harry now."

"Yes, of course. Well, you'll be glad to know: She's safe. So, come on." Max patted Harry's shoulder and led him out another way, passing beyond more busted columns. Full darkness had found them but Max navigated no problem, forcing Harry to feel at the back of his brother's cloak-coat as they moved along.

"See that ironwork over there?" Max said.

Harry peered. "No."

"That's because it's all melted clumps. That used to be the stage. The firebombing was so hot here that it melted metal." Max was shaking his head. "Demolished just like my career."

Harry said nothing. What was he supposed to say—that it wasn't Max's fault?

"Funny, here we are, on an October Friday evening in the State Theater," Max continued. "It might have been an opening night."

"Only problem with that is, the year is 1946," Harry said.

"And don't I know it, Heinrich? Sorry—Harry."

Out on the street, Max kept them close to the walls and doorways. Harry wasn't sure what dangers Max wanted them to heed, but he told himself not to ask too many questions or deduce too much—for once. Not yet. Harry wasn't sure what he would feel. For so long he never expected to see his brother again. He guessed he'd feel bitterness and certainly not the warmth he was feeling. Was it Maxie's old flair doing that? That had always been the biggest shock to Harry—that a gent with so much pizzazz chose a one-tune playhouse called Nazi Germany. Max had seemed tailor-made for New York City, or at least for what Harry imagined of NYC.

They were talking in a mix of English and German, and it was as awkward as when they were young immigrants in America—Harry always going for the English and Max the German.

"Your English is really something," Harry said.

"Thanks. Have lots more practice since you Amis stole the show."

"I'm sure. Ma and pop will be glad to hear it—that you're okay."

"They already know, Harry. Come on, around this corner here—"

"They know? How? And where we going?"

"Due time, kid, due time. I know you must have questions. A man is murdered and then suddenly I show up. Come on, this way. I have something for you, to show you. It will mean spending some time together, making up for lost time to be sure. You mustn't be home tonight, right? Good. There's a good brother."

The way Max had proposed it, Harry half expected Max to kick things off by taking him to a nightclub he was headlining or even owned. They would celebrate with champagne and girls who felt like dancing all night. It was nothing like that. Max asked Harry if he could get a dependable but inconspicuous car (a German make, if possible) with lots of gas in the tank.

"Please don't get a jeep," Max added. "I really do not like riding in your jeeps, not at all."

Then Max asked him if he could spare a couple days. Harry said he had the whole weekend. Then they finally shared a clumsy hug, Max all forced smiles and Harry's face feeling numb from the shock of it all, as if he'd spent too long at the barracks dentist.

By 8:00 p.m., Harry had an Opel sedan from the motor pool. Max had told him to dress as if he were going hiking, so he wore expensive Swiss alpine boots he'd been given but never used, wool trousers, and a thick sweater, wrapping it all in an even thicker mackinaw jacket of faint dark green plaid. He stowed a Jerry can of gas in the trunk and drove out beyond the main train station, parallel to the tracks. As Max instructed, he entered the courtyard between the remains of the Pschorr and Hacker breweries, a dead end of battered wooden kegs and brick walls, loading docks and fences. As he wheeled around, backing in to face the entrance, his headlights flashed on a couple kissing between stacks of kegs in a corner. Harry could tell from the shine of the man's black hair and the way his arms cradled her up high, erect and yet tender (like a man dancing well), that it was Max.

Harry switched off the lights, stood out at the front fender, and let them come out to him. They would want to see that he was alone. He lit a Chesterfield to confirm it was he.

The woman approached the rear fender. She wore a dark hooded poncho.

"Irina?"

"It's me, Mister Harry," Irina said in her German with the heavy accent. She pulled back the hood and rushed over and hugged him, kissing both cheeks.

"Pretty happy to see me for not wanting to see me," Harry said.

Irina laughed. She grabbed Harry's cheek and twisted it like a grandmother to a tot.

"Got a vise grip, sister," Harry said.

"Ah, that didn't hurt," Max said as he walked up.

Irina stepped back and compared the two brothers, Max sharing a smile with Irina as they studied Harry. Max nodded in approval at Harry's outfit and then shook his head at his own worn-out great coat. "If only I had such a jacket as yours, perhaps in a fine loden cloth," he muttered.

Irina nodded. "One could not tell you apart."

Harry pinched out his smoke, his mood darkening. "I got news for you—I'm not him."

Irina dropped the smile, but Max just shrugged.

"You really left me in the lurch," Harry told Irina.

Irina lowered her eyes.

"You can blame me for that," Max said. "For everything."

"That right? How would I know? First thing I need here are some simple answers. Before we go any further."

"It's nothing sordid."

"Says a guy I don't really know."

"You'll understand. You will."

"Let's try some basics. What papers you carrying?"

"I have my old army paybook." Max pulled his Wehrmacht *Soldbuch* from inside the greatcoat. "It has my name in it."

"But no domicile?"

"Domicile? These days? You want the bombed one or the fire-bombed one?"

"You're telling me you have no registration with local MG, *Polizei*, no POW papers, nothing."

Max forced out another smile. "Sorry, Harry."

"You were drafted, I hope."

"What on earth do you think?" Max held out his palms. "I was an actor here as well. No one needed actors in the end. Mass murder demands far more of a man than a musical."

What Max claimed wasn't that uncommon, Harry told himself. Former soldiers still roamed the land, homeless and heartbroken, their girls shacked up with GIs now. But they were asking for trouble without permanent papers. Irina knew about a murder, and Max might have ended up Hitler's valet for all Harry knew.

"I never know if you're joking or not," Harry said.

"You don't need jokes right now, Harry."

"Or trouble. And neither do you. You know what I think? Maybe I'm committing too much to you and whatever this is and just because you're my brother."

"Or, perhaps you have not committed enough? Am I right? You like to take a chance."

Harry started. "Hey now look, don't go supposing you know me . . . that you know what I'm thinking even for a second."

"No. I don't suppose anything, not anymore. I only know what I see and I hear," Max said. "So? Here is what you need to know: Let us say there is a lifeboat. Out at sea. Water freezing, sharks all around. One mad fellow in the boat wants to kick out all the rest out, so that he alone can live. What does one do?"

Harry threw up his hands. "Now it's riddles I'm getting."

"No riddles. We're talking about fate. The mad fellow, he's out. Let him swim with the sharks. Done for." Max slid his hands against one another, slapping them as if clearing off dust. "That's your answer. For starters."

"And, that was the man I saw with a saber through him?"

"Yes, I'm afraid. The very one."

# Eleven

MAX AND IRINA SHOWED HARRY SUITCASES, boxes, and bags full of food, blankets, and tools. They loaded up Harry's Opel, which flattened out the springs so much the city streets' holes and lumps hit them like hammers banging the chassis. Max had offered to drive, but Harry didn't want his lack of papers causing trouble. Irina had squeezed in back between cargo, shrouded under her poncho and hood. This food and these blankets and even tools seemed harmless—so far, Harry reminded himself. He fought the urge to press Max and Irina on the name or the why of that corpse as Max had him head northeast out of Munich using a secondary highway with only a narrow lane each way. A US jeep or staff car passed once or twice, and they spotted refugee campfires here and there flashing from within woods or barns.

"I made that poncho for her from an army blanket," Max said. "Amazing what a man learns." He chuckled to himself, a bitter laugh that was new to Harry.

Harry found Irina's hood in the rearview mirror, her head bobbing. "Gerlinde was worried about you," he told her.

"Her food was excellent. Will you thank her?"

"I will."

Harry brought real coffee in his chrome canteen. He had Max pour some into its red cap and they passed it around. Harry said, "That was some embrace you two showed me back there when I picked you up. Max always grab you like that, plant one on you?"

Irina shrugged. "Perhaps. Perhaps it's another of Maxie's props."

"Like his cane," Harry said.

Max didn't respond. He sipped, staring at the road ahead.

"You're laying low. Yet you wear that jaunty scarf," Harry said to him.

"The slightest nod to civility," Max said. "One can't be all storm and stress, can they?"

They passed Landshut and then Dingolfing. The headlights lit up endless trees and the occasional small meadow, village, or villa. Snowflakes swirled at the windshield but didn't stick. Irina was snoring, a low rumble that mixed in with the engine's drone. The coffee had warmed and quickened Harry, but he wondered how long it would last. Max still hadn't told him who the dead man was. Harry would get to that. Right now, he had other complaints.

Max knew it. He was watching Harry, his eyes pinched. "All right, have at it," he said in English. He added a glance at Irina as if to make sure she was sleeping.

"Your being over here?" Harry began. "It only made it worse on pop. The authorities hauled him in. The Alien Control Boards, the FBI even. They badgered him about having family here. Did he tell you that?"

"No. But I guessed as much."

"How long you been in contact with them?"

"A few months now. Letters. I have occasional access to a—what do you call it? *Ein Postfach.*"

"Post office box."

"They are happy to hear from me, Harry. Oh, don't look so shocked."

"Who's shocked? It's just that they never wrote me about it."

"I asked them not to tell you—until I could find you. I wanted to tell you myself, once I had something to show for it. So here I am." Max opened his arms wide and grinned like a dancer in top hat.

Harry kept a stone face.

Max dismissed it with a wave. "I'm not used to calling you Harry."

"You'll get used to it."

"I must, so I will. In any case: It wasn't like I was living it up with Nazis."

"Who knew what you were doing? We heard all kinds of rumors."

"What could I do? Japan attacks the US, Hitler declares war, and suddenly America gets in the ring. It all happened so fast. By then, I figured Mutti and Vati would only get worse treatment if they started receiving letters from me. So I held off, kept telling myself that it would end—"

"We heard you went and joined the SS."

"This is bullshit. Who told you that?"

"Relatives, up north. You been up north?"

"To see relatives? Yes. But that was . . . before. I'd lived in Hamburg, you know."

"No, I don't know." Harry added, "Then we hear you're Missing in Action."

"Missing in Action? I'm right here, aren't I?" Max patted at his chest.

"You said you were drafted—in the army, just another sorry *Landser*. What front?"

"Eastern front, Western front," Max said, his voice rising, straining. "What does it matter now? What, Harry, huh?" He looked out the window, into the blackness, searching it.

He let his forehead rest against the window.

Harry offered him a Chesterfield. Max nodded in thanks and slipped it under his ascot and into an inside breast pocket.

An hour passed in silence. Max was still staring out the window but sat increasingly rigid, his eyes alert to any changes in the dark country night. They passed through Plattling, which had a concentration camp during the war. Then an American armored car was parked along the road keeping watch. Harry let off the gas a little as he passed it. "Next one could be blocking the road. Never know—"

"Anyone stops us? We're relatives," Max blurted and his voice sounded like someone else's. The tone was monotone, metallic. He reminded Harry that their Opel had legit US MG stencils and plates as if trying to convince himself of it. "Me and you? We are looking for more of our relatives, who used to live in this area. This is what we tell them."

"Fair enough, Max. Calm yourself. I'll quit with the questions."

Max's head turned to Harry, mechanically, his shoulders fixed. But his face softened. "You must trust me. Please."

"We're carrying food. Bulk grain, lentils, dry meats. We have blankets, overcoats. Some hand tools."

"It's not black market. Just like I said. It's for people who need it. I don't want you to know in case we're stopped. You'll know, once we're in the clear. I promise, Harry."

The headlights found a green mass in the road up ahead. Soldiers. They had an armored car with a cannon and heavy machine gun, and enough jeeps to block the road twice over.

"Checkpoint," Harry said.

"We're helping people, Irina and I," Max added. "That's what you want, right?"

"We'll see."

Max had his Chesterfield in his mouth and he banged his old lighter on his knee, all out of flame. Harry thumbed open his Zippo and lit him. In the rearview mirror, Irina had lowered and slumped, her hood just another sack in the dark.

The soldiers formed a line, blocking the road left open by a gap between the jeeps. All had light machine guns instead of rifles. They wore the new overcoats and Ike jackets with bright yellow scarves and a red-yellow stripe circling their helmets. Harry whistled under his breath as he slowed.

"Know who they are?" Max said, eyeing Harry.

"All too well." It was the Constabulary Corps—MG's occupation police. This constabulary troop had the border beat. Theirs was not to fight but to catch a person in the act. Smugglers, illegal refugees, fugitive Nazis. Slowly, keeping one hand up high on the wheel, Harry slid on his horn-rimmed glasses. Max nodded at Harry in tense approval.

Harry slowed more, probably more than he should have. The key with checkpoints was to keep your speed steady. He tapped at the brake.

"Is there a problem?" he said to Max. "I mean a big one—something you want to tell me now? Before we get too far."

"No. Let's just do this." Max puffed away, filling the cab with the smell of profuse American tobacco.

A sergeant approached.

"All right. Follow my lead." Harry braked to a stop, showing off a big smile as he rolled down the window. He placed his MG liaison ID on the window jamb. "Evening, boys."

"Sir. How do." The sergeant was a square-faced Joe who from the steel in his eyes might actually have been in the war. The rest of the line probably graduated from high school the previous spring from the looks of them. The sergeant had his flashlight out.

"Any action tonight?" Harry said.

"Not near enough." The sergeant shined the light around the cab.

Max smiled back showing twice the teeth than Harry had ever seen on him.

"Sir, if you keep going this direction, you'll hit the frontier," the sergeant said to Harry.

"The frontier?" Harry said.

"Czechoslovakia. What they call the Soviet zone now."

"The border? Ah, right. No problem. It's some village on this side we're after."

The sergeant had bent down to check out Max again. "You two brothers?" he said.

"You got a way with faces," Harry said. "We have relatives that are supposed to be around here somewhere. If the war didn't get them. But, what can you do? We promised dear old mom we'd find 'em."

The sergeant walked around the car, flashing more light. He ended up at Max's window. Max rolled it down. His grin spread wider.

"What's the town they're in? Maybe I can help?" the sergeant said to Max.

"Some town called Zwiesel? Say it's right up the road here," Max said. "What you think, Sarge? Any warm bodies still there? Ten'll get you twenty, bound to be some kraut there looks like us two mugs here."

Harry's head whipped over to Max. Max's American English had turned silky smooth, with nearly no accent anyone could pin down. He might have been from Pennsylvania or Ohio. He'd pronounced Zwiesel like only a Yank would.

"You all right, sir?" the sergeant said to Harry.

"Fine, fine," Harry muttered.

Max took it from there. He told the sergeant that their cargo was for the relatives. Since none of it was worth a smuggle, let alone an arrest, the sergeant peeked in a couple sacks and let it go. Max introduced Irina as his current Gretchen. She pulled back her hood, twinkled her eyes.

And the sergeant waved them onward.

Harry drove on. They rounded a bend. A light snow returned, speckles of wet on the windshield. Max had shrunk down, his ears about level with his shoulders. His face was pale, reflecting the faint dashboard light.

Max had the thousand-yard stare. Harry knew it from Joes who had been on the front line. Combat. He supposed he'd had it too for a time after his battle on the train.

"All right, maybe you were on the front," he said.

Max said nothing.

"I know you're an actor," Harry said after a while, "but I never heard any accent like that on you back home—"

112

"It's not me," Max snapped in German, his hand out flat as if to karate-chop the dashboard. "It never was. I was just doing what I had to do. We clear on that?"

Max's voice had changed again, to a bolder tone Harry hadn't heard in years. He remembered it from when the kids in New Hampshire called Max a Hun and a kraut, and when Max vowed to get as far away from them as possible. The last time he heard it Max was leaving for New York City, telling their father that he was going to do big things with his acting.

"For now I am," Harry said.

Max blinked. He nodded.

Harry drove on. After a while, he slid off his horn rims and tried to polish them with one hand.

Max took the glasses and shined them with a fine cloth he'd produced from his overcoat. "These helped. Back there. Every little bit helps."

"I know. You do realize, I'm the only one whose ID that sergeant saw."

"I do," Max said.

"My liaison ID, my papers were ideal back there."

"I'm not using you, Harry. For something nefarious. If that's what you'd think."

"You said you had no papers. So why am I thinking that you do? Papers that aren't quite legit but would have just done the trick back there, if need be."

"Because you're the smarter of the two brothers," Max said. "Without a doubt."

Irina had returned to her snoring. They passed through a tiny junction with a few squares of window light, and then the road turned darker.

"In a few kilometers, there'll be a little road up here on your right," Max said, gently now as if telling a child how to bury a dead birdie. "Go ahead and turn there. That's the way."

The town of Zwiesel was straight ahead. "We turn there, we'll be heading dead east," Harry said. "You sure? That's what you want?"

Max was nodding. "I'm sure."

# Twelve

MAX SAID THEY WERE HELPING PEOPLE. *But where are they?* This was
Harry's first thought as he woke and it had been his last thought
before collapsing into sleep. He heaved himself up from his bedroll
and sat at the little pine table, taking in his sparse surroundings.
His hut was eight-by-eight with a floor like clay and an oven in the
middle, its fire gone out as he slept. His back was stiff, and a slight
headache pinched at his temples, and no wonder. The drive had
taken longer than Max hoped because the final few winding roads
had twinkles of ice on them. Then they left the Opel in a barn,
contents and all, and Harry and Irina rode on a cart that Max and
two other men pulled along a trail that crept ever higher, deep into
forest. Harry wanted to pull but Max's men refused. "You'll have
your turn to pull weight," one of them told him in clunky accented
German. When the forest began to descend, the men turned back
with their cart and Harry, Max and Irina had hiked onward in the
dark, through ravines, around patches of clumpy snow, and along
a stream.

Harry checked his watch: Nine o'clock in the morning, Saturday,
the twenty-first. He heard the birds outside and a trickling stream
even though the hut's walls were of a thick and lumpy old plaster.
He pulled his gray wool blanket around him, stood, and opened the
door. A deep fog found them when they'd arrived but had now given
way to murky sunlight. Around him, Harry saw a settlement along
the stream, more like a junction than a village, but there wasn't any

main road, only paths that connected the few thatched-roof farm huts, some of them stone and plaster, some wooden. Beyond was all tree trunks, their bark blotchy white and the leaves dark, the trunks so dense together that the fog stayed there, within that tall wall that loomed all around like the very horizon itself. They had to be miles and miles from nowhere. This place could have been hundreds, no, thousands of years ago—he wouldn't be surprised to find an undiscovered last tribe of Visigoths still hiding out from Roman times. Two long low barns stood close but at haphazard angles, and a rustic old watermill stood along the stream—the waterway having surely been the main road into here, once upon a time. In the middle of this outpost, all paths led to an open patch of pitted cobblestones with a rudimentary well fountain of stones and wooden lid. This must have served as the village square.

Harry stood outside leaning against his hut and waited. He saw no one. He saw stacks of wood vivid in color—freshly cut—and two carts whose wheels sported shining, freshly hammered metal rims.

"Morning," Max said, passing Harry's hut. He strode out onto the little square, where he stopped with hands clamped on his hips and one foot out in front as if about to deliver a few lines of famous monologue. Irina followed him out, wiping the sleep from her eyes but smiling. She sat on the edge of the fountain and, seeing Harry, waved him out to them.

Harry walked out and gave his blanket to Irina, who hugged it for warmth and said what must have been good morning in her language. Max turned to Harry. It was the first time Harry had seen his older brother in the light, up close. Dark complexion under his eyes had consumed the freckles he'd once shared with Harry, and his fleshy eyelids made him look less sleepy than simply tapped out. He still had his dark and shiny hair, but Harry could see his scalp up top where the strands had thinned. And yet Max still looked handsome. It had to be in his eyes, how they lit up, and the way his face could relax for you and only you. He was doing it right now,

Harry saw—smiling as if Harry was the one about to deliver the monologue.

"What? What is it?" Harry said.

"Wait for it." Max stretched out an arm, directing his hand at the settlement around them.

Women and children appeared in windows, in doorways, and from the fog of the woods. They wore the usual refugee rags, though Harry noticed more babushkas than he was used to seeing in Germany. Then horses were snorting and stomping their hooves, stepping out from behind corners, barn doors, woods, and where the stream cut into the woods. Towheaded children sat atop a few horses here and there. Men held the horses by their reins. The men had mustaches and most wore thick sable hats. Harry, pivoting to take it all in from his spot on the square, counted roughly a hundred people and a good twenty horses.

"What the hell's going on here?" he said to Max, but not taking his eyes off the people as if they could vanish any moment like the ghosts they seemed to be.

"You're in the Šumava," Max said.

"That's not what I asked. Wait—where are we?"

"Šumava. Germans call it the Bohemian Forest."

"The Böhmerwald?" Harry spun around to Max. "This is Czechoslovakia."

Max nodded. "That's right, Harry—we are just inside the Soviet Zone of Occupation. We passed over in the night, after your cart ride. Yet the Czechs and—most important—the Russians don't know that, you see. They don't know we are here. Any of us."

"Please do not ask questions of these people," Max said. "They will not answer you. I will tell you what you need to know—or as much as I can tell you now. Otherwise, do as you like."

Harry walked around and mingled among the people. He let them follow him and watch him, the boys and girls with their hands clasped in front of them and the women who stroked the kids' hair. He watched them cut wood. He cut the wood with them. He ate with them—saw what they ate. The sacks of grain made various porridges. Otherwise, fish from the stream, small woodland animals, and turnips and cabbages seemed to be their regular sustenance. They shared some grain with their horses, since their stock of oats and barley had dwindled to a few bags. Their sole possessions seemed to be bedrolls and packs, like soldiers on the march. Harry had learned all this using improvised sign language—they'd smiled for him, but they wouldn't answer his German or English. Harry couldn't help asking questions. He just didn't get this. Refugees hoped to be discovered, fed, and housed. That's why they wandered the land out in the open and clogged the roads, aid offices, and camps. That wasn't the only thing. From their babushkas, sable hats, mustaches, and towheaded children in peasant shirts, they looked like people who should want very much to stay well within Joe Stalin's half of Europe where the Soviet Army would feed them and deliver them home.

"Are they Czechs?" Harry asked Max. They were back in Harry's hut, warming up around the fire oven that someone had re-lit for him. Harry kept stealing peeks outside where the children stood in little groups stealing peeks back at him, as if he was the one who seemed an apparition from a previous century.

"No, they are not. I can tell you that." Max told Harry these people were maintaining an uneasy relationship with a few local Czechs, farmers and smugglers whom they bartered goods with and paid well to reveal nothing about them to their Soviet occupiers. But none of these local contacts knew where the people lived— there were only a few experienced people here who always went out and found whom they needed, and if they were ever followed, the follower would regret it very much. But it was getting more dangerous. Smuggling goods and people across the zonal frontiers was becoming big business, especially with winter approaching. Despite the increased border patrols of the last month or so. "There's always someone from the outside who offers to go on the take," Max said, "who lets you through or gets you through—or who screws you just the same."

"Are these people smugglers too of some sort?" Harry asked.

"No. It's not like that."

"Then they're refugees?"

"According to some. Not to most others."

"Are they gypsies?" Harry said.

"Good god. Regretfully no."

"All right. Then, how long have they been here?"

"About a year."

"It looks like a few days."

Max smiled with pride. "We can pick up and leave anytime. We have and then come back. We leave few trails."

"What about smoke? From cooking."

"Quite simple. They light as few fires as possible, and when they do? We keep watch around the perimeter, to make sure it's safe. We also use the cover of the frequent fog. They vent the smoke into the woods using fans made of branches and boards. Other boards redirect the smoke into tunnels we've dug, with small vents poking out along the way. Much of the meat and fish is cured, usually by drying." Max shrugged. "You get used to it."

"Why? Why do you have to?"

"I . . . can't tell you."

"But you brought me here. In Munich—Irina's corpse. He was one of these people?"

Max shook his head.

"Then why? Why bring me here?"

"Irina told you. Some have heard what you did with that train, with the Jews' belongings. You found a way to get it back to them so they could start over. You did it despite all that was against you, against them. It seemed impossible. That train was done for, sold off.

Another victim of greed. And yet you did it. It's quite impressive, Harry. My little brother has it in him."

"That was why Irina came to me," Harry said. "But what about you?"

Max's head jerked back as if Harry had taken a swing at him. "Me? What about me? I don't matter."

He muttered something about "making the rounds" and left Harry alone in the hut.

By the late afternoon it began to snow, lightly. The people watched it fall. No one smiled in wonder. The children glared at the snow-flakes as if each one had just slapped them on the face. Then a wind came through the trees, the temperature dropped, and the people retreated to their huts and barns. Harry watched as Max circulated with the people. His brother moved in and out of the buildings, haul-ing items, giving commands, and best of all for Harry, playing the clown for the children. He kept his chin high when working but he was genuinely on his tiptoes for the children, dancing around them and grinning, singing their songs and show tunes no one knew. That was the Max Harry had remembered. So much looser and lighter than Harry. Harry was the Ami now, but if one watched the two from behind soundproof glass, their clothing not telltale, one would think that carefree Max was the American.

But then, as Harry kept watching, he saw another Max. When wisps of smoke drifted by and Max, his face contorted, fanned and swung at the smoke to make it dissipate so that it would never give them away, not even this one little bit. When the clouds returned to block the sun and more of those few snowflakes swirled around and Max stood with his feet planted far apart to glare at the ice gray sky. He caught the flakes and held them in his hand, moving them around, checking their details. He was a botanist and this pestilence falling might be a new strain of insect come to lay death upon the land. He spoke to mothers and children and patted them on the shoulders and their little heads, nodding, but after they left with their heads high, reassured, Max would turn from them, his fists balled and shoulders tightened up, and he would grimace at the earth, his brain searching for some answer he hadn't considered.

"They've already suffered through one winter, you see," he told Harry.

In the hut, Max, Irina, and Harry shared a dinner—dried meat with rare dark bread. Afterward, Max sat upright on a stool, his hands pressed to his knees. Irina sat on the floor with her back against the cold wall, the thinning purple light giving her face a harder cast.

A boy appeared in the doorway, just half his head showing. The little guy was about five. Harry saw him first but only because he happened to be glancing that way. Harry never would have heard him, he was so quiet. Harry pretended to look away, and then he glanced back and showed a smile and then a wink, until the boy, now smiling, showed all of himself in the doorway. Yet he held onto the doorframe as if he was peering out of a fast-moving train. Harry recognized the boy as one who had stood far back during the day, the only one over time, sometimes behind a tree, sometimes behind the leg of a horse or the hip of an old man. He had blond hair, a square face, and enough layers of worn clothing and trimmed blankets to last him a year on the road. They doubled his size. From a great distance he surely resembled an adult, if not a soldier, a forward scout in dark camouflage. But there was just a scared skinny tyke under there.

Harry glanced over at Max and saw Max gazing at Irina. She stared at the boy with a tense smile on her face, beholding him as one would a rare forest bird that hadn't been witnessed by humans for decades. Max gave Harry the slightest shake of his head that said, *Don't disturb them.*

She whispered something to the boy in her language and gestured for him to come in. He vanished. They waited it out. The boy showed himself again. All three smiled for him. Irina rose from the floor and crouched on her haunches, ready to grab him.

The boy whispered something back finally and Irina, gasping with joy, rushed over and enveloped him so fully that he disappeared under her. She rocked back and forth, hugging him in the doorway. *As if saving him from falling from that speeding train*, Harry thought.

"He likes Harry," she said to Max, then she beamed at Harry and exited into the darkness still swaddling the boy.

Max kept smiling until she was out of earshot.

"He's a shy one," Harry said.

"He has his reasons. Irina likes it that way. Helps keep him safe."

"Hers?"

Max nodded.

"The father?"

"Died fighting. Near the end."

"What's the name?" Harry said.

"Oleksandr. Alex, perhaps one day. One hopes."

"He will be."

Max just stared at the doorway.

"So we get them west," Harry said. "That's what you want, right?"

"I'm afraid it's not as easy as all that."

"What, do they think I'll sell them out?" Harry said.

"No one's saying that, brother. It's not you. It's the people outside who could stalk you, or use you for this information. You must be very careful. They can come from any corner. This is the new world now. It's not about fighting head to head, a clear enemy. It's about infiltrating, and deceiving, and betraying, and all the fear that's created by that. Are we clear? Judas can be anywhere—here, Munich, everywhere."

"Is that what happened?" Harry said. "With the murder?"

Max glared at Harry, his lips pursed tight. He sighed. He stood and left the hut.

After a while, Harry looked out the doorway. He saw Irina walking with Max, tugging at his shirt and pleading at him in her language.

Harry finished eating. The fire smoldered and he let it. He pulled a blanket around him.

Max came back inside. He held a bottle of clear spirits. He was smiling again. He sat at the pine table and poured them out two tin cups.

"I don't want a drink," Harry said.

"Yes, you do. She wants us to."

"First I want you tell me something. A confession. Anything."

Max had his tin cup halfway to his mouth. He held it steady as if it was full to the brim with nitroglycerine. "Very well: We tipped them off, Harry."

"Tipped who off?"

"Your Military Police. We told them about the corpse. We were the ones."

# Thirteen

HARRY LUNGED FOR THE BOTTLE and Max flinched, raising his other arm in defense. Harry wasn't going to hit Max—he needed a belt. Anger surged in his head and he had to check it somehow. He took the bottle, took his belt. Fire wasn't the word for this juice. It burned his throat and the back of his skull like Chinese mustard. He crouched hissing like an old cat kicked out of its bed.

Max crouched with him. "I'm sorry, little brother."

"I should punch you in the mouth," Harry growled, wiping at his stinging lips. "Man, this hooch is stiff."

Max downed his cup as if it was cool spring water. "I told you you'd want a drink."

Harry hauled a stool to the table, slammed down the bottle and sat, his shoulders level with Max's. They were so close that Harry could smell the booze on their breath, but he couldn't tell whose breath.

"You told me to confess," Max said.

"Major Joyner could have tossed me in the stockade. He pressed me for answers. He still can. You do understand that, right?"

"You were getting out of control. Please don't give me that look. Yes, you. You were starting to attract attention, and we can't have that. I had to reign you in."

"Reign me in? What am I, the dog loose in the backyard?"

"No. You are definitely not that."

"I'm not the one playing the fugitive—if that's what you are doing. Because I really don't know what you are doing here."

"I truly am sorry."

"Your tip-off really was anonymous, I hope. Tell me that it was."

"Yes. Oh, yes."

"You don't know Major Joyner?"

Max shook his head. "Not personally. But I knew he was the one you'd seen—"

"And the very one who hunts Germans—I bet you didn't know that? No? That you were tipping off the very people you appear to be so afraid of." Harry slapped the table. "And Dietz? Shit. What about him?"

"I don't know that name—ah, you mean the police detective? No, he had no clue either as far as I could ascertain."

Max poured Harry more. Harry drank. It helped, all burning aside, to remind Harry that runaway anger was a Joe's worst enemy. Dearest Reason was always the best defense. He calmed himself, focusing on the knotty gray wood at his fingertips.

"I guess I should thank you all the same," he said. "You did help me find Irina and then you."

"Please, nothing to thank," Max said, attempting a smile.

"So, where are we at? These people here—you want to get these people west. Look, I know this woman at the DP camp in Munich."

"It's not that easy."

"That's what you say."

"They won't go, Harry. Believe me, I want them to go. They need to go."

"Why won't they?"

"They need to be convinced to go. They need to be convinced that you—that the Americans—will not treat them like the Soviets are, like the Germans have."

"What makes them think I would? That we would?"

"They have their reasons. And, I suppose I have my own reasons too," Max muttered. He stood and paced the small room, stopping to warm his hands on the oven although it was barely lukewarm.

Harry looked out the window. A few of the men were sitting on a log and arguing in hushed tones, their gestures slivers of moonlight, their orange cigarette embers rising and falling. Those men belonged to a clan, Harry saw, and let nothing escape outside it. Max, on the other hand, had become a clan unto himself. Nothing escaped his soul. And that was a hard safe to crack.

Max was sitting on the floor now, on Harry's bedroll, his palms upturned as if from exhaustion. He wore a long frown that in another setting might have looked forced, like a clown's scowl. Harry brought the bottle and cups over and sat like Max, his back up against the hard uneven plaster. He poured one for Max and Max closed his fingers around the cup.

"I'm not going to force it out of you," Harry said.

Max drank. He held up his other hand and let it drop. "They've had a tough go of it, and it's left some scars, I can tell you."

"No one knows of this, back in Munich. That must make you feel better."

"You sure? Someone we haven't considered—or you considered. There's always someone."

"All anyone knows back there, and there's only a few, is that a guy was murdered who is hardly an American and an Eastern European refugee may or may not have murdered him. So. What's that got to do with this here, with these people? Us? Nothing, Max. Nothing."

They kept drinking. Max loosened up. His eyes gained the sparkle. They talked about their parents, Manfred and Elise. Max was delighted they had written back to him. They only wanted their son alive and happy in the end, they wrote. Ironically, the war had settled Max and his father's feud. Vati didn't hold a grudge anymore. Sometimes you take a wrong road, their father had written. Often, one doesn't have a choice in the matter.

Their parents were the ones who revealed to Max that Harry had been transferred to Munich. Harry had become a fine upstanding man and could certainly help.

"They didn't mention New York. I didn't. But someday? I hope we can talk about it," Max said. The clear hooch had slowed his voice and thickened his tongue. Yet he was talking.

"We haven't seen each other in a long time, me and you," Harry said. "Yet you trust me. Take a chance on me. Still, don't go thinking it's a one-way street. I have to trust you, too."

"I know. I do know that."

"So what happened?" Harry said.

"What? Where?" Max glanced at the door.

"No, look at me. Start anywhere you like. Start with New York City, how's that? That much is safe to talk about, isn't it? It's been over ten years now."

Max's head hung. The sparkle in his eyes dimmed, submerged in a gloss of memory.

He couldn't get a break in America, he told Harry. First, he couldn't get a decent gig performing in New York City and then he couldn't get any job at all. He lost his American gal, Lucy, to California. Then Hollywood was too late for him, just another émigré German among far too many. He lost his will to scrape and fight and get ahead. He almost lost his will, period. New York was where he was going to prove himself to all, but it had become an utter dead end by 1939. Then, suddenly, Germany was looking like a Shangri-La, at least according to the kind German man from the embassy—a cultural attaché he'd called himself—who offered to cover Max's fare back home. Great things were happening back there, the attaché had promised. So many new opportunities opening up.

Harry didn't push Max. He didn't ask many questions. Max had obviously never talked about this to anyone for many years and he wanted to now. As he talked he sighed often, from deep within. Irina came and went and left them snacks of dried apricot. Such treats were rare here too, but she must have been able to see that whatever Max was saying to his brother in their English was definitely needed, and she only wanted to keep it going. Harry and Max stayed down on the bedroll, their backs to the wall.

"I loved America, but it didn't love me back," Max told Harry. He added an incredulous laugh that made him shake his head. "You? You were lucky. You came over earlier with Mutti and Vati. By staying behind in Germany and finishing my baking apprenticeship— just as Vati wanted, I was already eighteen when I made it over to you in New Hampshire. Do you know what that's like? I always felt like I was getting a late start. Funny thing. I guess I still feel that way."

"You left our home, and you left your baker job that he set up over there. Dad had to answer for that, you know. Make up for it. I had to help out."

"I know—"

"At some point they just wanted news of you, Max."

"I kept thinking that something good to report was right around the corner. That big break of mine. You know? But the big long city street just kept stretching on and on, ever longer, no corner in sight. My letters got vaguer, farther apart. This is why."

"If we got any letters at all. I wanted to visit you there in the city. You never responded."

"It was like I said. What had I to show you?"

"You—I wanted to see you."

"*Ach.*" Max waved at the air. "You were still a kid, what did you know—"

"Mom and dad wanted to visit. To see you. Jesus, Maxie. No one expected to find you in a penthouse wearing a top hat."

The bottle was empty. They let minutes pass in silence. Max smoked and nodded to himself deep in thought as if, Harry guessed, reliving what had come after New York. Harry wasn't going to press him on it. They would get there. Harry would have to eventually.

"Before you left, you wrote mom and dad from New York," Harry said. "You said you were only going to visit Germany."

"What could I say? I didn't want it to shock them."

"Shock them? What was left to shock?"

Max released a bitter laugh and his lit butt dropped to his trousers. He patted at the embers. "Now you shock me. We gave up on the corpse. We risked getting you tossed in some clink. We made contact with you."

"Because I was out of control—I know, I know," Harry huffed.

"It's one thing to bend the rules. Keeping that corpse on ice like you were doing. But you were going around in public offering Irina amnesty. A *Straferlass*? Please. You can't give her amnesty. How were you going to manage that?"

"I was going to find a way," Harry said. "Somehow."

Irina was standing in the doorway, leaning into the doorframe. Her look said: It was time for Max to come to bed. To her and her little Alex. Max, grunting, muttered something to Irina in broken Russian and gathered the blanket around him. She came over to him, nuzzled her head into his shoulder, and tucked a hand under his arm.

Max said to Harry, "I want you to know that, whatever happens, whatever you hear about me or even these people here, you will know that we are not monsters. We are simply caught between the trunk and its bark."

"A rock and a hard place, you mean. At least that's the English version."

"We need the Americans' help. They're the only option left. But it must go through you. Through someone who can understand. Forgive. Who knows how to find a way. Good night," Max said, and he gave a little bow and a flourish of his blanket as if it were a magician's cape.

Harry woke in the middle of the night, right when he'd told himself to. He had a flashlight. He switched it on, keeping it under his blanket as he navigated the room.

Max had left his overcoat out. Harry checked the pockets and found his brother's *Soldbuch*, his German military paybook. Harry flipped it open and saw a drab photo of Max in a regular army uniform looking offended. Name: Maximilian Kaspar. Max had been drafted in summer 1944, into a regular unit on the Russian Front. No awards. A common footslogger. But the record of postings ended in October 1944. A full seven months would pass until the surrender came.

Harry slid the *Soldbuch* back into the pocket. He fell asleep. At some point, he awoke to hear Max deliberating with others outside. They were arguing possibly. It was hard to tell. Harry fell back asleep.

Then Max was shaking him awake. It was early, the light a dark blue-gray.

"Morning," Harry muttered, the kinks in his back battling with the aches of hangover in his head.

"We're taking you back to Munich," Max said. "But first, I want to show you something. Give you something. Because, we have decided."

Max led Harry outside with his blankets still wrapped around him. They passed into the woods, into the fog. The older men were standing in a line, by a tree. They stared stone-faced, without gesture. Max halted Harry at what looked like a loose pile of underbrush piled up against a fallen log. Max eyed Harry.

"What?" Harry said.

"Your eyes should adjust first. Are they?"

"Yes."

Max rolled the log away and heaved the underbrush to the side. Underneath was a board. "Go ahead," Max said. Harry lifted it away to reveal a narrow ditch, like a rectangular foxhole. Harry stood over it, looking in. Two naked corpses lay in the ditch, their skin a bright blue-white in the fog, their midsections covered with a blanket. They lay on their stomachs. The backs of their heads were matted with dark, dried blood. They had a slight gamey smell, but the corpses were effectively on ice here and didn't give off much. Still, Harry's stomach cramped and rolled, his feet floated, and he had to close his eyes.

Max rushed over, steadied a hand at the small of Harry's back. "You okay?"

"Yeah. Yes."

Max turned Harry away from the ditch. From somewhere in the fog, Irina had appeared and was replacing the board, underbrush, and log over the two corpses.

"They're males, I take it?" Harry said.

Max nodded. "Soviet Army soldiers. They stumbled upon us a few days ago. Probably just AWOL, if not deserters, in which case they'd be shot. But you never know, and it's only a matter of time. Who knows who they are really?"

Max walked Harry to a tree trunk. Harry leaned against it. "What about the uniforms?" he muttered.

"Burned. All of it. They were two yokels from the steppes according to their effects. Farm boys most likely, but we had to be sure. Some of the people here are talking about eating them. I can only hope it's their dark humor."

"It wasn't just me out of control," Harry said. "You had other reasons. This."

"Yes. The thing you must know is the Soviets will find us. You're giving me that look again. But you asked for it. You wanted answers."

"Last night—you were arguing with those men," Harry said. "They didn't want you to show me this."

"That's right. But I won." Max held out his hands like he did. Lucky him.

"And they want my help now."

"They do. But the only problem is the Soviet Union is still your ally."

"Thanks for reminding me." Harry felt at the bark of the tree, a white birch—the bark was rough and jagged to his palm, but the sensation revived him. "Well, here we are. What did you call it? Between a tree and its bark?"

# Fourteen

"Did you know who he was? That corpse of yours? You got any idea at all?" Major Warren Joyner bawled at Harry. Joyner's office was now the interrogation room. The major had pushed Harry's chair close to the desk so that Harry's kneecaps pressed at hard oak as Joyner stomped around him in circles, huffing and puffing, the major's face turning red as if he'd drank a jug of wine. Only he wasn't drunk.

"No, sir," Harry said. It was eight a.m. on Monday. He had returned to his billet late Sunday evening from Max and Irina's refuge in the Šumava. When Gerlinde ran outside to him as he parked the Opel, Harry suspected it was Maddy trouble, but no—a major named Joyner was demanding that Herr Harry report to him first thing in the morning about something called "pronto."

"You really do not know? You got no clue. Well, you better not. Because you told me—gave me your word—that this wasn't going to involve a German."

Harry said, staring straight ahead, "I'm afraid I don't follow exactly, sir—"

Joyner slapped the desk, rattling drawers. Harry felt the soft old floorboards shudder under his chair as Joyner moved behind him, felt the major's hot puffing on the back of his head.

"The man was in the goddamn SS!" Joyner shouted.

Harry recoiled. Joyner might as well have slapped him hard across on the cheek.

"That's right—an *SS-Mann*," Joyner said, spitting it out, "God-damn it, Kaspar, why in the Sam Hell did you not report the death of a kraut who fought in the SS?"

"That's a good question, sir. Only, I didn't know he was SS." Harry's face was reddening like Joyner's. *Why the hell hadn't Irina told him?* That was the real question. Most any civilian east of Poland would be proud of killing an SS soldier even if just a private.

"Not only did you not report it—you were hiding his death. Jesus, Kaspar."

Joyner didn't have to tell Harry how this could look, and the fact that he was German-born wouldn't help matters. But Harry had been hearing it long enough. So if this bull of a major wanted to make something of it, Harry was ready to buck back. He sat up, clamping his hands to the desk. "Like I told you already: I had no knowledge," he said through gritted teeth.

"All right, Captain, easy," Joyner said.

Both of them eased off. Harry's hands found his lap and Joyner's shoulder the window, where the major consulted the gray Munich moonscape. He still had one fist tight to his side as if ready to jam a pencil into his leg. Harry tried to keep in mind what drove Sheriff Joyner. After two years of war, and worse, a fighter like Joyner was a lone wolf. Too independent for the career officers, had no love for the silver spooners who'd come over craving more silver spoons, and too old for the boy GIs who rotated in on a treadmill. Harry could relate. He was used to being an outcast among certain Americans on account of him being MG and a kraut to boot. The only problem was that Joyner was looking even more like one of those certain Americans.

"Can I ask a question?" Harry said. Joyner nodded, still gazing out the window. "What was the name?"

"The dead man? It's classified."

"Classified by whom? Sir."

Joyner turned from the window. His face had lost the redness. "Counterintelligence identified him. The CIC. They had it in their records. This bastard had been on the lam a while, and they'd been on his trail. It would've been a good catch, I reckon."

"I gather he was more than just a private? In his deeds, I mean?"

"I can't tell you that."

"Would it help if I went to the CIC and talked to them—"

"No! Absolutely not. Truth is, I shouldn't be telling you any of this. And God only knows why I am." Joyner scanned the room as if checking for any guests who could overhear. "Something tells me you did not know. Tells me, makes me hope, that you would've wanted a scum like this caught alive just as much as I."

"More than dead even," Harry said.

Joyner didn't respond. He sat down, his big frame made the desk look child-sized. He spoke in a near-whisper, his voice reedy like it was coming over a telephone. "This SS swine? He was part of the strike force that slaughtered our boys back in December of '44."

"Hürtgen Forest, was it? Or the Ardennes?"

"The latter. Battle of the Bulge. Ardennes Offensive, krauts called it. The bastard was in a special team, one of those who got behind our lines and posed as American soldiers. SS spies. We nabbed most of them, but this one had cut loose and tried to strike at anything he could—gas dumps, radio towers, generals I reckon if he would've got that far."

An uneasy feeling churned in Harry's gut. *Why the hell hadn't Max told him this?* He lifted a Chesterfield to his lips, hoping Joyner didn't notice his shaking fingers.

Joyner shot him a hard look.

"Oh sorry, sir. I won't smoke in here."

"Damn right." Oddly, Joyner's mouth had curled up on one side into something like a smile. He leaned forward. "I got you riled up though, didn't I? I'm telling you, this swine had no business getting away, dead now or no."

"And I hear you. Loud and clear."

"Good. So, keep on listening."

"Meaning, sir?"

"If you ever need help with whatever game you're playing—with whatever you're up to, you know right where to come."

# Fifteen

Harry wondered just who major Joyner supposed he was. Some sort of renegade Nazi hunter? A special assassin run by some new intelligence office? First Maddy and now Sheriff Joyner supposes he's a special operator and Joyner even offers his help. *If only matters were that clear-cut—then all could be fixed*, Harry thought as he marched back to his office in frustration, his wool service cap crumpled in his fist and his belted officer's overcoat hanging wide open letting the cold wind lash at his chest and neck and face.

If only he could tell it all to the likes of Joyner, or stroll right into the CIC duty station over in the Ludwigstrasse and ask for real help. That or he could even inquire, discreetly, with the reputed US Trade Council Representative at the far end of his floor with his overcoat draped over his shoulders and wide-brimmed hat. Harry had been wondering about the man, about his true operation. Munich was seeing a growing share of intentionally nondescript US officials like this, and surely some were covert operators. A man like that might know exactly what to do for the people trapped in the Šumava.

Harry marched on into his building and headed straight to the far end of his floor. The hallway was empty. He stood at the door for the US Trade Council Representative and listened. He heard nothing, no typewriters tapping, no voices, nothing. He stifled the urge to knock.

*If only*, he reminded himself. Sure, he had his own past to consider. But then there was Max.

Why would Max want to hide the identity of an *SS-Mann*? Could Max really not have known? The very idea of Max deceiving him— his own brother playing him for a fool—got him even hotter under the collar, and there wasn't enough cold outside to cool it down.

Back in Harry's office his secretaries passed in and out, a chain that he created by demanding each successive staffer fetch another so he could complete all tasks in his neglected inbox. He inhaled a sandwich and couldn't recall what it was. A secretary told him he was sweating and looked red in the face. "I suppose I don't feel so well," he said. "I'll have to go home."

He marched outside and flagged down a jeep for the stretch across the river into Old Town. From there he made his way on foot heading west of the train station, traversing debris-laden rail yards, bounding across the tracks and ties and gravel. Gimps and fiends approached. He shouldered them out of his way.

He had worked himself into a fit. What had Max taken him for? Did Max think family would trump all? Max could just tell Harry his sad tale of NYC and expect to be trusted?

Harry had dropped Max and Irina off near the train station after they came back from the Šumava. His billet was too visible; they opted for a bolt-hole they used in urgent situations—a deserted passenger rail car that had gone off the tracks and into the wall of a gutted building and hadn't been moved, Harry saw now, because it helped keep the wall standing.

The car was scorched and rusty on the outside. Harry headed right for it. A short but stocky man came at him demanding the password. Harry shoved him aside. He grabbed at a handle and charged up the car's steps, all shoulders and snarl.

Max was bounding down the corridor toward him like a man itching for a fight. He wore a thick wool cap, darned GI gloves, and a German overcoat dyed black, the very picture of a broken Munich rubble dweller.

Harry kept going. They grabbed at each other's lapels.

"You didn't use the password!" Max shouted.

"I'm your goddamn brother!" Harry shouted back.

"And coming here in uniform. People will talk!"

"Don't feed me that shit."

Max's eyes flashed around wildly. "What? What is it? Something's wrong."

"You bet it is."

Harry tried to free his grip on Max but Max grabbed at him firmer, reminding Harry that Max was stronger than he looked. They'd fought like this as kids, no punches, just shoving and holding ground like wrestlers trying to throw each other down. It was all in the stance, Max had always told him.

"I gave you answers, Harry."

"Did you?"

"You tell me what's wrong!" As soon as Max said it, his face paled as if he didn't want to know the answer.

They backed off each other, filling the corridor with their wide stances. Sweat was rolling down Harry's face. He tore off his overcoat. Max, sighing, took Harry's coat and cap and shook the cap into shape. He led Harry down the narrow corridor to a compartment with one bench intact and a larger table they'd hauled in to replace the bench opposite. The car had once been first-class, Harry saw. The woodwork still had polish and the bench a velour fabric the color of Burgundy wine. Amazing what survives, he thought, calming himself. Max slumped down on the bench, his elbows on the table. Cigarettes came out. Max pulled the curtain closed tight, and Harry slid the door shut.

"Just what do you want from me?" Max said.

Harry had the end of the bench closest to the door, trapping Max up against the window and table. He would let Max figure out the answer. He had decided on a new tack—he wasn't going to reveal he knew about the *SS-Mann*. He'd rather see where his actor of a brother took this.

Max was shaking his head, snorting, working himself up. "If you won't trust me, then—"

"Then what? Why should I? Give me one good reason."

Max kicked at the table to free himself, but the table was too big. Harry had him boxed in.

Irina heaved open the sliding door, glaring at them.

"I can't do it," Max said to her.

"Then I will," she said. "I will," she repeated to Harry.

First, Irina brought food to the table—actual meat stew with lentils and that rare brown bread. Max ate quietly. Harry wolfed down his stew, wanting to get at the real story, but he was also damn hungry having had only coffee for breakfast. Irina watched them in silence. She removed their metal plates and bowls. She came back with a chair, which she placed in the doorway facing them, and sat.

"*Kosaken*," she said in her clunky German. She patted her chest. "We Cossacks. You understand? Cossacks."

Max was nodding for her. Harry nodded.

"In Old Russia, we live as free. The Reds, they want us Cossacks to die. We fight Russian Civil War. After this, the Red Soviets persecute us. So when Germans invade, we fight on German side. We fight for us people, for Cossack people. We not fight for Hitler, for German people. Germans offer us a way to fight on. With our identity." Irina stopped to catch her breath.

Max said something in her language, adding in German, "It's not a race, dear. Take your time."

Irina focused on the ceiling as if recalling a street address. She pointed at Harry. "And then, your Mr. Roosevelt and the Mr. Churchill, they meet the Red Joseph Stalin in Ukraine, in Crimea. You make treaty with the one who wants us dead. Treaty say all Russians, Ukrainians, Soviet Citizens must return to Soviet Union after war."

Irina meant the Yalta Conference of February 1945. Roosevelt and Churchill had met with Stalin to consider postwar borders, occupation zones, reparations, and organizations, and to reward Stalin for sacrificing so much to help them all beat Hitler. Repatriation was key to clinching a deal. Sabine Lieser had been sure to remind Harry of it.

"It was all decided at Yalta," Max added. "All citizens of the Soviet Union were to be handed over regardless of their consent."

Harry wanted to raise his hand, stop them right there. Policy was one thing. 1945 was long gone. This was 1946. The Americans and British weren't as chummy with their ally Joe Stalin.

"You must understand," Irina said. "For many Russians now, if they don't want to return, it is no problem. We hear the rules are not so strong now. But we have no friends. No one will touch us. We are different, you see. Cossack armies retreat to west with Germans. We women, children, old people, we live and move with Cossack army. Our horses. Where we go now? Where? Red Russian Army came in fast from East, killing all like us, especially us. We are to them worse than Germans almost. The Germans, they promised we Cossack people receive new homeland in Northern Italy, near Alp Mountains. Thousands of us, you see. Hundreds of thousands at that time. Many Cossack fighters and officers and Atamans—generals— make way back to join us. We wait. We hope for homeland. Then your armies come from south. Then Soviet Army comes from east."

Irina had clasped her hands together as if praying. She swung them, back and forth. She said something. Max translated: "Stalin has made them enemies of the Soviet Union state, Harry. Age, gender, innocence do not matter. Only the number of souls matters. 'Stalin collects souls,' is how she put it."

Irina told the rest of the story in spurts, stopping only to glare at the ceiling. When the Allied armies advanced from the south across the Italian Alps, the Germans ordered the Cossacks northward into Austria. British army units overran the Cossacks near Lienz and interned them, cramming them into a canyon on the banks of the Drave River. The Cossacks surrendered without a fight. The British fed them and led them to believe they'd be protected from undue retribution by the Soviet Army now advancing well into Austria, only a few miles to the east. The Cossacks believed the British. They dared feel something like comfort, like safety.

At the end of May 1945, the British, still pledging protection, disarmed the Cossacks' couple thousand officers and generals and trucked them to the town of Judenburg.

"Where is that?" Harry asked.

Irina shook her head. Her face had gone pale.

"Judenburg was just over the Soviet lines," Max said.

"You're telling me the British handed them over," Harry said.

"If you want to call it that," Max said. "Many of the older officers had emigrated years before—during the Civil War—and were not even Soviet citizens, so they were technically exempt. But the British did it anyway—for Joe Stalin."

"What happened to them?"

"There are grim rumors," Max said. "Treason trials. Executions, mass lynchings. Labor camps. This happens not only to Cossacks, you understand. The rumor is, it's anyone—any Soviet citizen—who's been occupied by the Germans. Peasants. Forced laborers. Even POWs. To Stalin, anyone who got caught or was 'touched' by the West is now contaminated. All we know is, little word comes back from those millions Stalin already took back."

Tears were streaming down Irina's face. Her mouth opened, but no words came out. Harry moved to touch her but she pulled back, grasping at the doorway.

"She'll be all right," Max said. "For the Cossacks, the officers were only the start," he continued. "The Brits' 'sacrificial' deportation had left thousands despairing in the canyon on the Drave—the woman and children, the old ones, the poor regular soldiers who were fathers, sons, brothers. Three days later, on June 1, their own hell began. Troops of British Tommies, under orders, the poor bastards, prodded these helpless people at gunpoint into cattle cars and trucks. And in a panic bayoneted some. Mind you, this was happening across Southern Austria. Mayhem, all over. Many committed suicide. Or begged to be shot. Ghastly scenes, Harry. They'd brought their thousands of Cossack horses with them. These were children to them. Loved ones. How to leave them behind?"

A sick feeling constricted Harry's waist, as if a belt was being tightened. It drew all blood and power from his legs. This couldn't be true. He couldn't believe it. Irina had to be exaggerating, to save herself. "No, we wouldn't let that happen," he said, his head shaking.

"Who wouldn't let it happen, Harry?"

"At high levels, we'd be protesting it to the Soviet brass. Our officers. Diplomats. Somebody." Harry knew it wasn't true. He'd stopped believing back in Heimgau.

Max translated for Irina. Howling a laugh, she pushed at Harry's shoulder. "Or politicians, maybe?" Max said. "Your local congressman?"

"I'm just trying to understand. You think you know so well," Harry said to Max. "But were you there?"

Max looked to Irina.

"Don't look at her. Well, were you?"

Max's face softened. "Little brother, I—"

"Don't call me that," Harry said. He stood, but Irina had the doorway and he had nowhere to go either. He grabbed at the luggage rack and glared down at Max and Irina. What did they expect? These Cossacks fought with Hitler, and now they wanted a free ride out of it? Harry clenched at the cold metal of the rack, turning away from them, squeezing his eyes shut. He had risked his life once, but that was for a people who'd done nothing but existed, played by the rules, and even died in wars for the ones who ended up burning them and gassing them, their women and children, their old ones, their babies. What of those poor souls in the Šumava? Just days ago, they had killed two Russian soldiers to keep their secret quiet. Irina had killed a man who, it turns out, had been in the SS. But Max and Irina did not want Harry to know that?

"He does not want to help," Irina blurted, "I told you. He's like the rest. This is why I do not bring my Alex with me. Not yet. He's safer in a lost forest, separate from his mother." Glaring at Max, she pushed her chair clear of the doorway and stomped off down the corridor.

Harry slumped against the wall. He rubbed at his tired, itching eyes.

"Ages you, doesn't it, brother?" Max said.

Harry didn't answer.

"You're scared of committing to this. To me. Well, I cannot say I blame you. But I don't have a choice. You see, I was there at Lienz. That's right. I'll tell you." Max gazed at the window, into the curtain as if it was that stark canyon with its fast moving mountain river. "The British assumed I was a Cossack too. I had mixed in with them. Oh, they had us all right. And when the people found out what the Brits were really doing? They started stabbing themselves, pounding themselves with rocks, whatever they could grab, leaping into the fast river if they could reach it. Others fought it, tooth and nail. When the trucks came . . . horrible. People tried to break the Tommies' barrier, in great mobs, children and old women. And only so they could jump into the river, off bridges, find the tools to kill themselves. Even when the trucks started off, they leapt out, breaking their backs, getting run over, the trucks not stopping for them. It was mass hysteria." Max paused, took deep breaths. "This was not a brief mass hysteria. This played out over days."

Harry had sat back down.

Max went on: "Some of us escaped before the Tommies got to us. The Tommies were starting to crack from the strain. They couldn't take it. Could you? They had started looking the other way. That's when we escaped."

"Irina. You and little Alex and that group in the Šumava."

Max nodded. "Some came from other forced deportations—the woods and hills were filling with us, but, yes. And there is one thing you must keep in mind, brother. The woman and children there? The old ones? They did not fight on Hitler's side. Why should they pay the price?"

"I understand that, I do, but . . ."

"It would be as if, back home, the FBI took Mutti and Vati away simply because I had been part of a Germany that became Nazi. Without due process. Just suppose the President and his party used fear itself to terrorize and tyrannize America? Your Mom and Dad are labeled a threat. And we never see them again."

"There was a time, during the war, when I thought that might happen."

"Ah, but it didn't. Did it? It could not happen there." With that, Max ended his confession.

"I see," Harry said eventually. He wandered into the corridor. He trudged out of the car, and Max let him go. He stood looking out on the rail yards, smoking a Chesterfield. A group of ragged children approached, rooting around the tracks for scraps fallen from trains. Even though Harry was wearing his uniform, the kids kept on going, grabbing here and nabbing there, their little arms poking away like so many beaks of birds. Harry sighed. There was a time, and not long ago, when these kids would have rushed the American for candy, butts, whatever he had, even if to exchange a few words of broken English banter. Even if, more recently, to dupe him somehow. These days they didn't bother. A quick pass over the greasy gravel and rail ties could offer more hope than some sunny Ami. Maybe they had gotten used to their fate. This was what bothered Harry most. He pinched out his cigarette and left the butt in the gravel, hoping the kids combed back this way.

He ended up back in the compartment. Max was sitting in the same spot.

They sat there a while. The rail cars and tracks made Harry think about his train job, about what had made him do it. The story Max and Irina were telling him was, on a higher level at least, even darker and deeper than his sordid tale involving that bogus colonel and his deadly racket. This was the bone-crushing machinery of the world of power at work, its levers pulled by self-seeking deal-makers who just a few years before had been the warmongers.

"Have you ever seen a dead child?" Max said. "Not just dead, but left for dead? I have. I used to count how many. I stopped."

Harry had no answer for that. They sat a while longer.

"A story from a year ago is not good enough," he said finally. "You're going to need proof."

Max dared a little smile.

"Okay—we are." Harry held up his index finger. "But that's not why I came here, is it, brother?"

Max stiffened as if he were holding his breath. "No."

"You know it, and I know it," Harry added. "You told me about that place. About her people. You both showed me them. Irina gave it to me straight, as far as I can tell. But what about you? What about Max Kaspar?"

"Yes. What about him?" Max said. "I tell you what: If you see this out with me, help me with this job, I will tell you what I've done and what I've seen."

"But? There's another 'but,' isn't there, Max? I can see it on your face."

"I'm afraid there is. You see, it turns out that I have a visitor. From my past. And he demands an audience."

# Sixteen

MAX KASPAR KNEW THAT HIS SUMMONS was menacing simply from the venue. He was to appear at a spot called Kino Maritim. The "Maritime Cinema" was a confining name in itself since Munich was as landlocked as anywhere in Central Europe. But it was more ominous than that. Two crucial moments in his life had transpired in a venue with a stage. First, the SS found him taking cover inside a theater on the Eastern Front—and forced him into their last-ditch special mission. Then his dear younger brother Heinrich—Harry now—reunited with him in an opera house.

When he confessed to Harry that he must face a visitor from his past, Harry had said, "I'm going with you, and don't gripe about it. I'm going to keep watch for you."

Max wanted to reject the notion or even trick Harry if need be, but he had already been pushing things too far with his brother. Besides, he had to admit he could use the reinforcement and he needed someone he could trust. He didn't like the twinge he felt in his gut. All he really knew was that someone had left a note on his bench in the rail car: "It's high time for a reunion show, Herr von Kaspar. I know your talent and I hope to see more of it." At that he thrust open the car window and hung his face out in case he vomited from his head spinning.

Few alive knew him by his short-lived, one-time stage name of von Kaspar. The worst part was that the handwriting looked American.

It gave the location and time: eleven-thirty at night. The late show. In better times, in better moods, he might have told himself all these theaters were only foreshadowing his return to acting, down the road perhaps. Ah, but who was he kidding?

He had expected something grander nevertheless. Even the provincial theater in Poland where the SS found him was grand compared to this. Piles of rubble loomed around the building so it was hard to gauge how the middling splendor of the cinema's faux nautical facade stood up to the rest of the street. Kino Maritim had a quaint, two-door entrance, ticket booth in the middle, and modest marquee not up too high that read *WIR KOMMEN ZURÜCK*—this was hardly the name of the last moving picture shown but rather the owner's promise to reopen someday. Max wondered if the cans for one of his films were inside somewhere. The briefest of roles, they were, but they still deserved to survive.

For disguise he wore his cloak and fake beard and used another cane. He approached along the sidewalk, his head down, his eyes under the brim of his hat. A man on a rickety clacking bicycle passed, his knees stuck out sideways as he pedaled on by. Max, affecting a slight hobble, continued past the entrance and gave the insides a glance as he tottered onward. All he saw was the slight reflection of his cheekbone in the ticket booth window.

He stopped at the next corner and lit up a butt, leaning on his cane for actual support now. He was tired. Yet he used the pause to listen. He heard a faraway jeep or truck but the sound was thinning out, moving away from him. He took a glance back toward the empty street, then tossed the butt out onto the pavement.

Tossing the butt was their signal. But nothing happened. After a moment, Max's insides started to constrict. Where the devil was Harry? He had expected to hear something, anything, since Harry would be emerging from the rubble across the street. Still there was nothing.

Just as Max took a step to make his way back he caught the silhouette of Harry, crouching as he worked his way across the street while sticking to the long shadow of a spire. Max sighed, and the constriction lessened. Smart fellow, his little brother. That shadow was the only good cover with this strong moonlight.

The plan was thus: Harry would give the perimeter of the building a good going over and then wave Max in. Harry wearing the typical natty, mismatched clothes of a rubble dweller. If the coast was clear, he would reappear on the sidewalk and cough twice.

Harry reappeared. He coughed twice. Well done, little one. But then Harry turned to him and gave a signal involving two fingers that Max recognized as an American military-style gesture. Harry disappeared back inside the rubble skirting one side of the theater.

This was not in the plan! Max hobbled along the sidewalk stabbing with his cane, the anger rising hot up his neck. Harry was supposed to stay outside and watch the door after he went in. Dammit! This was not in the script at all. Harry could ruin the show.

At the entrance, Max leaned a shoulder into one door but it did not budge. Peering in through the glass, he could see furniture piled up against it. He tried the other door. It swung open and almost pulled him in with it. His cane saved him. Yet the door let out a mighty squeak.

He let out a booming sigh, not caring who heard now that he'd made so much noise. Maybe it was for the best that Harry was coming inside to get closer. Max hoped. Harry could be watching him at this very moment, or perhaps he had found his way up to a balcony or a box balcony if there were any. Not that Max could see them. It smelled moist and a little earthen in here, not from death but from seeping leaks and mud dried and re-soaked many times over, carrying with it, within it, who knew what pestilence.

He felt his way along in the dark, down the aisle, feeling at the chair rows as he went, descending down toward the stage. The note hadn't said where to go. So he would pull himself up onto the boards and sit. Where else were they supposed to find him? Selling sugared popcorn? Checking coats? Not his style.

It had been a cinema of late but naturally it would have a little stage—before the age of film it had surely seen recitals and plays, *Kabarett* und *Varieté*. It was so dark, Max couldn't see his hand. He pulled off his glove and stared at it and couldn't see it. Using the cane like a blind man, tapping around and not worrying about the sound, he found the stage and climbed up. He probed with hands and feet. His toe met something light and it scooted, what he recognized as a wooden chair on stage.

"Hello, Lieutenant Price."

A torrent ran through Max, electric and cold-hot and stiffening him with fear. The voice, of a male, had come from about fifteen feet away. He knew the voice. It has lingered in his head like the headaches other Germans got from the smog and debris of a destroyed city.

Max forced out a nervous chortle. "No, you seem to be quite mistaken."

"Let's not be coy now. You're not going to try that business again, are you?"

Sweat ran down the inside of his shirt. He wanted to call out to Harry, but only to make him run and flee and fast. He didn't want Harry to hear this. Damn! What was he thinking, letting Harry come here?

"I'm not trying a thing," he said to the man. "I'm only responding to a request."

"Your English is still excellent. That's so good to hear."

The piercing shot of fear was coming to a boil in Max's blood, converting into anger. It certainly helped disguise a measure of his shame. There was a time when he would have glossed it over with a light little musical number, tell a joke, buy a fellow a drink. But no song-and-dance, knee-slapper of a tale, or slug of schnapps could put a shine on this.

"Look here. Don't get angry," the man said. "It's not going to help either of us."

"No? Then why don't we turn up the lights and get this over with, eh?"

"They're out. Someone absconded with the circuit breakers—the whole unit to be precise."

Max reached inside his coat for his matches. He would shed the light on them. The horrid finality of his move made him pant as if he'd just carried a box of books up stairs.

"Wait a moment: Isn't there something you'd like to tell me?" the man said.

"Where would I start?" Max quipped.

"You brought someone with you. This is all I mean."

"Ah. Yes. Always a step ahead, aren't you? But never mind that. This is between you and me here. Is it not?"

"Yes. I suppose it is."

"May I?" Max said.

"Please do," said the man.

"I only have matches. The times being what they are."

"That's all right."

Max fired up his match in one strike.

Aubrey Slaipe was sitting bolt upright, but he looked relaxed, his head to one side a little. Like this he might have been watching a recital performed by children. He wore civilian clothes—a dark overcoat draped over his shoulders that was fine in its plainness, elegant without the swish and probably nicer fabric than Max had seen in years. It didn't stand out though. Only a man looking for it would notice the fibers. Slaipe's left hand rested on his left knee. It held a black pipe, cupped in his hand. He had removed his dark hat. It rested on his right knee, a surprisingly wide-brimmed fedora. He had that balding head and his hair was graying, although Max remembered they were roughly the same age. For Aubrey Slaipe was no more than thirty-six. Even in the dim flickering light his skin was pink, clean-shaven. His observing, detecting eyes so large with so much white. Max's match was burning out. He held the last flickers of flame to Slaipe's right arm. There, just under the overcoat, the sleeve of his suit was folded up and pinned flat to his torso.

Max let out a deep sigh. It extinguished the last ember, bringing smoke. His eyes squeezed shut in a mix of relief and stinging pain.

"It's still me, Max."

A lamp flashed on at Aubrey Slaipe's feet. Max hadn't noticed it there. Slaipe had set his pipe in his mouth to reach down with his one arm to switch it on. He seemed agile despite the injury.

"You're alive. I'm relieved," Max said, unknowingly in German.

"I can tell you're relieved," Slaipe replied.

"Tell me—can you walk?"

Slaipe stood. He held out his one good arm, showing it off, holding his hat with it. He pivoted around, revealing the pinned-up sleeve where his other arm used to be.

"Why did you wait to turn that lamp on?" Max said.

"I wanted you to find me your way. The way you wished to. This reunion can't be easy for you."

A silence found them. Slaipe kept his eyes fixed on Max. The look reminded Max of a keen boy at the seashore, studying tide pools for tiny creatures to emerge.

"I just realized we're speaking German," Max said finally. "Yours is so much improved."

"Thanks. I've been practicing," Slaipe said. "It wasn't until the surrender finally came that I began to realize I might still require it a while."

Harry found the side entrance and moved inside the movie house, feeling with his toes for debris and stray papers, anything that made a sudden sound. Dust grated under his soles as he shuffled and felt his way along down a narrow corridor and reached what had to be a backstage area, no wider than two people side-by-side and lined with timbers and boards and supports that could strike his head at any moment. Good thing he had on a thick cap.

He heard someone speaking, then two people. From the echoes, he could tell it was Max and another man, out on the stage. He couldn't make out what they were saying, but it wasn't heated. It sounded direct yet careful—that "what are you doing here?" sort of conversation he heard so many times between ex-lovers at some staff party or liaison to-do, bombed-out occupied Europe being such a damn small world . . .

The possibly shame-tinged tone made Harry wonder if Max wanted him to hear this. Max hadn't asked him to act as the backup inside, to play the mean face if need be, yet here he was. But who would he play the mean one for? Max still hadn't told him the whole story, and it was Harry's fault for not pushing his older brother.

A match flickered. Harry could see Max facing him about ten yards away out in the middle of the stage. Another man had his back to Harry. He sat in a wooden chair. They faced each other as if waiting for the lights to come up and they were the panel for a presentation on something humdrum yet vital like the return of Bavaria's wheat exports—better yet, it could have been a talk on the importance of prewar New York theater in the New Germany, with a number or two at the end performed by Max Kaspar truly. Then a lamp went on at the man's feet, what looked like a camping lantern. The man stood and turned in a full circle, holding out his wide-brimmed hat with one arm and revealing that the other arm was missing under that overcoat draped on his shoulders like a cloak. And it hit Harry:

*It had to be the man from his building*—the reputed US Trade Council Representative. The overcoat looked the same, and the hat. The erect yet relaxed posture.

Max's voice sounded thinner, under strain, and they switched to German. But Harry could not hear their words.

Max wondered what Harry was seeing, hearing. It was nearly absurd to imagine now that this man Slaipe and he had been enemies just last winter. Why hadn't they just stopped it all then? Say, look friend,

I know the forces that wish us to kill or at least imprison us are overwhelming in their pressure and pressing ever stronger, but what do we have against one another? If we met on an ocean liner, we'd probably make fast friends and proceed directly to the cocktail bar.

"Look at the two of us. It was always so ridiculous, was it not back then?" Max said to Aubrey Slaipe, switching back to English and trying to keep it light. If he didn't, he thought the arteries to his heart might explode.

"Some of it was, yes. Some of it was simply a job that had to be done. Finished off."

Slaipe had not changed. Max had his arms out to convey a lighter mood but they felt heavy, as if he was holding dumbbells. They lowered to his sides. "And, Justine DeTrave? What happened to that woman?"

"She's dead, I'm afraid. Oh, she survived your bit of business, but that brother of hers in the Walloon SS returned right about when the war ended and by then the Belgians were really looking to strut their stuff. They hanged her in the nearest town square, next to dear old brother. Her jaw was still wired shut, by the by. You did a number on her with the butt of that rifle."

"My god." A heat welled up behind Max's eyes, and his heart ached now, but it wasn't for Justine.

He lunged at Slaipe and hugged him. Slaipe stood rigid but let him. Max was crying. The tears ran into his mouth, down his neck. He pulled away and the tears splashed hot on his fingers.

"You're on stage. But I can see this is no act," Slaipe said.

Max wiped at his face, gasping. "I'm just glad you're alive," he muttered. "Of course I feared the worst. But what could I do? I only wanted to get free. Flee. From all of it. I told you that was all I had planned."

"Yes, you did. One could say that you saved my life. That DeTrave woman probably would've shot me again to cover up her silly plan. Or I simply could have bled to death right there in the snow. Not far from Smitty himself."

"Perhaps. Poor Smitty. Good god . . ."

"In any case. One could also say that you left me there to die," Slaipe said.

"Certainly," Max said, sniffing up tears. "I liked Sergeant Smitty, you know. Your right-hand man hated me, but I liked him. If I only could have known she was going to do what she did, I would have stopped her earlier. I would have."

"I want to believe that. But, the sad truth is, you did not want to know. Even when she gave you the clues."

"But who was I to tip off you? Eh? Just say to you: Look here, good fellows, I'm a German soldier spying in an American uniform, but never mind that; here's what you really ought to know—the woman we're staying with here while we're stranded in this snowstorm like we are? She's planning to do you two in because she's the only resolute Belgian Fascist left in this part of the Ardennes and we, we three poor devils, just happened to stumble upon her snowbound house all at the same time." Max had turned to face an imaginary audience, standing center stage. It was instinct, old habits dying hard, but the effect probably cheapened the truth. He turned to face Slaipe, shrugging, a little ashamed. His words were true enough. He shuffled back over to Slaipe and, although Slaipe's face was shadowed, he saw the glints of Slaipe's eyes and wanted to believe that their wet gloss was from sympathy and not the sickest schadenfreude there ever was.

"You shouldn't have run, Max. I do understand why you did. Supposing you stayed with me, helped me stop the bleeding, helped get me back to my lines."

"I would have had to finish her off."

"Kill her, yes. Let's call it by name. Would it have been so very difficult?"

"In hindsight? No. I would do it. I know how now."

"You see? But even if you had—what was I to do with you then? What would the forces that be have demanded I do, despite whatever pleas I might have made. Yes? Are you with me?"

"Yes, yes. That's about it. Just so."

Slaipe leaned closer. "And yet the most important thing is, you did save me from her."

"I see."

"Do you? It does appear that you do. It's kind of a wash, you see. We're back where we were. I still have to make good on my word. We have unfinished business, me and you. I'm going to have to tie back the threads together."

"But, the war's over," Max said.

"Is it? Which war? Did we have a signed contract based on such and such a period of armed conflict? I'm afraid not. Your obligation is to us, not to a war. Me. You remember what I said?"

"I do."

"I said that you would have to go back to your own side, but working for us."

"There's always a war," Max muttered.

"That's right, Max. That's correct."

They stood there a moment. Slaipe leaned on the back of his chair. It creaked like a tree trunk cracking. Oddly, sourly, the sound took Max back to those frigid, death-laden Ardennes woods that had delivered him right into Aubrey Slaipe's hands—just when he thought he had a chance at breaking free from it all.

"I'm sorry," Max whispered.

"So am I," Slaipe said. "We're all victims of it. But there are jobs that must be done."

Slaipe was supposed to be dead—this was what Max had ended up telling himself. No one had known of the seed that Slaipe now reaped. Max could not let Slaipe and Harry share notes, deliberate, collaborate. He shuddered at the thought. Pretending to shiver from the cold, he glanced around for Harry but he could see or hear nothing.

Slaipe was watching him, an odd smile forming on his face. He looked over his shoulder. No sound came from backstage. That was where Slaipe was looking. Backstage.

"What do you want from me?" Max said.

"At the moment? I only wish to confirm that it's really you."

"Listen. Look at me, please," Max said, hoping to keep Slaipe's attention. He broke into a grin. He offered his right hand for a shake, then yanked it back out of shame. "Let's go get a drink, just you and me, Captain."

"It's Major now, actually. But I'd prefer that you call me Mister."

"I . . ." Max heard the creaking of floorboards.

A silhouette appeared on the stage, just out of the light.

Harry.

Harry felt he had no choice. After Max had hugged the man, which was shocking enough, Harry began to make out a little of their conversation. The man spoke with assurance and used particular words but as if his careful word choices were never an issue for him and hadn't been since childhood. A man who knew what needed to be done—that it would get done. Then Max's grin became a grimace, making him look like an actor who'd forgotten his lines as he suddenly kissed up to the man. Harry had to know what had made Max stoop so low. And, he could admit, left backstage he was feeling a little bit like he had as the youngest when the older ones played a joke on him. We'll meet you down by the river, Henry—wait for us at the abandoned mill. Of course, Max had never taken part in such jokes as older brothers often do—Max was always the one who had come and rescued him.

So there Harry went, out onto the stage. The man turned to him.

Max froze. In better days Harry was certain that his brother would have strode on over, cradled Harry's elbow and showed him off to his old acquaintance, introducing them profusely. Now he just glared and shook his head at Harry behind the man's back.

The man nodded Harry over. Harry stepped forward, into the lamp light. The man held out his hand. "You must be Harry Kaspar," he said.

Harry shook hands, nodding. He didn't ask the man's name, for Max's sake, and the man didn't look like he cared much either way. His intent eyes showed they had more important matters behind them.

Harry stole a glance at the man's missing arm.

"The war," the man said.

"Come again?"

"I lost it in the war."

"Oh. I'm sorry."

Harry wanted to get things done, same as this man. But he was never quite sure what those things were until they were smack in his face. It had always been that way with him. That was what had gotten him into trouble back in Heimgau with the train business—he had let the wrong man tell him what needed to be done. He liked to think he knew better these days. So he pressed the matter:

"On the front?" he said.

"Of sorts."

"What unit?"

The man paused, cocking his head back a little. Harry kept his eyes on the man and could hear Max moan nervously.

"Counter Intelligence Corps," the man said.

Of course. This CIC agent had the same manner that Harry remembered. A fake colonel named Spanner had it, and Spanner even claimed to be a CIC agent himself, and it had all helped con Harry so much that he ended up having to kill that man. But wasn't Harry like that now, too—that kind of operator? He was a freelancer when he had to be. People knew about him. Some even knew about the train.

"What's your posting these days?" Harry said.

"Oh, we'll get to that eventually," the man said.

Max scrambled off into the darkness. The man's chin went up and his mouth parted a bit, like a cat sniffing at air. Max came back with two more chairs, rearranging all three chairs just so like only someone who'd worked on the stage would do. They sat.

Harry stared at Max and the man and said, "So, what's this all about? Who's going to tell me?"

Max eyed the man, who gave him a little shrug.

"Where does one begin? Let's just say that your brother Maximilian and I here share a certain, well, past."

"Maxie?" Harry said to Max. Max stared at his crotch as if there was a tarantula crawling across it. Harry added in German, "Well come on, out with it."

Max jerked his head up. "Don't call me Maxie."

"Don't call me Heino then," Harry shot back.

"Whoever said I was—"

"Gentlemen, please," the man said. "I see you are brothers, aren't you?" One corner of his mouth wrinkled into a smile. "It's up to Max. He will tell you when he's good and ready."

But Max only went back to staring at his trousers.

"I can say this," the man added, "I simply aim to confirm that you two, once reunited, will seek to perform the sort of deed that I imagined you would—so this applies to you too, Harry."

"What? So we're circus seals, that it?"

"Hardly. 'Subjects,' more like."

"Don't you mean, your 'marks'? So you're sort of like a flimflam man?"

"In actuality, you make a good point. I think the con men—the skilled ones, anyway—must have similar talents. And salesman. They judge and predict to the point of knowing. In this regard I am rather like a scientist, you see. And now that my findings are being confirmed? I'd say that you two are welcome to continue."

"With?" Harry said.

"Whatever I think you will respond to."

"And, why in the hell should we do that?" Harry said.

"Heinrich, *bitte*," Max said.

"Don't call me that either," Harry said.

"Actually, for now, it's more about what Max will do. You are on board if you choose, but I believe I know what you will choose—based on your past—so let us assume for the sake of rational science that you will respond."

"Oh yeah, and what do I respond to?" Harry said. "You said you knew. So what is it?"

"Well, the truth, of course," the man said.

# Seventeen

Harry didn't pressure max on the way back to his billet. Max didn't speak the whole time. His mouth was too busy hanging open like he was going to retch.

Back inside the mansion, Harry poured Max and himself whiskeys in the living room. He made a fire. They sat near it, staring into the flames. Gulps became sips. Max smiled to himself, shaking his head, and then he moved closer to the fire rubbing his hands together. A man like Max, holed up so often like he was, probably dreamt of mansion fireplaces.

"My compliments on your abode," Max muttered. "It's truly magnificent. Kudos."

"Thanks," Harry said. "I wonder—how did that man lose his arm?"

Max started. "In the war!" he barked. "He told you."

"Take it easy. I thought you were doing better."

Max rubbed his hands faster like he had too much lotion on them; he was going rub the skin right off if he kept it up. "You don't know," he muttered. "You weren't in the war."

"No, but aren't I getting all the shit that it left."

"Too true. I'm sorry."

"Don't be. And do not worry yourself—I don't want the man's help either," Harry said.

Max beamed at him. "Truly?"

"Truly. I don't even want to know his name."

Harry was relieved that Max, despite his apparent obligation, did not want to involve the onetime CIC agent if he could help it. Harry hadn't told Max he had seen the man in his building, on his very floor at the far end of the hall from his office. The man may be legit on some War Department letterhead, in quadruplicate, Top Secret even, yet he still came from those same higher powers that pushed war, incubated a corrupt racket in Heimgau, sent in a fool like Harry's former CO—one Major Robertson Membre RIP, and created a monster with a death wish calling himself Colonel Spanner. Now the predicament was Yalta policy. Now Harry worried the man might have an office there just because of Harry, to keep an eye on him along with his brother. So Harry had his own cards to keep close to his chest. At least the man coming for Max had not proved to be a German and especially not one in the style of the conniving Nazi at large who only appeared after dark. If a man like that had something on Max, they were in for it. And these days the tight spot had two ways—a chameleon ex-Nazi might even be under the employ of Joe Stalin.

Max's smile faded. He turned back to the fire. "But, you will want to know in the end."

Harry sipped his whiskey, then set it back down with equal pressure on all sides of the bottom, as if pressing it into sand. "It's like the man said: Only when you're good and ready."

"Okay. All right, Harry."

The man knew they were up to something. Before they left the movie house, they had each told him, without giving anything away, that they were working on an operation on their own and didn't need his help. Each had their reasons. The man didn't ask just what it was they didn't need his help for. He had simply shrugged his overcoat forward onto his shoulders, set his hat on his head, and exited the stage. Max was holding out his arms like he was going to hug the man again, but he had held back.

Max puffed up his cheeks, held it, blew out air. Harry poured him another whiskey.

"Me, I didn't like the way the man was talking," Harry said. "It wasn't his implying that we should commit to him and his organization, whatever that is. It's that he thinks he's so damn sure of our next moves. We're not mice in some lab."

"Let us hope not, brother."

They downed the whiskey. They turned from the fire, faced each other, and began to work out their plan. Sleep could wait. They had even less time to lose.

"Suddenly you must know so much?" Sabine Lieser asked Harry. "No one ever wishes to know."

"Someone has to," Harry said. He sat with Sabine in a small *Konditorei* in Schwabing near what was left of Munich's grand university. The unlit pastry case contained two half loaves of bread and three turnovers of dubious vintage, the mold surely scraped off daily. Yet the place had white marble and mirror tiles that helped show off the polished metal coffee machine, all more than ready for that day when the *Kaffee* was fine again. Harry imagined smells of pastry glaze and hot sweet milk, but all this place could offer for now was a faint smell of detergent. It was the morning after the man in the movie house—after Harry and Max worked up a plan till late. Harry had called Sabine first thing; this secluded spot was her idea. At a table in the back corner, they drank ersatz coffee they poured from little pots that they cupped their hands around for warmth. The place had no heat this time of day so Sabine had left her coat, scarf, and gloves on. Harry had fought off a sudden urge to rub her warm, all over. It was the first time he'd seen her outside of her work. Her fur hat softened her face and she smiled more, making her look like the playful sister of the hard woman who helped run the Standkaserne DP camp. When Harry began by asking her about repatriation and about deportations specifically and how they took place, her face softened even more. Her eyes had fixed on him in that way that made some Americans uncomfortable. He had no problem with it.

"And, you wish to know what exactly?" she said.

"Supposing I found Irina—not that I did. Let's just suppose I did. Problem is, she has a couple friends—refugees—she wants processed too."

Harry thought he saw a sparkle in Sabine's eyes, or maybe it was a flash of window light reflecting off the coffee machine's chromium plating. He expected her to ask him flat out if he truly had found Irina. Another sparkle wouldn't help him keep his secret.

"Processed how?" was all she said.

Harry stole another look around. The cafe was empty. The two women running things were in back.

"We're safe here," Sabine said. "They used to be refugees of mine. Why do you think I picked this place?"

"Well, processed, as in, brought over from the Soviet zone into the West."

"On their own?"

"Yes—not sanctioned, for lack of a better word."

"I see." Sabine lifted her coffee cup. "Depends what the refugees have for a past. What identification is required. Depends on who's willing to help, and, in turn, who's willing to be bought off. Everyone from smugglers to officials to soldiers could help, but it's risky. The crooks and double agents are multiplying by the day."

"Everyone's either greedy or desperate."

"That is correct. Winter is coming. The Soviets."

"So, no normal channels? No official agents."

Sabine gave a little shrug of one shoulder and sipped. "If they come through Munich, through the Displaced Person authorities and the camp system, they would seem to be better off under my control, but they really are not. In camp, they are slaves to policy. As for your official agents? I should think not. They only represent the same big men who dreamt up Yalta . . ."

Sabine stopped speaking. A haggard man and woman passed out on the sidewalk. The two looked in but seeing the case near empty, moved on. And the view was safe again—all Harry and Sabine saw was the slab gray of the banal building across the street.

"Why do the dreary buildings always survive?" Sabine quipped.

Harry smiled. "Search me."

She raised a gloved hand as if to take his hand in hers, Harry hoped, but she only set it on the table.

"So," he said, "should I gather that you—or people such as you—can help some unfortunate refugees *outside* of camp? Using your expertise, that is."

"This also depends," Sabine said.

Their faces were drawing closer, ever slowly, as if by a slight change in gravity's pull, a strange sideways current. Sabine's gloves came off. She pressed her slim fingers to the table's edge as if to halt the pull.

"Would you do it?" Harry said.

"Do what, my dear?" They were speaking in German now.

"You know what. Rock the boat of your masters?"

"Be specific."

"If a repatriation meant certain death—would you work to stop it?"

"I know what I would do. But do you?"

"Yes."

"I said be specific, Harry. There's no time."

"I am. I would work to stop it."

"Against policy? Against orders. Against threat of death. With eyes on us possibly."

"Yes. I would. And I will."


Over the next couple days, Harry bent the ears of American officers who knew the score. He'd been to enough parties with Maddy Barton to still know people who knew people staff level, the types who felt the latest scuttlebutt like a nurse measured pulses. To keep it casual, Harry had to navigate like a river captain. He bumped into officers in their buildings and on street corners. He surprised the officers on his floor with his friendliness. Meanwhile, he kept clear of the far end of the hallway and never saw anyone coming or going from the office of the trade representative. He hit the officers' clubs day and night. He bought them and their Fräuleins' drinks. It emptied his pockets and left him hung over, but it had to be done. Many didn't want to know about repatriation while others shook their heads as if they might know but wished they didn't. When Harry pressed them, lit their cigarettes, bought them another, all confirmed Sabine Lieser's take. Flouting the repatriation regulations was touchy business. Refugees whom the Sovs clearly intended to persecute might be helped, but if those refugees had sided with the Germans in any way, it was probably a wash. There were other issues. The US Constabulary had stepped up border patrols. The Sovs were doing the same on the other side. Some now harbored genuine fears the Soviet Army was about to invade. Then there were the Soviet spies lurking around. It was a fine line. Even finding a sympathetic voice was a crapshoot. This was 1946 and all was in flux—with wartime agencies disbanding and new ones arising, too many internal battles had to play out first. Don't rock the boat was the game more than ever. No one needed another war now, not with Joe Stalin. Not with so many careers being remade. The big showdown would come later. The new men, the comers, they first needed to stock up on shiny stars and fruit salad.

Gossip bred gossip like so many rats, and Harry's inquiries ran the risk of new tales propagating. All it took was one Joe to whisper that MG liaison officer Kaspar was up to something. Kaspar had to have a racket going. Was Kaspar trafficking in people? Could he really be dealing with Reds, or was it Nazis on the lam? Gossip could also turn cruel. After receiving Harry's letter, Maddy Barton had arranged to have her belongings hauled from Harry's garage. Harry had been expecting one last knockdown with her. But he discovered on his gossip tour from multiple sources that Miss Barton was taking it well. She had even taken up with a young colonel, a real mover and shaker. This was the part that gave Harry that hangover.

He kept clear of MP Major Warren Joyner—until Thursday. The MP clerk said Joyner was in that morning, but Harry found Joyner's office door closed. He knocked.

"What?" Joyner barked from inside. "Come in," he added before Harry could answer.

Harry entered into near darkness. The major was sitting at his desk with the curtains drawn. A silhouette. The air was warm and stale and sweet with whiskey.

"What is it, Kaspar?" Joyner's shadow said.

"Should I turn a light on, sir?"

"No." Joyner stood and ripped open the curtains and faced Harry. His face was more pink than ruddy, eyes bloodshot, his jowls fleshy and lined. A guy who looked this sad probably couldn't get too drunk if he tried, Harry thought.

"Everything all right, sir?"

Joyner didn't answer. He just stared at his desktop, at the inbox, pencils, files, and folders as if presented with them for the first time.

"I could use some chow," Harry said. "Could you?"

To Harry's surprise, Joyner said yes. He took Harry to a former small beer hall that had evolved into one of Old Town's unofficial officers' clubs. To keep a good thing going, the aging waiters spoke broken English and shaved off their Hitler-style mustaches that had once been so harmless everywhere from here to Nebraska. It was a long narrow hall with dark stained glass windows of colored circles framed in lead. The tables were knotty, the benches about as comfortable as pews; and red, white, and blue ribbons draped the old pillars like giant 4-H awards. Joyner ordered scrambled eggs, toast, and coffee. Harry, coffee.

"I come here for the breakfast," Joyner said. "Plus, got to say, reminds me of my Grange Hall back home. Go figure that one out."

"I can see it," Harry said.

"Just what do you want, Kaspar?"

Harry asked if Joyner had any experience with repatriation efforts—forced repatriation to the Soviet Union, specifically. Joyner had not, but he had heard things within the Military Police. Down south in Austria, the British had sent home thousands against their will. American troops had been forced to do it, too, right here in Bavaria—sending away people like so much cattle, just like the Germans had done. It was part of a deceptive and brutal campaign called Operation Keelhaul. It gave everyone a bad taste in their mouths. Meantime, fewer trusted the Soviets by the day. Yet just because an American officer hesitated to offer someone up to the Soviets didn't mean they were going to help someone either. For the most part, folks were on their own.

"Enjoy your new freedom, peoples of Europe," Joyner quipped. "Why you asking?" he added.

"Because I knew you'd give me an honest take."

Joyner grunted. "During the Great Depression? We had a score of poor Okies come out west looking for a place to hang a hat. We helped them then. My town took them in. Done. No complex regs necessary."

Two young GIs passed, joking around, their caps pushed back. Harry was about to ask if the major knew Sabine Lieser in the Standkaserne camp but Joyner had clenched up, digging his elbows into the table as if wanting to bore right on through it.

"What's the matter, sir?"

"What? Nothing." Joyner's head dropped, and for a moment Harry expected the major to heave up his eggs.

"I'm sick of missing him," Joyner muttered.

"Him, sir?"

"My son. My boy. If he came back right now, walked into this room here, I'd probably kill the damn kid I miss him so much."

Harry gave Joyner a moment. "What was his name?" he tried after a while.

"Harry." Joyner added a bitter chuckle.

"A fine name."

"Maybe that's why I haven't shut you down yet."

167

Harry fought the urge to pat the man's shoulder. "Can I ask how he bought it?"

Joyner stared, but his eyes lost focus. "Northern Italy. Kid drove a tank, when he wasn't fixing them. Took a direct hit, his CO letter said. A quick death."

Harry wasn't so sure. Tank deaths were ghastly. He'd seen one charred body protruding from a tank hatch and that was all he ever needed to know about it.

"You like me to order us something stronger?" Harry said.

"No. No . . ." Joyner began to say something but stopped. He shook his head. "Do you know I volunteered for this? At my age. I had to. I wanted in because my boys had gone."

"You have more?"

"One left. In the Pacific. Martin. He's rotating out soon." Joyner looked away, glaring at a waiter who hurried along. "Mary, my wife, she wasn't much for me coming over."

Joyner asked about Harry's family. Harry mentioned Max but said he was still MIA—besides Max was dead to him for hurting the parents and shaming the family, he added. It was close enough to the truth. He had no choice but to play it like this. He didn't know enough about Max yet.

They sipped coffee. Joyner pushed away his plate, his breakfast half eaten. "I thought you wanted chow," he said.

"I wanted you to chow. Looked like you could use it."

"I'll survive," Joyner said.

"I have no doubt of that."

"You sound like my nurse."

"I was the Public Safety man in my previous posting," Harry said. "A burg south of here. Then I was the detachment commander. Skeleton crew, small town . . . had its challenges."

"You know what you're doing. That what you're trying to tell me?"

"I'm telling you that I once knew a man who hated Germans. He was a major too. You would've hated the bastard to no end."

Harry was ready for Joyner to burst. He even grasped onto the table frame. But Joyner only broke into a grin so big that Harry imagined him pushing back a cowboy hat. "What, you my preacher now too, Kaspar? That why you here? Asking me to forgive?"

"No. That part, it's up to you."

Harry left it at that. He couldn't involve Joyner until he had something more concrete. Joyner said he'd be waiting. Harry was his nurse and his padre, so why not his savior?

That afternoon Harry was crossing the Luitpoldbrücke, the usual chilling river gale whipping into him, when the erstwhile CIC man in the overcoat and wide-brimmed came right at him. Harry stiffened—he couldn't help it. The man held out his one arm as if to say, fancy meeting you here, what a coincidence. They stood eye to eye in the middle of the bridge, all alone, not one jeep or a bike clattering by. If Harry didn't know better, he would have sworn the man had requisitioned the whole stretch.

"Well, well," the man said.

"Am I supposed to acknowledge you?" Harry said. "I never even asked your name."

"I can't answer that."

"Can't you? I thought you always knew the play."

"No. I predict an outcome. The rest, it's up to you . . ."

The wind fluttered the wide brim of the man's hat. The hat jumped, Harry lunged and caught it coming off. He pressed it to the man's chest, and the man held it there like a door-to-door man paying a visit.

"This is your chance, Kaspar," he said. "Yours alone this time."

Harry sighed. He looked up at the low gray clouds. He turned and ended up stepping in a full circle, weighing the gloomy sky pressing down on them, the bombarded spires of Old Town so grotesquely jagged, and the brown-green river hurtling past underneath them.

"I'll take my chances," he said.

Harry had expected the man to pull out a top-secret order reigning him in, or signal for a constabulary jeep to roar onto the bridge and cuff him, or at least to shake his head at him in disappointment. The man was just smiling. It was a nice smile. It almost made Harry ask him if he had children back home.

"Bravo," was all the man said. He patted Harry on the shoulder, set his hat back on his head, and strolled onward.

On Friday morning, October 26, Harry met Sabine again in the *Konditorei* to talk strategy. She had come up with a solid plan of her own to help them. Afterward, as he was rounding the next corner, he ran right into Hartmut Dietz.

"Why, Herr Kaspar," Dietz said. The detective grabbed Harry's shoulders in an improvised hug, since Harry had an unlit Chesterfield in one hand and a two-day-old *Käsestange* in the other. "Of all the people."

"I should say the same."

Dietz had a grubby briefcase under one arm and wore a different overcoat that was ragged even for a German.

Harry held up his meager cheese breadstick to share.

"Thanks, no," Dietz said. "That's not real cheese, I'd guess. Take powdered milk and color it, bulk it up with grease, margarine if they can get it."

Harry slid the thing into a pocket. "I'm hoping this one's better than that."

"Certainly. I'm sure that shop does a fine job . . ."

They stopped talking, stuck on the corner, the building's sandstone blocks pressing into their shoulders. Harry moved to light his cigarette. Dietz offered his lighter, eyeing the sidewalks as he did so. A couple people passed. They were alone again.

"How goes your investigation? Is she still worth the trouble?" Dietz said.

"Possibly," Harry said.

Dietz placed a hand on Harry's arm. "Say no more, Harry. I know you're still at it—you're not the type to quit. But please know that I am at your service, should you need me. I know you trust me. I certainly trust you."

"I appreciate that." Dietz wouldn't be offering his help if he didn't mean it, Harry knew. The detective could likely help as well as two Sabines or even a Joyner but going local, as Harry also knew all too well, had its own set of complications. "Let's just say, it's become an internal matter—for now," he added.

Dietz pulled his hand from Harry's arm. "Very well."

"How are the *Kinder*? Wife? Need anything?"

"No, but thank you." Dietz slid his hands deep into his pockets, and his eyes lost a little gleam.

"Look," Harry said, "I've given you enough grief. This mess is mine now."

"I understand. I do."

"Good." Harry held out his *Käsestange*. "Here, take it. Maybe you won't eat it but one of your kids might. So don't go trading it."

"Thank you. That's very kind." Dietz lifted it to his nose. "You know, this one might just be real cheese at that."

And there they left it, Harry heading on back to his mansion, his stomach creaking not so much from the hunger of losing his cheese bread but from the absurdity and longing in that moment. It had been like running into an old girlfriend or an estranged buddy—an awkward reminder that whatever they'd shared had never been completed. Dietz might as well have been Maddy, Harry thought and sucked on his cigarette and marched across the cobblestones searching for a notion that might comfort him. Then he found it. He imagined Dietz retreating to a nearby doorway and devouring the pastry himself, an act that Harry should have found despicable but in these times was just about right.

Back at the mansion, Gerlinde met Harry in the foyer, happy to report that his *Herr Bruder* had decided to stay. Max had eaten soup and sausage and even drank a beer at lunch. Harry didn't need to tell her Max was a Kaspar; she had figured it out with one glance. He found Max holed up on the sofa. The sofa was pushed closer to the fireplace so that no one could see him from the windows—and he had the drapes shut as well. He had on the mansion's requisite velvet smoking jacket and, using hair tonic (Harry could smell it), had combed his hair back neatly. He had a Shakespeare anthology open on his lap. He sat up straight for Harry.

"What, you have an audition?" Harry said.

"Of a sort, yes."

Gerlinde had a good fire going. It crackled and hummed. Harry sat on the ottoman before Max, his hands hanging off his knees, letting the flames tingle his veins. A couple other books stood at the sofa leg. Next to them lay Max's *Soldbuch*, his army paybook.

Max had pursed his lips together as if holding his breath. "How can you help me—help us—if you don't know who I am? It's not fair."

"No. I guess it's not."

"The man who called me to that stage? His name is Aubrey Slaipe."

"I told you I didn't want to know."

"He knew me as Julian Price—one US Army Lieutenant Julian Price."

"Oh, boy," Harry muttered. He stood and backed up into the nearest chair.

"You need the full confession," Max said. "So if I'm going to sing it, then it might as well be from the top."

# Eighteen

MAX TOLD HIS BROTHER MUCH of the worst of it. He had been a flameout in New York and a would-be comer in Nazi Germany. These were only the first two acts. He lost his love, the opera singer Liselotte Auermann, in a Hamburg air raid of 1941. He lost faith. He lost roles. The final act came in the fall of 1944, when the Wehrmacht called up English speakers for an assignment with unknowable prospects. As a drafted foot soldier, he was already under contract. He fit the part perfectly. He had no idea it involved a secret mission as part of the surprise Ardennes Offensive in which American-speaking German soldiers were to infiltrate the American lines. Worse yet, the Armed SS recruited him for the job. Max had no choice. So he would rewrite the role. Once behind the American lines, he would desert and go on the lam in France or end up a POW playing the forlorn, clueless *Soldat*. That would be his way out. He might even get back to America this way. He was that naive then.

He confessed all that he dared. The curtain was up and it was break-a-leg time. Harry had listened with his usual patience, his usual poker face. Harry was still his little brother, make no mistake, with the same broad, freckly cheekbones and those bangs wanting to curl, same neat dress and now those horn-rimmed glasses when it suited him. Max thought he'd seen hints of silver-gray in Harry's sideburns. Overall, Harry had the look of the boyish yet competent officer who was too capable for the great career rise. Max knew a few of Harry's breed in Nazi Germany. Shocked by the sticky, downright greasy ways the world really worked, they fought the corruption and cronyism, greed and incompetence at first and then, once grasping the overwhelming superiority of decadence and cynicism in sheer power and numbers and policies, found small but effective ways to undermine the dark machine. Leak a scandal to the press. Approve an exit visa. Divert funds to hospitals, rationing efforts. And yet Harry's deeds revealed there was something more to him. He had hijacked a train like Robin Hood, it was said, and now here he was breaking steadfast MG regulations for a refugee girl's word and a hunch of his own. Working together, he and his brother were about to give a wayward tribe a chance at salvation. This was the stuff of epics! Harry had the reasoning and deduction, confidence and bravado of men Max had only played on stage— had only seen on stage.

The sad part was that all men stumbled on the stage of real life. The world may offer epic stuff, but it rarely results in epic men. Life was tragedy without the plot.

Max didn't tell Harry he saw him like this. He confessed to Harry about that first morning of the Ardennes Offensive, what Amis were calling the Battle of the Bulge. He, a fellow soldier named Felix Menning, and the two other amateur impostor-spies in their team, Kattner and Zoock, were crammed in an American jeep. Then Felix Menning and Kattner killed two American MPs at a checkpoint. Max had only wanted out, away, beyond the war.

"But you were there," Harry stated, as if confirming the price of a hat.

And Max nodded, his head hanging low as if he'd just admitted to personally murdering hundreds. Thinking, his brother was always so much more matter-of-fact, so much more Prussian. Max had expected this would doom young Harry when he was older. But look who was doomed now?

He told Harry: He thought he had freed himself from Felix Menning. Yet Felix was relentless. Felix returned. Felix found him.

"The murdered man—whom Irina was with. He was this Felix Menning," Harry said.

Showing that damned smart analysis once again. Not that Max wasn't expecting it.

"Yes," Max confirmed.

Friday afternoon had dimmed for evening. Harry had moved to sit on the floor, on the area rug. Max had done the same after throwing off his blanket and pacing the room to tell his story. He was sweating a little from reliving it, from the warmth of the fire, his back against the sofa, facing Harry. They might have been two brothers on a sublime skiing trip. Sipping mulled wine? That would be something.

"Was that how this Aubrey Slaipe tracked you down? Through this Felix Menning."

"I believe so, yes. The CIC wanted our scalps, Harry. They had our names. Slaipe was hunting Felix. He was the big prize. Felix was supposed to have been caught, during the war. It was said he faced a firing squad like the others who were apprehended. Felix had not been caught, however—Felix had escaped. He became a one-man show. He left a trail of destruction behind the American lines, raiding US depots and offices all over. After the war, this had Slaipe thinking Felix could lead to me as well eventually. As if all of us two-bit secret agents had holed up in a ridiculous underground redoubt or some such notion. Because I had disappeared too, you see. For Slaipe, Felix's trail ended southeast of Munich. Meanwhile, Slaipe knew that my American little brother Harry was in Munich and, through the grapevine, that Harry was seeing a climber by the name of Maddy Barton."

"Wait. How do you know all this?"

"I ran into Aubrey Slaipe, Harry. On a dark side street, just he and I. He set it up that way, I should think. The street was all his."

"I did too," Harry said. "He might as well have slapped an off-limits sign on Luitpold Bridge. It was so nice and cozy, just the two of us."

"Oh, dear. Well, I'm not surprised."

They shook their heads. They eyed each other.

"I told him I'd take my chances," Harry said. "On our own."

"He told me not to botch things up. He also told me not to disappear, because he would find me." Max held up a finger. "But he did not threaten me."

"Hold on," Harry said. "You think he had Maddy keep an eye on me?"

"It is possible. He likely figured following you would lead to me, somehow, and then to Felix."

"Jesus."

Max said, "But Felix is dead. And now here comes his hunter. I'm his booby prize."

"No. That's not what he wants—he doesn't want to hand you over. Not anymore."

"No. Because there's a new war coming." Max shook his head and he told Harry more: "I thought I'd lost that trickster goblin Felix. I fled my supposed secret mission. I just walked away. I found some farmers' clothes and I headed back into Germany like any other refugee, pushing old folks' carts, riding on fenders, but mostly just hoofing it, and then further on I went, fleeing your troops. Spring came. On into Austria I went, and why not? I could hole up in some Alpine village, make cheese the rest of my days with some happy gamey farm girl. Problem was, old Austria didn't turn out so idyllic, Harry. Sorry fact was, in those last days, thousands got crammed in down there, a giant traffic jam car wreck of broken armies, refugees, and stragglers—and absconders—and from all points, that rare tiny pocket of Central Europe not overrun with US or Soviet troops."

"This would have been . . . what? About May of '45?" Harry said.

"Yes. This was when Felix found me. It was less coincidence than sick fate, considering the traffic jam." They wound up in the same small valley along with hundreds of others, waiting, huddling. The

British Army was one valley away. Felix persuaded Max to keep running. They did and they found the Cossacks who'd massed along the River Drave. Max stayed, but Felix would leave and keep coming back with food and other items. So he was a blessing and a curse.

"Problem was, you owed him your life," Harry said.

"Yes. That was the tough bit."

Felix was up in the hills when the British trapped the Cossacks, watching, sizing up his options. He followed Max when Max escaped with his Cossacks. He helped them on their trek, warning them of checkpoints and double-dealing smugglers. He rejoined them in the Šumava. The war was over by then. Summer. Felix had various aliases. He'd even scored the fatigues of a deserter GI, passing himself off as a GI Joe with his Ami English—

"Earvin Posey," Harry said, getting right to the point. So like Harry. Probably good at carving meat, Max thought.

"Posey died months ago, and it wasn't from old age," Harry added.

"There you have it. Felix surely offed Posey before Posey could Felix." Max gave a sigh, for Harry. His brother liked the doom and gloom, and one had to serve one's audience. "So there I was, stuck with Felix. My ghost found me and taunted me and hounded me like a devil's dog."

"Then comes Munich," Harry said. "Felix Menning gets a saber in his gut."

Max told it straight. He and Irina had been venturing into Munich to do black market trading for the Cossacks. Increasingly, Felix had insisted on coming along. This time they would sell Cossack sabers—a desperate measure, but winter was coming and sabers were their only fine wares left. Felix insisted on impersonating the GI, which was a huge gamble in Munich. He would help them move their goods but wanted a straight cut off the top. By then, Max trusted Felix less and Irina didn't trust him at all. Max and Irina argued about it. She was scared that Felix might use her boy

Alex as leverage. It was only a matter of time before Felix would sell them out, and the man had options—either the Americans or Soviet Repatriation agents could reward Felix for handing over enemy combatants in hiding.

"You and Felix had a fight?" Harry said.

"Another one, yes. Felix was talking to someone we didn't know—he wouldn't tell us who it was."

"Did you find out who?"

Max shook his head. "Irina and I were tracking Felix. The person was a shadow. They'd meet at night in doorways, under bridges."

"A male tryst?"

"No. Conversations. Small packages passed between them."

"Drugs? Meds?"

"Who could afford such a racket? Not Felix. I'm guessing it was cigarettes, small amounts of cash, to string Felix along. Don't forget we're all bottom tier, Harry. Our narcotic is calories."

"Information, then?"

"Certainly. Whatever it was, it was giving Felix a swagger. Felix was wearing that Ami uniform again. The costume was not convincing, Harry."

"I could've told you that even with all that blood on it."

"That's the way Felix was—he wouldn't listen to reason."

A great mass had built up in Max's chest like when he needed to cough onstage and held it in with all his might. He rubbed at his face so Harry couldn't see his pain.

"Irina didn't kill him," Harry said.

"No, brother of mine."

"You had to do it. He was pushing you to do it."

"I stabbed and I stabbed and kept stabbing into the same spot. I had to be sure. I had to finish it. I kept stabbing through that blade striking wood, the blood it was everywhere, strings of it, all over his face, how does it get everywhere?" The sweat returned, itching at Max's scalp, running cold down his sides from his underarms.

Shivering, he wiped it off his neck. He sighed at a grim thought: The same impulse running through his very marrow that used to make him need to perform and delight and dance and sing had demanded that he snuff out this scorching wildfire that was Felix Menning. Watching him, Harry nodded as if understanding. "But you must realize," Max went on. "It was to save Irina and her people. Her boy Oleksandr. All the children. Not for me. It was true I had let him become who he really was, a monster. I had practically made him. We were a team at one point. Felix saved my life once. I didn't want to do it, he made me do it, to save them . . ."

"You're not on trial, Max. But, what I don't get . . . You fled the scene. You left Irina."

Oh, Harry knew how to carve a bird, all right. Leaving Irina behind like that had been the real torment. Max's hands rose high, as if tugged by wires. "You think I wanted her there? Every woman I touch? You heard what happens."

"It was her decision. She wanted it that way."

"Yes, yes. We argued again, naturally—how we screamed, Harry. We knew you were in Munich. I told her. I didn't want to see you, not yet. Why burden you with me and my suspect past? But Irina, she was going to find you. She demanded it. Based on my hopeful assessment of your good humanity. We had only minutes, I tell you. Seconds. A decision had to be made."

Harry looked away. He consulted the fire, his eyes etched with the reflection of it. He stood. It was his turn to pace the room. He traversed the room once, past the windows, the entry, the book-shelves. He faced Max from the middle of the room, arms crossed at his chest, needing more.

"I warned her," Max confessed. "I told her the tough position we would put you in, what with my brother being a naturalized Ameri-can now. Congratulations by the way—I never told you."

"Thanks. You didn't trust me."

"Would you, were you I?" Max pressed at his chest.

"No. The same goes for me, Max."

"So here we stand."

Harry sighed. Max sighed.

"Irina found me through Detective Dietz," Harry said.

"We'd made too much noise. Someone from the block alerted the detective to us, so Irina had no choice but to try him. What can I say? She got lucky there. His price wasn't too high either. I never met this Dietz. What do you think?"

"Seems on the level. A survivor, like anyone. Why did she run from me? I had her here at my billet. What? Look at me, Max."

"She said that your girlfriend could not be trusted. That's all it was, I'm afraid. Women."

"Her name is Maddy. I'm not with her anymore."

"I know. That impressed us, your shedding her. So we'd decided to try again. After all, you'd worked a masterstroke by putting Felix's corpse on ice. You bought time. I was proud of you. But we'd just track you, see how you'd respond. See if you could live up to this reputation you have."

Harry turned away. He stared at the window leaden gray with murky clouds, not so much looking out that window as assessing its dimensions. When Harry turned back around he was smiling, to Max's wonder. Harry went to the fireplace and stoked the fire. Then Max watched Harry stride over, pick up his army *Soldbuch*, and throw it into the fire.

"But, that's the only proof I have of anything," Max said.

"You're starting over," Harry said.

"It didn't include that I was forced to serve in the SS. It might have helped."

"Would it have? Months and months are missing from that book."

Harry was a fine *Mensch*, to be sure, so much so that Max felt an immense sadness swell up in him. Max himself could never be that good, not after what he had done.

"Thank you so much. You could have turned me in," he muttered.

"I could have," Harry said. "But you've changed."

"I just want others to survive. I don't care about me."

"There you go. It's rare for a person to change."

Together they watched the last embers of Max's army pay book vaporize into ash.

It was now October 26—two weeks to the day since Max had plunged a saber into Felix Menning, at about the same time that his Cossacks hiding in the Šumava, frantic from fear and hunger, had to kill two Soviet soldiers or risk detection.

"Tell me something," Harry said. "Would you do it again?"

"Kill Felix? I never thought I could kill a man."

"That's not what I'm asking."

"No. Then, yes—yes I would."

Harry nodded, at the flames.

"So. Here we stand," Max repeated.

"Still standing, Max. And you know what I think? Belgium back in 1944, that was certainly not your final act."

# Nineteen

HARRY WAS READY FOR ANYTHING. He had made his decision. Yes, it was tragic that the Cossacks felt compelled to snuff out those two apparent Soviet Army deserters even if those Ivans were repatriation agents. Yet the Cossacks were only a cog. And Max was only a cog. By committing to Max, Harry could help his brother free himself from the grinding machine of doom and leave his worst days behind. Together. They would liberate helpless, hopeless human beings from the methods of the madmen in charge. The notion was dramatic as hell, but this was what Harry told himself. He ignored the other voice in his head. It whispered to him that, after the hard vengeance he'd wreaked on one fraudulent and murderous colonel named Spanner—real name of Virgil Eugene Tercel—he only hungered again for violent action and for its own sake, repercussions be damned. Even if those nightmares returned.

So when Harry got a call from Major Joyner the following day, he said, "You just name the place, sir."

Major Joyner was sorry to call on a day of rest, but he said he had something new for Harry. The major met Harry in that same officer's club-beer hall Joyner hated to love. This time Harry had the eggs and toast though it was pushing dinnertime. The place was half-full with officers drinking liter steins of beer, and Joyner took Harry to a booth in a corner.

Joyner brought up the subject of repatriation right where Harry had left it. Harry didn't tell Joyner just who needed saving, and Joyner did not need to know—not yet.

"You'll have to figure out yourself if they can be saved at all," Joyner said. "Based on what I'm telling you."

And Joyner dumped the sorry facts on Harry.


Harry, his head and stomach aching with worry, returned to his mansion showing a smile he'd worked hard to stick on his face. He'd spent the whole walk back hoping the glue would hold. It only gave him a worse ache.

Max met him in the foyer, his face pale. "Brother of mine, you are the worst actor I believe I have ever seen."

They went into the main living room, passing the fireplace and sofa and chairs, shuffling impulsively toward the two broad tapestry armchairs set at the base of the column at the farthest edge of the room. Voices did not carry here. No clear sight line to the window. It was the same spot, Harry realized, where he'd questioned Irina.

"Irina is taking a bath," Max told Harry. She had returned to the mansion, sharing Maddy's old room with Max. Harry had insisted that she and Max stay put here, at least for a few hours, to prepare for what was soon to come.

"Good, that's good," Harry said.

Max sat with his hands pressed to the armrests as if ready to hear about an audition lost or a bad review.

"We, meaning the Americans, have a new policy called McNarney-Clark," Harry began.

"Sounds like a songwriting duo," Max said, adding a bitter laugh.

"It's not. I've asked some American officers what they think, you know that, but the stark reality is expressed in the McNarney-Clark Directive. Every American officer must obey it. The Brits signed off on it, too. The intent was good, I think. Someone finally realized that last year's broad and indiscriminate repatriation was too harsh on certain groups that did not want to return to the Soviet territories. It was also doing a harsh number on the Allied officers, GIs, and Tommies who had to enforce it."

"You sound like a clerk. Don't disguise this for what it is."

"They wrote McNarney-Clark specifically for cases like ours. The directive is crystal clear, Max: No one, not even Soviet citizens, now has to go back against their will."

Max's eyebrows went up. Harry held up a hand.

"Easy for them to say, though," he added, "since so many millions have already been sent back. There's now only, what—twenty-thousand or so up for grabs?"

"That's still a lot to Joe Stalin. He wouldn't have agreed to this easily," Max said.

"No, not without clear conditions. Which brings me to the real rough part. So that the Soviets wouldn't protest, Allied policy-makers formulated a clear opposing distinction—a counter balance, if you will."

"Ah. A volte-face," Max said.

"An about-face to be sure. Policy language would read something like this: 'certain precise categories are now liable for return without regard to their wishes and by force if necessary—'"

"Stop, let me guess: Those captured in German uniforms. Those who fought on the German side. Those who rendered aid and comfort to the enemy."

Harry nodded. "Before, there was a good gray area. At least there was that. Now there's no breathing room for ones like the Cossacks. So that others can stay off the hook. Officially."

"And the families? The innocents?"

"That's still unclear, policy-wise. Way I heard it, it's proving different in every case. The Soviets are demanding that all be returned. There's been a couple near international incidents, but . . . The thing is, Americans just don't want to know about Cossacks who fought with Hitler. Intelligence isn't touching matters like this. MPs, Constabulary, CIC. Everyone wants them to just go away."

"And die. I see." Max's hands had slid off the armchair, hanging from the sides.

Harry gave him a moment.

Max growled, "You're not finished. So get on with it."

Harry sighed. "Yes, well, that was the good news, I'm afraid. Your Cossacks are technically over in the Soviet zone. So none of this really applies at all, technically."

"Not until we got them over into the US zone."

"Right. But even then? It could be worse for them. The Sovs are becoming the new bad guys and fast, so anyone coming over from the Soviet zone could be looked upon with even greater suspicion than if they'd fought for the Germans."

"Soviet spies? These are Cossack women and children, old men, a few broken boy soldiers." Max hissed out a laugh, threw up a hand. "Oleksandr, Alex . . ."

"All I'm telling you is, it's got to be watertight all down the line. Getting them over. Getting someone to take them in when over. Finding someone who will refuse to send them back. Eventually, someone who'll get them to a third country, where they can start over. Look, Max: The Soviets are still our allies, and we made an agreement to give them what they want. But things are changing fast—"

"We can't wait any longer."

"I know, I know." Harry rubbed at his temple. The coffee hadn't helped the ache of worry Joyner had given him. He should have had the beer. And Max didn't even know that he only had a couple weeks of duty left. After that, he'd have little more power than Max or Dietz.

"Harry?"

"I said 'officially.' It's the official policy. But I'm guessing—betting—that I know a higher-up in US uniform who could be convinced otherwise." Harry didn't mention Major Joyner by name. If Max had heard the legend of Sheriff Joyner, he might just take his chances with Joe Stalin. Yet Max didn't know Joyner like Harry did, hadn't seen how the man, deep down, must loathe his grim obsession with hounding Germans. It had to be eating away at him. How could it ever avenge his son's death?

"Harry, stop rubbing. Stop thinking for one goddamn second. I know you have a new plan. Why else keep me here in Munich?"

"You're right. I do. I hope I do."

It was all about showing the Soviets' intention. Harry and Max would have to prove, without a doubt, that people were in immediate danger of execution. Sabine Lieser told Harry how to prove it. Now Harry needed the tools. That Saturday evening, well after dark, he bought Detective Hartmut Dietz a beer in Dietz's least favorite local pub—a damp and smoky shanty with candles for light and more prostitutes than ashtrays and fewer ears on them than the summit of an Alp. Before that first thin beer was down, Dietz was sure he could get what Harry needed. Sunday evening, Harry met Dietz in the rubble of the National Theater of all places (Harry picked the spot—it worked for Max). They stood in the dark, using the light from passing military vehicles, neighborhood cook-fires, and failing street lamps that flickered and flashed and bounced around inside this giant pinball box of debris.

"I appreciate your letting me help," Dietz said.

"Don't mention it—you've proven yourself," Harry said. "Well, do you have it?"

From his overcoat, Dietz extended a brown bag into Harry's hand. Inside, Harry felt, was a small rectangle about three inches by one. "No bigger than that cheese bar you gave me," Dietz said. "Delicious, by the way."

"Good to hear. This is it? I didn't think they made them this small."

"We are still in modern Germany, don't forget. Go ahead."

Harry drew the odd camera from the sack and held it up to the dim flutters of light. All metal, a uniformly dull gray, it looked like a small gun cartridge.

"Gray, so that it doesn't catch sunlight when you use it. It's a Riga Minox."

"A spy camera? You went out of your way, Detective."

"And why not? It wasn't so hard. You know how many fine German cameras are floating around? They're our hundred-mark notes now. But be careful with your shots. I could only get one film cartridge. It's in the camera."

Dietz, reveling in the workmanship, showed Harry how to shoot by pulling on the rectangle, like cocking a pistol slide, explaining in greater detail than Harry needed, like a schoolmaster to a farm boy.

Harry set the camera back into the sack and pushed the sack into his pocket. "How do I develop it?"

"Not so difficult. Surely you have a photo man somewhere in your ranks—that is, if it's someone you trust."

Harry didn't know anyone in Signal Corps. None of the MG men he knew took photos. He simply hadn't considered this part. He lit a Chesterfield. He lit up Dietz.

Dietz shrugged, releasing a barrel of smoke. "Cameras like this," he whispered, "they are not used for tourist photos, for shooting castles or a Fräulein's long legs."

"I'm not some kind of spy," Harry told him. "If that's what you're thinking."

"Clearly," Dietz said, adding a smile. "So, what's it for?"

From his overcoat, Harry held out a larger sack. In it was a hundred occupation dollars and a one-time pass to the main Munich PX. "It's for this."

Dietz didn't look down at the sack. He kept his hands in his pockets. A strand of thin hair hung loose from under his hat.

"This means no questions," Harry added.

"It's something to do with that girl, isn't it? The Russian. Irina. That what she is, Russian?" Dietz was grimacing now, and soft tails of smoke snaked out from between his teeth.

"It's Military Government business," Harry snapped.

Dietz held up his index finger. "I know—it's your brother? What is his name?"

Harry yanked his Chesterfield. "What did you say?"

"It's all right. I know about him coming back. You're reunited, yes? Just like you wanted. Please, do not glare at me. It's nothing to be ashamed of. We all have secrets—"

"Who's ashamed?"

Dietz held his hands up. "Say no more. Say no more . . ."

Harry wasn't about to grill Dietz, not now. Harry was the one who'd gone asking Dietz about Max in the first place. Besides, did he really think Max would remain a secret? The man and his girl were staying in an MG officer's billet. Gerlinde might have even mentioned it on the black market unintentionally. It could have been anyone. The occupied were constantly gathering around and the thrill of a sale makes happy chitchat, which loosens lips.

"Max," Harry said. "His name is Max."

"Well, I congratulate you both." Dietz stood close to Harry, and Harry caught a whiff of Dietz's warm and stale cigarette breath. "Look here. Why don't you let me help? Tell you what—why not let me do this with you? As your photographer. I know my way around. I can work a tiny Minox well enough."

"Suddenly you're the eager beaver? Trying to double up on me, that it? No."

Dietz pulled back. His eyebrows pinched up. "Have it your way. But remember: Not all of this is about money," he hissed and stomped off around a pile of bricks and charred lumber, the steam and smoke pulsing out his mouth and nostrils in balls of fume like so many fists.

"All right. Come back," Harry said. "Listen: I might need you. I just don't know yet."

Dietz strode back around the pile to face Harry. "The film developing, for example? I could do that. So let me know. 'On the QT,' as you say."

"Of course. I will. And I appreciate it."

"Excellent," Dietz said and, in his excitement, clicked his heels.

His lips tightened from embarrassment, but Harry ignored it as if Dietz had only passed gas.

He offered a handshake. "Thanks."

"You're very welcome. Yes, yes. So, you know where to find me—anytime," Dietz said, and turned to leave, bouncing as he stepped, his toes dancing a path through the debris.

"Wait," Harry said.

He was still holding the sack. The detective had forgotten his payment altogether.

# Twenty

WEDNESDAY MORNING, OCTOBER 31. Harry and Max, hunkered down on a hillside, cursed the bitter cold and the thick birches and pines that shaded them from the bright autumn sun rising at their backs. Yet the trees hid them well, and their high perch offered a prime view. Opposite them stood a squatty, rockier hill. Down below ran a rail line between the two hills, like a river through a gully. A small valley held a station house that was little more than a half-timbered box and a cobbled road that led through a short pass in the hills to the village of St. Stephanus. Beyond the station stood a large wooden barn and a valley meadow that was muddy as if trampled by cows or feet, but Harry saw no cattle there. The meadow stopped dead before another squat rocky mount to the north—a steep wall of granite. A modest sign along the tracks read ST. STEPHANUS. Atop that, dwarfing it, stood another sign:

SOVIET ZONE OF AUSTRIA

In four languages. Atop that, from a tall pole, fluttered two red Soviet flags.

The leaves were tawny and rust and amber and they floated down, coating the near frozen earth with the thinnest layer of crunch. Harry and Max wore a mix of threadbare clothes and gear, all with enough holes and tears and stains to remind that unexpected and horrid incidents always threatened. Harry in a German greatcoat from two wars ago, Max in a fur-collared cloak of unknown militia. Max had given them their role—they were harmless vagabonds. Central Europe was full of them, those who'd refused to participate any longer in a world that only dumped war and death and sorrow on them. Most local troops let such outlanders be, and Harry could only hope it was the same here.

Sabine Lieser gave Harry the tip when they last met in that Schwabing cafe. She had gotten word that a couple hundred other Cossacks were being repatriated back to the Soviet Union from a detention camp in the British zone of Austria. The train would make its first stop in the Soviet zone at St. Stephanus. The setup had McNarney-Clark written all over it, Harry recognized. Sabine only wanted to observe the train from its last stop in the West, see how the Cossacks and their dependents were coping. Were there suicides? Attempted escapes? It might be enough proof, she said. It wasn't good enough, Harry knew after hearing what Warren Joyner had revealed to him. A Military Policeman like Joyner knew the score, how this worked.

They needed concrete evidence. And Harry needed to see it for himself.

Harry and Max had entered Austria's Soviet zone through Bavarian forest, paying off a smuggler to show them the way. The smuggler got them into Austria before sunup. Once they were in the village, a couple Soviet Army officers walked right past them; Harry and Max kept their heads down and mumbled in Austrian-accented German. Then they asked a passing local man if camping in the nearby hills would bother the Soviet Army, to which the local grumbled in dialect, "Wherever you likes it. All these brigands care about are drinking, fucking—any Nazi they find goes on a meat hook and all our machinery sent off to Mother Russia."

They had spread out their bedrolls on the dry leaves. They rested against their rucksacks, stuffed with the usual vagabond chattels—tarnished silverware, jam tins, hats, stockings, anything wool, dried sausage, cigarettes and butts, a couple broken watches for trading. Harry didn't dare bring his top-grade paratrooper knife, and certainly not his immaculate Mauser pistol—these would surely give him away if caught. They had an antique one-cylinder opera glass but tried not to use it. So far, they could see a lot from their roost with their naked eyes.

A truck of Soviet Army soldiers had arrived along with two staff cars. The soldiers hoisted more red flags, large placards of Stalin (peering down, with one fist at his stomach like a priest clutching a rosary), and more signs in Cyrillic script. They unrolled barbed wire, so new it glimmered in the sun, and strung it high to seal off the only open end of the meadow. A couple local morning trains passed through, but the troops took little notice of them. A village shuttle *Pendelzug* of five rickety cars pulled in, and locals passed through unchecked. Many looked like Harry and Max. This boosted Max's spirits, Harry noticed. His brother opened a prewar can of beans and they ate the cold slop right out of the tin, sharing the spoon, and Max, smiling, wiped the spoon with a clean hanky until glossy.

Max nudged Harry's shoulder. "Hey, brother, today's the thirty-first."

Harry smiled. "Halloween? In America. You remember it."

"I always loved that holiday of theirs. Yours. And look—we have our costumes on."

Harry kept smiling, but he couldn't help thinking that Hallows Eve meant ghosts, and specters, and calamities that haunt to no end.

Afternoon now, about 12:15. The train from the West was to arrive at roughly 1:00 p.m. The scene below was set—red flags and giant Joe Stalin, Soviet soldiers and so much barbed wire.

Harry smoked a Russian cigarette. It made him wheeze but he liked its warmth. He smoked it down to the butt, daydreaming. He hadn't told Sabine he was taking things this far. He wondered whether she would slap him or love him. He was betting on the latter. In the café that morning, it was all he could do not to caress her face and kiss her. Now, as he thought about her, tracing the mechanics of how he came to meet her, he realized what should have smacked him across the forehead that very first day.

Of course! He was no genius, but he could paint by numbers.

He looked to Max, who was reaching for the cigarette. "Sabine Lieser," he said.

"Come again?" Max said, though he pulled back his hand.

"You know her!" Harry jabbed his index finger into Max's arm.

"*Aua!*" Max slapped Harry's finger away. "Oh, she's the one who runs that DP camp, right?" he tried, playing it coy.

Harry formed a fist, showing it off.

"Okay, yes, of course I do," Max said.

Harry lowered the fist. "I wasn't going to hit you. I'm not even offended. I think I even understand."

"We were never involved, brother—if that's what you're thinking."

"It's not. Let's see if I can get this straight . . . back before Felix's murder, you went to her, searching for me. You'd heard she was sympathetic, a maverick, what have you. So you two were in on this from the start. She's known about your Cossacks all along."

"Yes, she knows."

"She wanted to help, but she can't go through normal channels."

"Harry, I want you to know one thing. Please. She was not using you. Deceiving you. She simply had to feel you out first."

"Like I said, I got no problem with it," Harry muttered, fighting a smile.

Max wagged a finger. "Look at you, how you blush—"

"Am not, it's these damn cigarettes. But, I guess I should thank you."

"Nothing to thank. You did all the work."

It was 12:30 now. Half an hour to go. Harry parceled out hard grainy bread and dried sausage, sawing away at their ration with an old butter knife. They would need their stomachs full for whatever was coming.

"First, I had to find her though," Harry said, flipping open the ceramic cap of a tall beer bottle they used for water. "That's where the bearded man came in, the one who followed me home that night . . . who told me he'd seen Irina at Sabine's DP camp. You paid him to do that, didn't you? So that Sabine and I, two people with common sentiment, could discover each other."

Max had tilted his head, smiling. He wagged the finger again.

"No! That was you? The bearded man?"

"Most certainly, *Mein Herr*." Max affected a little bow.

"How?"

"The beard, glasses, the teeth gap wax, these are simply props. I scored them cheap on the black market. Who needs stage costume these days?"

"Actors," Harry said, feigning disgust. "Some outfit."

"Me? What about you? A bowler and sable collar? You looked like a butler out there, pining away for his lost lord. I'll bet you raided your mansion's closets for it. Ha—you did, didn't you?"

"You got me. I confess." Harry laughed.

Max, smiling, pressed a hand to his heart.

They heard loud music down below—stirring, pounding military music.

They squinted and scanned the area. "Don't see a band," Harry said. "No, it's loudspeakers," Max said. A jeep pulled up towing a trailer of speakers. Staccato drums and shrill horns filled the glen and sent echoes up the hill, so loud that Harry couldn't hear the rustle and crunch of the leaves. Birds had scattered from the trees, off beyond the hills they flew. The few civilians near the station scurried for the village, hands pressed to their ears. Then the music stopped.

"They're checking the sound," Max said. He had the opera glass out, scanning the valley. "Officers, look, gathered around the speakers."

Harry opened his rucksack and felt around for the Riga Minox. He set the camera between his legs. A part of him wished for a belt of whiskey now, but he knew better; when he drank at dire moments, he got an acute need to defend someone's honor and too fast.

It was 12:50 p.m.: Max scanned the opposing hills with the opera glass, to make sure no one was staking them out. He reported only bare rocks and more trees.

Down below, the Soviet Army soldiers split into two rough groups—one lining either side of the tracks and the other forming a gauntlet before the doors of the warehouse. Any locals who were nearby had vacated the station and valley.

Harry and Max heard the thumping and clacking of a train coming in from their left—from the West. A small locomotive towed five freight cars and one passenger car, the cars decorated with Soviet flags and banners. "Welcome banners," Max grunted, the opera glass pressed to his eye. The train pulled up to the platform, the station house obstructing the locomotive, but they had a good view of the rest. Harry held up the Riga Minox. He could get a wide shot from here, but it wouldn't detail much. The locomotive hissed and clanged, then petered out. The freight cars had vertical wood slats and narrow windows up high. Faces showed in the windows, but there were no waves or smiles. Two Soviet officers stepped down from the passenger car, followed by what looked like a British officer and an American officer. Liaison officers. The American there because the train had passed through the US zone of Austria on its way. Seeing the liaison officers, the faces up in the windows began shouting then screaming in Russian and broken English and German—amazing what Harry could hear after those speakers and the locomotive were done—piercing shouts that sounded more like shrieks of birds, carrying through the valley and upward.

Two polished staff cars were waiting at the rear of the station house. The Soviet officers were trying to direct the American and British liaison officers that way, but the two had stopped well before the staff cars. What followed could only be described as a heated argument, a flurry of puffed chests and arms flailing. Harry snapped photos, hoping he was close enough.

The Soviet Army soldiers along the tracks had hoisted their guns at the ready, a fence of rifle and machine gun barrels directed at the freight cars. The American and British liaisons marched back toward the train and passed through the line of soldiers and moved along the freight cars, stopping at windows, shouting back at the faces inside the cars.

"Not a lot they can do," Max said.

The music started up again, drowning all sound. The Allied liaisons cupped hands at their mouths to shout louder, and then they threw up their hands. They couldn't hear a damn thing. The American wandered off with his head in his hands, his fellow British officer moving him along by an elbow like a nurse with an elderly patient. The Soviet officers rejoined them, escorting them to the staff cars. The cars sped off.

"It's back to the West for those four," Harry muttered. "Mission accomplished."

"Some gig," Max grumbled.

The Soviet Army soldiers fanned out to form cordons at each freight car door. The Cossack refugees climbed out, the Soviet soldiers pulling them down and herding them along the tracks. The Cossacks included woman and children. There were boys and girls as young as Irina's Alex. Most of the refugees were men wearing new British fatigues, a bon voyage gift from the Brits. Surrounded by the troops, the people stood in throngs, facing inward, facing outward, what to do now? Well inside the throngs stood old officers in antiquated dress uniforms and Cossack style hats.

"I count about two hundred men—like Sabine said. About another hundred women and children, elderly," Harry said as if under oath, trying to stay matter-of-fact. Information was everything now.

"They need to run, do something," Max said.

An elderly Cossack man stepped out to approach a Soviet officer, supplicating, hands clasped together. The officer pushed him back. The music droned on. The soldiers were herding the refugees down toward the warehouse. Three heavy troop trucks had backed into the gap between the station and the warehouse. The soldiers charged the throngs and began separating the women, children, and elderly from the men. A woman fell to her knees before a soldier, another soldier kicked her in the face, and she tumbled back into the crowd. The music droned on. A man charged a soldier trying to grab his rifle. The soldier swung the rifle butt into his face and the man collapsed, blood streaming out.

"You capturing this?" Max said.

"Yes."

The Cossack throngs lost whatever fight was left in them. Now separated, the woman, children, and elderly climbed into the trucks, shoulders sagging. The men watched the trucks roll away, faces slack, some people on their knees, hands pressed to their heads.

"Where they going? Another train? To the East, far East? A labor camp? Shit, shit." Harry knew the answer. Gulags, Irina had called them.

"Never see them again," Max muttered, "never, ever again."

The speaker music droned on. Soldiers prodded the men toward the warehouse, the Soviet officers following at a casual pace, smoking and gesturing. Harry and Max had to crane their necks for a full view of the warehouse and the meadow beyond. They were standing now, their toes digging into the leaves and hard earth so they wouldn't go tumbling down the hill. The Cossack men shuffled along, heads down, into the warehouse.

Harry moved closer, advancing along the trees, propelling himself by pushing off the trunks. "Keep going," Max said as he followed. A ridge led to the end of their hill. Harry took the opera glass, Max the camera. They each hugged a tree trunk and peered down, drawn ever closer by the details now coming into view. The old wood warehouse lacked a roof in many spots. There they could see through the gray timbers.

Inside the warehouse, the Cossack men stood naked and huddled in groups, stomping at the cold, grimy hay. Their clothes—their new British fatigues—lay in piles. Soldiers had followed them in and shut the doors after them. The Soviet officers stood out in the meadow along with another team of their soldiers. Facing the warehouse, the Soviet officers shouted commands.

The old Cossack officers shuffled back out naked, hands over their genitals, their pale skin bright white in the sun. Five stood out in the open meadow, peering around for any way out, hopping frantically now like shaved monkeys inside a cage. The soldiers stood in a rough line, about fifteen yards from the bare old men. The Soviet officers shouted. Their soldiers raised barrels, fired.

Cracks, pops, echoes of it combined with the marching music. Harry gasped. His throat clenched up and he tried to breathe slow, deep breaths, fighting hyperventilation, a panic attack. Max had grabbed at Harry's sleeve, a fistful of it to keep Harry steady, and Max was snapping photos with his other hand. Harry watched without the opera glass. His eyesight seemed to gain power from the intensity of it all, the shock, the madness. Back inside the warehouse, the soldiers had fixed bayonets to their rifles. They charged and stabbed the naked men, who tumbled, climbing over each other, scrambling, more blood than flesh now, and some men charged, clawing at the soldiers, their last acts, while others ran out into the meadow. Barbed wire, a wall of granite loomed. Corpses of their leaders, mentors, fathers. They plowed through the mud, trudging on in circles, grasping at each other for support and screaming. The soldiers fired at will. A Soviet officer grabbed a machine gun and joined in. The music droned on.

They heard clear voices, shouting. How could they from up here? Harry looked to Max, who turned. Behind them, three Soviet Army soldiers stood over them, their barrels trained. They were kids no more than twenty. Harry and Max's hands went up. The soldiers lunged.

Something burst, a bomb in Harry's head.

# Twenty-One

*I SHOULD FEEL LUCKY*, MAX TOLD HIMSELF. *Lucky I'm not dead.* He tried to sit up, wheezing from the tender pain—*tender like someone had shoved a grand piano between my ribs*, he thought. He had his back against a crate, his lungs tight from the pain, the trauma.

Harry sat across from him, his shoulders slumped against the pocked concrete wall. "We're alive," he muttered.

"You're awake. Welcome back."

Feeling themselves for blood, bruises, and holes, Max and Harry pieced together what had happened. Harry had taken a good blow to the back of the head—a rifle butt, and Max confirmed he'd been out a good few minutes. Max got a butt to the ribs and a boot to the face. The boot only grazed him, leaving a scrape on his temple, but the butt was dead on—thus the grand piano. He might have a cracked rib, but he didn't tell Harry that. Harry didn't need more worry.

Max patted his pockets for a nail to smoke. None. Of course, they had taken them. The four young Soviet Army grunts—Ivans, Americans called them—had searched Max and Harry but greedily with random slaps and jabs, hoping for valuables. Max and Harry only had the grimy, bloodied clothes on their backs now. Their rucksacks and bedrolls, food and water were long gone. Good and nabbed, he and Harry were. How were they to know that four Ivans had been roaming those hills above the train station?

The Ivans had dragged Max and Harry straight down the hill, letting the tree branches whack at them, and a couple trunks managed to strike their shoulders, faces, shins. Harry was out cold for most of that. He only came to when they neared the little train station. Max, having become quite the tragedian, was certain those Ivans would drag them straight over to the meadow and stack their corpses atop the Cossacks. But, no. Comedy lives on—harsh and wretched but a comedy of errors to be sure. And so Max and Harry ended up in this cold sandstone room, dismal and gray, the floor a rocky dirt, the shelves storing more grease and dust than stocks. Cobwebs hung at every angle and intersection.

The window was high and their only light was a square of shadowed daytime. Outside they heard occasional shouts and vehicles roaring about.

Harry pulled himself up, peering around. "We're in the station house, looks like," he said through grunts, "in the cellar." He was coming to his senses. Good man.

"That's right," Max said. He had an old hanky around his neck, a hint of respectability for his vagabond outfit. He scooted over and, wincing with pain, wrapped it around Harry's head to help stop any bleeding.

"Thanks, brother," Harry said. His hand was sticky with drying blood. He stared at it and wiped it on his trouser leg.

"You rest," Max said.

"The hell I am," Harry said. "We rest, we're dead. They are."

Apparently Harry could handle more worry, even with that hole in his head. "Bravo," Max said. "So, what's next?"

"You know what," Harry said.

"Do I?"

"You should know better than I." Harry leaned closer. He whispered, "They're going to send the big bad wolf in here, give us the third degree. Who the hell are we."

A shudder of dread moved up through Max, seizing his aching ribs. Harry was right of course. Whenever had he not been? Still, Max had to protest their lines being rewritten with the show only minutes away. "But we're just vagabonds," he groaned. "Wasn't this the plan?"

"Before we got caught, it was. Look, I'm telling you what you already know—as an actor. To be believable? Every good role, every good story, it has to have a kernel of truth in it."

*I must have some kind of a death wish*, Harry thought. His head still throbbed and Max's hanky probably wasn't helping, but he left it there to mollify Max, to help prepare him for what was to come. In the cellar darkness, in whispers, he told Max the way it would have to go down. They would admit they were not simply vagabonds but deserted American GIs wandering the land. It was more rare of a catch but also a more sensitive case for the Russians. As the Soviets' Allies, American citizens were harder to make disappear.

They had one good shot at this.

Max's face had paled, his upper lip damp from a cold sweat. "I vowed never to do it again," he whispered. "I told you. The last time I played that role to the hilt . . ."

"No choice now," Harry said. "Besides, we've been speaking in English this whole time."

"Oh, yes. So we have." Max held up a hand to the heavens. He sighed, from deep in his chest, and it rattled a little with regret.

"Just one more time," Harry said.

"*Zugabe*," Max muttered. The encore.

Harry whispered, "But, what about the camera—"

Shouts. Boots. Heels pounding down the stairs, to the cellar.

Max shook his head. "Later," he whispered.

The boots stopped at the bottom of the steps. Harry expected the cellar door to fly open. Max pressed his shoulders against the wall to brace himself.

A soft knock sounded at the door instead.

Harry looked to Max. Max took a deep breath, let his shoulders relax, and crossed his legs with one stretched out lazily. He shouted,

"What, ya need an invitation? Come in already!" in his best American English.

The door opened. In walked a Soviet officer flanked by two soldiers with machine guns slung on their shoulders. The officer was little older than his young guards. He spoke in Russian and the two Ivans stayed by the door. He walked the ten feet over to Harry and Max and folded his arms on his chest, which only served to show how lanky the kid officer was.

"You are speaking English?" the officer said in German.

Max looked to Harry, shrugged.

Harry attempted an American's broken German, sputtering, "*Bitta sprecken langsam. Vee nix versteh' Deutsch goot.*"

The officer blew air out one side of his mouth and left. The two Ivans stayed at the door. Harry recognized one and thought about thanking him for the dent in his head.

Half an hour later the cellar door flew open, banging against the stone wall. The Ivans stood at attention although the man who came through the door wore a drab brown civilian overcoat over a simple gray suit. The Soviet man had close-cropped hair and a soft, doughy face. He scanned the room as if looking for a lost storage box. His eyes passed over Harry and Max. He kept looking for that box. His eyes found Harry and Max again. "So. One hears your German is not so good, what?" he said in accented yet solid British English.

A rush of relief loosened the knot in Harry's stomach. If they'd gotten an American-educated interrogator, they would have even less of a chance. He shrugged again and replied, "Hey, it's a tough language, Mac."

And Max said, "We're your Allies, see, and you go treatin' us like the krauts?"

The Soviet man stood before Harry and Max, looking down on them, his blocky rubber overshoes inches from their feet. "You are Americans. But what sort are you?"

"Sort? Ain't it clear? Ones who picked the wrong place to camp," Harry said.

"Minding our own business, see," Max added.

Harry thinking: *Don't tell them we're deserters because that would give them an excuse. Let them assume what they assume.*

"Is this so?" Soviet man said.

"The hell's it look like?" Harry released a snort of contempt. Max shook his head and cleared his throat. They were a real couple of born losers, the two of them. Such was the plan.

Soviet man drew their opera glass from a pocket. He held it to an eye and looked out the window. He looked at Harry and Max with it. "How, then, do you explain this?"

"Explain it? A Joe's got to see where he's heading, don't he?" Harry said. "Cost me half a Lucky on a Graz street corner."

"Me, I jus' love da opera," Max added.

"Graz is not in the US zone. We are far removed from your zone," Soviet man said.

"Our zone? Forget that!" Max blurted.

"Ain't no zones for the likes of us," Harry muttered.

The Soviet man shook his head. He left.

The night came and the cold with it. Harry and Max tried to sleep, huddling under a sooty, oily blanket they found in a corner. For Harry, it was an ache-filled sleep, his head feeling as light as cotton and then as heavy as a concrete block. At some point he heard what sounded like a mouse hissing. It was Max, sobbing in his sleep.

Harry woke later with a sensation rushing through him, cold then warm under his skin, and he couldn't resist it: He found himself wishing that Max's bogeyman Aubrey Slaipe was directing them after all, if not with them now. The man could simply watch over them. There to pass a tip or nudge him the right way. But then again Harry had wished that about his own bogeyman, Colonel Spanner.

They got a beating in the middle of the night, this one unauthorized judging from the smell of grain alcohol on the Ivans' breath, the squealing laughs to go with it, and the flashlights throwing stabs of white light. It was messy business with wild kicks to the head and stomach, but most swings missed. And then more chilled darkness came.

# Twenty-Two

Max felt the overwhelming urge again, like a relentless thirst—
he found himself pining that Aubrey Slaipe were near, if only there to
observe them like his drama teachers used to do for him. He yearned
for the approval, the recognition. He wondered if it was the shock or
possibly hypothermia setting in. In any case he had to fight it. Slaipe
would be the only thing worse for his health right now. Groggy, he
could only make out faint vertical lines in the darkness, like venetian
blinds in a fog at night. The air hung stale and thick.

Then he remembered. After their beating from drunken Ivans,
they had attempted something like sleep again. A voice rattled them
awake: "Wakey wakey . . ." The Soviet man was standing over them
in the dark. "Now listen to me, you lot. You may be deserters. You
may not be. If you are not, then we hope your experience here—our
little stay with us—shall help send a clear and resounding message:
The next spies we catch shall visit the Gulag for a frightfully long
time. Understood?"

He remembered those loutish and still-drunken Ivans had pulled
a black burlap hood over their heads, tying it with rope at the neck.

He felt for the rope, fingered the knot loose, and ripped the hood
off, gasping for the fresh cold air that wafted in between those vertical lines that, he now saw, were the slight gaps between the slats of
the wall.

It was daylight, Thursday morning—November 1. Before dawn,
Max and Harry had been locked in some sort of rectangular shack,

with hoods on. The plank floor had clumps of dirt and straw and smelled like dried shit. Nothing to sit or lie on, so they'd hunched in a corner with their backs up against the slat-wall.

Harry slept on. He had been moaning in his sleep, Max recalled. The daylight let Max see the dried blood coating the side of Harry's neck. His hood lay across the floor.

His eyes popped open.

Max smiled for his brother.

"What are you doing?" Harry said.

"I was thinking about taking in a musical. Or maybe just stroll Broadway, watch the pretty girls go by."

Harry smiled. "I could tag along. Popcorn's on me."

Max chuckled, which made him wince again. "One good thing about a little pain . . . it helps keep the hunger away."

"You did good, Max," Harry said.

"Likewise. Where are we, you think?"

Harry started to speak, but his voice cracked. He tried again, "I'm afraid we're sitting inside a freight car."

A freight car. Of course. Thus the slats for walls. Max hadn't considered it, but his brother would certainly know a train when he saw one given his renegade past liberating a freight of ignoble plunder. Harry would rather be back down in that grimy cellar.

"I'm sorry, Harry."

Harry showed him a thin smile. "I always tell myself, never set foot near another freight train again."

Two narrow windows were up high on either side. The door was metal, a black square as high as the ceiling.

"Already tried the door," Harry added. "Locked tight."

"Window?" Max said.

"It'll take both of us. But, do we really want to see?"

"A fair point."

Were they only waiting for the locomotive? A train of more prisoners? They heard nothing outside, not even the rustle of fall leaves.

Harry said they must be sitting a ways down the tracks from the station, on a side spur, waiting.

"Better not to think too much about it," he added, and he let his head slump.

Max had never seen Harry like this. Luckily he knew just how to cheer up his brother. He had planned to wait, but it had to be now, timing was everything. He sat up and clapped his hands. Harry lifted his head. Max straightened out his arms and shook them, letting his cuffs dangle. "Now, for my next feat of magic . . ." He extended his right arm nice and long like he was doing the old Heil Hitler and then wiggled his shoulder until the Riga Minox poked out from his cuff.

Harry's eyes lit up. He heaved himself upright. He looked both ways as if anyone was bothering to peer in through the slats.

"Don't worry. One good thing about a locked freight car—we're all alone."

Harry grinned. A curl of his hair hung down and he pushed it away. "How'd you do it, Max? Huh?"

Max's ribs ached from the performance, but he disguised his grimace as a grin to match Harry's. He raised his arm over his head, and let the harmonica-shaped camera slide back down to under his armpit. "Those Ivans were too busy thumping us to do a proper frisk job. And this old arm of mine with the camera way up its sleeve? Too busy clutching my ribs in pain to give them a good angle for the frisking. Then they found cigarettes on me and a gilded pocket watch in my trousers. Then they must've found that opera glass on you, figured those were the choicest goods. Plus, knowing a few magician's moves didn't hurt. Then, there was luck—for once there was that."

"What now?" Harry said.

"I keep it in my armpit."

"Do you think that's wise? Supposing where we might be headed."

"What are we going to do, develop it here? With shit and straw and blood?"

*Hope is a question, waiting to be answered,* Harry reminded himself.

They heard activity outside the freight car. Harry heard men chatting in German and men shouting in Russian. Max said he smelled cigarettes. Harry thought he smelled something like coffee. Hoping, the two of them. The metal door clanked and rolled open with a roar, and the daylight made Harry and Max shield their eyes. The door rolled shut again. Harry looked around, squinting. A loaf of brown bread and a canteen lay on the matted shit and straw.

They ate two, then three chunks of bread, being careful to ration. Then they sat in silence, the fear and worry creeping up in them like shiny black winged ants crawling up their legs and torsos from the feces-floor all around them. Harry had to counteract it somehow, anyhow.

He told Max all about his train job in Heimgau, with every grisly detail and why he did it. The corrupt American whom he fought, phony US CIC Colonel Eugene Spanner, was a criminal deserter who had proved no better than the Nazis they came over to defeat. Harry's risky job stealing the colonel's freight was the only way to stem the terror the man had unleashed in the secluded rural county of Heimgau. The colonel had killed Harry's CO Major Membre and Harry's fellow conspirator, a fine German as it turned out and a baron by title—von Maulendorff was his name. Then Harry thought he was a dead man. But he kept fighting and ended up with only a knife that he ran through this fiend who seemed indomitable if not undead, Harry stabbing and stabbing through the man until the knife was hitting metal floor. It had happened onboard the train. In hindsight, it was almost like Spanner wanted him to do it. It gave Harry a heap of nightmares. And yet Harry would do it all over—just like Max had with Felix Menning.

Max listened enthralled, as if being read a play script. "My own little brother," he said, shaking his head, grinning again.

They didn't talk about all the blood.

"One thing I wanted to ask you," Harry said. "Did you know the actress Katarina Buchholz?"

"Not personally. But who doesn't know of her? Men had pinups of her in bunkers from Normandy to Stalingrad . . ." Max sat up. "Wait. You know her?"

"She was my partner in the train job. It's one part no one knows about."

"You were lovers," Max said.

Harry nodded, then shook his head. He told how Katarina had left Germany to join Emil, the Jewish refugee partisan who made unloading the train heist workable—to whom Harry had given all the contents of the plunder train. The two of them lived in Palestine, the last Harry had heard. "I probably shouldn't be telling this, but what does it matter now?"

With that, he let his head slump again as if those Ivans were lowering that black hood back over him.

"Hey, now, brother, stop with the storm and stress," Max said.

"It doesn't matter. What's done is done."

"I'm sorry," Max said.

"Don't be. You've lost girls too. You've paid some steep dues."

"I suppose I'm getting closer, yes."

A jolt. A boom, like a howitzer, so loud they pressed their hands flat to the floor. Dust and straw floated down from the walls and the floor churned and wobbled. "Our car—they're hooking us up to others. Yes. I hear a locomotive," Harry said with precision as if reading out a duty roster. Then they were moving, in fits and starts. More jolts and their train was rolling along the tracks, clacking and thudding ever closer together from the speed of it.

A few hours later, a stop. Harry and Max's hearing had dulled from the constant roar of riding inside a rolling freight car, like being underwater in a rushing spring river. They listened as intently as they could, leaning forward to the slats, and detected a droning they couldn't identify. They picked out shouts in Russian and German. "Wait. It's people. People? Must be hundreds."

The door thundered open. A throng of refugees climbed up and inside, their faces slack from fatigue and worry. Women. Children. Men. Taking little notice of Harry and Max, they huddled in the middle of the car as a woman shouted at them to stay put while she swept up the straw and dried excrement with an old short broom she carried in her coat. She only glanced at Harry and Max once as she did so, shaking her head. The door shut, the car started rolling again. The sweeping done, the families spread out across the car's floor. Someone set out a bucket in the other corner closest to Max and Harry. The toilet.

They were shouting over the roar at each other and speaking a clunky old German, not Austrian *Deutsch* at all. The adults kept their backs to Harry and Max. Only the children started looking at them.

"Hello. We go west?" Harry shouted at a young boy, keeping his German wooden and true to character.

"Not exactly," a mother shouted for the boy.

"We were in Austria, north part," Max hollered, in character, an Ami deserter with bad German.

"You're well north of there now," barked a man.

"Bohemia," yelled another. Czechoslovakia.

"Probably passing right by the Šumava," Max shouted into Harry's ear. "Wonder if my scouts could hear this train."

Another stop, more people. Someone reported that the train had gained six more cars from its original ten, some of them open cars and the people in those had it much worse. The children finally came over to stare at Harry and Max's wounds. Harry and Max offered their bread, and everyone's food was shared all around. Harry and Max got used to the urinating and defecating in the bucket and even joined in. People emptied the bucket by dumping it out the narrow windows up high—a complicated, circus-like maneuver that required a pyramid of helpers with a child at the top, best done at those times when the train was almost at a halt.

Another stop. A few more refugees came in, these ones speaking what sounded like Russian with some quaint old German words thrown in.

"It's Polish," Max said, losing any spirit left in his voice.

More jolts, starts, and stops. The light was dimming outside. By the time they got rolling again, it was near dark. The train barreled on into the darkness, yet at half the pace as before.

"Why so damn slow now?" someone shouted.

"Different locomotive," shouted back one of the Poles. "Red bastards keep the ones from the West and send back the rickety old ones from the East. Like this one we got."

More food was shared, rationed out by bites. Harry and Max joined the crowd, and the women tended to their wounds. The refugees on this train, they learned, were ethnic Germans the Soviets were expelling from the East—forced to vacate countries, cities, villages, homes they had lived in for hundreds of years, some of them. Thus the strange German, if they had any left at all. Many only had their German names left, but even that was too much for Joseph Stalin.

Harry and Max slept, their heads on the soft wide laps of women they didn't know. They did not stop for hours, the tracks clicking and clacking and thumping. An icy wind whipped at the car and forced its way in between the slats. They woke to a dim light and then sat up. All paced the car. Friday morning. Organized looks out the high windows revealed countryside much like that of Austria, Czechoslovakia, Poland. "A sign!" someone shouted. "I can't read it."

The old locomotive raced on as if barreling downhill. Harry hoped it had the steam to stop itself. He and Max retreated back to their corner, alone again, hanging on to each other's sleeves, anchoring their feet to the walls. If this thing wrecked, at least they wouldn't be killed by the bodies of other people. He hoped.

"Hold on, Max, hold on!" Harry shrieked, and then muttered it to himself.

The train slowed. Brakes squealed and the car wobbled as it switched tracks, once, and then twice. Another look out the window was attempted, this time by a young man who climbed back down with a stern look stretched across his face.

"It's all destroyed! All of it, for so many kilometers. Even the horizon. Where are we supposed to go? Who would take us here?"

Full stop. The refugees cleared the doorway, and the woman shielded their children. The doors rolled open, bringing blinding sunlight and a gritty dust that swirled in the car and bit at their noses. It meant rubble. A city in ruins.

Max and Harry helped each other up, leaning against one another. A few men approached the door. They stared out a moment, into the light, and then, with a shrug, waved the rest on out. Harry and Max waited until the last were outside. They hobbled to the doorway of the car and peered out.

"I've been here . . . before," Max said.

Their car, attached to the middle of the train, stood half inside the great rail station and half out. Yet that hadn't stopped the sun from streaming in, because the station's great hall was a creaking, gnarled skeleton of iron beams, pocked and charred stonework and iron frames that had long ago lost all of its glass. The refugees moved along the platform, their heads craning at the great hall, clutching each other. The platform sign read:

NÜRNBERG HBF

# Twenty-Three

"THE TRAIN ENDED AT NUREMBERG," Harry told Sabine. They were back at Harry's mansion. It was that evening—Friday, November 2. Harry had asked Gerlinde to call Sabine, and Gerlinde and Sabine had cut a deal over the phone. Gerlinde would clean and dress Harry's head, then Sabine would arrive and make Harry stay in bed. Gerlinde, still showing Harry disapproving looks, propped him up with pillows against the headboard so that Sabine could get a good look at him thusly repaired. When Sabine arrived less than a half hour later, she sat in a chair next to the bed, her fingers feeling at Harry's duvet as he told her about Max and him on the packed train of ethnic Germans, just one of so many human trainloads that Joe Stalin had expelled from Eastern Europe—"Uncle Joe" had his own brand of Europe in mind, and it was already sure to look and behave like no other. To counteract the sick foreboding this gave Harry, like a bag of sand in his chest, he gazed at Sabine as he talked. She wore no makeup and as far as he was concerned didn't need it. The low, soft light in the room, from candles Gerlinde lit because of outages, made Sabine's skin glow. Her concern showed in her hard-set cheeks and full eyes. Her lips were a little chapped, with a darker spot on her lower lip where she must have been biting it. Was she worrying about him? Harry hoped so.

"What about security?" Sabine said.

"Wasn't hard to avoid the controls with all the people. We got outside the station, onto the street . . . grabbed the first MP I saw, told him I was regional MG and I'd been roughed up by some deserter gang, took the clothes right off my back. Didn't mention the train or the Soviet zone."

"And Max?"

"I told them he's my brother. They didn't ask questions. From there, all it took was one call from Nuremberg MG to Munich. Munich regional verified me. Nuremberg even drove us back in an army ambulance." Harry tried a laugh. "Max, he wanted us to rush us straight back over the border."

"To the Šumava? To be with the Cossacks."

Harry nodded. "I feel for him, after what we saw, but he's too banged up to go just yet. He's got the bedroom down the hall—Irina's with him."

Sabine laid a hand over Harry's and held it there. Harry told Sabine the rough part about their venture. The Cossacks' families were trucked off, the men shot down like rabid pigs. Yet Harry and Max got it on film.

"Now we have the proof," Sabine told him. "And you used a top-notch Riga Minox? Such boldness."

The story of Max's magic trick to hide the film made her clap. And Harry had another revelation for her: He had figured out that she and Max knew each other from the beginning, from before Harry found Max, and not only that: "You've been working with him all along."

It made Sabine blush, which Harry was sure to point out.

"One thing not even you knew though," he continued. "Max himself sent me straight to you at the Standkaserne, can you believe that? Used a disguise to hit me up on the sidewalk at night, of all the things."

Sabine shook her head in wonder.

"Bet you didn't know actors had so much moxie?" Harry said, adding a smile, but it pulsed hot in the back of his head like that Chinese mustard and suddenly he wasn't smiling anymore. He said, haltingly, "What we saw, it was like something the Germans did—the Nazis did."

Sabine squeezed Harry's hand. "You can include me in that. The Germans did it, and I'm a German. Now the game changes fast, does it not? A year ago? Right after the war ended? This was happening every other day, what you saw—to normal citizens. Anyone Russian or Soviet who had the misfortune to be caught in the West. POWs. Forced laborers. Even their own spies and underground fighters. You sent back over two million—you Americans, the British, the French. All for policy."

"Hell, let's not coat it with sugar," Harry said.

Sabine checked Harry's wound, re-dressed the bandage, and stroked his hair. She undressed, tugging her blouse off her shoulders, and she wriggled her skirt off her hips. She unclasped her white corset lingerie that shined in the candlelight. He wondered, watching it billow to the floor in one last shimmer, if she had worn this just for him. She slid into bed with him. She was so warm, and he told her so, and they promised each other, fighting chuckles, that they would behave themselves and only sleep. Sabine, feigning anger, told Harry he was too banged up to even think about making it with her. Harry had been hard far too long yet managed to keep his pajamas on. She kissed him on the forehead and on each cheek. She blew out the last candle. They fell into sleep.

Harry woke, in the dark, must have been the middle of the night. Sabine had clasped onto him in her sleep, one leg over his hip, her arm tight around him. Like a brave woman hanging on for dear life. Her cheek pressed against his shoulder. Then she was kissing him, her lips chapped no more. Harry was hard again. His pajama trousers came off and his shirt, so fast she'd done it like the veteran nurse she was stripping a bed. She cradled his head on a pillow. Re-lit the candle. She was all seriousness—not focused in a sterile way but rather bright-eyed, as if she were gazing out at a grand mountain view. His hands all over her now.

He felt scars, on her back and on her shins, and dents there, and he knew where it came from. Few survived the Gestapo without something to show for it. Her fingers found the scar on his left thigh, from his death bout with Spanner.

"Me, I walked into a door," he whispered.

"Is that so? I tripped on the sidewalk."

"A likely story."

"I'm not ashamed," Sabine whispered.

"Neither am I."

They stopped, to stare into each other's eyes. Then they were kissing again, with tongues, her contours velvet in the light, and he was reaching for all of them, finding them. Finding her.

The next morning, Harry reported to regional MG with the same story he'd told Nuremberg MP and MG. The gash on his head and one oversized bandage from Gerlinde didn't hurt his tale, and he had little trouble getting sympathy. That was some tough luck for a Military Government Officer on his way out the door, they said, because the quadruplicates had reached Munich HQ spelling out that Captain Kaspar had no more than two weeks left. He could push the papers for redeployment if he wanted such a thing, but time was ticking. Harry still hadn't told Max, and he should've told Sabine last night. He refused to think about it this morning. It was a Saturday, the sun made the November breeze tolerable, he felt lucky to have his skull in one round piece, and there was so much to get done and fast.

The Minox cartridge needed developing. Using Harmut Dietz made sense, Harry reckoned. The detective had given him the camera, after all, and this way no one else would have to know. Dietz was a good egg. Sure, the detective knew about Max, but he hadn't made an issue of it and hadn't gone around prying as far as Harry knew. Sabine had demanded a shot at developing the film herself, but she didn't know a photographer she could trust, she admitted, since so many good ones were dead or emigrated. Yet she vowed to find someone or would learn to develop it herself if need be. No, Harry had argued—this needed doing pronto and right. He said he knew a person and Sabine didn't ask questions.

Harry called Dietz at the *Polizeipräsidium*, saying only that he had hit a snag. Dietz said he'd meet him in one hour.

To kill time Harry strolled through Old Town, lit up a Chesterfield and thought about Max back at the mansion, hopefully charming Gerlinde right about now into making her famous *Kaiserschmarrn* even if they didn't have raisins. He passed St. Peter's Church, thinking of Sabine again. She'd been up and working for hours, no doubt. The most surprising thing about Sabine in bed was that it had been fun, a hoot. They had laughed. Maddy had always made it so formal, like taking some ancient rite. One would think the German girl would be the ceremonial one, Harry thought, wearing a smile as he turned corners.

He stopped. Maddy Barton herself was coming up the street. She wore a buff fur coat with matching bonnet. A squared-jawed hunk of a GI in crisp new US Army green followed eyeing pedestrians who got too close. Harry had no choice. He gritted his teeth and continued on, locating the gears inside his head that would somehow put a pleasantly innocent morning smile on his face.

Seeing Harry, Maddy stopped a moment and then made straight for him. "Well! Captain Kaspar," she said. Then stopped again, waiting for him to come to her. Always the formality.

Harry took a puff and kept coming, not faster or slower, just on his merry old way. Square-jawed GI stood in front of her. Harry gave him a once-over. "Madd, I think there's a tree trunk got between us. And he doesn't salute much either." Only then did Harry realize he had his civvies on.

The GI broke a smile. Teeth wider than Harry's fingers.

"Oh, let me at him," Maddy said and the GI stepped back. "Go on, take a breather and ogle some dames or something," she told him.

She rolled her eyes at Harry as the GI found the closest wall to lean against. Two Gretchens passed, already eyeing him. Maddy's face looked a little paler but in a nice way, like an Asian woman with powder on her face.

"What's with the goon?" Harry said.

Maddy shrugged, the fine fur billowing. "They made me take him. I don't care for it either if you must know."

"Made you? Ah, right, your new general did."

"He's only a colonel, Harry." Maddy blushed, feet together, swinging her hips a little.

"Yeah, but he's staff caliber, right? So he'll be a general. You deserve a general." Keep this civil, Harry. He put on another smile. "I mean it, Madd. Good for you."

But Maddy's mouth had scrunched up. "Hey, wait—turn around, you." Fur hooked onto his arm and she spun him around, making a tsk-tsk sound.

A small square of *Pflaster* had replaced Gerlinde's big bandage on the back of his head, expertly applied by Sabine. "Oh, that? Heck of a thing. It's not too bad," he said, giving her no more than that. Maddy shouldn't have been able to see the bandage from her angle, but then again she didn't have to—she'd surely gotten word through the MG grapevine. She probably even knew his assaulted-by-deserters story. Come to think of it, why would she just happen to be waltzing up this very street? They had no dress boutiques, candy shops, or even a swanky bar within blocks. He wanted to point that out to her, but he was being a good boy today, and she a good girl. "Say, just where you heading anyway?" he added.

"Never mind me." She turned him back around to face her. She was pouting, her lips two cherries. They had always been sweet—he had to admit. And they were going to start asking questions and rapidly like a tommy gun. Too many Americans and Germans were like Maddy, all flash and gossip and snooping. The Maddys of this world had too many connections, which meant too many allegiances. What did they care about those Cossacks? Not unless the poor saps were privy to a truckload of gold bars, rare bibles, or a secret map to the Fountain of Youth.

He had to curb her powers somehow. He blurted, "Hey, you know a man named Aubrey Slaipe?"

The cherries parted, flattened. For the briefest moment, nothing escaped from between them. "That a doll or a guy name?" she sputtered.

"Guy."

"Who's asking?"

"I'm asking. Just me. Calls himself a trade representative. Might be CIC or whatever the new flavor is."

"Well, I don't, Harry . . ." Maddy looked around before she continued. The GI was talking to two other Gretchens. "What are you up to, huh?" she whispered. "Soon as I'm out of your life, you're off getting in all sorts of trouble."

"You're hearing it or you're knowing it?" Harry said.

"A gash like that? Someone meant to do you some harm. I don't want harm done to you, see, whether you believe that or not."

"I'm glad you're not sore at me."

"Sore at you? Heck, best thing you could do was give me those walking papers. I was about ready to seize your whole billet. First your fancy bathtub, tomorrow the world . . ."

"Thanks. I mean it." What if he just out and told her now? He fought the urge. He couldn't know what she'd do, what whistles she'd blow or bells she'd ring. She might just call him a sucker. "I'm doing all right, Madd."

"It is quite a serious to-do though, isn't it?" she said.

Harry took a long drag of his Chesterfield, wondering how to play it. She was obviously keeping tabs on him. She may or may not know Slaipe but had probably heard of him even though the man didn't seem like one for castle parties. She might even have taken a little of what he preached to heart. Yet that fur was saying otherwise—that her priorities were always her own.

Maddy hadn't taken her eyes off him. The cherries were back.

"Your brother," she said. "Does this have something to do with it?"

Harry yanked his cigarette. He hadn't meant to and it gave him away. She planted her gloved hands on her hips, expecting him to fess up. The grapevine, that goddamn grapevine, it grew faster than any ivy, stronger than any iron.

"Who told you about him?" he grunted. Not that he expected an answer.

"Word gets around. They say he looks like you—only ritzy," Maddy said but she added a sympathetic raise of eyebrows where he'd expected a devilish grin. "Look. Maybe I could help."

"Maybe you shouldn't."

"Nothing shocks me, Harry. You know that. And now? Let's just say I'm wising up, see. You may not believe this, but I've given some thought to some of those things you laid on me that night. You mean well. I know that now."

"That's good," Harry muttered, still stunned by her knowing about Max. He should have seen it coming. Her pale and beautiful mask of a face was so impenetrable. What did she really want? Was this the look of contrition? It might as well be part of a complicated plan of deceit. She was only trying to peg something on him. Something she could do to make him pay for kicking her out. How could he know with a gal like this?

She was doing that damn pout, again.

"I can't, Madd. Sorry."

"That's all right. Though I would love to see him someday—see how the big brother measures up."

"Sure, sure," Harry said, knowing better than to antagonize her after she'd backed off. "I'm happy about your colonel. Are you happy?"

"Yes, Harry, if you can believe it. I think I am. But remember—if you need anything at all, you do know where to find me. And I you, too . . ." Maddy patted him on the chest, kissed the air, snapped her fingers for old square-jaw, who removed himself from the soft clutches of the two Gretchens, and she was off.

Harry met Dietz at his local pub. As Harry strode in, he sensed something and turned around to find Dietz behind him. Dietz could see Harry's bandage from there. "What happened? What is it?" the detective said.

"It's no bother."

Dietz grimaced inspecting the damage.

"I'm fine, it's fine," Harry said, waving a hand. "Don't worry about it."

"*Quatsch.*" Dietz gave the bartender a stern look and the man disappeared in back. The failing front door swung back open and Dietz pushed it shut, which oddly made the place draftier than it already was. It gave Harry a shiver. Dietz moved to fetch them a drink.

Harry grabbed him by the arm. "No time," he said. He handed over the film cartridge from the Riga Minox.

Dietz, nodding, dropped the cartridge into his overcoat pocket. He patted Harry on the shoulder. "I understand."

"Thanks." Harry shoved occupation dollars into Dietz's pocket, but Dietz pressed them back into Harry's hand.

"I told you: I understand."

# Twenty-Four

Max sat in a cell. He was in jail. He almost wanted to laugh and find a song he could belt aloud to mock this bind he was in, it was so surreal. He'd been avoiding it for so long. He should have been sitting in a Nazi prison two years ago. After that, the US Army should have had him before a firing squad. And when his time came, it was the feeble Munich police who collared him? It did make him chuckle a little. But there was no song for this.

His cell was not so bad. It had a bunk, a sink, a toilet, and even a window that looked out onto a courtyard. He didn't know where he was, but the paddy wagon drive had been only a few minutes. He guessed it was the *Polizeipräsidium* or the justice buildings.

He squeezed his eyes shut in frustration. The problem was, he was losing time. They had to get back to the Šumava and get those people out.

Harry said he must recover, but he had enough convalescing and had hit the black markets early for anything they could take, if only a stuffed bear for Alex. Someone must have fingered him. Because the Munich bulls were working damn hard for a Sunday morning. The raid came right after he and Irina reached the square at Sendlinger Tor, their very first stop. He'd seen his share of black market raids. Usually one heard the cars and vans coming, if not the shouting, and any wise fellow was gone. The ones who stayed either had no goods or were too dumb to notice. But this roundup was a small raid aimed at only one corner of the square. They snuck in, parked blocks away, and held their tongues. Max was across the street by then yet they—at least six of those bulls—came right for him. As if looking for him. He hadn't fought it. He held up his hands. He didn't have any goods on him. They ran him in anyway. They were gentle with him, these new German police with their blue American-style tunics and silver badges that had them looking like Hollywood extras in a hold-up picture rather than bloodthirsty cavalry. His ribs made him howl with pain when they carried him along by his arms, and he pleaded with them to let him walk on his own. And so they did! So congenial, these new bulls. They even let him light up a nail for his troubles.

About a half hour after they locked him up, a German official came in—a weary-looking paper-pusher in an ill-fitting suit, but those types could be the worst kind. Max had been contemplating, over and over, the usual offenses they could pin on him. He did not have a residence. He had no ID. He also had not, they'd discover if they went looking, filled out a *Fragebogen*, that damning question-naire all suspected Nazi sympathizers and party members and former SS still had to complete. They would want to know what he had done during the war. Max had already taken his deep breaths, looked in the mirror, and paced the room as if waiting for a stagehand to call him backstage. The official had a clipboard under an arm like a stagehand. Max was sitting bolt upright on the bed, his chin high. He stated, "My name is Max Kaspar. I used to be an actor. I was conscripted in the last year of the war, nothing fancy, replacement foot soldier on the Eastern Front, me and my scared-tight asshole retreating with all the rest of Germany's finest cannon fodder."

"And then what happened to you?" The official's voice sounded thin, dry.

Max held out his hands. "Look at me, friend. I simply walked away from it, didn't I? Been wandering ever since."

It was that easy. This was the first time he had told anyone—besides Irina and his brother Harry—his real name and identity since the fall of 1944. Max's name didn't seem to register with the official. The man went on to state that the new regulations required him to tell Max he was an investigator with the Justice Department. Again, so congenial. He asked Max about his ribs, why they hurt him so.

"I appreciate your concern," Max said. He made a big monologue out of it. He told him that he was riding on the outside fender of a crowded Old Town streetcar—without a ticket he had to confess—when at the next turn an American MP was lying in wait for them, like they did, and the Ami gangster chopped at them with his long billy club and sent them tumbling off like dominoes. Max went head over heels right into a kiosk. *Autsch!* Just his tough luck.

"You seem to be a constant target," the official said.

Max shrugged. "Now, if I may ask you, good sir—why come nab me today? Your bulls were aiming right for me."

"It was on a tip," the justice official said, and he left.

That was three hours ago. That first hour, Max had kept it together. Then he started pacing the cell again. He realized, with horror, that the walls in here were taller than they were wide. He began to shiver even though the cell was warmer than most hovels. This could get much worse, he was realizing. They could hand him over to the Americans, who might prosecute him for war crimes if they found out who he was. Other Germans who'd taken part in code name Operation Greif had been shot, some within days, others after pacing cells for months. He'd seen it in a *LIFE* magazine dated June 11, 1945 that a GI left lying in the street. "Firing Squad: Army Executes German Spies Caught in US Uniforms," read the headline with before and after photos of three of his fellow commandos tied to posts for the big show. That was closer to the war then, but they still needed sad sacks like Max for the papers these days. Wrong place, wrong time, right command of American English. Talk about tough luck. Max was perfect. He'd participated in an easily identifiable, notorious act. Not only that, he was an actor, and you know what they said about thespians. Degenerates, all of them.

*He was losing time. They had to get back to the Šumava, get those people out. Four hours now. How long were they going to keep him? This could go on for months. Did Irina even know where he was? Would Harry?*

He thought about asking for an American named Aubrey Slaipe. He drove the notion from his head by slapping at his forehead repeatedly.

He went over it again in his head. That was no black market raid. They had come straight for him. A tip, the justice official said—yet who could have tipped them off? Was it someone who knew Harry? Someone had to be watching Harry's mansion, to know who was coming and going and how Max tiptoed out the back way off into the English Garden and then through to Old Town. Another possibility was, one of those black market scoundrels had tipped them off, filling some quota, hoping for a handout. No great coin in that, but there were new reputations to be cemented, what with the New Germany coming. Lives were being reinvented. Some concentration camp inmates who'd survived were common criminals but were now passing themselves off as diehard anti-Nazis or even Jews. They were giving the poor victims a bad name and fast. *Probably was a Nazi himself who sold me out,* Max supposed.

It was too dark a notion. The black moods will kill a man. *Quit pacing, Max.* He lay on his back, upside down on his bunk and stood his legs up against the wall, wiggling his socked feet. *Think of the good things.* At least Irina had gotten away—his brief sprint across the street had given him just enough time to see her make a break for it. She was trading in a different crowd. When the raid came she started for him, but he gave the signal—two slaps to his upper arm that meant *run on your own, we'll meet back at that spot along the Isar River.* She wouldn't have fled right away—she would've stayed long enough to watch him get nabbed, he was sure of that. She was a smart young lady, his dear Irina. This was why he loved her. She was going to raise Alex into such a smart boy.

His ribs ached so he sat up on the bunk and rocked back and forth, carefully, trying to stretch away the pain. The only thing he could do now was wait. But who would open that door next? Another German in a nicer suit, or in the new police uniform? A so-called liaison from the Soviet Repatriation Mission on a ruthless mission for SMERSH? Or, an American officer who would ask him: Did you once encounter a man named Aubrey Slaipe? Back in 1944, in Belgium, middle of winter? Sure you did. You remember. The man was a captain in the CIC.

Max could still feel that Ardennes Forest chill clawing at his joints, could see the grime worked into his every pore, could smell the bitter aroma of that cellar on Christmas Day, 1944. He had ended up stranded in a snowstorm together with Slaipe in a villa owned by the woman named DeTrave. Justine. Max was done for. Slaipe had figured out Max was a secret agent—the worst spy ever known to the world—but one nevertheless. Yet Slaipe was going to give Max a chance. He said he wouldn't turn Max over outright; Max would have to spy for the Americans instead. Max was unsure. He'd been fooled so many times. Then Justine fooled them all. She shot Slaipe. Max was engorged with rage, the first time in his life he wanted to strike someone. He hit Justine's jaw with the butt of a submachine gun, surely broke her jaw. He could have helped Slaipe at that point. He ran instead. He could not conjure up the faith in Slaipe.

He wandered south into Germany that spring disguised as a refugee and ended up in shattered old Nuremberg, a jagged gray wasteland of rubble and hollowed spires and craggy facades barely standing. He lived in doorways and cellars, wherever, sharing his dark and dirty hovels with crippled ex-soldiers, the elderly, and many who'd lost their minds, anyone who needed him.

One afternoon he thought he heard a symphony. Beethoven's Fifth. The sound led him to a scorched gothic chapel without a roof. Inside, at the altar, surrounded by blackened stonework and shattered stained glass, a small orchestra was playing for ladies in minks, the wounded of all stripes, pale old men, laborers. Max sat on a pew in back. The Beethoven ended to respectful applause. A blond woman stood at the altar and sang opera—von Weber's *Der Freischütz*, but her voice wavered. The crowd applauded nonetheless. Men shouted "Bravo, bravo!" There was a time, and not so long ago, when Max would have snickered at such bourgeois hokum. He cried openly, his face in his hands.

The US Army took Nuremberg. They distributed newspapers that told the horrid story of the concentration camps, with photos to prove it. On the battered Frauenkirche, someone painted in huge white letters: "I'm Ashamed to be a German."

American soldiers filled the city. Counterintelligence officers roamed the streets in open staff cars. Every time Max saw one, he feared it would hold Captain Aubrey Slaipe—or fellow Americans out to avenge his death.

One humid morning, he was searching for a new hovel in the rubble hills of Old Town, pressing his unwashed hanky to his mouth to block the grit-filled wind. He had a nasty cough now—they all had it—and it left him shaking and shivering. Narrow lanes wound through the ruins.

He heard shrieks, and short gasps, what had to be a woman. He started toward the sound. Then he stopped. What could he do about it? Freed forced laborers and GIs were known to rape Fräuleins. Screams were heard day and night. It was considered to be part of the price to pay. He turned and crept away.

The shrieks grew louder, making dogs bark and crows shoot into the sky. Max turned back. Grasping at stones and protruding beams, he climbed to the top of a giant heap and peered around. Below him, he could see into the exposed first story of a house.

A woman lay on her back, atop a vast slab of fallen wall. She wriggled about with her knees up high. Max yelled down to her: "Was that you? What's wrong?"

The woman's face jerked his way. She was a teenage girl with chubby cheeks and braided pigtails. "My cat died," she shouted back, "what do you think?"

Her stomach was huge, a medicine ball. "*You're having a baby? What can I do?*"

"Are you a doctor?"

Max sputtered a laugh. "An actor."

"You're no help. Go away!"

The girl let out a shriek that made Max jump.

"Hold on, girl, hold on . . ." He scrambled down the pile, knocking his ankles on busted stone. He sprinted down the narrow lanes for two blocks, then three streets over.

Out on the Königsstrasse, two MPs were surveying the endless traffic of American trucks and jeeps and staff cars. Max ran up and, catching his breath, shouted in crisp American English: "Gentlemen, you must help! I need a nurse, a doctor. A poor girl's life is at stake—her baby's life. She's all alone."

It was the first English he'd spoken in months. It shocked the MPs into action despite his appearance. One yanked on white traffic gloves and dashed out into the busy street. An ambulance came, the MP directed the driver to the curb, and an American doctor jumped out of the passenger side, a captain with graying sideburns—a neat Cary Grant type.

The cough hit Max, and he screeched and spat but was able to explain the situation.

"Where?" the captain said as the driver handed him his doctor bag.

Max and the doctor climbed the rubble and scrambled down to the girl. Max translated between her gasps and moans.

"You'll have to find clean linen," the doctor said. "Go!"

Clean? In this hell? "I'll be right back," Max muttered and headed off. Two streets over, he kicked in the window of a tailor's shop and grabbed the first white fabric he saw—a wedding dress with veil and flowing train.

The doctor was hunched over the girl's knees and stomach, his sleeves rolled up. Max passed him the dress, and the doctor gave it a double take and kept working. Max wanted to look, but the smell was thick and earthy like a sick man's saliva, buckets of it. Eventually he looked. The baby's head protruded, its skin gray and the veins blue and bright red, and the liquid flowed out in sloppy drops that gelled on the stones and shined in the sun.

Max turned away, his stomach rolling, and he vomited.

The baby screamed and squealed as Max wiped his beard clean with his sleeve. The doctor passed the baby to him in the veil, kicking and slippery. It was a boy. Max showed it to the girl. She grinned and tears ran down her face and into her ponytails matted with sweat.

Max handed the girl her baby boy. She hugged it to her breast and laughed so loud that the doctor chuckled and shook his head. She was not beautiful by a long shot, but at this moment she was one hell of a beautiful wonder to behold.

The doctor sat on a chunk of sandstone. He wiped sweat from his nose. "You the father?" he said to Max.

"Oh, god no. I don't even know the girl."

The doctor looked to the girl. She seemed to understand. She shook her head, no.

The doctor stared at Max, long and hard. It reminded Max a little too much of Captain Slaipe's stare.

"She needed me," the doctor added. "Her baby, it wasn't coming out."

Max smiled. "And why would it want to? Just take a look around, Doc."

The doctor was not smiling, but he wasn't frowning either. His lower lip stuck out as if he was concentrating on a medical chart, Max imagined—an interesting new case only a new medicine could cure.

"Why did you do such a thing?" the doctor said. "Go out of your way? Here. In this place. Where everyone is looking the other way—including us."

"Why would I not?"

They sat staring at each other, listening to the girl babble to her boy and kiss him.

"What I'm getting at is, what's your story? Your English is stellar, it seems, and your ability to take action, well that goes without saying . . ." The doctor gave Max's tired refugee getup a once-over. "Look, maybe I can help you. At least do something for that cough of yours. I have a fair amount of pull."

No doubt this victorious doctor had pull. Max could use something for his cough, certainly. Pressed new clothes would be a fine thing, too, and he really would like to shed his awful beard. Perhaps it truly was time for a new role.

He stood, and he gave the doctor a little bow, from the waist. He wanted to thank the doctor for showing him that, now that the Nazis were out, maybe a new way of living was possible for him.

But he did not. He only backed up and scrambled away, then climbed over the next pile of rubble. All it took for him to lose his role was one American who knew a fellow who knew Aubrey Slaipe from the CIC.

He walked out of Nuremberg. He ran again, kept running. On a country road, a farmer smoking a curved pipe told him the news— the Führer was dead, and good riddance.

Summer came. He wandered south, on into Austria, where he found Irina.

Where Felix Menning found him.

And here he was now, pacing his Munich jail cell, thinking, pleading, *please, I must get back to the* Šumava *and get those people out.*

# Twenty-Five

As HARRY LEFT HIS MANSION Irina ran up to him shouting, arms flailing, her hair in her eyes wet with tears.

Harry's first thought—*my brother is dead.*

"You must help," she shouted. "They have him!"

Max was in a German jail, she told him. Harry put a good face on it, holding her close as he ushered her inside and onto the sofa. His initial relief turned to dread when she recounted the details.

"It was black market raid but different. The bulls search only for Max and they push many people out of way to find him."

It was all Harry could do to get Irina to stay put. Gerlinde wasn't there on a Sunday morning so he brought her soup, but she refused to eat it. She began crying. He told her she had to stay at the mansion while he figured this out.

"You must help," Irina cried, "you must," and lunged for him and grabbed at his lapels. Her eyes were wild. Tears streaming down her cheeks again.

"Can't you see I'm working on it?" he said, hoping she couldn't hear the strain in his voice. He managed to get her up to the bedroom she was sharing with Max. He stood back, blocking the doorway. Irina curled up in a ball on the bed, squeezing at the very pillow Max slept on, but her breathing calmed. She looked up to him.

"I know you will try," she said. "I'm sorry. Go and do what you must."

Harry turned for the door.

"Mister Harry? I'm sorry for wound on your head."

"So am I," Harry said and, to make sure Irina was not thinking stupid thoughts, added, "If you flee from here like you did that first time? I cannot help you. I cannot help your Alex."

Harry wondered who could have fingered Max. It was as if Max's old nemesis Felix Menning were a ghost, playing the trickster, tripping up Max for evermore. If Harry went to Military Government, it might trigger even more snafus and troubles unforeseen. He thought about trying Warren Joyner, but his plan had been to hold out for that. Joyner had to be ready. The timing had to be perfect. Harry again considered the inscrutable Aubrey Slaipe but ruled out the option. He didn't want Slaipe selling both of them down the river. Max could have been mixed up in more than he had admitted. He hadn't meant to be, Harry was sure of that. And yet Max had left a sinkhole-sized gap in his story stretching from the end of 1944 on well into '45. At least Max was sitting in a German cell and not a US stockade—not yet.

If he couldn't get Max out, what would Max want him to do? Max would want him to do what Irina wanted: He had to get the Cossacks over, no matter what. That was everything. It was November 4 already. They had to get back to the Šumava and get those people out.

The Germans had Max, so Harry would keep the bleeding isolated for now. He had to keep the matter from the Americans.

Hartmut Dietz was working that Sunday. Harry went straight to Dietz's desk at police headquarters. Dietz took Harry by the arm and led him down a dark and narrow hallway. They faced each other, each man's back to a wall.

Dietz said, "Something's gone wrong?"

"Where's the film?" Harry said.

"I have it. Just developed it. But I have work. So I couldn't come straight to you . . . wait here. No, better yet, wait downstairs, outside by that statue of the general."

Harry waited down by the statue sucking on a Chesterfield, wondering if Max was in the same building complex somewhere. But where? It had to be a different unit, another jurisdiction. Maybe they simply had him on a black market crime. It could be denazification. Or there was some other ridiculous act Max had committed as a carefree actor, now come back to haunt him?

"Let's go." Dietz wore his overcoat and carried his scruffy briefcase. He led Harry on a roundabout way to the pub that was draftier with the door closed. There he paid the bartender three cigarettes, the bartender then told his three drunk patrons they were closing a while, and the three men stumbled out. The bartender locked the door and disappeared. Dietz pulled down the shade. The detective laid out the briefcase and drew out a few blurry prints. These were the most damning ones. Harry made out the figures of men running panicked back and forth, as the soldiers fired at them. Other victims lay sprawled in the mud, their dark figures mixing in with the shadowy earth. In one corner of the print, a Soviet flag hung from the warehouse. In another, Harry could see the sign for the St. Stephanus station. A person would be able to make that out with a magnifying glass, he assured himself.

Dietz brought over two thin beers and set them on a free corner of the table. "These may be blurry shots," he said, "but they're damn good for a Riga Minox from that distance."

Harry nodded. Another print showed the families being herded into the trucks with the warehouse in the background. He leaned over it, peering at the pleading children and sagging, resigned old men.

"Just what the hell is going on here in these photos?" Dietz said.

Harry told what he could. It had to do with his brother Maximilian. Max was involved in safeguarding one of the last hideouts of Cossacks who had fought with the Germans—Cossacks from the Ukraine, Harry admitted to Dietz, who listened sitting upright and respectful, his glass of beer untouched. Irina was a Cossack.

Harry didn't need to state the obvious. If the people Max was safe-guarding got sent back, the Soviets would shoot them down just like those men in the photos—who'd themselves come from another group of Cossacks. This was their hard proof.

"This is damn brave of you," Dietz said. "You went into the Soviet zone for this?"

"I wouldn't call it brave. We were supposed to be in and out by afternoon. Then they gave me this souvenir of mine." Harry felt at the scab forming under his hair.

"And they're still in hiding? *Mein Gott.* The Americans and British were sending them all back last year. Not just Cossacks. All. Families. Millions went back."

"That's right. For Cossacks, it goes on."

"For how long?"

"We don't know," Harry said. "Times are changing, but . . . the thing is, we're trying to do this our way, in secret. My brother, others, they always say there are spies around, Soviet Repatriation agents and various weasels on the Soviet take. I wasn't listening. Maybe I should start."

Dietz nodded.

Harry needed Dietz to know all this about Max before he sprung the rest on him.

"Max got fingered this morning," he said.

"*He what?*"

"It was at a black market raid, right here in Munich."

"Ours or yours nab him?"

"Yours."

"Oh. All right. Go on, fill me in . . ."

Harry told Dietz about the way Dietz's fellow cops had picked Max right out of a crowd. Dietz rubbed at his face, his shoulders slumping. A cop was used to hearing tales of friends and family of friends getting unfair treatment from the police, but Dietz seemed truly concerned.

"Someone must have told them," Harry added. "I just wonder if it was someone trying to put him on ice." Hot blood pulsed through him now, and he wanted to pace this tiny closet of a room. He stood, sat back down. He lifted his glass, set it down.

"Look, we should not panic here. The police haul in plenty of people, for many reasons. People finger each other all the time. Your brother might have been buying or selling on some other Hans' corner and Hans wants him gone. All sorts of reasons."

"What if it's denazification?"

"Was he in the party?"

"No. Well, he didn't say he was. But, he served other ways. You all have."

Dietz looked away, at the shaded window, as if wondering if he should dare ask what Max had done. Who was he to ask? They had all done something and each was paying in their own way. The detective finally took a drink of beer. "Did he have ID on him? Papers?"

"No. He shouldn't have, in any case. He never does."

"That's good, actually. A denazification court jail cell is the best place for your brother. They take forever. They don't call in other agencies. You Americans don't care about them anymore. Then, often they just give up. Not enough resources. So many records have been lost, burned. So, I will see what I can do."

"What about the Cossacks? Can you help us?" Harry blurted. He hadn't meant to say *us,* but he couldn't take it back now. He took a drink of the beer, wishing it were a hot shower he was taking instead. He couldn't help feeling a little unsavory here. So soon after the war, and here he was asking Germans for too many favors. So much had changed indeed.

Dietz paused to think, swirling his beer. "Possibly. The rules keep getting revised. But it might take time."

"You know I'm going to make this worth your while."

"That's not why I'm doing this now."

"Why are you then?"

Dietz took his time with his answer. He looked away again. He looked into his beer. His chin quivered, his eyes went a little glossy. He looked up, and he glared at Harry as if he'd just been slapped. "It's time we all start stepping up. Germany's starting over. We cannot look the other way, not this time."

"Thank you," Harry said.

Dietz sat forward. "Now. Tell me where they are, your Cossacks. How many. I would need all the information if I'm going to help."

"What do you think you can do?"

"There are plenty of ways. Papers. Trucks. Connections. Trains even. I have connections. You know I do. You saw me at that club playing cards." Dietz lifted his beer with both hands as if it were hot tea. "So? Where are they?"

"I can't reveal that," Harry said.

"Fair enough, fair enough," Dietz said. He drew out more of the prints and lay them out, standing over them like a field marshal. He pointed at images, eyeing Harry.

"Austria. Right? St. Stephanus is Austria."

Harry nodded. He wouldn't tell outright, but Dietz could guess all he wanted.

"But, that's not where your Cossacks are," Dietz said.

"Of course not. They would be dead."

"But, they're close? Somewhere between there and here. They would have to be."

Harry nodded again.

"They would have to be in a forest, a deep forest . . . The mountains are too high, they would freeze . . . no, somewhere dark, and yet with access to water, animals, smugglers . . ." Dietz held up a finger. "The Bavarian Forest?"

"Close."

"Give me a hint, Harry—this isn't children's play now. Your brother is sitting in a cell."

"Close, but, it's not called the Bavarian Forest where they are."

237

Dietz's eyes widened. They rolled up, consulting an imaginary map in his head. "The Šumava? In Bohemia? But Harry! That's Czechoslovakia."

"The Soviet Army doesn't know," Harry said as if stating the obvious might help.

Dietz shook his head, baring teeth at the grimness of it all. "True, but they will soon. It's only a matter of time."

"You said you could help. You saw these photos. You know what will happen."

Dietz stared at the wall, deep in thought, and his eyes rolled up again as if consulting something else. What? A calendar? A payment? A litany of small crimes and white lies he might erase with this job? He sighed. Harry lit him a Chesterfield, but he waved it away. Then his shoulders gained bulk and width.

"These people," Dietz said, "I'm guessing they're getting excitable. Being cooped up here has not helped them? Right, this is what I thought. If they were crates or animals even, it would make it easier. Humans are such unpredictable cargo. A shout misplaced. Someone shits from their mouth—how do you say it, you Amis? 'Loose lips sink ships'?"

"They're keeping it together," Harry said. "If they weren't they'd be dead already. Besides, no reason to panic, just like you said—"

"Fear is necessary," Dietz cut in. "It keeps a people vigilant. And then, suppose we do get them over to the West? You can't be sure the Amis—your colleagues—back in Munich or Frankfurt or wherever wouldn't suspect Soviet spies among these people. I know I would."

"That's absurd. Max has been with these people through thick and thin. They fought alongside the Wehrmacht, for Christ's sake."

"I'm just pointing it out. People's loyalties can swing widely when the pressure turns on its head."

Harry's blood ran hot again. "What are you trying to say, Dietz? Can you help or not?"

"Of course. But we must play this very safe. Whatever you do, do not let those people leave there, even if those Russian patrols get closer. Especially not in any direction east. Keep them right there. It's the safest place for them. I doubt the Soviet Army will find them in the next few days, week even. My guess is, the Russians are only worried about the border itself. Right under their noses is often the best solution in these cases. Don't you think?"

"It's been working so far. I'm afraid you might be right."

They toasted to it, each drinking their beers empty. Eyeing each other.

Harry slid the prints back into the briefcase.

"Keep it," Dietz said.

"What? They're my prints."

"No, I meant the briefcase. Easier to carry them out that way."

"Thanks." Harry felt around inside. "Wait. There's only prints in here."

Dietz broke into a grin. "*Ach*, yes, of course. You'll need the negatives too. I almost forgot." He produced an envelope from his overcoat pocket, and he slid that into the briefcase. "So careless of me. How could I forget?"

# Twenty-Six

THAT EVENING, WITH MAX STILL STUCK in a Munich jail, Harry worked out the angles at the mansion. He introduced Hartmut Dietz to Sabine, who shook Dietz's hand with one quick thrust, all business, neither smiling. Dietz had come straight from the jail. He couldn't get in to see Max, but they told him to try back Monday morning. Irina hugged Dietz for helping, and Dietz playfully admonished Irina for having fled Harry's mansion, but his joke seemed forced.

A runner had reported in from the Šumava, Irina told them—the Soviet Army was erecting white posts along the zonal border, the Russian patrols were increasing, and the Cossacks' food was running lower. The four shared strategies, timetables, the possible allies. Sabine would handle the Cossacks once they were in the West while Dietz would see to it that no one witnessed them crossing over. Harry would land the necessary American commitment. He didn't tell them how tricky this was. Warren Joyner was his best bet but still a gamble, and Harry wasn't the best salesman—a born German and an émigré liaison officer who spent his days doing who knew what. And now this Harry Kaspar character comes looking to save sorry old Slavs who fought with Germans? His priorities looked skewed at best. The alternatives had no better odds. He couldn't just go waltzing into Aubrey Slaipe's office and ask for help, not until he knew the full story between Slaipe and Max—and now he couldn't even confer with Max. He certainly couldn't go begging a general in his castle. He needed more than a defined mission for that. He needed benefits that he could produce for a general—kickbacks, political gains, a reputation made, if not all the above. He should have been more of a climber, an opportunist. Maddy always told him that. Now he feared that she might have been right for once.

Later, after Dietz left, Harry showed Sabine the prints of St. Stephanus, laying out the harsh images on his bed. Sabine's eyes became wet, and her face darkened. "This is exactly why we must be careful," she said.

"Of course. In what way exactly?"

"Your policeman—I do not trust him."

"You mean Dietz? I wouldn't worry about him," Harry said.

She and Dietz had kept their distance throughout the evening, addressing each other with formal German—the detective was the *Herr Kriminalkommissar* and she Frau Lieser the *Mitarbeiterin*, a colleague. Yet each listened intently to the other's opinion, heads cocked as if listening for incoming bombers. Harry hadn't told her what Dietz had whispered about her when he got Harry alone: "Frau Lieser was a Communist, did you know that? She probably still is."

"I knew that," Harry had replied. "She was imprisoned for it, too. Scars to show for it."

Dietz just shrugged. "Well, I just wanted you to know in case you did not."

That night, Harry could not sleep. Sabine heaved heavy breaths as she slept. She finally woke and rolled over to him. They were lying on their backs, staring into the stout web work of the timbered bedroom ceiling.

"You were a young Socialist, right?" he asked her. "But, what about the Communists?"

"What about them? We Social Democrats, we mostly fought with the Communists. And that was our downfall, in part. We didn't join forces soon enough. The Nazis used that against us. That's politics for you. The infighting, it destroys the cause."

"Were you a Communist ever? I read that a lot of activists changed teams, late twenties, early thirties."

Sabine's voice hardened. "Harry, you must remember that I was barely an adult then. A girl really. This was a good excuse to skip lessons, run around with boys, smoke cigarettes with girlfriends, wear a leather cap like the workers." She added a sad chuckle. "So, later, the fascist thugs beat me for that. For playing revolutionary."

A few moments passed. Harry said, "Why are you so suspicious of Dietz? I'm not questioning. Just trying to learn here."

Sabine took a while. She sighed, once. Shifted her head on her pillow. "Maybe it's because I'm a German. Not like you—rather, as someone who lived through these last twelve years here. The detective, he seems different. He seems to me . . . well, like he didn't live through it."

"Not sure if I follow. So he trades and hustles. He has connections. Everyone does that."

"This is not what I mean."

"Some of the worst Nazis weren't even in the Nazi party. There's no way to track them. That what we're talking about here?"

"Perhaps. But I mean, inside a person. It shows through the eyes. For those who suffered, really got dragged through hell whether at home or on the front, there's a shock, a sadness, a determination all rolled into one look. For me, this Dietz fellow has something different, and I do not like it."

Harry kissed Sabine and promised to keep an eye on Dietz. Yet the sad truth was, and he didn't have to say it, Hartmut Dietz was looking like all that they had.

Harry's foyer filled with the sound of singing, from the front door.

Harry, Sabine, and Irina were huddled before the fireplace with maps, going over roads and rail lines. "Who is it, who's there?" Harry shouted as Sabine and Irina rose and retreated to the safety of the back hallway.

Gerlinde ran in grinning, arms raised as if she had just scored a goal. Dietz followed her, with Max.

"Max!"

Max and Dietz had arms around each other. They sang loud and not quite in unison: "*Ach Mutter, bring' geschwind was Licht, Mein Liebchen stirbt, ich seh' es nicht . . .*" It was the Faithful Hussar song—a soldier leaves the front to return to his true love who's sick and dying. Harry could smell booze on them. Their hair was drenched from the rain.

Harry hugged Max. Irina rushed back in. Max held her face and kissed her on the lips.

Dietz stepped back, a frown on his face. He held up a glass flask, nearly empty. "We celebrated on the way here—to lift Max's spirits. Fruit brandy. I hope this was all right?"

Harry slapped Dietz on the chest. "Forgiven. Kind of you to indulge him."

"It's prewar *Obstler*, Harry! Take a swig," Max said and shared a laugh with Irina.

"Now tell us how you sprung him," Harry said.

Dietz waved at the air. "It was nothing much. I simply talked sense into them."

"All I know is, your man here's a miracle worker," Max shouted over more of Irina's kisses.

Sabine emerged from the darkness of the hallway. Harry could feel her at his back, eyeing all as if meeting them for the first time. She held a forced smile on her face.

"Look! Look who we have here," Harry said to her.

Sabine directed her smile to Dietz who stared back, his face slack and blank. "Yes, it is quite a miracle," Sabine said. "Congratulations."

Dietz gave her a nod in thanks.

Harry brought chairs and the five sat around the sofa. The rest of the *Obstler* was poured and Gerlinde brought beer. Harry asked her to brew coffee and make it strong because they were going to need it later. They toasted, laughed, and their wide smiles turned taut as Dietz told the tale.

"It was easier than one might think. First, I said to them, you don't even know who this man is for certain. In a Democracy such as we have now, you cannot just hold a man indefinitely, simply on a suspicion or a tip. A tip, from whom? I asked them. They did not know. Well, if we start acting on blanket imprisonments and incrimination alone, then we're no better than we were under Hitler. And that's when I had them! They had no proof that he's even Max Kaspar. I said, 'This man may be an actor but he could be Peter Lorre for all we know.'"

Harry and Dietz laughed, but Max only rolled his eyes. "I'm not completely off the hook. I must register my domicile in Munich and report once a week until they find documents that identify me and show what I have or haven't been up to."

"It was terrible in there?" Irina said, stroking his arm.

"Not worse than a foxhole on the Eastern Front or some big city air-raid shelter on a night of firebombing. I tell you, I expected the worst. I had a sinking feeling my next visitor would be the one who damned me. I hardly expected it to be this man here." Max patted Dietz on the knee, and Dietz showed them all the closest a German came to an aw-shucks grin.

It was Monday afternoon, November 5. They worked on their plans into the evening, spurred on by the coffee. Sabine needed forgers to replicate documents, Dietz offered to help her with that, and Max and Irina could get a list of most of the Cossacks' names. Dietz could get some trucks, but Harry might have to procure them trip papers. Sabine could free up a couple buildings in the Standkaserne, though Harry should try to score a barracks just in case. Best to keep all of the people together, at first. They had been so close together for so long.

Harry vowed to them that he would do his best. He had an ace in the hole. He knew a major named Joyner. The man was certain to come through. Harry was feeling better about it.

Late that night, after Sabine and Dietz left and Irina was asleep, Harry found Max outside on a balcony, staring out. Harry watched his brother from inside, his fingertips on the chilled window. It was getting colder, Harry could feel it, and the light rain was turning to a snow that would blanket his back garden white. Yet Max wasn't wearing a scarf. He had no coat on, no hat. He just stared, into that bleak whiteness, as if waiting for the white to consume all.

# Twenty-Seven

TUESDAY, NOVEMBER 6. EARLY THAT MORNING, Harry drove a jeep out to the infantry base. He was towing a covered trailer full of silver, whiskey, and tapestries along with a couple Nazi flags and SS daggers thrown in to spruce up the barter. He'd added the valuable gifts from his office. For the lot, the base quartermaster filled the trailer and back of the jeep with new wool blankets, boxes of rations and even a carton of Hershey's. On his way back Harry swung north of city center, and it was all he could do not to go see Sabine in the Standkaserne where he would find her as busy as ever, barking orders, keeping everybody in line. A gal like that had more grit than ten Maddy Bartons, he thought, steering on into the city now, along the Ludwigstrasse heading south past the university. Given Maddy's American passport, looks, and powers of persuasion, it was a shame that she didn't want more out of this life than a shiny ring and an open bank account. Or so it seemed. He had wondered if there was more to Maddy.

He had the tarp roof on the jeep, a newer model with zip-on canvas doors. He turned the heat up. The rig even had a radio. The new Munich station was playing the latest swing tunes. Hail was coming down, mixed with snow. It rattled and pattered at the canvas around him, but he only turned up the heat, the radio, the wipers. Nothing was going to stop him. He was going for broke and out with a big bang. He had received a letter from Frankfurt about his replacement—arriving at the end of November.

The streets were emptying from the weather, so he shifted up and gunned it for the final stretch back to his mansion.

Five minutes to noon. Harry pulled into his front drive and around to the rear courtyard where he parked in front of the garage. He'd get help later heaving his haul into the garage because the jeep didn't need to be back to the motor pool anytime soon. Pure snow was falling again, the ground still white from last night. He walked the path around back. The wind hit him there, a barrel of it that had funneled through long stretches of the English Garden, giving him a shiver. Onto the rear terrace steps he went and he almost slipped. *Be careful, Harry*. He shivered again, the snow floating off his shoulders and hat and . . .

The rear door was cracked open. The wind was trying to pull it open further, but the heavy door only gave an inch, and then it banged back again, and again.

Strange. Gerlinde must have forgotten to lock it. Sure, he thought—and Reichsmarschall Hermann Göring was one nimble ballerina.

Then he remembered—Gerlinde was gone all day. She had family visiting and she was cooking for them; it was someone's wedding.

He stopped at the door, expecting to feel heat from the house. He got another shiver, and it wasn't the wind this time.

He stayed outside and stepped back, keeping close to the sandstone wall, out of sight of the windows. He didn't have a pistol on him or in the jeep. Not in the garage either. No reason why he should. He did have his paratrooper pocketknife with him, and he moved it from his breast pocket to his trouser pocket.

He scanned the tree line out along the English Garden. All he saw was the snow coming down in sheets. He tiptoed around to the windows on either side of him and tried to peek in, but the curtains and the reflection from the white outside gave him nothing.

Back at the cracked door. His heart was racing now, his blood pumping, heating him up, the sweat trickling down under his wool shirt, his heavy overcoat.

He told himself not to panic. He didn't need his Mauser or his Colt or even his knife. Someone could have just left the door open. Max or Irina could have. They all had so much on their minds. He pushed the door open with one finger, making sure it did not creak, and stepped inside. Pulling the door shut. He stood against the wall, listening.

He heard nothing. It was cold in the main room, no fire in the fireplace. He kept his coat on. Feeling at the spring button on his knife in his pocket. With his other hand, he picked up a poker from the fire set.

He tried to be methodical. He locked the back door and the front, to make a tough exit for anyone who might try to escape. He did a thorough walk-through, first into the den, then Gerlinde's guest room, and down into the pantry and kitchen and cellar. Nothing. Back up to the ground floor. The doors were still locked shut, and so quiet. He stopped to smell. Oddly, it smelled like nothing at all in here, like a bare refrigerator. That was what the cold did. It equaled all.

He was still warm, with sweat behind his ears, but he kept his coat on—in case he would have to chase someone down. The second floor was next. Up the stairs he went, crouching, one hand grasping the poker, the other clenching the pocketknife, taking a good look around with each step. He checked the bathroom, his bedroom, the upstairs storeroom.

Down at the end of the hall was Max's room. The door was cracked open.

Harry stood at the crack. He looked on through. He saw flesh. A hand. On the bed. A woman's. Someone sleeping? Please, let it be so.

He cracked the door open farther, pushing it open with his knuckles tight around the poker. The door, well oiled, swung open.

"No. Oh, god, no," he muttered.

Irina lay on the bed, facing up. Arms and legs splayed out. She wore a long blue overcoat, her hat on the floor. The white of the snow and clouds from the window cast a pale bright light on her face and neck. Her skin was purplish blue and bloated, dotted with darker spots, her tongue a dark blue ball bulging out, dwarfing her lips. The beige bedspread showed a circle of blood, from below her neck. Harry gasped. Across her throat, he saw, was a thin dark line.

# Twenty-Eight

*WHERE COULD MY IRINA HAVE GONE?* Max thought as he circled the Viktualienmarkt one last time. The open-air market with its ramshackle stalls and tents, kiosks and umbrellas and carts could easily conceal a girl, especially this morning as the snow came down thick for the first time this year. No one liked it coming, and how could they? People walked with their heads bowed and some even swiped at the flakes as if they were venomous bugs flying in their faces.

It was Tuesday, eleven in the morning. He and Irina had planned to meet here and sell their last two Cossack sabers. Irina was going to carry them inside a long blue overcoat hanging from two loops she'd sewn inside. They had laughed about it back at Harry's mansion. He'd seen watches, silverware, pans, sausages, but two infamous sabers inside a long coat? Now he had seen it all. His girl had a blade for each hand. Irina was his pirate—a ravishing Cossack raider.

He stopped to huddle in a side street and survey the square, seeing mostly old women schlepping carts and bags with their old men following. He eyed the traders and what little they had to offer a poor soul to get a starving family through the winter. They brushed snowflakes off each other, off the ragged roofs of their tents and stalls, as if it would help. At least the snow helped keep the bulls away, Max thought, and any confederates of the Soviets sneaking about. To keep warm, he stomped his feet and rammed his fists into his pockets.

They were supposed to meet a half hour ago. Maybe she had the spot mixed up?

A fountain stood near the middle of the square. He bounded through the snow, jumped up onto the fountain rim, and held onto the statue he didn't recognize with so much snow on it, possibly a drummer boy or a girl singing. Here he stood a few feet above the people's heads, in line with the umbrellas and tops of kiosks, but it didn't help him see a thing. It only blurred whiter up here and felt colder.

Noon. Max could see Harry's mansion through the trees in the English Garden as he marched home, his toes numb from the cold. The truth was that he didn't know where else to go. He'd tried the obvious black markets nearby. They had given up their rail car bolthole. Irina didn't have any other haunts or habits here in Munich.

He crossed through the hedge of Harry's rear garden. He stopped, dead in his tracks.

Harry was standing out on the terrace, facing him. Harry didn't wave, or even nod. His arms hung slack at his sides and looked shriveled to the bone. His face, paler than the snow.

Max felt a clogging in his throat, putrid like someone had poured used motor oil down it. His lungs felt flat, he heaved to breathe. He slogged up the steps, his legs like cement now—wet, thick cement. Harry's eye sockets were pink. Harry had something down the front of him. It looked like stew. Then Max smelled it. Vomit.

Max stood face-to-face with Harry, the steam pulsing out of them, onto each other. Harry's chin was quivering. Max pushed at his shoulder. Harry opened his mouth, but nothing came out. Max pushed harder. "What is it? You tell me!" he shouted.

Harry held out his hand. Max's hand found Harry's, and Harry squeezed with both of his.

"I'm so, so sorry," Harry said.

He led Max inside. The mansion was chilling cold as if no one had lived here for months. Harry sat Max down in the den, a serious, somber room of dark woods and a monstrous desk. A room like this offered only a grim reality. Again, and again. Max was so sick of dens, of bureaus, cells—masters, officers, bulls, anyone with rank for rank's sake. They could all go to hell. They were bringing this on him, again.

He surrendered to the urge to run upstairs and jumped up, but Harry grabbed at him and pulled him back into the den. Harry was fighting back tears, and this shocked Max back into the room. He shook Harry's lapels. He said to Harry, "The Cossacks—that what's happened? Someone got to them."

"No, not them," Harry said.

Max's head spun. All turned white, like the snow outside, and the grimy thick oil clogging up his chest seemed to fill his lungs. He couldn't get air, couldn't feel his legs. He was staggering. He felt for a chair, wall, anything. All went black.

Sometime later, Max found he was sitting on a small dais built into the corner of the den. At first he had thought it was a raised platform for a map table or a painter's easel, but, no, it was a stage. Of course it was. There were even holes for stage lights, capped with metal discs.

Certain things came back to Max: Harry had been holding him upright here at the edge of this stage after he had fainted and then flew into a hysteric wail.

The heat from that episode had left Max's head, face. His tears had dried, leaving his windblown cheeks feeling parched. He smiled for Harry, who came back over to him sitting there. Harry had shed his vomit-stained overcoat. Two whiskeys stood on the desk, untouched.

"I must see her," Max told Harry and marched out the den, his little brother in tow.

Two hours later, Max and Harry were back downstairs in the main living room.

"It was strangulation, correct? That's what it is, so let's call it by its name," Max said. It was three hours after his beloved Irina was murdered, and here he was questioning Harry like a homicide lawyer, like a man he had never imagined himself capable of becoming.

He had no choice. They had no time.

"Are the prints safe—the negatives?" he asked Harry.

Harry nodded toward the den. "There's a concealed safe under the floorboards. I have the whole briefcase in there."

"Good. What was used, you think? A cord? A belt?"

"Looks to me like something thinner," Harry said, somber.

"A blade."

The tables had turned. It was as if Max were Harry the rational scientist and Harry was Max, the emotional artist. He had made Harry change all his clothes so that he didn't smell.

"This is going to trouble Gerlinde to no end," Harry said, shaking his head.

"Any reason to suspect her?" Max said.

"No. Absolutely not." Harry said she owed her life to him. Harry had found her sleeping homeless in the English Garden and, assuring her that he wouldn't hurt her, gave her a job just to prove it.

Max had to ask questions. He had to stick with this logic, with this focus that he had somehow found deep within him. It was the only way to proceed. It was true that it seemed every woman he got close to ended up astray, or leaving him, or dead. He didn't care at this moment. He would wail again later. Irina would haunt him, she would, but he couldn't run away from it as he always did. *Face it. Investigate why. Act to correct it.* He was sitting on the sofa facing the raging fire that he and Harry had built together muttering to themselves about how they were going to find the goddamn killer and do him in good. This was going to give him the strength. Reason. Vengeance. Justice done.

Harry found his way back to reality. He splashed his face with water. He slid on his horn-rim glasses, then took them off and put them into a drawer. They spoke their thoughts. They stared out windows, retracing their steps. They paced the room, considering any suspicious connections. Harry had searched the mansion once more and then gone outside, he reported. He had looked for footprints out there. But the snow had covered all. He sat on the edge of the sofa with his back to Max, glaring at the rug. Then he came over to Max and they stood before the fireplace, Harry's shirt collar open, his collarbone lit up hard by the flames.

"I think we should go to this man of yours," Harry said. "Aubrey Slaipe."

Max was prepared for this. He paused a beat, then another as if giving the idea hard thought. "I'm afraid we cannot do that," he said mechanically.

"What if I told you something? Slaipe has an office in my building."

Max's gut squeezed. "He what?"

"It's on my floor in fact. It's not him by name. It's some kind of cover. A trade representative."

"Have you been there? Tell me that you have not been there."

"I have not. I don't think he wanted me to be, or even to know he was there."

The oil filled Max's lungs again, boiling hot from an overworked engine. He lowered himself back down, feeling for the sofa, and sat. "So he was watching you too," he muttered.

"It's likely." Harry didn't sit with Max. He stood over him. "Maybe that's why this Slaipe wants us to continue the way we are, or so it seems? His people or new agency can't touch what we're doing, not officially."

"If that were the case, then all the more reason not to go to him. We can't know what his true aims are. What he or his agency will do. We must keep this isolated."

"We might not be able to."

"No! He might sell out Irina's clan. We dare not let him . . ."

"Just what is it with him and you? Huh? Tell me that."

Max glared up at Harry, who only glared back at him. Max had kept things bottled up. He couldn't tell Harry that he had abandoned Slaipe. They still had choices. They had each other. Max shook his head.

"He might also say that you have been performing quite well on your own," Harry said.

Max slapped at the sofa and bolted up. "How do you know that? How can you?" he choked and spat, "he may claim just as well that I've been doing more damage, and we don't even know to whom. And then he has me in his clutches even tighter. You can understand that, can't you? I know you can."

Harry left a pause where he might have nodded. He turned back to the fire and stared into it a while. "I just thought I should offer the possibility," he said.

"I know. I understand."

"So, it's me and you. We're going to take care of this," Harry said. "I'm talking about Irina's killer now."

"Yes. I am too."

"We do it for her. We do it for young Alex."

"We do it for all of them."

"We'll have to act fast."

"Of course," Max said.

"We do it right before we go."

"But we don't know who it is. We haven't a clue."

"Don't we? Don't we?" Harry turned to Max, a snarl spreading on his face, the flames turning it grotesque.

"You know? You know who it is?"

"Yes. I'm afraid that I do know. And so do you."

# Twenty-Nine

Late afternoon, tuesday, november 6. The light was thinning over Old Town as Harry and Max locked up the mansion with a note for Gerlinde to take a few more days off because Herr Harry was going on a trip. He left money to cover her lost hours and added a little more in case she'd need something to get by on. He only hoped that she wouldn't sense the death in his house, since Germans had become so accustomed to such keen perception.

Harry had told Max the reasons why Irina's killer could only be one person, and Max, calmly, agreed with his assessment. They had cared for Irina's body. Harry suggested he clean her up himself and wrap her in a blanket, spare Max the heartbreak, but Max said, "No, no, I must do it." Harry helped Max carry the body into the bathtub, and then he shut the door behind him on the way out of the bathroom so Max could be alone with her. From his bedroom, as he changed into a warm union suit, Harry heard the water running, and Max was speaking to her in the hushed tones of promises, but there was no wailing, no crying. When Max was ready, they would carry her down to the cold cellar where she could lie hidden and undisturbed.

Harry wore a watch cap, a leather overcoat with a thick black scarf, and wool trousers tucked into double-buckle combat boots, looking nothing like the privileged American official, while Max in his wool cloak, buckskin car coat, high boots, sable hat, and green cashmere scarf tied ascot-style might well have been, on another quest in another era, something like the successful actor he'd always wanted to be.

Yet neither was playing a role, not anymore, not today. Harry felt natural like this and he could tell Max did too, just by his defiant posture.

They had called the *Polizeipräsidium* and asked for Detective Dietz and, after being made to wait three times and transferred twice, were told that *Kriminalkommissar* Dietz was out and they would simply have to try back. Now they cased the street outside police headquarters, working the corners with hand signals to each other, eyeing the officials coming and going.

They found Dietz in the front courtyard out by the scorched statue of a general. A man in a long coat had just hurried off after meeting him, hobbling along, and Dietz watched him while smoking, blowing out a long barrel of the blue vapor like a mistress after good sex.

Harry and Max came up from behind Dietz, from around the statue.

"Dietz," Harry said.

Dietz whipped around. "*Ah, meine Herren.* How goes it? So the good brother's here too." Dietz was holding his cigarette straight up, between two fingers. "What? What's the matter?"

Ten minutes later Harry and Max were leading Dietz north, away from Old Town. Dietz had protested that he couldn't come along because he was on his way home to his family, but Max had stated, "We need your help with something," and Dietz complied. He happened to be wearing warm gear much like Harry's, a bulky wool cap for his head. "Going mountain climbing, Detective?" Max said to him, to which Dietz emitted a thin, squeaky laugh.

It turned dark as Harry led them through the ruins of the university, ducking in and out of doorways, arches, rubble piles. "Where the devil we heading?" Dietz said.

"It's in case we're tailed," Harry said.

They came out again and crossed the Ludwigstrasse heading northeast.

"Sabine Lieser? That where we're going?" Dietz said. "The Standkaserne's this way but it's a good walk from here. Why don't we hail a lift, eh? One of your GI taxis."

Harry said nothing. "No," Max grunted.

Max led them into the English Garden and on through the woods, well north of Harry's mansion now. Max had picked a stretch of dirt trail that made no sound under their feet.

Dietz set a Lucky Strike butt on his lips—Harry snatched it, shoved it into Dietz's pocket.

"No light," Harry said.

"We shouldn't be rushing into anything. I can see something's eating you, but—"

"But what?" Max said.

"Nothing." Dietz shrugged, peering back over his shoulders into the darkness.

They came out of the woods and the cold hit them, stinging Harry's cheeks. He liked it. It kept him fresh. He was getting that old feeling back, surging through his legs and making them lighter, stronger. As they hiked he felt the paratrooper knife in his breast pocket, against his heart.

They reached the bank of a calm lake—the small Kleinhesseloher See, no bigger than a couple football fields in any direction they could see. Max crouched at the gently lapping water a moment, cocking his head one way, and then the other. He headed off along the bank, leaving Harry and Dietz to follow.

A little rowboat was tied off at a crop of water shrubs, the boat camouflaged with branches like a sniper's helmet.

Dietz peered at a darker patch out in the middle of the water. Out there was a little island, about 200 feet long by 150 at its widest. "I don't really care for boats," Dietz said.

Harry said, "You were in the Navy. Weren't you? That's what you said."

"Hah! Yes, the irony," Dietz said. "You know I've never been on this lake? Homegrown Municher and I've never been on it."

"Well, I have," Max said.

The three were crouched in the shrubs around the rowboat, the calm water washing up against it like a giant smacking his lips.

"Get in," Max added.

"Why don't I stay here? Keep watch," Dietz said. "There's a plan."

Max shook his head.

"No? At least let me piss. This cold, this water—"

"No. Get in."

The three stepped in and Max pushed off, Dietz in the middle, Harry up front and Max in the back paddling, all so close their knees could touch each other. Harry faced Dietz and Max, his back to the bow. He never cared for black water of unknown depth either but suddenly he welcomed it, loved the things it could do to a person. He and Dietz rode bolt upright, keeping their balance centered, lean either way and the little boat could pitch over. Steam pulsed from Max as he rowed, his eyes boring into Dietz's back.

About halfway to the island, Max stopped rowing and let them coast toward its bank. A wind had picked up, stirring the waves. Patches of ice floated by. Dietz had hunched over shaking, hugging himself from chill. The detective's face showed nothing.

All was on ice here. Just like Felix Menning in the morgue. Just like Max, in jail. Harry, all this time.

"Irina is dead," Max said.

Dietz's head popped up. He showed a frown, a sorrowful raise of eyebrows. "No . . ."

"Someone killed her."

"Oh, dear. I'm sorry for your loss. I really am."

Max only grunted. Harry pulled his stubby Mauser HSc pistol from his coat and trained it on Dietz.

Dietz seemed to fight a snicker. "Harry? What in the devil are you doing? You know that's a German cop's pistol? Come on now."

The safety was already off, Harry made sure of that. He cocked it.

Max said, "Irina, she must have found you in Harry's mansion."

"What? Me? No." Dietz whipped his head around. The boat rocked and he grabbed at the edges, all white knuckles. "Now you two listen. You got this wrong! Someone's been feeding you a line."

"Yes, they have," Harry said. "When I came for those prints? I didn't tell you that Max was sitting in a jail cell, not exactly. I only said someone had fingered him to the cops. Never said they kept him or what for exactly. Yet you already seemed to know. I can see that now in hindsight. Sure, you're a cop, but you're in a different section. So how could you know—unless you tipped them off yourself?"

"It was a tactic to keep me frozen, until you devised a way to serve up the Cossacks," Max added.

Dietz formed a broad smile. His teeth and eyes glistened from some unknown, faraway light. He held up a hand. "Please, gentlemen—"

Harry grabbed at the boat's edges and rocked it violently, splashing water onto their shins, feet. Let them pitch into the black, icy water, he only wanted Dietz to shut the hell up.

Dietz glared at Harry.

Harry said, "You were glad to put a corpse on ice for me because it kept you in the know. On the scent. Do anything to help, wouldn't you? You were always there at the ready. Take the day I stepped out of that *Konditorei* after meeting Sabine Lieser. You just happened to run into me."

Max said, "You were dealing with Felix Menning. He was a contact of yours. But then I happened to off the little bastard, didn't I? Mine was a necessary ploy, but it was none too splendid for you because it was only a matter of time before he gave up the Cossacks to you—and to the Soviets."

Dietz shook his head.

"Irina, she went back to the mansion for something, who knows. Maybe her coat wasn't long enough for those two sabers. Something. Any case, she found you there. Looking for those negatives. But you didn't find it, did you? No. Because I had them safe."

"Now you listen to me one moment."

"Someone—your controllers, whatever you call it—needed all copies, all the negatives," Harry said. "Who are they? Our friends at the Soviet Repatriation Mission? The ones who like to court Sabine Lieser? But she wasn't the marrying type, was she? Wouldn't give them a thing. Or is it some other Soviet patron who uses you, but less polite, same old thugs but with a new playbook? Someone who knows more about you than we Americans do?"

Dietz held up a hand with his arm at a right angle, like a man taking an oath or, not so long ago, giving the Hitler Salute. "Hold on. Gents, listen. I understand your pain. Your girl bought it, Max, and that's a rough thing to bear, but—"

"You didn't even ask how she bought it," Max said. He leaned into Dietz, the steam of his breath swirling around Dietz's face. "She was strangled, from behind her back."

Dietz's eyes twitched.

"You were doing all right," Harry said. "Especially after I was stupid enough to tell you about the Cossacks, where they were even. I almost, unwittingly, sold them all down the river, all those people my brother works so hard to save. Irina, and . . . You were going to let me."

A grimace spread across Dietz's face. His arm had lowered, and he added a sigh. "Well, I can see that explaining is pointless. So. Let's just get ashore and off this icy water, shall we?"

# Thirty

Harry and max calculated that holding Dietz captive on the island would force him to confess his vicious game. He would tell them he killed Irina. He would tell them if he'd yet betrayed the Cossacks' hideout to anyone. The tiny isle had a dim gray bank ringed with skinny black birch trees that trickled from the wetness, combining with the lapping of the waves to sound a menacing peal like the percolation of a steam locomotive. This wasn't exactly reassuring, but they had chosen it for inaccessibility: Even if they were followed, Dietz's accomplices would have to find a boat somehow.

Their rowboat eased onto the bank with a little thud and shifted sideways in the soggy earth. Here the snow survived only as wet clumps soon to be mud.

Max had Harry's service Colt pistol. It extended from his fist. Once it would've stunned Harry to see his brother the actor wielding a gun, but now it was probably stranger to see Max in stage makeup or reading a script.

They frisked Dietz, which produced a pack of various American cigarette butts, his wallet, and a tarnished metal German pocket-knife in his sock. They tossed the knife far out into the water. They walked Dietz to the center of the island, Dietz with his head up, peering around.

Harry said, "That man with you at the statue? In the long coat? Probably hobbling from two sabers in his coat. Do I have it right? Sabers that you sold him?"

Dietz snorted, shaking his head.

It was tough to tell where the far bank of the island ended—it was so dark there. In the middle of the island, a clearing held a trench half-covered with tent cloth and camouflaged with grass and shrubbery. The T-shaped trench had a fire pit branching off the main dugout. More tent material had been laid out as a barrier to the mud. Down inside were crates and boxes and bedrolls.

Seeing it, Max sighed from deep in his chest. This trench, he'd told Harry, was where he and Irina first holed up in Munich when the weather was still fair. Irina hated it here, as had Felix Menning, so Max scored the three of them that cellar hovel where Harry met the corpse of Felix.

Max shoved Dietz down into the trench. Dietz stumbled, the groundcover shifting under his feet. The detective climbed onto a crate, sat on it, and looked up at Harry and Max standing side by side and staring down on him from the edge.

Dietz snickered. "So, what is it now? Torture me? If that is your game, then, oh sure, I confess everything—I killed your girl for a couple swords. But listen to me first. Make sense of this. Please. Why would you find me in plain sight if I just killed someone? I would hide out, would I not?"

"You don't have to," Harry said. "You're a plainclothes cop. Know everyone. We're the ones underground."

Dietz stared at Harry. He seemed to take in Harry's darkly utilitarian outfit for the first time. Something appeared to click in him, as if he realized he was misjudging the American Harry. "Harry, listen to me," he said. "I have a family."

Max cleared his throat and spat.

"You saw them," Dietz continued to Harry. "My wife. Why would I do this? Why?" he clasped his hands together.

"That's exactly what we want to know," Harry said. "We're going to hold you here until you tell us all of it. If you don't, we bring in someone who will help your memory."

Harry didn't tell Dietz who. The truth was, they had no one. Aubrey Slaipe was not an option. Max could have found a thug on the black market. Harry might have tried getting Warren Joyner onboard for this. *Like a Nazi-turned-Red opportunist all to yourself, Major? We got one for you, and he's a killer to boot.* They had lots of rope here and a rag for Dietz's mouth, not to mention Dietz's handcuffs. They could keep him here for days. Harry knew that he or Max would gladly get Dietz talking. They didn't even have to discuss it. Each had done far worse.

"I'm telling you all I know," Dietz said.

Max jumped down into the trench. He heaved Dietz off the crate, Dietz landing on his back. Dietz tried to scramble away. Max was sizes bigger than Dietz or Harry and had broader shoulders, yet Harry had never seen Max move like he was now—like a linebacker after a backpedaling quarterback. Dietz's arms and feet flailed in defense as Max pounced on the cop. Max roughed him up and good. Harry heard grunts, smacks and thwacks, pleading. Max finished by patting Dietz down. He climbed back out of the pit huffing, scowling. His green cashmere scarf hung off a shoulder, and he used it to wipe the mud from his face.

"Careful of your ribs," Harry said.

"They're no worse. No handcuffs, but look what I found." Max held up a compact Sauer 38H.

They heard a bleating sound from the trench. Dietz might have been sobbing, *if a snake like that was capable of it,* Harry thought. They gave Dietz a moment, only so Max could catch his breath.

They looked down to find Dietz huddled against a crate, his face a patchwork of bleeding and bulges. He spat blood, and again, and the whimpers subsided.

"I am not a spy," Dietz said, "and that is the sad part about this whole affair." He spat more blood. "It was an accident, all of it. She had a compulsive, irrational suspicion that I was a spy. She was going to report me to the Amis. And when she saw me at your billet, well, one could just imagine—"

"What were you doing at my billet?" Harry said.

"I went there to find you! Irina was there. She came back because of those sabers; they were too hard to carry, as you say. She started up again with this spy business."

"She never mentioned a suspicion to me," Harry said.

"Me neither," Max said.

"She didn't want you to know probably . . . she wanted to prove it herself, I imagine, then she would come to you."

"You strangled her. You slit her throat for good measure," Harry said.

"With a saber," Max added.

"No. That was not me. It was an accident."

A rattle of a sigh left Max. "Did you fuck her?" he barked.

"No!" Dietz pressed his bloody knuckles to his chest. "Listen, let's not get irrational. There was simply something about me that she suspected. The way I survive. She didn't trust it. Everyone needs an enemy, a conspiracy to fear, is that not so? To justify themselves. It's what you're doing here right now. The Allies, the Soviets are starting it all over. I mean, look at us here. Please, *meine Herren . . .*"

A twinge of doubt rippled through Harry's stomach.

Dietz must have sensed it. He shouted: "You will not kill me! You two? What are you, a failed actor, and this Captain Kaspar of legend? The Jews' Robin Hood? Sure, Harry, you are rumored to have hijacked that plunder train once upon a time—if it's even true—but you had a clear purpose then, didn't you? But now? This is not your style. It's too debatable. Your good conscience could not take this. So you're stuck, aren't you? And if you turn me in, then I simply finger your Cossacks to the Amis instead. I would simply have to."

"Go to hell," Max said.

"I'm already there, it appears." Dietz laughed. He stood at the edge of the trench, his head just above it, his fingers digging into the mud of the wall. "You were all set," he said to Harry. "You wear your conqueror's uniform, good posting, fancy mansion, the pretty Ami girl. You could have done so much more with that—"

Harry kicked Dietz in the face. Dietz disappeared with a thud.

Max had turned his back to them. He was glaring up at the black sky, wheezing, muttering at the night. Harry wondered if he had any doubts.

"Maybe we do call in your Major Joyner," Max was saying under his breath, gritting teeth. "You said he's the one who can help."

"No, we need to work on Dietz, get more out of him," Harry said. "Something to show Joyner as proof. Photos might not be enough for him."

Harry and Max stood yards from the trench with their backs to Dietz. The cop had fallen silent, sulking down in the trench.

"What more do you want? He killed her," Max said. He punched at the air and stomped in a circle, glaring at Harry.

How could Harry tell him? If he went to Joyner now, he wasn't certain what Joyner would do with Max. What if Dietz was speaking some truth? The detective might not be enough of a prize. Harry didn't doubt Warren Joyner would help with the Cossacks. Yet, for his efforts, would Joyner also want Max's head on a stick? It was only a little less gamble than Aubrey Slaipe.

"Just say it, why don't you?" Max stepped close, his voice rasping with anger. "You still don't trust me. Think I look a bigger catch than that pig-devil Dietz down there. So suppose I am, Harry? We should take that chance."

Harry didn't have an answer. He could only stare back. They could wait a while. Dietz would lose his cool. He'd already admitted murder. He only called it an accident.

"Give me your pocketknife," Max growled, glaring into the trench.

"No. We don't need more blood, not yet. We need information. First, we let him stew a little."

"Then I need a walk, to clear my head." Max wandered off, out along the tree line where the water slapped and loomed, his silhouette blending with the trees' shadows and the black water as he shuffled along, out toward the far end of the island.

Harry crouched at a far edge of the trench smoking a Chesterfield, keeping one eye on Dietz down there, head lowered, a dark lump. Was the detective praying? Planning his next lie? Harry thought of offering the swine a cigarette, but he spat into the mud instead.

He heard crunches, grunts. He peered around but couldn't see Max. Then he saw shadows flailing among the trees and water, all of it dark shapes. Shadows? There were two?

A shot.

Harry dropped flat to the earth and pulled his Mauser out aiming, but at what?

"Max!" he shouted.

Max had crawled back into view, just inside the tree line. He faced something, someone at the dark end of the island behind trees. He had his Colt out. He lay still, his cloak spread out like wings. Was he hit? The shot hadn't sounded like his Colt.

"Stay down," Harry muttered. He regulated his breathing so he could hear. He heard a long groan but couldn't tell where it came from as if this very island itself was giving it off, sick of the violence it supported. He switched his aim to Dietz's trench, where he thought he'd seen Dietz's head. He wasn't sure now.

He heard simple German and broken Russian. It wasn't Max. It was between Dietz and someone else—another man on this island? Dietz must have had a tail as backup. His tail had somehow followed Dietz here. They were snarling at each other, Dietz at the far end of the trench and the other man somewhere behind the trees. Dietz insisted his man come to him, but the man refused to show himself.

"Calm now," Dietz was saying. "That's it. Now, go to the one closest, get his gun."

"What about the Ami? He'll shoot," said the man.

"No, he won't," Dietz said. "Just do it."

Max was only ten yards from the man behind the trees, while Harry had to be forty. The man moved out into the open to get at Max, a slow crawl. Harry aimed but had no good shot. He might hit Max from here.

"Max! Max!" Harry shouted.

The man reached Max. Max's silhouette barely moved, he didn't seem to fight it. The man wrangled the Colt out of Max's hands. Now he used Max's body as cover.

"It's over," Dietz said to Harry from his trench. His voice had lost its shriek. It was somber, as if he were a cop again, telling a family member of a traffic death. "You're no cowboy gunslinger, Harry."

# Thirty-One

HARRY STOOD WITH HANDS UP. He set his Mauser down on the ground so that Dietz could see it. Dietz climbed out of the trench, picked up the Mauser, and frisked Harry with the other hand, methodically, the plainclothes cop doing his job. He took Harry's paratrooper knife and dropped it into his pocket. He patted down Harry a second time.

Harry stood poised, his legs pumping with blood like a sprinter reading to launch. Dietz said, "All right, go ahead."

Harry rushed across the clearing to Max. Dietz's man had flopped Max onto his back to frisk him, Max groaning. The man was staring down at Max with terrified eyes set in a thick brow. He moved away, backing up toward Dietz who urged him over in Russian.

Max stared up at Harry, his arms propped up like a baby waiting to have its diapers changed. Blood was seeping through his sweater and ascot, from the chest. Harry tore at Max's sweater and shirt as Dietz and his man argued again in the distance, Dietz demanding his Sauer pistol back. Blood soaked everything under Max's shirt, sticky, wet, hot. Harry kept feeling around, his hands turning gooey until Max finally grunted, "*Aua*! Quit poking around—it's up on the chest somewhere, the shoulder. *Autsch*."

"You! Come back over here," Harry barked in German at Dietz's man.

Dietz let his man return. He produced a flashlight. Harry grabbed it, flicked it on. Seeing the wound, he heaved a sigh of relief. He slapped Max's hand onto his upper chest where the shoulder and arm met. "Keep pressing there and do not let go," he told his brother.

Dietz kept Harry and Max down in the trench. Dietz's man—his hired stooge—looked like any other refugee in his mismatched fatigues and patched wool. He could be anyone from a Yugoslav to Ethnic German Pole. He also had cheekbones like cobblestones, a nose mangled sideways, and Max's Colt now along with his own gun. Harry could care less. All he knew was, the man had offered to help Harry lower Max down to him. Harry ended up telling the stooge to go to hell and expected a smack for it, but he only got a gentle shrug from the stooge. It might be something to exploit.

Dietz knelt over the trench and boasted how his man had trailed them and somehow found a rowboat, waving Harry's Mauser for emphasis. "Earned his lumps today," Dietz said, shouting it for his stooge who now stood out in the middle of the island looking bored as if waiting for a streetcar. Harry sat and placed Max next to him, propped against a crate, Max's hand still pressed to his shoulder to stop the blood flow.

"Spent time on the front, did you, *Kamerad*?" Dietz said to Max. "Look at the irony of it—only now do you get wounded. Well, it's only a graze. So you're lucky."

"And you?" Harry said. "You're a dead man. Anywhere you go."

Dietz spat out a laugh that he cut short with a wince of pain. An eye and the opposite jowl were swelling, grotesque in the shadows and scarce light.

"What, you starting to realize it? You're the man who's on the run now. Sabine Lieser knows where we are. And one Major Joyner of the US Military Police. Yes, Sheriff Joyner. If we don't make contact soon, well . . . it's just a matter of time. He has a whole squad and they have a motorboat."

Harry had to bluff. He'd been a damn fool. They had decided not to tell Sabine because they didn't want harm to come to her. Sabine didn't even know Irina was dead. There had not been time.

Dietz opened his mouth to speak, but no words followed.

"You want to cover your tracks?" Harry went on. "Then you're going to have to kill us. But you've never killed anyone, have you? Maybe a young woman named Irina. But, no, I bet one of your other goons did the job while you kept watch like some spooked weasel." He howled the words at Dietz, it forced its way out like hot spew. "That was the accident—she wasn't supposed to get the blade too but that's all a goon knows when a job goes fubar."

Dietz had stiffened.

"That about right? Maybe you even handed him the saber. You panicked, see."

Dietz aimed the Mauser back on them.

"You're not man enough. Because you set up others to do that kind of work. Like your thug there. Your toady." Harry shouted toward Dietz's man: "What's he paying you, huh? Not enough, I'm sure of that!"

"Leave him out of this—"

Harry laughed. "You're vermin, Dietz. Doesn't matter who's running the show, what regime, as long as there's a weasel's work to be done, you stand ready, the ready rat-fink . . ."

Dietz sighed. "You don't think I agonize? I do."

"Tell it to Joe Stalin," Harry said.

"Uncle Joe put you up to this," Max added.

Dietz stared at muddy earth.

"Why don't you do it?" Harry said. "Do it now, right here. Only problem is, Joyner's squad might just collar you on the way out and then what?"

Dietz said nothing. He twitched. His thoughts must have been screaming at him so loud inside his head he wouldn't hear himself talk if he tried.

A silence crept in, and it settled them, he and Max down in the trench, Dietz's stooge standing alone, and Dietz, all alone. The dripping of the trees and slapping of the waves returned as a belching, slapping clamor.

"You're running," Max said to Dietz. "That's your plan."

Dietz looked to Harry. "You know, my wife, she knew nothing of this . . ." His eyes had glossed over, welling up. "My children," he muttered.

"I can see that they're taken care of," Harry said.

Dietz sighed, and his voice wheezed, oozing weariness suddenly. Harry recognized that fatigue. POWs sounded that way. It was finally over for them, and their lungs gave it away.

"What about your wife?" Harry said.

"I'll get her over, somehow," Dietz said.

A born Municher, following her traitor husband without her children to the Soviet Union or some equally ghastly protectorate? The Soviet zone of Germany alone would be horrifying for a Catholic wife from the Free State of Bavaria. A woman like her would never go.

Dietz straightened up. He was standing on his toes. Squinting, peering around. He shouted, "You get back here!" He hissed under his breath, "Shit, shit."

Dietz's stooge was long gone. Dietz shouted for him again and got nothing, only that lapping water and the whistle of a little icy wind coming on.

Harry said, "Looks like your new boy scout's gone run out on you, Detective."

Max started laughing, from deep in his belly. It had to sting bad but he couldn't help it, and he groaned between his laughs.

Dietz jumped down into the trench, grabbed a pair of cheap binoculars, slung them around his neck, and climbed back out. He sloshed through the mud toward the end of the island, Harry's Mauser and his Sauer in each hand, keeping one barrel pointed Harry's way.

"I can see that stooge already, back in his little boat rowing away," Harry said to Max.

"Row, row, row your boat . . ."

Dietz shuffled back to them. His pistol dangled from his hand as if it might drop any second. The butt of Harry's Mauser bobbled from a pocket.

"Look at it like this—it's a wash," Harry said to Dietz.

"Your man didn't like what he saw," Max said. "You aren't worth the cabbage."

Dietz laughed, a sad chuckle. He waved his gun at them one last time. "I sincerely hope that I never see either of you two ever again," he said and turned from them.

Dietz headed off hobbling, dragging one foot after the other and one shoulder lower like a hunchback, and he had the face to match. His steps made sucking noises as he headed across the island, back for the rowboat they had come in on.

Harry pulled himself up, grabbing at the edge of the trench. "The Soviets are going to kill you too!" he shouted after Dietz. "We saw it with our own eyes. You saw it. Those photos."

Dietz's silhouette blended into the tree line, finding the darkness. Somewhere out there was a man who hated boats.

Half an hour later. Down in the trench. Max was shivering. Harry found the driest possible blanket and draped it over him. He made Max keep his arms to his sides and pressed the wound at Max's shoulder. They should be dressing the wound, but Harry had little to work with. There was nothing here but mud and sand and ice-cold stagnant water.

"He can't know where the Cossacks are, not exactly," Harry told him. "In the Šumava, sure, but it will take him time."

"Save it," Max said. "Next thing you'll be telling me we just had tough luck, is all. So American of you. You don't understand. For me and so many this is the way it is. Our natural state. That wind of fate never blows right for me. That's what scares me, you know? That cruel wind could have—could still—lead to the gallows for me. But for you, it's like you've been riding on a steel track—like it's your birthright. Always has been."

"Till now. So don't go and tell me you're envious. I went right off the rails today. I gave it all away to Dietz. And now look at us."

"One must try," Max said.

Harry placed a Chesterfield in Max's mouth. "I thought we were better at this, the shit we've both been through."

"I don't know. Maybe he did us a favor, in one way."

"How you figure?"

"Let's not kid ourselves. One of us was going to kill Dietz. Perhaps this was why we really brought him here. I know I wanted to do it, the more he sang."

Harry thought about it. After what he had once done to a wicked and heartless man, doing in Dietz would have been a cakewalk. His pleasure. "Supposing we'd just killed the bastard at first sight out on the street, dumped him in a rubble hole."

"That's being too good at this."

Harry nodded. He glanced around the trench for items he could use to make a fire.

A tear ran down Max's cheek. "Listen, brother. If anything happens to me? Just lay me down in your cellar with Irina. It's cold enough down there to preserve us both until buried. That's where I want to be—"

"Shut up with that. Melancholic actor. Besides you're no Gary Cooper."

"Says you."

Nothing was dry enough to make a fire. The trees had to be soaked through. A light rain began to fall, laced with wet snow, tapping at the half-cover of tarp. Harry watched as little pools formed on it. How long would that last before it started dumping into the trench or come crashing down on them?

"Bastard took my pocketknife," Harry grunted.

"I liked it better in that freight car," Max said.

"Me, I beg to differ," Harry said but he felt a shiver, and another. He tried to cloak it with coughs so that Max wouldn't panic. Harry's arms were stiffening as he pressed at Max's wound. How long could he keep this up? His wrists felt like they were falling asleep from it. Or was it the cold?

Three hours gone. Harry and Max huddled together, against each other, Harry using his weight to press his shoulder into Max's wound.

"They used to say on the Eastern Front that the cold, it just takes you to sleep. And that's it," Max said.

"Stop it, will you?"

Four hours. Harry checked Max's pulse—Max was only sleeping. He heard something. He heaved himself up, slapped Max's hand on his wound, untangled himself from the blanket, and stood, his legs stiff and his toes numb.

Men were shouting. Light beams flashed and shot up into the sky, the rays rippling along the water. Headlights. Harry ran to the tree line behind them along the far bank. He could make out silhouettes across the water. The opposite shore was closer on this side. Men in uniform, men with shovels. Flashlights.

"Over here, over here!" Harry shouted as he rushed over bouncing off thin trunks and sagging branches as he found the bank. "Over here!" He stomped into the bitterly cold water, splashing it, waving his arms.

The flashlights shot his way, the beams not near long enough to reach him. Yet they had heard him.

# Thirty-Two

MAX WOKE. HE LAY ON HIS SIDE. Daylight in the room made him squint. He faced black shelves on burgundy wallpaper. On the shelves stood dark little statuettes of gargoyles, winged serpents, warriors with horse bodies, African warrior heads. Max felt a twinge of pain in his shoulder. He felt for his wound. It was bandaged. He was wearing an olive green wool shirt, US Army issue. He turned onto his back, craning his head to face the room. He saw a chaise lounge exactly like his—purple with black fringe—but this one was empty with a pillow and folded blanket stacked neatly atop it. The burgundy wall across had more black shelves with more of the arcane statuettes. It seemed like a psychoanalyst's salon but for twins. He wondered if it was Freudian, or was it Jungian? Either way it was far too odd. *This room could use a piano or a bar, something with pep*, he thought.

Then he remembered. Irina. Dietz. The Šumava. Young Alex was still there.

His eyes burned and he wiped at them, but no more hot tears would come out.

He remembered a predawn work detail had appeared on the opposite bank of the lake—GIs with German POWs. The GIs made the POWs rustle up a boat. Harry had the GIs take them straight to a Major Warren Joyner with the US Military Police.

Max was lying in Major Joyner's billet.

An American medic had sewn him up and dressed his wound. After that, Max woke once to see Harry sleeping across from him as the dawn streamed in blue-gray from the bay window, a Wilhelmine behemoth with vast panes, ornate framework and enough lace curtains for a window double its size.

It was Wednesday. November 7.

Hartmut Dietz was long gone.

They had to get the Cossacks out and now.

Blinking, letting the full daylight shock him awake, Max heaved himself up to sit and scanned the room for his clothes. He rotated his arm and stretched it out, the pain beating his heart faster but not adding much more pain. He could keep going like this.

He heard voices behind the shut door. "Harry?" he said.

The door swung open. A man strode in wearing the same olive green shirt as Max but with the sleeves rolled up. Max remembered— this was Major Joyner. With his red face and bull-legged stance, the major did look like a sheriff. Max could see him guarding a log cabin with a rifle like on the cover of a Karl May novel. This must be a good thing, Max told himself.

"What time is it, sir? Still morning?" he said.

"The corpsman told me it's only a graze, but a close one just the same," Major Joyner replied, his voice booming but hoarse. "You're one lucky man."

"Thank you, Major. Me, lucky? I doubt this very much. I do appreciate the medical attention, but what time is it? Where's Harry? We must get moving—"

Harry entered holding a mug of coffee. Max could smell it. Harry's other hand carried Dietz's shabby briefcase with the prints and negatives of St. Stephanus. Harry patted Max on the leg and sat on the chaise lounge opposite. "How you doing? Take some coffee? It's real."

Max shook his head. "What time is it?"

"Eleven in the morning."

The room had a writing desk of what looked like black marble with a matching chair. Joyner picked up the chair as if it were made

277

of cardboard and set it between the ends of the two chaises. "This is one nasty room," the major said. "I never go in here. It's the way I found it when they billeted me here."

"We're just happy for your help," Harry said, not looking at Max.

Harry was acting different, Max saw. He wore his uniform even neater than usual. He spoke with a deference Max had never heard. Max realized he'd never seen his brother among his fellow American superiors. Was Harry always like this, or was it because Harry had pinned all of their plans on this man?

To push the issue, Max added, "I'm indebted as well, Major, but we must get moving."

Joyner looked to Harry, who said to Max, "I've told Major Joyner everything."

"Everything?"

Harry nodded, slower than usual. "I told him about our stranded refugees."

"It appears you showed the major the photos as well." Max looked to Joyner, who nodded. "And, did you tell the major who they are—"

"He told me," Joyner cut in. "Cossacks. Ukrainian Cossacks. The white kind—as in the kind who don't like Soviets. The kind who fought with the Germans. Your brother didn't want to tell me that. I made your brother tell me that."

"Ah. I see. But we must go. The Soviet Army could be combing the Šumava by now," Max continued and moved to stand.

Joyner only stared back at Max. His hands were planted on his knees like a commando ready to leap from a plane. The major reminded Max of those wartime Americans who knew exactly why they were over here and what they were doing. Sergeant Smitty, rest his soul. Aubrey Slaipe. Harry was probably like that too back in May of '45. And yet, something about Joyner was knocking even Harry for a loop, Max could see. Harry gazed at Joyner and then at Max as if the major were a stranger who'd just burst into the room.

"You want something first," Max said to Joyner. "Is that it?"

Joyner's lower lip protruded, and it was all the confirmation Max needed.

"I will tell you all about me," Max said. "If that's what you require."

"Tell me what exactly?" Joyner said.

Harry stood up and cut in, cracking a nervous smile, "Maxie here, he was just a German grunt private. That's what happened to actors in Germany. What happens to them everywhere. They're disposable. Right, Max?"

"It was not just actors that it happened to," Max said.

Harry turned to Major Joyner. "You know about the Cossacks. I told you about that Felix Menning character, how he found Max with the Cossacks, but this Felix was one nasty type—"

Max grabbed at Harry's elbow to shut him up. He had used his bad arm and it stung, but what was a little more ache? "You mustn't protect me, brother," Max said. "This man here needs to know, and I want him to know."

Max told Warren Joyner everything. About Operation Greif, about their false flag operation in the Ardennes, about Felix Menning and Kattner killing the MP GIs. Max wanted to flee all along but couldn't. Yes, they had hastily inducted him into the SS, but he killed no one and didn't even fire his gun and he certainly had nothing to do with the Malmedy massacre that was transpiring at the same time—with Max's sort of luck, those SS would've shot him as an American prisoner.

As Max spoke, Harry slumped, staring at his fingers clenched with nothing to grasp. But Joyner wanted it all, and Max gave it to the man.

Max finally did run, he told them, but this only led to the snowbound, cursed DeTrave villa. Then he told the part that not even Harry knew. Cruel fate left Max, posing as an American lieutenant, stuck together in that villa with an American CIC captain named Aubrey Slaipe and a sergeant named Smitty. The DeTrave woman, a Belgian fascist, deceived Max and attacked the Americans. Because of that, and of Max's own failure to act, he caused the death of Sergeant Smitty and conceivably Captain Slaipe. Max ran. Slaipe could have died. He lost an arm instead. Max could have saved it by sticking with Slaipe instead of fleeing underground, back into Germany.

Harry had turned to Max and he stared, unblinking. One tear had leaked out, down along Harry's nose. Harry had to be thinking of their parents and what they would think of this.

"Thank you for your candor, Herr Kaspar," Joyner said.

Max and Harry watched the major leave his chair. Joyner stood over at the window. Joyner sighed. He cleared his throat.

"Sir?" Harry said. "I talked to Sabine Lieser. She's ready to move on her end, just like we talked about. Sir?"

Joyner said nothing. He touched the lace curtain, feeling it with fingertips. Staring out at the wind that was stripping the trees of last leaves.

"Major, I will turn myself in," Max said. "Tell your men anything you wish, just as soon as we get them out."

"I checked with the Munich police," Harry added. "Hartmut Dietz hasn't shown up this morning, no one's heard from him. We have to assume he's already fled east, made contact possibly . . ."

Joyner turned to them, filling much of the large window with his frame.

"No," Joyner said.

"No?" Harry said.

"You see, I'm rotating back, Captain."

"Stateside?"

"In two days. An early release." Joyner flashed a smile, but it looked more like a wince. "Truth be told, I'm not in the best of health." The boom had left his voice, leaving only a wheeze.

"I don't understand," Harry muttered. "Wait, you mentioned a nurse once."

"Yes. They're saying it's something to do with my blood. Getting weaker, and fast."

Harry opened his mouth to speak again. Joyner held up a hand to stop him and he gave Max a hard look. "So, here is what I'm prepared to do," the major said. "I won't do anything. I won't run you in. I will simply go home."

"But sir—"

"Shut up, Kaspar. Just so that we are clear—it's not because I'm sick. Do you know that those Ukrainian Cossacks fought for the Germans in Italy? That is exactly where my son bought it. And this man here, your own brother . . ."

Max felt weak in his gut, his stomach rife with a consuming nausea. He closed his eyes to this, what was happening, what he heard. "You can't do this," he blurted.

"I can," Joyner said. "I refuse. I came here to fight Germans, not Soviets."

"Who's fighting?" Harry said.

"So stand me against a wall for it!" Max shouted. "I'm yours. Just go help them."

Joyner shrugged.

"So that's it?" Harry said. "You just leave those people in the lurch like this?"

"Let fate have them," Joyner said. "The same fate that took my son."

Harry stood and lunged, waving at the air, shouting spittle: "Those people didn't kill your son, Max here didn't kill him—"

"Didn't they? Didn't he?" Joyner stood with his chest out, daring Harry to keep coming at him. "I am helping, in my way. I could do a lot worse—to you even, Captain. All right? So that's it. You two are on your own," the major said calmly, as if concluding a meeting about clerk assignments.

He left the room, closing the door behind him.

Max and Harry, mouths open, heard the major walk down the hallway to his foyer, leave his own billet, and slam the front door shut.

Fifteen minutes later, Max rode with Harry in the rear seat of a staff car that cruised the broad avenues west of Old Town past neoclassical ministries and museums and onetime Nazi party temples and manors of nobility, many of these fine sandstone frontages and granite columns largely untouched from the bombs, bullets, carnage. Joyner had called for the staff car and instructed the driver to take Max and Harry anywhere the men said. It was his final act. Max and Harry sat in silence. Max glared at their young driver's big ears. He felt an unnatural urge to tear at the fine leather of the seats. Harry had a Chesterfield hanging from his lips, but he hadn't bothered to light it. The briefcase of prints and negatives stood between them.

"You picked a hell of a time," Harry said.

"I had to tell the major. I should have told you sooner—much sooner."

"No, you did the right thing," Harry said after a pause.

Max could tell something was lodged in his brother's brain, nagging at him. He kept touching the briefcase and jerking his hand away as if the thing were a pan too hot to handle.

"We're still doing this, correct?" Max said.

"I should be the one asking you. I fucked it all up, Max. First, I misjudge Dietz. Then Joyner. 'You're on your own,' the man says—some sheriff he is. Every man for himself? Is that what we came over here for?"

"I can't blame the man," Max said. "Pain, fear, they can destroy any old dream."

Harry yanked his cigarette. "Look: You did what you could at that villa in the Ardennes. What could you do? That Belgian woman was determined, and she saw no way out. War brings it out in a person."

Max threw up his hands. He'd gone over it so many times. He should have given himself up sooner. He should have informed on Justine earlier. He should have done a mess of things differently. Stayed in America and given up his acting passion. Come to Germany but joined the Nazi party for better acting gigs. Later, once he'd recognized the evil, he should have joined the anti-Nazis. And so many variables in-between. He too had his steel track, only it wasn't gilded and neither was Harry's now, it seemed.

They sat through a long pause in which one of them might have shouted: So what in the hell are we going to do now? It didn't need to be said.

Harry was staring out the window, still deep in thought. "I picked the wrong goddamn horse," he muttered.

The staff car turned north at the Königsplatz, slowing for the narrower street that would skirt them around Old Town and deliver them to Harry's mansion. On the horizon, the broken spires and towers loomed above the scraggly trees.

"The major's right, in his way. He's still helping by not helping," Max said.

Harry wasn't listening. He was sitting bolt upright. The sun blazed through a break in the clouds and was streaming into the car, lighting up Harry's whiskers as he peered out, checking the street signs. He was clutching the briefcase to his chest with both hands.

"Harry? What is it?"

"Give me one hour," Harry said. "I'll have the driver drop you off at my billet. I'll meet you back there. All right? And get Sabine there and quick."

# Thirty-Three

Harry stood before the door at the far end of his office hallway—the plaque reading, US Trade Council Representative. Waiting, clutching his briefcase like the sorriest door-to-door salesman there ever was. He had knocked. No one answered. He'd turned the door handle. Locked. He took a deep breath and let it out, telling himself to stay calm. He had made his decision. He was going to cut a deal, whatever it took. On the ride over from Joyner's in that staff car, he saw that Max was brooding, again, about the many things he should have done differently but he couldn't have. There were mistakes in life. There was inescapable fate. Harry wasn't going to let error and sorry luck crush him any more than Max had. He came here to do what he should have done before he let Max talk him out of it.

The door had a peephole. Harry glared into it. He thought he saw light in there. He knocked again. He waited, tapping his foot then grinding it into the floor so hard he could start a campfire from all the friction. He felt someone watching him. He whipped around, but the hallway was still deserted. When he had entered the vacant foyer downstairs, a lone secretary rushed out of the elevator giving him the old up-and-down as if he was just coming off a bender judging from his disheveled state. Harry told himself he wasn't going cuckoo, wasn't letting the old fury get up on top of him. It was the noon hour, sure, but not everyone could be out to lunch. He had never seen or heard it so empty here. He pressed his ear to the door. He swore he heard something inside. He took another deep breath, preparing for action. He knocked hard, rattling the hinges. Nothing. He shouldered the door, harder, then with all he had. *Bang, bang.* It gave, creaked. He stood back a step. Still no one answered.

Slaipe was forcing him into this. He was forcing himself into it. Only action mattered now. Keep moving was the rule. Slaipe was practically begging him to do it.

He took a few steps back, launched off his toes, and hurtled his shoulder at the door with his knees up. The crash clanged down the hall behind him. The frame had cracked, split. He backed up and lunged again. The door gave all the way and sent him scurrying into the room.

It was pitch black inside. He could hear his own scream echoing out in the hallway—he'd shrieked throwing himself at the door without realizing it. His shoulder throbbed. He squinted. The dim beam of hallway light coming in caught no corners of furniture, windows, nothing. He felt at the walls for a light switch. He found one, pressed it. Pressed again. No light came on.

He shuffled backward out into the hallway, shaking his head.

"You there, what's this all about?" a voice said in German.

Harry whipped around. A man in faded worker's overalls stood facing him.

"*Herr Kapitän* Kaspar?"

"Where is he?" Harry barked.

"Who?"

Then Harry realized that it was old Peching the *Hausmeister*, his building's fully vetted janitor and super, depending on the need. Peching held a toolbox in one hand and a brown bag in the other, looking like each was heavier than a cannonball but might explode if he dropped one.

"Oh, it's you, Peching," Harry muttered, pushing sweaty stray hairs off his forehead.

"What happened?"

"Nothing, I . . ."

"Should I call the police, the MPs?" Peching stammered, and his thin tone made it clear the real question was, should he be calling them on Harry? He glanced at Harry's briefcase like it was the loaded cannonball.

Harry rubbed at his face and formed a smile with it somehow. "I was looking for him, you know, the, uh—" He cut himself off, realizing he shouldn't be giving out names. He nodded at the plaque on the door.

"Ah, that," Peching said.

"That what?"

"It doesn't mean anything."

"Please, be clear, Herr Peching. It's very important."

Peching set down his toolbox and paper bag. He produced a flashlight from his vast pockets, stepped into the room, and shined it around. Harry followed, peering in.

The room was small, smaller than his office, and completely empty. With his senses adjusting back to normal, Harry now smelled the musty odor of an attic long unopened. It had parquet flooring sorely in need of refurbishing, wires hanging from the ceiling where there once was a light fixture, only one window covered with tarp, and another door.

"That—where's that lead to?"

"Closet." Peching added a shrug.

"Okay, okay," Harry said, stepping back out and rubbing his face again. "How long has this been empty?"

"Oh, this was always empty," Peching said, meaning since before he was here and he was here well before Harry.

"And the sign?" Harry rubbed at his sore shoulder.

"Was the standard work order," Peching said. "It wasn't due, but you know me—I might be too punctual. Your trade representative on your plaque there is not expected here for some time. Good thing, too." He stood inside the doorway, eyeing the frame, his hands planted on his hips.

"You're going to have to fix this door yourself, aren't you?"

Peching nodded. He didn't seem the least bit curious. The first war and the Great Depression and the last war and now the Americans simply happened, like the worst nasty weather. A man such as Peching didn't ask too many questions because he would not like the answers. Maybe he was a wiser fellow than all of them.

Harry sighed. "Look, I'm sorry about this."

Peching shrugged again.

"I'll make it worth your while. We clear?"

"Clear." Peching held up a hand. "And, I know, I know, you don't have to tell me—mum's the word."

Harry marched down the broad sidewalk, his arms cocked so tensely that his briefcase kept banging at his leg and his other hand wouldn't stay in his pocket. The sun broke through again as he crossed the Königsplatz, and he shielded his eyes from the sheets of sparkle along the wet avenue. He didn't know where his sunglasses went and did not care. He had no other choice left. He first considered it on the way over with Max as they passed this, the King's Square, but then forced it from his mind because he'd resolved to try Aubrey Slaipe on his own. But after finding only a void behind that door, he'd bolted back downstairs and told the waiting staff car driver to drop him off on a corner near the Königsplatz and make it quick.

The address was not far from Warren Joyner's billet. Harry was walking down a tree-lined avenue now. In hindsight, he understood just how cool Slaipe had played it. When Harry noticed Slaipe that one time on his office floor, the man had surely not meant to be seen and was only standing at that door at the end of the hallway with his back to Harry so as to look inconspicuous. Slaipe knew how this would look to a go-getter like Harry. Harry could have sworn Slaipe turned the handle and went inside, he being the supposed new trade rep, but had he really? As Slaipe himself said: Like a con man, he judged and predicted to the point of knowing.

The mansion was less imposing than he expected—no bigger than his or Joyner's, with a low iron gate and an ivy-covered arch over the front steps.

Maddy Barton answered the door herself, wearing a shiny white bathrobe with more of that fir trim. She gave his meager duds and drawn face a once-over and let him in without a word, as if awaiting his arrival. She led him into a corner sitting room similar to Joyner's, only the dark tone and the freakish statues were replaced by floral wallpaper, etched mirrors, and clusters of porcelain figurines. She sat Harry next to her on a green leather love seat. Harry noticed she sat upright, and her robe stayed closed.

"Coffee? Tea?" Maddy said.

"No, thanks. Not right now."

A young woman appeared and Maddy waved her off, saying, "No thanks, honey."

"You got a maid now?" Harry said.

"You don't think I have this place all to myself, do I? We let three other gals have rooms."

"Rough on you?" Harry added a chuckle so she knew he wasn't here to rehash it all.

"In the Army now. A girl's gotta make sacrifices."

They shared a laugh.

"I can see it on you," Harry said.

"Can you? He does love me, Harry."

"And you him?"

"I think so. Yes." Maddy batted eyelids, but it wasn't at Harry. And Harry thought, for the first time, that he'd witnessed Maddy Barton embarrassed. She added, "He wants to take me back with him, you know—stateside like."

"That's good, Madd. I'm happy for you."

"And not as his mistress, either. His wife, you see, she left him."
Maddy was wearing less makeup, Harry noticed. It didn't look half
bad. He thought she looked younger. Who could've guessed her skin
had a natural radiance?

"*Silberstreifen*," Harry said.

"Say again?"

"Silver lining. Every cloud has one. You know."

Maddy repeated the German word.

"That's good. You're getting better."

"It's a start." She gave him a second once-over. "And you? I hear
you've basically deserted your post. What the hell, Harry? Look at
you. You're all banged up."

Harry hadn't thought out how to play this. "I'm all right," he
said, stalling.

"Sure you are. It's your *Silberstreifen*."

"Touché."

"It wasn't my one true goal in life, you know. Marrying the brass
with prospects. Getting the big house in Virginia or wherever we go.
Falling in love."

"I—"

"Just listen. You think my big MO is conspiring in the bedroom
to get ahead. There's more to a gal than that, Harry. Someday women
will be running corporations and even countries, and they're not
going to do it by fucking."

"That will be a good day."

"I want more," Maddy said. She practically shouted it, as if speaking over a loud band.

"Come again?" Harry said.

"I told you. I tried to. I want to do more. Just like you."

"I didn't believe you."

"Well, you can now. So, what is it? You came to me. This is your
last chance."

Harry looked her in the eye. "Do you know how to contact the man I mentioned, this Aubrey Slaipe?"

"You know I don't. But if you need a man like him, I'm your gal."

"Good. That's good."

"Well? It's down to just you and me. You knew it was or you wouldn't be here."

Harry didn't respond. Something held him back. His knee was bouncing and he slapped a hand on it.

"Geez. Don't be so goddamn stubborn, Harry. Do I have to give you a lashing? That what you want? Well, then you're one hell of a dolt. How's that? If you would've gone to more of those to-dos with me, maybe you would know someone special who could help you out better. Sooner."

"You're right."

"You're lucky to know me, you know."

"I know."

"Swell. So why don't you quit your sorry sidestepping and show me what's in that wretched briefcase of yours?"

Four hours later, Wednesday, November 7. Harry was back at his mansion billet, down in the cellar kitchen, sitting around the large prep table with Max and Sabine Lieser. He was holding hands with Sabine below the tabletop. Sabine had cried for Irina when hearing the news of her murder but, having seen so much, and knowing how much they had to do, only needed Harry's hands warm in hers now. Max was pacing the kitchen, a big open area for onetime servants and cooks, all white tile and wood shelving painted a neutral cream color. Harry imagined servants eating at this table, stout women rolling dough on it. Now they had maps out and empty cups of coffee, ashtrays filled. Their gear sat ready in a corner.

Harry had been back here for two hours. He'd told Max and Sabine they would give Maddy Barton four hours. If she didn't come through by then, they were on their own.

The high and squat kitchen windows showed the last dim charcoal-gray of daylight. More wet snow pelted the glass, oozing down, a white sludge.

"It will be snowing there. We should not rule out freezing rain," Sabine said, a statement most Americans would've taken as pessimism. Harry and Max only nodded.

The doorbell. Voices, footsteps. All three stood, gathering in a line before the table. The footsteps were coming for them, down the short flight of stairs.

A man stood at the bottom of the stairs, the sopping flakes still sliding off his leather overcoat. The man had dark hair touched with gray at the sideburns, a strong jaw, and bright eyes, much like a businessman in a shaving cream ad.

Harry couldn't help smiling. Max blew out a breath of relief. Sabine Lieser glared at all of them, including the man, and said in her passable English, "Who in devil's name are you?"

The man let a smile curl a corner of his mouth. He nodded at Harry. "I'm Maddy Barton's colonel, that's who."

# Thirty-Four

THURSDAY, NOVEMBER 8—4:00 P.M. "Keep down, down," Harry whispered in broken Russian. Crouched in the mud and rocks, he had an arm tight around two children, a boy and a girl, a weak but icy stream trickling around their feet. They crouched close, grabbing at him. Harry peeked up ahead. The thirty or so women, old men, and children were crouched just as they were down in this deep, narrow ravine, so isolated that little of the snow falling in the Šumava and adjoining Bavarian Forest could penetrate the dense birch trees here, not yet. Harry was checking for too much steam from their breath. He'd told them all, in sign language and German, to cover their mouths or breathe down into their clothing. Only for a second. Only long enough to let the Soviet Army soldiers pass.

Harry kept his head down. He could hear the soldiers crunching through the snow and underbrush above the ravine. Far away he could hear the idling drone of a military vehicle, possibly a light tank or armored car, waiting for the men to work their way along this thick and dark stretch of the forest. No vehicle was going to pass through here.

Harry and Max had taken two groups through already. As they returned to shepherd another, other groups passed them heading west escorted by Cossack scouts. It was a constant chain, following the stream that snaked through the ravine.

It had been over twenty-four hours since Harry showed Maddy Barton the photos. Maddy fought back tears imagining those poor people being shipped back to the Soviet Union to die in labor camps or be shot outright, and for what? For belonging to a family? For being loving mothers of men? Less than twenty-four hours since a Colonel Bill Partland, boyfriend of Maddy, showed up in Harry's kitchen to offer his services. Colonel Partland was involved in earlier repatriations, he told Harry, Max, and Sabine. One of the largest was the previous winter at a camp in nearby Plattling, the former concentration camp. They sent the Cossacks detained there back at bayonet point, forcing them from bunks in the middle of the night, using force and fear. The Cossacks resisted.

"I saw these Cossack men bash their heads into windows and slit their throats with the glass," Colonel Partland began. "Others started fires in their barracks and threw themselves onto their own goddamn pyres. Meantime, men were hanging themselves from rafters. We couldn't reign them in. We had to deploy tear gas. The delivery was worse. They threw themselves from our trucks. Had one man scream at my horrified translator that we are condemning them—and their children—to die by sending them back, all while stabbing himself in the chest with a railroad tie, a rusty goddamn railroad tie." The colonel paused a moment, his stare blank, distant. "And that was before the Russians got their hands on them. The lynching started before I could even get my men out of there. Through the trees, my boys had to see the poor bastards they'd just handed over already hanging from branches."

Shameful to the core, Colonel Partland called it. It made them all, from the lowliest grunt to Partland himself, feel too much like those SS camp guards they had liberated so many from. Never, ever again, the colonel told them. Max poured him a Scotch.

"The McNarney-Clark Directive, it's just cover for the politicians, the diplomats, the brassy desk generals," Partland declared. "An officer—a good soldier—should never obey an order he believes to be immoral. If nothing else, hasn't this war proved that much?"

"We should be so lucky," Max replied.

"I'm going to help you," Colonel Partland told him. "I have a regiment at my disposal. All I need is one good unit. You give me the details, I'll be there for you and your refugees."

Colonel Partland could keep the Constabulary Corps clear of that sector of the border for just long enough. The colonel also understood the Cossacks might not trust another American involved, especially not a military officer after what had happened at Plattling, so he typed a letter for Max and Harry to carry to the Cossacks—a personal assurance that they would be met and transported to safety. But Partland's plan only safeguarded the people so far; it depended on Harry, Max, and Sabine having a solid plan. He demanded it.

Harry and Max assured him. "I have my end all worked out, Colonel," Sabine told him.

Partland wanted Harry to stay with him on the US side of the frontier. He could not help if Harry were caught on the Soviet side.

"You're already helping enough," Harry told him.

Harry and Max had reentered the Šumava overnight. They had found the Cossacks huddling in groups clutching their few bags, some crying, others arguing. They had traded away the last of their beloved horses for food and for assurances from the few smugglers and farmers who knew of them that they would keep their mouths shut.

Then Max found young Alex, off on his own with his back to them. Harry followed at a respectable distance. Alex was holding onto a skinny birch trunk as if keeping it from tipping.

Max got on his knees and whispered to Alex in his language. Harry's chest squeezing up like he was holding his breath. Eventually, Alex nodded. He turned and looked up to Harry, this time not smiling, his little square jaw set hard. Harry nodded back to him, and with that Max walked Alex over to join a group of women who gathered around him, enveloping him.

Max trudged back to Harry, his eyes wide but unseeing, holding out a hand clawed as if feeling for something to hold onto. Harry wrapped an arm around Max's shoulder to steady him.

"I told him she is there waiting for him," Max said, a tear running down and off his chin. "It was the only way. The only way . . ."

The Soviet patrol passed and it kept going. Harry looked up ahead again. Max was there at the front clutching two children just as Harry was. One was Alex, huddled so close he was inside Max's coat. A young Cossack man—their scout—clattered up the ravine and peered out over the plateau of forest, making sure the patrol was gone. He took a while. Making double sure. Then he clattered back down and they moved on, a chain of hunched backs.

They were higher up than it seemed down in the long ravine. The mountains around them brought fog along with the powdery snow, which helped cover them. Yet they were dressed lighter, for fleeing, so they could never stop long. If one of those Soviet patrols stopped to make a fire, hunt, or wait for a vehicle broken down? They could freeze to death hovering in hiding.

Harry pushed them along, holding hands, patting backs, whispering encouragements. Ahead as behind, as all around, the narrow birch trees loomed, all but the tops having lost their leaves like an army of giant fish skeletons standing in wait. The group skirted a small meadow, passed through more forest, and moved along a larger clearing, a high valley dusted with snow. They stood at the tree line huddling, looking across.

Harry looked to Max, who said, "Listen, everyone. We have just crossed over into Germany—into the American Zone of Occupation."

There came no excited talk, hugs, or tears of joy. The people only stared, wide-eyed, expecting more instructions.

"Look across that valley. Look very hard. You see those objects just beyond the trees? Those dark shapes? Those are the soldiers of the American Army. They are here to help you. The refugee official is also there." Harry looked down the line. All were holding hands, the women, children, men, some propping each other up. The line ended at Max.

"You are all very brave," he told them. "Now, come along."

They walked through the trees now, huddling no more. They talked openly, and Harry even heard joy in their voices. But they were so tired, and the steam pumped out of them. In the wood on the other side of the valley, American GIs waited, standing about in little groups, smoking. They kept their guns out of sight. Harry and Max had been clear about that—the Cossacks didn't need to see more guns. Two troop trucks stood inside the wood. Colonel Partland sat in a command car with Sabine Lieser and two assistants from her DP camp. As Harry and Max led the group of Cossacks in, Sabine rushed out and watched from the hood of the car so that they could see her, a civilian. "They should see a woman," she had told Harry.

Alex was wandering the clearing looking for his mother. Max followed him as a parent would a toddler walking for the first time. Eventually, he took Alex's hand and walked him over to Sabine. She smiled for Alex, crouched down low to him. He stared up at her, his face blank. "Tell him, like we talked about," she said to Max. "Do it."

Max spoke a few words in his ear. Alex nodded. He went away with Sabine.

"I told him that his mother is a great hero. Sabine will take care of the rest. I fear that boy will hate me forever," Max muttered to Harry.

"He will not. Just look at me—I did not," Harry said, patting his chest.

They shared a grim smile.

Farther back, Sabine had a tent set up with a little table inside where she took their names—and gave new ones. A trunk had stacks of passports, most the so-called Nansen passports, created in 1921 by the League of Nations largely for Russians left stateless by the Russian Revolution and the ensuing Soviet Union. To obtain them, Sabine had gone to consulates, used up all her favors, wheeled and dealed, and in the end, accepted many she knew could not be real. The rest of the passports were a mix of nationalities, some of these also fake. Yet they were good enough to get these people where they needed to go.

The Cossacks wandered into the clearing that held the trucks, Sabine's tent, and Partland's command car—this was the way it went down every time, with every group. Like cats in a new home, they were allowed to simply sniff things out, look around, get used to their surroundings. No one touched them until they were ready. The trucks were open, but no one called them up into them. In the trucks waited those from previous groups. They stared down, a few calling out a weary welcome. Then they exchanged words, questions, demands. They whispered.

"No one's hurting you, forcing you?"

"No. It's all very casual, no hurry at all."

"It isn't a trick, you think?"

"I can tell you it is not, friend. Come on up . . . when you're ready."

They could take their time. Sandwiches, water, and coffee were set out in Sabine's tent. The children, women, elderly stood in the clearing nibbling the sandwiches. Talking. Keeping close together. Eyeing Sabine and the odd green soldiers who stood around so casually and took no notice of them. With time, the people climbed into the trucks, and their friends and family helped them up. The women helped up young Alex. Max waved at him. Alex waved back.

And Harry and Max were already off again, to help the last group over.

Near midnight. The last group was the Cossack men.

On the way back to the settlement, Harry and Max had another close encounter with a Soviet Army patrol. This patrol moved with purpose as if it had a clear destination, coming up on Harry and Max so fast they had to lie flat under the remains of a fallen log.

They found the settlement deserted. "I know where they are," Max said.

Farther south, they discovered the Cossack men hunkered down in a hut along a stream, thirty of them crammed in there like too many chickens in a coop. They had left behind the few rifles and pistols they had. They had all agreed on that. Their meager worn guns wouldn't help them against so many Red troopers and would only start a war if not endanger the rest making it over the border. Harry and Max carried no weapons, not even a new pocketknife. What could a Colt or a Mauser do now that it could not before? Harry wasn't up against one man anymore but the relentless machine of a system.

"The rest have made it," Max told them, and it raised the men's spirits enough to get them moving. They navigated through the mud and underbrush and fog and snow like the smallest rodents in the forest, taking an hour to move ten feet if they had to, speaking little, using hand gestures. Soviet soldiers were everywhere. They could hear engines and occasional shouts. The settlement was probably the Russians' command post by now, Harry couldn't help realizing.

They came up to the valley from the north. After climbing on his stomach to the peak of a small hill, and then shinning up a thick birch tree, one of the Cossacks returned muddied, scratched-up, and panting to report that Soviet soldiers had taken up positions at the tree line on the eastern edge of the valley. He saw the soldiers below him there, their silhouettes mixing in the moonlight and snow of the valley—the Red troopers stood right on the border, keeping watch.

Could Colonel Partland know this on the other side? Could his binoculars pick up any of it? Had he sent out scouts? Harry and Max would just have to trust him.

"I only hope the Cossacks over there don't know, or they'd suspect a deal," Max whispered to Harry. "They might panic."

"They'll have to trust us," Harry said.

Harry and Max and the Cossacks decided to wait until later when the Soviet soldiers were at their groggiest. They then would make a break for it, taking out a soldier on watch if they had to, because some of the hardier Cossacks still had their daggers. They didn't want to reposition farther south because they could not know what the Soviets had there. They only knew they were safe here in their pocket. But not for long. They squatted like rugby players in a scrum, some whispering prayers, others rocking back and forth, humming, then hunched over, stomping their feet and interlocking arms to stay closer.

Five a.m.—Friday, November 9. They could see purple on the horizon, fading to a uniform gray. The sun would be up in an hour. They huddled around again, this time like before a big game. They were thanking each other, grabbing at each other's shoulders, passing along messages and love in case any of them didn't make it. Harry could make out tears in the dim light.

Max had moved over to Harry. He put his arm around him and gave him a squeeze. "Let's go."

They moved along in a chain, from tree to tree, rock to rock, hole to hole, downed trunk to trunk. It took longer than Harry wanted. The sun was coming up, the grayness rising fast into the sky as the sun rose up behind the clouds. Harry was in the middle of the group, crouching behind a snowdrift that had blown in from the valley. They had to be right on the border here. It was all he could do not to make a break for it. The dire need was straining all their tired and frantic minds.

Shouts, from inside the woods. It was Russian. Soviet Army regular soldiers rushed to the tree line north of them. The Ivans were everywhere. Others were coming through the trees, shouting and charging from every direction.

The Cossacks ran now, breaking off into little groups, some only two together, in every direction. Harry found Max. They grabbed at each other, panting, and sprinted on.

"Look, look!" Max gasped.

At the opposite tree line at the other end of the white valley, Colonel Partland's GIs were advancing out into the white open. Some Cossacks were running that way.

Harry and Max moved along, ducking behind trees. They traded urgent glances. Should they do the same? Would the Ivans shoot?

Behind them a group of four Russians had three Cossacks surrounded, aiming their rifles. The Cossacks charged before the soldiers could get a shot off and tackled them wielding daggers, but more soldiers bounded over and absorbed the three Cossacks. Screams rang out. Shrieks. From other parts of the forest too.

"Look, more are out there," Max said.

"We go. It's time."

Harry grabbed Max. They sprinted out into the white valley, their legs heavy, the snow pulling them down. They ran in a zigzag pattern, grasping at each other for support.

Soviet soldiers advanced into the valley with their barrels lowered yet in a line, as if moving to surround the thirty or so Cossacks huddling out in the middle of the valley with arms up. The Cossacks were backing away towards the GIs who were advancing out to them just the same with their barrels lowered. A line of Soviet soldiers pushed forward behind Harry and Max. Harry and Max ran, joining the Cossacks who held their arms out to them, urging them on as if they were swimming to a lifeboat.

The Cossacks kept backing up, in a half circle as if hiding something. One was panting, growling, muttering fierce words to himself, and none could console him. He broke off from them and charged the line of Soviet soldiers raising a dagger and the Ivans let him on through until the Cossack reached the trees where more Ivans surrounded him, rifles up. The Cossack swung his blade at them. A rifle butt struck his jaw and he dropped, and the Ivans dragged him into the dark forest.

Harry huffed at the sight, sickly, incredulously. Two potent adversaries were like something out of the old Battle of Waterloo now, each side in tight aligned formations. A line of American GIs stood about forty yards away, out in the valley. On the other side of Harry, Max and the Cossacks stood a line of the Soviet soldiers.

The Cossacks kept to the middle of the valley, close together on a muddied patch of snow, the steam billowing out of them.

"Stay there!" came a shout from the American tree line, repeated in Russian and German.

"Do not move!" came a command in Russian from the Soviet side, repeated in German.

# Thirty-Five

THE SUN CAME UP AND OUT, breaking through clouds and illuminating the snow all around them with a blinding whiteness. Neither the Soviet Army Ivans nor American GIs advanced, heeding the commands from either end. The opposing troops each stood in their lines, each man roughly three yards apart, stealing looks back for further commands from the tree line. Out among the Cossacks, a few cigarettes came out. They shared them, the sun bringing warmth to their pale, white faces. It didn't warm their numbing cold feet. They slapped their hands together.

An hour had passed. Harry imagined frantic wireless communications on each side, reinforcements called in. Harry could make out Colonel Partland at the Americans' tree line. Partland appeared to give him a thumbs-up. Harry only nodded. At this point, he didn't want to try anything that made the Soviets think he was more than a common Cossack. His exhausted mind had been racing through the possibilities, around and around, an endless oval track of comeuppances. As Partland had warned him, an American captured among this group could be used for all manner of propaganda, as proof of aggressive US intentions. A show trial. And in concert with his brother, the former SS man? It was tailor-made for propaganda. He would, at the very least, make a useful prisoner for swapping someday. He wondered if they knew of him already. It depended on how far Hartmut Dietz had gotten with his disclosures, and how much they would believe him. Harry looked to the Americans' trees again and realized he was looking for any sign of Aubrey Slaipe there. He saw none but somehow felt his presence, like a man standing on a train platform sensing that a train was coming.

"Do be careful what you wish," Max muttered to Harry. He was scanning their trees too.

A Soviet officer arrived at the Soviet tree line using binoculars. Soon a man in a civilian overcoat flanked him wearing a large black sable hat that bore a red star badge. A commissar.

Another hour passed. The rich aroma of the cigarettes gave way to the terrified, metallic breath of the Cossacks around them.

"It's like being on that damn island again," Max said.

"That or in a train car."

The Soviet officer and commissar advanced out into the snow and kept coming, right past their line of men. From the US side, Harry saw Colonel Partland doing the same, flanked by a young captain. The opposing lines of GIs and Ivans each followed, but Partland and his counterpart from the Soviet side each waved at their men to stay put.

The group of Cossacks convened in groups of threes and fours, arguing what they would do under what conditions.

"The woman and children, the old ones made it over. We've done our work," said one.

"But that's no reason to lie down and take it up the ass," growled another.

"If it saves the whole?"

"We don't know just who's saved, not yet."

They grabbed at each other's collars, shouted at one another, hugged, shared whispers.

The Soviet commissar in the overcoat was grinning at them, and Harry half expected to see the man bounce on over and give them a touristy pitch on the positives of returning to the Soviet Union, their great Mother Russia that would welcome them as heroes. Yet as the commissar came closer, Harry could see the man's grin was one of ridicule. A rich man grinning at circus clowns. They were only pawns. Their opinions, wants, and wishes did not matter.

Colonel Partland and his captain met the Soviet officer and his commissar in the middle of the valley. Harry and Max stood as close as they could without leaving the Cossacks, straining to hear.

The four officers exchanged terse greetings. Hands were shook. The commissar spoke some English and Colonel Partland's captain translated the Russian parts. It went back in forth in Russian and English with some German thrown in. The Soviet talked of an exchange—half would go one way, half the other.

"Nothing doing," Colonel Partland said. "These men, they're now in the US zone."

"Can you prove it? They fled the Soviet zone, did they not?"

It went on like this. The Cossacks, their faces deathly pale, kept arguing among themselves as they eyed the deliberations. The thirty men had split up into two rough groups—ten in one group, about twenty in the other. This confirmed they were separating according to who had family that had made it over—these men went on to safety while the others would return as sacrifice. This wasn't a new arrangement. The men had often discussed the possibility, Max told Harry.

"Look, Harry, look," Max said.

One Cossack from the twenty trudged over to the officers deliberating. At the same time, the group of twenty started walking back to the line of Soviet Army soldiers, their knees arching high as they hiked through the snow.

"Wait, come back!" Harry and Max shouted, but the ten or so Cossacks who'd stayed surrounded them and hands slapped over their mouths. "All right, all right," Harry growled, pushing the hands away as Max did the same.

The Cossack representing the twenty deliberated with the Soviet officer, his arms flailing, frantic now as he eyed his men marching back to the Soviet line. As the Soviet officer listened, the commissar lit a cigarette and stuck it in the Cossack's mouth. Colonel Partland and his captain were standing back, their faces taut.

"They are doing it to save us—and to save you who have done so much for us," one of the ten Cossack men said in Harry's ear.

The twenty Cossacks neared the line of Soviet soldiers. The Ivans raised their barrels. The Soviet officer shouted and they lowered the barrels, but it didn't stop the Cossacks from raising their arms high about their heads. The Ivans turned with them, escorting them back to the tree line and into the forest that was the border of the Soviet zone.

Harry and Max and their ten stood there a long while, their feet planted in the muddied snow. Then things became calmer. The Soviet soldiers retreated from the tree line altogether. It looked like a normal forest anywhere. The meeting broke up. The Soviet officer and his commissar were strolling back to their side with their hands clasped casually behind their backs, moving through the deep snow as if it were a thin grass.

"Harry? Come on, let's go." Colonel Partland was standing behind them.

"No," Max said. "We can't just let them."

"We have to. It's all we have. It's over."

The last truck drove away, to catch up with those already heading for the Standkaserne DP camp in Munich. Colonel Partland and his captain had sped off to escort the trucks through any constabulary checkpoints. The Cossacks were on their way and Sabine's assistants were with them—feeding them, treating them, consoling the ones whose men did not make it over. The GIs had packed up the post and, as ordered, left the captain's jeep for Harry, Max and Sabine complete with trip papers. Colonel Partland had stood a bottle of Scotch on the hood, but no one felt like toasting. Sabine opened Harry's chrome thermos and the three drank coffee from the red cap. They had a little fire going. They smoked. Soon the Scotch made it into the coffee.

"Alex was quite the brave young man," Sabine said at some point to no one in particular.

Max kept standing at tree trunks along the clearing, surveying the Soviet line across the valley with binoculars. It was afternoon now. Low dark clouds had moved in and the snow had a grayish-blue tint, what would be a permanent dusk until the sun went down.

The Soviets' woods were dim, Max told them, but they were still there, inside. "They have a fire or two burning, moving around in there for certain. But they're farther back now."

They heard singing from the Soviet side. Max said it was a Cossack song. "Keeping their heads high," he said.

The singing stopped. Minutes passed, the three of them in silence. A half hour. Max sat on the hood of the jeep, a wool helmet beanie on his head pushed back. Like this he looked like a corn-fed American soldier—like he might have looked two years before as a half-baked spy on the loose in the Ardennes. Sabine sat with Harry on a crate. The only smells left in the world were tobacco, coffee, Scotch, the charcoal smell of their fire. The fire smoldered now as embers, and no one bothered to stoke it. They wouldn't need to stay here all night. All of them knew it.

Max heaved himself from the hood and stood at the tree line. He lifted the binoculars. He trudged on back, and he found his spot on the hood. "Soon," he said.

The Cossacks' singing started up again, faint but clear enough. All three could hear it from across the high valley. Then they heard pops, and screams, what sounded like the trees themselves splintering apart and wailing. The screams ceased. Yet the clacks of gunfire persisted, spaced a few random seconds apart, and on, and on, like the creaks of a slow, slow, heavy old wheel.

# Thirty-Six

"THEY ARE COPING WELL ENOUGH," Sabine said.

"Laying low, I hope," Harry said.

It had been three days since they rescued the Cossacks from the Šumava. Harry sat at the desk in his den. Sabine sat across from him in a smart blue pea coat, brown scarf, and modest black hat, her cheeks flushed from being outside. She'd just come back from the Standkaserne.

She nodded. "Those passports are a mix of nationalities, so all the more reason to sit tight. They play down their Cossack nature to outsiders, of course, but only until we can get them moved out. Then they're refugees again. They may become whoever they are."

"And young Alex?"

"Also well. We have many children who lost their parents, from everywhere. He is among them now. He plays with them. And he stays close to me."

"Is he talking to Max?"

"He slept by his side last night."

"Good. That's good. Have either of you told him yet?"

"No. That time will come. He must be ready."

"Supposing those Sovs come sniffing around—your friends at the Soviet Repatriation Mission?"

"The Nansen passports should protect them. Any case, I do not think the Soviets will bother. They got their spoils."

That weekend, Colonel Partland had met with trusted contacts from the US Consulate. The United States government could not help directly, but officials there would do what they could. It may take a while, Sabine warned. A vast number of Displaced Persons still needed homes, including those millions of Jews who would never return to Germany. Most countries' existing refugee quotas were completely inadequate and many didn't have new policies yet. The United States, the land of the immigrants, was well behind other countries in taking in the vast numbers.

"Will they have to split up?" Harry said.

"I'm afraid so, yes. It's the only way to find them homes. I expect most will go to the US, others Canada, Australia, South America even. Others go it alone. Some leave camp on their own once they feel safe. Just walk out the front gate. It happens all the time, and no one's stopping them. Rural Germany and Austria will make them their own eventually. And for some it's probably best."

Harry thought about young Alex. He wondered if, by some amazing chance, the boy would someday meet Little Marta, the orphan refugee from Heimgau who made it over to San Francisco. He thought about Warren Joyner, who was probably in transit to a hospital ship home by now. He would like to think one of these Cossacks would end up in Joyner's hometown, maybe with a job as a baker, making the pie his surviving son ate at the counter. Or doing hard work in Joyner's wife's front yard, since it was more than likely she was soon to be a widow.

"What about you?" Sabine said. "Where are you heading?"

Harry had told Max and Sabine that his tour of duty was ending, but he didn't know what came next. Today was a Monday. He would have to be back in his office this afternoon. Transport papers would likely be sitting in his inbox. It was November 12. He had four days, tops. He was now in the redeployment pipeline, so they might well ship him somewhere else if he did put in for more duty. Above all, his parents would want to see him—they deserved that, and discharging out would get him home quickest. He should at least get stateside for a spell. Maybe he then could land something civilian back over here in Germany, or attached to the military. But he wondered how long it would take to find a way back over the water—back to Sabine.

He played it light. "Maybe you'll give me a job," he said, stroking her ankle with his slipper under the desk.

"Perhaps an apprenticeship," Sabine said, grinning.

"Ah, so happy to see me?" In came Max with arms out and a steady grin like the actor he once was coming out to greet photographers. He gave Sabine a little bow from the hip.

"Well?" Harry said.

Harry had lent Max his dark brown suit from America. The sleeves and legs were too short but who was counting in this busted city? No one worth a damn. Max pulled at the lapel of the jacket. "Such boring dress you have, Harry. The cut, fabric—like English clothes but without the flair."

"So you told me," Harry said. "So tell me something new." That morning, Max had registered his domicile with the police and reported his first week with the denazification bureau. Harry's billet was the domicile. Harry was hoping Max could remain in the house for the next American living here. He could help Gerlinde with the chores. Harry's recommendation would be glowing, of course. Max could call himself a butler if he wanted.

"They treated me well enough. One clerk thought I looked familiar to him and I was going to ask him which of my movies he had seen—ah, but why bother? We move on." Max's grin had fallen away. "How about you, Harry? How did it go with Dietz's wife?"

Harry had gone looking for Frau Dietz twice over the weekend. She'd refused to see him. This morning he went back over, but this time he didn't ring her bell or knock on doors. He stood out on the corner as Dietz had done so often, eyeing would-be strangers, casing the street and front doorway. After an hour of this, Frau Dietz yelled down at him from her window to quit plaguing her and just come the hell on up.

Dietz's wife had her bags packed, a pile of mismatched suit-cases and carpetbags by the front door. She had sold the furniture. Her children watched from the hallway until she barked at them to disappear. She was wearing two overcoats, her arms crossed at her chest.

"I've been lenient with you, so please be candid: Did he contact you?" Harry said.

"No. I tell you the truth. But I'm leaving in any case." Her face was pinched as if she needed to clear her throat and spit.

"I'm sorry. I know that, whatever else he was, he loved you."

And she did spit, right against the wall. "I'll tell you what he was . . ." She told Harry all she'd known about her secretive hus-band. During the war, the Wehrmacht Military Police had indeed kicked Dietz over to the Navy because he was too much trou-ble, but it was all much more than Dietz had let on. No doubt he was running a corrupt racket, Frau Dietz said, and who knew how many deaths he'd caused if not ordered—German and local, Jew, it didn't matter, whoever might spill his secret. The records would show it. It was only a matter of time. Frau Dietz asked what the Soviets would do with her husband. Harry suggested that Dietz could make a go of it in the Soviet zone of Eastern Germany betraying fellow Germans there. Tears streamed down Frau Dietz's face, and she rubbed them away with her coarse woolen lapels.

"How could I ever go over there . . . and with my children?" she shrieked. "Hartmut, he'll only end up in a Gulag just like all those German POWs, those repatriated Russians."

"At least he's alive," Harry said, not caring one way or the other.

"Is he?" Frau Dietz said, showing about as much enthusiasm.

Harry couldn't do much for Frau Dietz. She was a German, not a Displaced Person—a German with nothing to offer. He could get her some food. Maybe she had relatives in the West. He told her, "I promised your husband I would help your children. He wanted to know that I would."

Frau Dietz had only glared at him. "Never mind him now. Do you have a jeep? You could give us a lift to the train station."

"And that was it," Harry told Max. "I gave the woman and her children a ride to the station. We wished each other luck. She didn't want to know what her husband did here."

"My guess?" Sabine said. "Dietz's gone deep inside. Maybe changed his name. They might put him to use. But after what we saw with those Cossacks? Anyone who's been touched by the West is a cancer to Stalin. I imagine you'll read the news one day in their big paper."

"*Pravda*," Max said.

"Surely. Execution of one Hartmut Dietz—Fascist Criminal. Found in the Soviet zone of Germany. Or perhaps imprisoned in Moscow. That is how they operate."

Gerlinde brought them bread smeared with butter and green onions, coffee. As they ate, gathered around the desk, they joked about how Harry would extend his duty, but Max would step in to play him for an extended run. With so much weight lost, he probably even fit Harry's uniform—all he had to do was let out the sleeves and inseams. After all he was an actor, and he had done impersonations before. Meanwhile, Harry would stay with Sabine and live like a local.

The doorbell rang.

The three of them froze, bread raised halfway to mouths. They lowered the bread and rose in unison. Max straightened up tall, shoulders squared, the closest to standing at attention that Harry had ever seen. They were expecting an undertaker to come for Irina in the cellar. The *Optiker* in the Seidlstrasse who made Harry's horn rims had an undertaker friend eager to help—apparently the mortician business was slower than one would imagine, the optician told Harry, what with the conquering powers managing all matters of death for the foreseeable future.

A sense of unease made Harry hesitate, a chill. He pulled on his Ike jacket and waved for Max and Sabine to stand back. The den door was open. He went over and peered down the hallway toward the foyer.

A man stood before Gerlinde, erect, almost German or at least British in his bearing. He held a black pipe cupped in his hand. His balding, graying head was pink from the cold outside.

Aubrey Slaipe.

That dark overcoat draped over his shoulders so fine and yet so plain that it had to be part of his official dress. Gerlinde was holding his wide-brimmed hat.

Slaipe turned Harry's way. "Good afternoon, all," he called down the hallway.

Gerlinde ushered them all into the living room, her face turning pale seeing Harry so troubled.

"My name is Slaipe. Aubrey. So very pleased to meet you, Frau Lieser," he said to Sabine in adequate formal German.

Sabine stole a glance at Harry as if to say, How does this man know my name? Harry nodded for her to continue. She faced Slaipe for a handshake.

Slaipe raised his hand holding the pipe and, to their amazement, lifted his other arm from inside his overcoat and took the pipe in his other hand, which was now a hook. He was wearing a prosthesis.

Sabine didn't blink. She'd likely seen more artificial body parts than there was chewing gum in the PX. They shook hands.

Max's face had gone white. Now it was red.

Slaipe declined Gerlinde's offer to take his coat. "I won't be long," he said, his eyes fixed on Harry and Max.

Gerlinde led Sabine away, Sabine eyeing Harry over her shoulder.

Harry, Max, and Slaipe stood in a triangle near the fire. Max scowled, twitched, and rocked like popping corns ready to burst from heat.

"Why didn't you spring me from jail?" he barked at Slaipe.

Slaipe held out his palm as if it were a clipboard to show Max. "I did not know," he said.

"That is a load of shit."

Slaipe made a tsk-tsk sound. "You made it quite clear that you did not require my help. As did your brother here."

Max turned away, muttering curses. Harry starting rocking on his own feet.

"I am sorry about your Irina," Slaipe said to Max. "Dearly. It took me by surprise as well. If I could have helped somehow, stepped in, I would have. Max? Please listen. It was not your fault."

Max said nothing.

Slaipe turned to Harry. "And as for you—I'm not anything like Virgil Tercel, you know. You do understand this."

"Who?"

"Oh, come now. Alias Eugene Spanner. Called himself a colonel, ostensibly in the CIC. Except that he was not. The man was a criminal deserter as crooked as a corkscrew and far more dangerous."

Harry snorted at Slaipe. "Did you know about Dietz all along?"

"No. Not until it was too late. By the by: You had to dispose of Tercel. If that is what you did. Because the man disappeared in the summer of 1945, last seen near Heimgau. You did the right thing."

Harry almost thanked him. He said, "Now your turn: Why the disappearing act? When we needed you. You tell me that."

Slaipe opened his mouth to speak. He turned back to Max instead and gestured with his hook for Max to venture a guess.

Max understood. "You know why, brother. He wanted to see how we would do. Perform. It was just as he proposed to me in that Belgian villa. He wanted me to reenter Nazi Germany as his spy, or at least an actor's facsimile of one." Max's face darkened and he stared at the carpet.

"And perform well you did," Slaipe said. "I could not have done better than your Colonel Partland in any case—Maddy Barton's boyfriend, I should add."

"You should add. She made it happen."

"Indeed. Bravo."

"So he's saying we passed some kind of test?" Harry asked Max.

Max nodded, his eyes closing. "And well enough to make the grade, I'm afraid."

"A good operative doesn't have to kill," Slaipe offered.

"Operative? Who you calling operative?"

"I simply mean," Slaipe said, "that there is much to be gained by allowing a certain malfeasant to live on and run. See where he's drawn to. There's one lesson right there."

Harry looked to Max, who only showed him a frown. "Now you listen to me," Harry told Slaipe. "You can't just march in here and—"

"But, there's nothing to reject," Slaipe cut in, his tone sharper. "You're already aboard, aren't you? In point of fact, you've been working for me all along. In its way. And I would say that you passed the test damn well. Damn fine. Though there's always room for improvement. One's never satisfied with even their best performance. Wouldn't you say that's how it is in the theater, Max?"

Max showed Harry another frown.

Slaipe, smiling, turned to Harry. "Say, you ever hear the one about the man who had three hounds?"

"I'm afraid I didn't."

Slaipe chuckled. "Well, the thing was he owned one, then two, and then three hounds . . . one for every ex-wife!"

"Is that supposed to be funny? I don't know what that's supposed to mean."

"We will, Harry," Max said. "This is what the man is telling us."

"Very good, Max." Slaipe nodded. "I won't keep you two any longer. Just wanted to pay my respects. Oh, I almost forgot . . . There's a man waiting outside, dark costume, looks like your proverbial undertaker. He reached your door before me, but I kindly insisted that he wait outside. Because, you see, I always come first."

# Afterword

THE FORCED REPATRIATIONS to the Soviet Union described in this book are historical fact. By early 1947, the United States, Great Britain, and allies had returned nearly two and a half million refugees, forced laborers, and prisoners of war to the Soviet Union as agreed in the Yalta Conference. These people were sent back forcibly, without consideration of their individual wishes and genuine fears. Moreover, thousands of émigrés who had fled Russia during the Bolshevik Revolution and the Russian Civil War—well before WWII—were sent back to the Soviet Union that they had opposed. People of Russian descent who never set foot in Russia were forcibly sent east as well.

The best overall history of the shameful repatriation efforts remains Nikolai Tolstoy's *The Secret Betrayal* (1977; British Edition: *The Victims of Yalta*). It's not easy reading. Many of the repatriated were tricked into going or outright lied to. When that didn't work, they were forced at gunpoint. The bloody sellout was already set in motion by the unconditional surrender of May 1945, when the so-called Soviet Repatriation Commissions were roaming Western Europe operated by agents of the NKVD and SMERSH. Sometimes the Soviet officials promised those returning that Stalin would give them amnesty, appealing to a yearning to reunite with family and loved ones. Many others knew what would happen if Stalin's agents got to them—they would land in a Gulag, if they were lucky. Some of these had fought with the Germans, the Ukrainian Cossacks fictionalized in this book among them. Roughly 50,000 Cossacks had ended up in British-occupied areas of Austria, some tribes that had fought with the Germans against the Soviets and, with their families, retreated westward as the Third Reich collapsed.

Faced with overwhelming numbers to send back, the British resorted to subterfuge, then brute force. It has been called the "Betrayal of the Cossacks" and the "Massacre of Cossacks at Lienz." Once the refugees understood their fate, they resisted with grim consequences. The horrific scenes that Irina describes happened. The Judenburg collection point in Austria existed—in just one incident over two days during the summer of 1945, the British handed over some 18,000 Cossacks to the Soviets at Judenburg, many of these reportedly Ukrainian Cossacks.

The execution scene is fictional. Surely similar incidents existed.

The Americans ran their own operations, most notably at the former concentration camps at Dachau and at Plattling where thousands of Russians were brutally repatriated by US troops obeying the McNarney-Clark Directive. The fictional savior Colonel Partland in this book had real-life counterparts in American soldiers who, as Tolstoy describes it, were left "visibly shamefaced" after one nighttime operation where they rousted the terrified Russians from their beds at gunpoint shouting and wielding nightsticks and herded them into trucks and, hours later, handed over their prisoners to Soviet trains inside Bavarian woods at the Czech border. The American death march was soon reaping suicide and murder: "Before their departure from the rendezvous in the forest, many [US soldiers] had seen rows of bodies already hanging from the branches of nearby trees. On their return, even the SS men in a neighboring compound lined the wire fence and railed at them for their behavior. The Americans were too ashamed to reply."

The crimes of diplomacy in this book are only a few among a vast, years-long and suppressed story of postwar treaty-dealing that sold out pawns and only created more death, more murder, more shame, and resentment. A sliver of hope in this sordid history was that some of the condemned civilians were able to escape like the group in this novel. No matter what the Cossacks did as soldiers, whether fighting to stay alive or even committing atrocities, it's inexcusable that innocent woman and children should have had to suffer for it. If there's a lesson in this, perhaps it's that we should always keep a careful watch on the victors no matter what evil has been defeated. We see it repeatedly, even today: Peace alone does not spare the innocent.

*Lost Kin: A Novel* is the third book in the Kaspar Brothers series. The story of Max Kaspar forced into a suicidal mission during WWII is told in the novel *The Losing Role*, while Harry Kaspar's deadly postwar rite of passage follows in *Liberated: A Novel of Germany, 1945.*

www.stephenfanderson.com
www.twitter.com/SteveAwriter
www.goodreads.com/author/show/3518909.Steve_Anderson
www.facebook.com/SteveAnderson-Author
www.stephenfanderson.com/mailing-list

Novels by Steve Anderson

*The Losing Role (Kaspar Brothers #1)*
*Liberated: A Novel of Germany, 1945 (Kaspar Brothers #2)*
*Under False Flags: A Novel*
*The Other Oregon: A Thriller*